Rekindled Prophecy

Abundant gratitude and thanks to all the guardian angels I've encountered throughout my life--the ones who encouraged me to be myself, to dream big, and to unfurl my own wings to fly.

Rekindled Prophecy

Greylyn the Guardian Angel
BOOK 1

KC Freeman

ISBN: 979-8-71534-114-3

Third Edition: June 2025

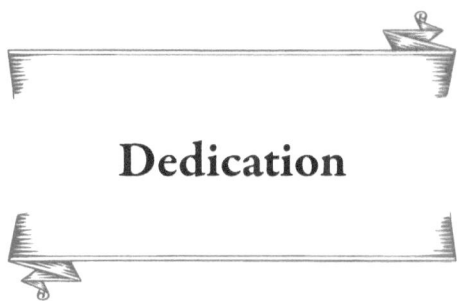

Dedication

Abundant gratitude and thanks to all the guardian angels throughout my life—the ones who encouraged me to be myself, to dream big, and unfurl my own wings to fly.

Prologue

London, England 1567

This would be her first test as a guardian angel. The very first time that she, and she alone, was responsible for the success of the job. No partner to bail her out if she messed up. No pressure...then why did she feel the need to vomit from the pinching pain in her stomach?

Her mentor, Jasper Moreau, had flashed a brilliant smile and pushed her hair back up under her boy's cap before shoving her out of the carriage a couple blocks down from the tavern. He'd said, "You've got this, darling. You're a natural." Greylyn was glad someone had confidence in her because she certainly did not.

She had spent the last few months learning how to fight, how to utilize her guardian senses, how to cover her tracks, and how to blend into society from Jasper. He had been an unrelenting task master, but kind after training was completed each day. The grueling physical training had been nothing compared to his endless lectures on everything from metaphysical sciences and world religions to telepathy and mastering the art of disguise. The latter came in handy for tonight's assignment.

Inside, her heart hammered against her ribcage. Cold sweat broke out on her palms. Peering through the soupy fog across the broken cobblestone street, Greylyn paused to stare at the entrance to the tavern. Women were not commonplace in bars, unless as barmaids or they practiced a certain profession. The tight corsets and stiff skirts did not work well in circumstances where she needed to fight. She prayed the ruffled shirt, vest, baggy britches, as well as the tight bandages that kept her bosom well-hidden and made breathing near impossible, were enough to disguise her femininity.

A tingling feeling spread all over her body from the moment she pushed open the heavy doors of the tiny, dim pub. The heat from too many bodies crammed together so closely and the stench of the smoke emitting from the corner fireplace smacked her in the face immediately. Sweat broke out across her forehead. She itched to wipe her brow, but her hands were shaking too violently. Swallowing the bile rising from her belly, she forced her feet to shuffle forward until the heavy door thudded back against the doorframe.

Five steps into the establishment and every nerve ending ignited like the fireworks Jasper had told her about from his last visit to China. This feeling was quite different from what she experienced when coming into contact with the innocent human she was charged with saving. The first time her guardian senses had picked up on Edward, the hairs on the back of her neck rose, her vision momentarily blurred, and there had been a faint tickling in her chest. But this feeling, she could not place.

Something was wrong.

She shoved her way through the throng of patrons to the bar. A sensation of being drawn to something, like a magnet in her belly, fought against her body's command to move forward. It demanded she stop and turn. Jasper had never warned her about something like this. Was it just nerves? Greylyn dug her fingernails into her palms.

Stay focused.

The invisible pull messed with her connection to the innocent man she was there to help. The ruddy-faced gambler was on the other side of the tavern. His eyes flitted around the room. His time was short, and he knew it. The man, Edward, had failed to pay his debt to a notorious card shark. He did not owe money; he owed his soul. No matter where he ran, the demonic enforcers would track him down. She had been sent here tonight specifically to save the man from having a harpy gorge on his soul like a meal of fish and chips.

He was her mission. But still her feet refused to cooperate.

What is wrong with me?

As her eyes darted around the room, looking for the source of her discomfort, her vision blurred, and her pulse quickened. Nothing seemed out of the ordinary until ...

A dazzling pair of eyes, flecks of gold practically glowing in a sea of burnt umber, stared at her from a corner table. The gentleman's eyes widened momentarily, and a slight tremor rippled through his expression. Dark hair with auburn highlights cascaded down past his shoulders. Rooted into place, time stopped and the world around her went hazy until his face transformed into a mischievous grin that sent tantalizing tingles throughout her body. Heat crept up her cheeks, but for what reason she could not comprehend.

A loud crash from across the tavern broke Greylyn from her paralysis. She spun around to see Edward bolting out the back door, followed by a group of burly looking men carrying a large potato sack and thick wooden clubs.

"Dammit." This was exactly what she was meant to stop. Before she could give chase, a tall, muscular form blocked her path. Citrus and sandalwood invaded her senses, which was strange, given the odor of sweat, stale whiskey, and ale that permeated the crowded tavern.

"Excuse ..." She looked up. Big mistake. Hypnotic eyes stared down at her, and a delicious smile curled the corners of a sensual mouth. Her own lips failed to form words.

"May I help you, young lad?" His voice washed over her, deep and somewhat familiar, followed by a throaty chuckle. Her mind screamed to get away from this man ... fast, but her eyes were locked on his, unable to break free.

An abrupt high-pitched cackling of a barmaid burst through her deaf ears, shattering his invisible hold. Forcing her feet to move, Greylyn spun around and sprinted out the back entrance of the tavern, desperate to find Edward before the demons captured him. Or worse.

Behind the bar, the backstreet was dark and stank of garbage piled in more than a dozen mountains against the weathered stone exterior. Her eyes adjusted almost instantly, but Edward was nowhere in sight. He must have gotten away or done a damn good job of hiding, because the demon thugs canvassing the alley cursed and hurled threats to no one in particular. One especially rotund demon-possessed man swung a large wooden slab at piles of refuse lined up against the building while the others slowly stalked along the alleyway. "Here, here, little kitty," one taunted. "You can't hide forever, stupid bloke."

Okay, now what, Greylyn?

Lost the innocent. Now she was stuck in a face-off with a band of demonic ruffians.

Jasper's voice rang in her head. *Brilliant job!*

She doubted Jasper would praise her efforts so far to save the human. Instead, she was in quite a conundrum.

No, her first lone assignment was not going smoothly. Not at all.

Greylyn took a deep breath before moving out of the shadows to stand in the middle of the alley. Yanking the cap off her head that had kept her long ebony locks hidden away, she whistled to get their attention. "Yo, laddies! Looking' for a good time?"

They turned in unison, each bearing the same slimy grin. The one in the middle carrying a meat cleaver of all things, stalked towards her. "What we got here? A wee pretty thing, tain't she?" He cranked his head left and then right, bones popping loudly. "Why ya covering up all ye assets dressing like a lad?" With that, he lunged for her arm.

Greylyn side-stepped, pivoted, and slammed him in the back of the head with her elbow. "What d'hell ..." were the last words he uttered as she slid in front of him with her dagger drawn, leaving a bright trail of blood along his now near-decapitated neck.

The others paused as the man fell to the ground, his head lolling. Crimson blood gushed onto the cobblestones to mix with the putrid liquid run-off from the piles of garbage. Greylyn stood tall ... well, as tall as she could for her barely five-foot frame. "Who's next, boys?"

Look who's the tough broad now? Me, that's who.

Spending all day, every day with Jasper, and his sarcastic wit had rubbed off on her. With her confidence reinstated from such a quick first kill, Greylyn's ego swelled with pride. However, this probably was not the best time to spout off to a demon gang, even if she was tough.

Tall, splotchy, and already sporting a black eye from another encounter, the man on the left advanced. "Such a lovely lassie," spit flew out between his blackened and rotting teeth, "t'would be a shame to spoil such a lovely lassie as yourself, but ..." he shrugged, "that'd be fun, too." He barreled towards her with a wicked smile. Whoosh! The air escaped her lungs when he slammed into her, tackling her to the ground. No sooner had she blinked away the stars in her eyes, his tremendous weight lifted off her. Greylyn flinched and screwed her eyes shut, waiting for him to punch or kick her, or outright twist her head off her body.

Nothing happened.

"What da bloody ..." The goon did not get to finish his sentence. The next thing she heard was him gasping for breath, then the tremendous thud when he collapsed onto the ground. Blood flowed from his mouth and his neck bent at an awkward angle.

Oh, thank heavens! Jasper had arrived to save her sorry butt.

When she looked over, the man smashing the other goon's face into the rock wall until his skull split open was quite obviously *not* Jasper Moreau.

It was the man with the predatory tiger eyes she had encountered inside the tavern. The one that caused her to mess up because the pull to him had been greater than her guardian angel connection to poor, hapless Edward.

Where the hell was Edward anyway?

Lying paralyzed on the ground, Greylyn watched in abject fascination as the handsome man savagely twisted the neck off the last member of the card shark's hit squad. From this vantage point, she could not make out his expression. His movements were smooth and agile, but also brutal. An exquisite and macabre dance of primal violence.

No more bad guys to fend off, he whipped out a handkerchief from his breast pocket with a flick of his wrist and wiped away the blood and gore splattered on his face and hands. He did it in such a nonchalant manner, as if it were commonplace to violently beat men to death. A chill ran up Greylyn's spine as he turned to face her.

Do I thank him or run?

In two quick strides, he knelt beside her. One hand came up to brush a tendril of hair out of her eyes and tucked it behind her ear. The angered expression he had worn just seconds before evaporated. His eyes softened. A small smile tugged at his lips.

A wave of heat originated from his touch, spreading out to her entire body. "Everything's alright now, Gr ..." His voice, smooth yet husky, trailed off but with a slight accent marking him as not English, but from someplace close ... someplace familiar.

A chill raced through her veins, freezing her in place as she watched his glowing topaz eyes widened before morphing to a deep crimson hue.

A demon?

No, not exactly. The hint of sulfur was missing. The way pinpricks of pain flashed out when one touched her skin did not happen. Oh, there were pinpricks of something, but not the same sensation. No, he was not a demon, nor was he possessed by one. Of that she was certain, but the realization something was different about this man was enough to jar her back to her senses.

Her fingers coiled tighter around the hilt of her dagger – a weapon bestowed upon her as part of her initiation into the world of guardian angels. The handle, intricately carved with a Celtic symbol interlaced with the sign of infinity and two opals of varying shades embedded in the center, now pressed into the soft skin of her palm. Months of intensive practice, it was now an extension of herself. Its sharp, jagged edges of an unbreakable shimmering blue metal were forged specifically to kill demons, to kill anything not intended for this world. Greylyn prayed it also worked on whatever this man was.

He had not moved. Just stared at her with those freaky eyes of blood. She slashed upward with the blade. He jerked away, but not in time. A gash appeared across his cheek and his hand flew up to his face. Greylyn used his momentary surprise to push herself off the ground to run away. Not two steps later, the man grabbed her upper arm, hauling her backwards into his chest with such momentum she felt, as well as heard, the cracking of her spine from the impact. The small bones of her wrist popped painfully under pressure from his much larger hand, forcing her fist to unclasp and the dagger to fall. His other hand snaked around her waist.

"Going somewhere so soon?" His voice held a gruff edge to it now, no longer velvety smooth.

Every instinct screamed at her not to, but she defiantly craned her neck to stare up at her captor. Big mistake. He whipped her around to face him. Now pressed against his chest, the thumping of her own heart against her ribcage mixed with sound of his own rose to a deafening level, blocking out all other sounds. His lips curled on one side, highlighting a dimple. Perfectly white teeth glinted in the dim moonlight. Warm breath caressed her face, smelling slightly of bourbon.

"Let. Me. Go," she ground out from clenched teeth. Her body shivered, but she refused to acknowledge the fear. Although it was likely she might not survive her first guardian assignment, Jasper's mantra that he had drilled into her head over the last year rang in her ears – *Never acknowledge the fear. A guardian does not have the luxury of giving in to fear.* Greylyn prayed her eyes reflected resolve and courage, not the terror coursing through her veins. Or whatever else was pulsing through her body.

A full grin broke out on the man's face. The red flames dancing in his eyes smoldered before returning to their topaz hue that had riveted her in place earlier. His entire face relaxed. "Now, love. Why would I do that? There's so much we have to discuss before ..."

Greylyn stomped down on his foot with all her strength. Considering their significant size difference, she did not expect it to work, but it startled her captor enough for him to loosen his grip. She wrenched her arm away while her other fist swung up and slammed into his face. Blood gushed from his nose, flowing down to drip off his chiseled chin.

Instead of an angry shout or a return punch, he glared steadily at her with no other outward show of pain or emotion.

"So much for civility then." The words were spoken so softly through thinned lips that she almost doubted he had spoken at all until his fist shot out. Excruciating pain blinded her.

The jerk broke my nose!

Strong hands gripped her arms and yanked her with such force her neck snapped as her body sailed across the alleyway. Colliding with the moss-covered stone wall of the tavern, all the air whooshed out of her lungs. A coppery tinge filled her mouth.

Pain and anger boiled up, fueling a surge of adrenaline that brought everything into crystal clear focus. All sound, except for her assailant's heavy breathing, stopped. She waited.

Why didn't he attack? Why did he stop?

She raised her head in defiance, blood and muck clinging to the strands of hair covering her face.

I am a guardian angel. No evil shall pass by me.

This man was obviously evil. Demon or not, evil was evil. She had no choice but to put an end to him.

"Like hitting little girls, do you? Not very gentlemanly." She clicked her tongue behind her teeth as her arms numbly pushed her into a squatting position. Sizing him up, this time as an opponent, Greylyn saw past the fashionable attire and good looks to the dark soul underneath. A blackness exuded from his aura, so dark it mingled with the night sky. How had she not seen it before?

The man straightened to his full height, hands at his side curled into fists. "You shouldn't be here, love." She had expected an angry retort or another attack, but his voice was soft and shaky.

Her eyes darted around the alley. She needed a weapon, preferably her own. Where had it gone? With the moon fully ensconced behind the clouds it was impossible to see more than his faint outline, even with her superior nighttime vision.

Greylyn rose to stand, her back against the broken stone wall. "Well, I am here. Ready to party." She had aimed for a daring, but jovial tone. The slight squeak at the end belied her inner fear.

"Looking for a good time, I see. Well then, how about a dance?"

He sprung at her in a blur, but Greylyn dodged just an inch to the left and he slammed into the same wall he had thrown her against. She pivoted to attack while he was still prone on the ground, but a sudden glint of blue caught her attention. Her dagger! Just a few yards away.

She dove to the right, her outstretched fingers grazed the hilt, but her hesitation cost her. A hand clamped down fully on the handle and wrestled it away from her grasp. He rolled her over roughly, straddled her hips with her arms trapped underneath his knees, and smashed her face with the fist holding her own weapon.

Pain exploded as bones and tendons cracked and blood seemed to spurt from every pore. The assault continued, punch after punch, blow after blow. Greylyn's world turned crimson just before a blackness edged her vision.

Her first assignment as a guardian angel. Her first failure, and quite possibly, her last.

Death was inevitable. Not even her own supernatural strength could save her from this monster. Despite the agony racing throughout her body, her mind clearly accepted her fate.

Even though I walk through the valley of the shadow of death, I shall fear no evil.

Silence fell over the alley. The rain of punches stopped. Greylyn's eyes opened to peek at her attacker. What she saw chilled her to her soul – the demonic red eyes had smoldered away, back to their original gold-flecked hue. The man's face transformed from pure rage to sadness as a tear rolled down his cheek. A tear? "I'm ... I ... Oh no ..." His trembling lips continued to move, but no coherent words formed.

"What in the bloody hell ..." An angry roar shocked her out of her stupor. That voice she recognized. Jasper.

Unable to move, she gaped as a tall shadow with piercing eyes of ice jerked her assailant away from her.

"You damn ..." He did not finish his sentence, just punched the man in the face while holding him by his lapel.

Greylyn gulped in air. She was not dead, not yet. Renewed energy pulsated through her body and gave her strength to push herself up on shaky arms. She stared, turning to look at each man as they circled each other. Both men with deadly intent etched on their faces. In between getting hit, and throwing jabs of his own, the stranger muttered, "Had to be you! It just had to be you!" One final uppercut to Jasper's jaw, and the guardian angel fell back.

Her mouth opened to scream for him to leave Jasper alone, but no words came out. He turned to her, his face bloodied, but with a sad smile. "Until next time, love." Seconds later, he vanished down the alleyway.

Suddenly able to move again, Greylyn jumped up and ran over to Jasper. "Who the hell was that?"

"Oh, I'm fine, by the way." With the indignant look he flashed she knew Jasper was far from being fine. Physically, yes, he was alright. But his icy-blue eyes spoke volumes of fury she could not understand.

"I'm so sorry ..." She checked him for injuries, hands roved over his body. His clothes were spattered with blood. Other than his pride, and a black eye that would fade in an hour or two, he was in perfect shape.

Greylyn knew she looked a mess. Hell, she should be dead. Instead, the blood had already dried and the sizzle of her bones mending underneath her skin comforted her.

I am not going to die. At least not tonight.

Jasper cupped her chin. "Yes, I know. It's my fault. It was too soon to send you out on your own like that. I realized my mistake and came to find you in case you needed assistance." A nerve twitched in his jaw. "And I find I was correct. You certainly needed help." Disappointment was evident in his tone.

"Oh, no! Edward? Did he escape? I came out here looking for him, but these guys," she waved her hand towards the corpses littering the alley, "were after him and ..."

"Yes, yes. I get it. You ran into the bad guys and as a bonus, you got a bloody dark guardian your first time on your own."

"A what?"

"A dark guardian. The exact opposite of us, darling. You are just lucky I came along when I did. That one would've carved you up like a porterhouse steak." He pushed himself off the ground. At his full height of well over six feet tall, he towered above her.

"Does this dark guardian have a name?" She did not know why it mattered that she find out his name. Jasper narrowed his eyes at her in obvious disapproval.

"That one in particular is Kael," Jasper spat. "Truly nasty piece of work. Avoid him at all costs. Hopefully, you will never have to see that creature again."

He turned towards her and grabbed her by the upper arms, leaning forward so they were nose to nose. An aroma of whiskey and tobacco wafted into her face. "Greylyn, promise me that you will stay away from Kael. If he ever crosses your path, either annihilate him completely with your dagger through his heart and then rip it out of his body while it is still beating; or run. Just run."

Centuries later, Jasper's warning still echoed in her ears. Kael arose every so often,

almost as if he were taunting her with his presence. He would toy with her, undo whatever good she intended to do, and just in general made her afterlife difficult. Every encounter etched into her memory, chipping away at her tough veneer. One day, she vowed, she would end him for good.

Chapter 1

The Dueling Hearts

West Memphis, Arkansas

Four Centuries Later

Stale beer and sweat assailed Greylyn as the gorilla of a bouncer pushed open the wooden doors to allow her entrance into *The Dueling Hearts.* The country western establishment was the hottest nightclub scene this side of the Arkansas/Tennessee state line. She sometimes wondered why she never had an assignment at a spa or a beach resort. Instead, it seemed she always ended up in bars and alleys seeking out people to save.

After jostling with other bar patrons for the lone bartender's attention, Greylyn ordered a bourbon with a splash of coke and settled in to wait. Trying her best to put out the *Don't bother me* vibe with a vacant stare and expressionless face, she sipped her watered-down beverage.

A tugging sensation in the back of her mind alerted Greylyn that her young charge, Jenna, had just walked through the door with some friends. She shook her head.

Last weekend, Greylyn had brushed up against a plain Jane with mousy brown hair barely able to make eye contact with anyone. All of Jenna's loneliness and memories of neglect had flooded her angel senses. However, she had not been sent to rescue the girl from her own fragile mentality.

Now the girl sported long, platinum blonde locks that went midway down her back. Her face was plastered with "southern beauty queen" make-up. The transformation was complete with typical clubbing attire –

short-short denim skirt, shimmering, hot pink tank top exposing substantial cleavage, and silver stiletto heels that she had obvious trouble walking in.

Poor girl is going to break her ankle in those things.

Unfortunately, the metamorphosis had done nothing to improve Jenna's emotional state.

She still could not make eye contact with anyone.

As Jenna headed towards the bar with her friends, Greylyn kept an eagle-eye on the door for trouble. She did not have to wait long. Trouble, aka Devon – a young, handsome man with a Cheshire cat smile and smoky-gray eyes – sauntered into the bar and made a beeline towards the girl. He was followed closely by an entourage of four strapping young cowboy-types. An annoying buzzing behind her eyes confirmed it … soul stealing demons.

Greylyn had encountered several soul stealers over the years. Seeing the results of their work – the zombies that their victims became as they continued throughout life without the ability to feel love, hope, happiness, or differentiate between right and wrong – made her blood boil.

Adding to her frustration was the fact this particular soul stealer had escaped her clutches before and gone on to inflict evil on countless other souls.

Tapping her toes to the upbeat country tunes, she vigilantly watched over Jenna, waiting for a good moment to confront Devon alone. But the group of demon cowboys stayed close together, forming a circle around the couple.

The tiny hairs on the back of her neck suddenly stood straight up. One of Devon's pals approached her, a squat-faced man resembling an NFL linebacker with long, shaggy dishwater blond locks tied back in a ponytail. His ragged designer jeans and uber-tight white t-shirt showcased his ripped abs and pectorals to perfection. Several female heads spun around, watching his every move, probably hoping he was heading their way. But he stopped right in front of her with an outstretched hand. "Care to two-step?"

Without waiting for an answer, he grabbed her hand and dragged her onto the dancefloor. He took every opportunity to press his face close to hers. The stench of the brute's beer breath could have leveled the entire establishment and made her eyes water. She continued to smile up at him while fighting the urge to flinch.

Despite his numerous attempts to hold eye contact with her – a common trick used to captivate innocents – her eyes darted around the room in search of Jenna and Devon. With all that twirling, Greylyn lost sight of them in the throngs of couples on the dance floor. Again, she cursed her shortness. The thug blocked everything in her line of sight.

After about the tenth time of swatting his giant hand off her buttocks, she had had enough. The twangy song mercifully ended so she wrenched herself away from his meaty grasp. Her heartbeat quickened. Neither Jenna nor Devon was anywhere in sight.

Shivers spread up her spine. Her charge was in danger.

Damn it! Where the hell is she?

Greylyn climbed up on the edge of the stage for a better view. She spotted one of Jenna's friends, a strawberry blonde in black denim pants and a V-neck top that plunged too far down when she bent over. The woman was sitting on the lap of a young cowboy with his hand sliding up and down her legs. She pushed past the throngs of dancers. Without waiting to introduce herself, she yanked the woman off her paramour.

"Where did Jenna go?" Starry, vacant hazel eyes stared back at her. The girl was blitzed!

With the gray tinge around her aura, Greylyn suspected she was quite literally drowning her sorrows. Placing the pads of her thumbs on the woman's eyelids, she whispered a quick spell in Latin – *Ostendo mihi Jenna.* The last image of her friend played back in Greylyn's mind – Jenna holding hands with Devon as he led her down a long, dim corridor towards the back bar area. The poor girl had even tripped in those insane high heels, but Devon caught her arm, dragging her outside.

"Thanks." She released the girl, but something stopped her from running out the back. A vision blinded her to all else. The thumping of the music stilled. All else around her ceased to exist.

The same woman, except dressed in ivory chiffon, stared out a high window. Although slightly obscured by a drizzling mist, terror radiated from the woman's wide eyes. A single tear slid down her pale, freckled cheek. Fear seized Greylyn's own heart and squeezed to near bursting. Then …

The rowdy bar roared back into full focus amid the crowd singing along to "Chicken Fried" by the Zac Brown Band. Shaking off the vision, Greylyn placed a reassuring hand on the woman's shoulders. "I believe I'll be seeing you again sooner or later." Glossy eyes stared blankly back.

Greylyn ran out the back of *The Dueling Hearts* to an unlit alleyway. Her vision immediately adjusted to the pitch-black night. In the right corner of the alley, Devon's entourage loitered around a stretch limo, smoking cigarettes. She sensed Jenna nearby but could not see her or the soul stealer anywhere.

Okay, Grey. It is now or never to put those acting skills to work.

After working as an understudy for a minor character from an off-off Broadway production of *Cats* for three months to keep the producer from taking advantage of the revolving door of innocent children into the theater, she took a bit of pride in her new dramatic skill set.

Mussing her hair a bit, she noisily sauntered towards the group. "Excuse me," she tried saying in her best drunken drawl, "could one of you handsome gents help me out?"

The men turned towards her, their eyes at first growing wide before narrowing at her approach. The way their gazes roved up and down her body, lingering too long on her chest, sent a wave of revulsion through her.

They advanced toward her like a hyena pack. Greylyn picked the weakest looking of the crew, a tall, lanky blond with pristine nails and hair frozen in place with product. Wavering over to him, she peered up into his slate-gray eyes as she placed her hand lightly on his chest. "Hi," she cooed seductively, followed by a giggle.

With a wicked half-grin, the demon placed his hand over hers while using his other hand on her chin to lift her eyes to his face. He drawled, "Hello, there. Just how can we help you, pretty lady?" He kept one hand on her face while the other lightly brushed her hand, which remained on his chest, just above where his shirt opened to reveal baby-smooth skin.

She batted her richly mascaraed lashes at him and giggled again. "You know, I think I'm lost. One minute I was inside the bar looking for the ladies' room, and then I was outside. Now I can't even figure out how to get back in."

He uttered a tsking sound as the others closed the circle even more tightly around her. With a sickeningly sweet, condescending tone, the demon stroked her cheek as he leaned in to whisper in her ear, "Poor little, lost lamb. Just what are we going to do with you?" At his last words, his irises changed to blood red orbs.

Greylyn firmly placed one hand against the demon's chest, her other fist struck out with all her might. Skin and bone gave way underneath her small, thin hands. Not a death blow by any means since he was a demon, but enough to incapacitate him while she dealt with the rest. In his shock, the demon's eyes quickly retreated to his regular human gray. Clutching his chest, he slumped to the ground as blood gurgled out of his mouth.

The others jumped into action as the injured demon lay on the asphalt, writhing in agony.

One down, three strapping demon cowboys to go.

They attacked simultaneously. Her squat-faced thug dance partner grabbed her arms from behind. She keeled over as the other two rained down punches on her face and into her abdomen. A sharp jab straight to her nose accompanied by a nauseating crunching of bone, Greylyn was blinded with pain.

Infuriated, she raised her face to glare at her attackers. "You're going to regret that." With one super-hard stomp of her cowgirl boots on the toes of the demon behind her, she heard a gush of air as he bent over in pain. She reared her head back as sharply as possible to collide with his face. He bellowed like a howler monkey before letting go. Staggering back, he cupped his hands over his face as blood gushed out of his broken nose.

"Who's next?" She swiped the blood dribbling down her own face with the back of her hand.

The other two advanced with more caution. Backing up to get a running start, she maintained eye contact with the bigger, more aggressive-looking demon. Greylyn reached behind her back to grasp the hilt of her dagger. Its power flowed from her hands and up her arm in a warm wave. She unsheathed it and pulled it in front of her, gripping the weapon firmly by the intricate Celtic crest carved in the handle. Its blade shone with a cold, pale light of its own and was sharp enough to slice through a single strand of hair as it floated in the air while its jagged edges could saw through anything. Not many things could kill a demon, but that was exactly what the dagger was designed to do. And it did its job well.

Greylyn sprinted towards the two standing demons. One turned and ran with a shriek reminiscent of a cartoon character's reaction to seeing a ghost. The other stared her down while waiting for her to strike. Just a step before reaching him she jerked to the right. He lunged for where he thought she would be. But with an abrupt pivot, she swung behind him. Her dagger thrust upward into his back, finding its mark, the place where a human heart would reside. The serrated edges sawed through the beating muscle then ripped upward. The demon bellowed in pain before falling lifeless to the ground, red, slimy blood gushing out of his wound and pooling underneath his corpse.

Panting for air to refresh her burning lungs, Greylyn peered around while wiping the blade on her jeans. Her dance partner had recovered. Rage peered out from under the blood-drenched hair partially covering his eyes. He stormed towards her, much like an NFL linebacker going for the quarterback sack. Blood cascaded down his face, his lips curled up in a menacing snarl.

"Hey, there sweetie," she teased as he stopped within a few feet of her. "Wanna dance?" His growl was all the answer she needed. They circled each other, never breaking eye contact. He moved first, swatting at her head with his long, muscular arms. She leapt back, but the palm of his hand whacked the side of her cheek with a resounding slap. Greylyn raised a hand to her face. Her cheek stung fiercely, but she grinned back at him.

She had not realized just how much she missed the rush of adrenaline and the thrill of the fight until this moment. Her last few jobs had been benign, involving talking desperate people out of doing horrible things or just not jumping. Nothing that required violence. Until now.

He barreled towards her with a guttural snort, like a raging bull in the arena. She quickly sidestepped and hooked her foot around his ankle. The thug face-planted on the rocky asphalt next to the back tire of the limo.

With the dagger suspended above her head, Greylyn pounced on his back, jerking his head back by grabbing a handful of hair. The knife sliced through the bulging muscles at his neck, through his jugular vein. A final death thrash threw her off him just as his body slumped against the pavement.

Asphalt pebbles wedged painfully into her skin. Before she could take a breath, the back door of the limo creaked open. Devon emerged in all his tall faux-cowboy glory. Red lipstick smudged his stark white shirt and around his mouth. Obviously, he had been enjoying his quality alone time with Jenna.

Please, Lord, don't let him have gotten his grubby mitts on her soul yet.

His eyes burned with barely controlled rage. He did not glance back as a clearly frightened Jenna ran, sobbing hysterically towards the bar. With relief, Greylyn noted that the girl's aura was still intact, meaning so was her soul. Her emotional state, on the other hand, not so much.

Devon's eyes narrowed with contempt as he assessed the carnage lying around the alley. In two long, quick strides he was within inches of her face. Greylyn stood her ground.

"If you wanted to get me alone," Devon's lips curled into a suggestive grin, "all you had to do was ask."

She wiped her bloody blade on her white tank top. The move was enough to attract Devon's attention. He blinked, causing his gray irises to flash their true demon red. "Nice knife. Looks familiar. A guardian's blade, I see. Should've guessed considering your," he waved his hand to indicate the bloodbath in the alley, "work."

Still, his eyes remained deadlocked on the dagger. Deciding to capitalize on his fascination with the weapon, she waved it in front of his face. Moonlight reflected off its pearly surface, the jagged edges darkened with demon blood. Devon made a lightning-fast grab for the dagger but came up empty-handed.

"Gotta be quicker than that, cowboy!"

Devon took a step back to get a better look at her. He shook his head, his long dark locks swished over his eyes as a pearl of sweat streamed down his face. He made another unsuccessful grab for the knife. "There's something familiar about you."

"Who I am is irrelevant. What I am is the means to an end ... yours." She lunged at him with whirlwind speed. As she attacked, she envisioned all the nasty, evil things he had done to countless humans. There were no telling how many lives he had shattered since her last failure to kill him. Tonight, those souls would be avenged.

They charged each other with roars of fury. He was strong and fast, faster than his entourage had been. With a powerful kick, the tip of his boot smashed into her sternum, knocking the breath out of her lungs. Falling, Greylyn barely escaped another bash to the chest from his boot heel with a quick twist to the side. She jumped up and sprang over the demon's head to land on the trunk of the limo. Her feet slid on the smooth metal, but she planted them firmly against a slight ridge on the edge. Despite the pain ravaging every muscle, despite the broken bones, and despite the blood gushing down her face making everything in her sight blurred in heavy crimson, she could not resist a grin at the riled-up demon.

He dove to tackle her. They both tumbled off the car onto the sharp, graveled pavement. Locked together in a battle for control, they rolled for several feet. Devon grabbed her wrists just as the dagger's point pricked the skin at the base of his Adam's apple. Her wrist bones snapped and sent shocks up her arms. Unable to withstand the pressure, her hold on the weapon weakened. Devon successfully turned the blade around towards Greylyn's chest. The tip pierced her skin.

She head-butted him with all her might. Blinding pain exploded through her skull. His head shot back with a howl of rage. The reprieve was just enough to loosen his grip. Greylyn twisted the weapon around, now clutched in her hands, and scraped the edge across the jugular vein throbbing in his neck.

Devon's hands clawed at his bleeding throat. She pushed him off her. Blinded by pain and blood, Greylyn crawled in the direction of the gurgling sound of the soul stealing demon in his death throes. Once she came in contact with his hard form writhing on the asphalt, she straddled his body while holding his arms down with her knees. He thrashed wildly trying to toss her off him, but she held on tight, digging her heels into his sides. Raising her arms high above her head, she thrust the dagger down with all the strength she could muster in her tiny frame – right into his heart. Greylyn felt the jagged edges tear through the skin, muscle, and bone to the beating organ. Another push and twist of the blade, the heart of the demon burst with slimy, blackish blood.

Devon the soul stealer was dead.

"Well, my boy," said the larger man in a Dolce & Gabbana suit while he slapped the other man on the shoulder. They had watched the petite guardian ravage the pack of soul stealers behind the bar. They had the best vantage point for the battle, hidden in the shadows atop a crumbling service station a couple blocks away. "You've done a fine job of keeping track of our girl over the years. I will admit that I am thrilled you defied my brother so long ago and chose *not* to kill her. Not many can get away with such disobedience. But this gamble has really paid off."

Smiling, Kael replied, "Always glad to be of service to you, sir." Teaming up with one of the most notorious tyrants of Hell had been dangerous, but he would not change a thing.

"Not much longer now until we can set things in motion with our little angel. I've waited long enough." Without so much as a farewell, the large, hulking man vanished into a whirling tunnel of air with only the sound of his laughter continuing to resonate in stifling humidity.

Alone, Kael breathed a heavy sigh of relief. Oh, he had every intention to keep a close eye on Greylyn. Things were just starting to go his way. After everything he had done, after all he had endured, an end was in sight.

He whispered out into the dark night, "Soon, Greylyn. I promise. Soon."

Her silhouette paused at the end of the alley and turned towards his location for a moment, her emerald eyes sparkling even from this distance. Kael knew she could make out his outline against the night sky, but more than that ... she sensed his presence. Undoubtedly, she had felt it before she even confronted Devon. The same way he always knew when she was near.

His lips curled up in a smile as he watched her instinctively grip her dagger again with one hand and the chain around her neck with the other. A second's pause, she turned away and raced off into the night as sirens blared in the distance.

Chapter 2

Gaelic Haven

5 years later

Wind ruffled her raven hair and pulled strands from her ponytail as Greylyn sped towards the closest thing she could find to Ireland hidden amidst the rolling hills of the Shenandoah. Every mile she drew closer, the better she felt. After battling vamps in Utah and saving a truckload of immigrants from a demonic smuggler in Arizona, she craved some rest and relaxation, preferably someplace with a milder climate and some green scenery.

Well, one did not get much greener than the foothills of the Shenandoah Mountains in early summer. Virginia was a vast landscape of varying shades of green during the spring and summer months, with spectacular red, yellow, and orange foliage in the fall, and dreary gray all winter long. Right now, the peaceful valley soothed her weary soul, but also stung with a bit of nostalgia for the never-ending hills and dales of Ireland.

Her memories of her homeland were scant, aside from the night of her rebirth. Those still replayed vividly in her mind. Of course, waking up in a grave would not be something one could forget. Anything before that fateful night remained a mystery.

One hand absently twirled a small, metal ring hanging from a spaghetti-thin platinum necklace around her slender neck while tapping her other hand on the steering wheel in time to a Kenny Chesney tune. The ring served as her only physical remnant of a life she did not remember.

Turning off the main highway, tension that had been hammered into her shoulders for months melted away. Two right turns and a hard left onto a shady tree-lined street, and she had her first sight of the inn. Greylyn drove up the ambling driveway, her breath taken away by its simplistic beauty as the magnificent manor stood atop a hill, framed by the rising mountains behind it. She had visited the Gaelic Haven Inn over a decade ago and had longed to return, but her job kept her busy.

Pebbles crunched underneath the tires of her British racing green, 1968 Camaro as she pulled into the mostly empty parking area adjacent to the main house. As the roar of the engine died, Greylyn immediately looked around for signs of the pint-sized, fifty-something innkeeper, Maureen. Just a few yards away, she was dressed in her garden scrubs, pruning rose bushes by the expansive white gazebo overlooking the rectangular koi pond where the loudest bull frogs in the southeast took up residence – guests were even provided ear plugs in each room to block out the continuous croaking during the nights.

Maureen had transformed the picturesque setting into her own version of a traditional Irish estate, as her very own *Gaelic Haven* for travelers and those looking for a peaceful retreat from the world. The hilltop Edwardian mansion had quite a history of its own, being the site of a notorious Civil War encampment. While the inn was maintained as a historical preserve, the crumbling antebellum manor and grounds had been renovated into the grand 19th century Irish estate it was today.

During her last visit, Greylyn had instantly formed a fast friendship with the chatty owner. She loved to hear Maureen's accent and could listen for hours to her yarns about her childhood in Ireland or interesting clientele.

She had barely placed both feet on solid ground before Maureen swooped her into a tight embrace. The smell of garden soil and lavender wafted through the air.

"Now, how have ya been, Sweetie? It's been much too long since your last visit. You promised to return every year, and now it's been over ten."

Maureen squinted a little, causing Greylyn to tense slightly. She had not considered that her unchanged appearance after so many years may raise some uncomfortable questions from her hostess.

"Why look at ya, lass! Ya haven't aged since I've seen ya last. Why your skin's as fair and smooth as a baby's bottom!" Maureen accentuated her remark by caressing Greylyn's cheek. "Yes, those freckles are still adorable! And not a single gray strand in that beautiful mane of yours!" In contrast, Maureen's once flaming red hair had faded to a muted copper.

She hooked Greylyn's arm with her own and began to explain that there was a wedding taking place that weekend as she escorted her to the Carriage House, a two-story brick building that had been added after the completion of renovations to the main house. It had a tower that rose above the building where folks could peer out from a higher vantage point over the hills. Both stories of the house had large porches for visitors to relax while taking in the beauty of the surrounding valley and the splashing of koi and frogs in the adjacent pond. "As soon as I got your call, I explained to the handsome gentlemen occupying the room for the wedding that he would have to vacate."

"Oh, I don't want to inconvenience anyone," Greylyn proclaimed, but she was privately grateful. She preferred the quiet and solitude found in the Carriage House suite, even though the bullfrogs were parked right outside her window. Luckily, she could effectively tune out the croaks. Being a guardian angel had its perks. She would take the bull frogs anytime over the racket that accompanied her usual digs in seedy roadside motels as she drove cross-country doing her job.

"Now don't be silly, girl! That is your room whenever you visit. Besides the gentleman was rather understanding about the matter." After a slight, meaningful pause that Greylyn could not miss, Maureen added, "He's not bad on the eyes either so I gave him the room above yours. I hope that's okay." Her powder-blue eyes twinkled with mischief.

Oh, no. How could she have forgotten that the woman was a hopeless romantic?

Maureen left Greylyn to settle into her room, with a promise that her guest hop over to the main house for drinks. "Don't take too long, dear. I'm dying to catch up."

The door clicked shut softly. Alone, she looked over the cottage décor. Everything was exactly as it had been on her last visit. An antique mahogany four-poster bed with a deep purple duvet cover and throw pillows anchored the room. Sunlight barely filtered through the antique white lace curtains, as the day outside was somewhat cloudy. Straight back from the bedroom was her favorite part: the luxurious bathroom. In contrast to the vintage décor of the suite, all the modern conveniences of a full spa soaking tub and steam shower had been installed. Last visit, she spent more time soaking in the tub than hiking the foothills of the Shenandoah.

But something was wrong. An electricity filled the air. Despite the comforting familiarity of the room, her hopes for a peaceful vacation sank. The air was more oppressive, heavier than the atmosphere outside. Considering the humidity in Virginia this time of year, that was saying something. Goose bumps sprung up all down her arms. The tiny hairs on the back of her neck stood up, too. Yes, something evil was here, or had been recently.

The room lacked the hint of sulfur that was a dead giveaway when demons were around. Although not the smell of rotten eggs, the lingering scent was oddly familiar. She just could not place it.

Thinking back to her earlier conversation, she guessed the recent occupant was more than he appeared. It had been too much to hope that she could go anywhere without encountering some form of evil being. She made a mental note to check the wedding guest out immediately. But preferably after a nice glass of wine with Maureen.

Dammit! For once, can't I catch a break and not have my R&R spoiled?

She scoped out the room for signs of non-friendly visitors or surveillance. The battle between good and evil had escalated to high-tech gear. She preferred to fight the old-fashioned way. High-tech gadgetry spoiled the fun.

One time she found a tiny radio transmitter disguised as a towel hook in a bathroom at a high-end hotel, where a certain rock star on the verge of suicide stayed while in the Big Apple. The human ear could not hear the incessant chanting in Latin that urged the drug-addled man to take his own life. Another time, a listening device was discovered in a corporate office intercom speaker for a tech company's charismatic CEO. Not overly high-tech for a dot.com. While amusing, these antics made it easier for her to locate the bad guys, not harder.

Satisfied that there was no surveillance, Greylyn pulled some sage and a small vial out of her knapsack. While burning sage to cleanse the air of malevolent energy and placing talismans at all possible entrances, as well as at the north, south, east, and west points in the room similar to a compass, she dusted a special mixture of ground salt and rosemary around the suite to keep non-human entities away while she was out.

Some holy water sprinkled along the doorframe, and the room was protected from any evil entities, whether in corporeal form or not. Determined to root out the problem quickly, Greylyn stomped over to the manor to investigate.

"No one is going to spoil my vacation. No one," she muttered under her breath.

He had felt her approach long before the Camaro's tires crunched on the long gravel driveway leading up to the house. That energy and magnetic pull intensified to a feverous point whenever she was near. Kael had waited for this moment for a long time, too long. And he was not a patient man. Things could not be working out any better if she had fallen right into his lap. A grin pulled at the corners of his lips as he listened to her exchange with the sweet-as-pie innkeeper.

"No, Greylyn. No vacation for you, I'm afraid. This weekend is going to be a wild ride."

Greylyn fought off a rising sense of frustration as she stepped out onto the small patio of the Carriage House. Perhaps Maureen could divulge more about the wedding party. If evil were afoot, that would be her first guess where it would likely raise its ugly head. If the male guest currently in residence had been in her room, and was giving off a supernatural vibe, that would be the most logical explanation. She had witnessed plenty of weddings targeted by demonic entities in the past. Perfectly planned weddings, days of love and celebration ... all ruined for no other reason than evil enjoyed destroying any inklings of happiness.

A frog splashed across the lily pads on the surface of the koi pond, just a few yards away. Slightly startled, Greylyn laughed at her own unease. "Come on, Grey," she muttered to herself. "This will be easy-peasy. No worries."

Glancing up at the main house, a large antebellum manor of brick, rock, and a metallic green roof, a jolt went through Greylyn's body as she was overcome by a vision ...

Droplets of rain fell. A cloudy haze blurred the gazebo where a small group huddled underneath. Soft piano music played but was cut off suddenly. The sound of a door banged like a thunderclap. Glancing over at the manor, an image of a figure in white looked out a second-story window. Her mouth opened wide in a silent scream.

With that, the vision receded like the flood waters of the Nile, leaving only a piercing pain behind her eyes.

Rubbing the bridge of her nose, she cursed her luck. Agitated, she stomped over to the main house.

Greylyn found Maureen in the large kitchen off to the side of the dining room, putting away the clean dishes.

"I'll be with you in a moment, sweetie. Just need to stash away the crystal. Make yourself at home. The pub's fully stocked."

During her visit ten years ago, Maureen had explained that the pub had been designed as a scaled down replica of her favorite bar back in Dublin – The Brazen Head, Ireland's oldest pub, dating back to 1198. It was even older than Greylyn. She had frequented the actual establishment in the early days of her resurrection with her friend and mentor, Jasper Moreau. Its miniature replica brought a smile to her face.

Walking into the dimly lit nook off the front corner of the house, she felt transported back in time. It was still daylight outside, but the dark wood floors and wall paneling cast the room in eternal night, with antique wall sconces providing minimal illumination. Greylyn took down two glasses from the under-cabinet stemware rack and yelled to Maureen, "I'll be out on the front porch when you're free."

The covered veranda overlooked the front lawn, furnished with old-fashioned rocking chairs. Flowerpots stretched across the railing and along the cobblestone floor. She took a deep breath of the fresh country air.

Hints of lavender and rosemary greeted her senses.

Ah, now this is more like it. Why can't I stay like this? Can't another guardian work this gig?

She pulled out her phone from her jeans pocket. Maybe, Jasper can take care of this instead. Part of her felt guilty for wanting to pawn a job onto someone else, but guardian angel burnout had set in long ago. That last gig, she had been so exhausted that she had completely missed the obvious signs of a Jinn-infestation until it was almost too late.

With a few clicks on the phone, the message was sent. "Help. R&R in jeopardy. Wedding to save."

She allowed herself a few moments to soak up the serenity Gaelic Haven offered. Birds chirped a cheery tune. A gentle breeze tussled her hair. Elegant calla lilies – her favorite flower – in colorful ceramic pots made her smile. With a sigh, she poured some wine into her glass and took a big gulp. Just a minute to herself. Was that too much to ask? Probably.

A blanket of iron-gray storm clouds off in the distance cast an ominous shadow over the landscape. She had been so engrossed in the countryside during her drive, she had not paid any attention to the weather. Usually, Greylyn enjoyed rain, especially thunderstorms. The sheer power and vitality of a storm had a strangely calming effect on her. Pure, unadulterated energy. However, she did hope the foul weather would not settle in for the weekend and interfere with the wedding. Most brides wanted glorious sunny weather for their big day, even though an old wives' tale stated that rain on a wedding day heralded fertility.

But now, the electricity in the air raised the tiny hairs on the nape of her neck. Was it just the storm, or something more?

As she poured another glass, she caught the hint of a shadow moving at the edge of the front yard, in the gazebo. It was darker than the surrounding shade and appeared human-shaped. The evil was there, watching, and biding its time.

"There you are."

Casually setting her glass down, she called inside the house. "Hey, Maureen. I forgot something in my room. I'll be right back."

Greylyn slipped back through the house and out the rear door. Instead of crossing the short, pebbled path to the Carriage House, she quietly snuck around the other side of the manor. The dense tree line edging the property camouflaged her approach. The shadow was still there, completely motionless. There was also a faint musky scent in the air. It was not offensive like the odor given off by lower-level demons, more like the lingering fragrance in her suite.

When clandestinely watching someone, the key was to keep your focus just to the right or left of your object of interest. Looking directly at someone could transmit the sense of being watched, and then the jig was up. Greylyn kept her sights directly on the side of the gazebo where her peripheral vision could still track the shadow in case it chose to bolt.

The shadow did not move. As she neared the gazebo, the scurrying of a squirrel up the tree behind her was enough to warn the entity of her presence. It still did not move. Either it was completely unaware of her, or it was waiting for her.

"Hello, Greylyn! Long time, no see. Did you miss me?" a husky male voice called.

Chapter 3

The Enemy Unveiled

C hills ran up her spine at the friendly greeting, and her breath caught in her throat. That voice belonged to the one dark guardian she never wanted to tangle with again. Kael.

She had never in her over four hundred years of being a guardian angel encountered the same evil being twice ... except for this one. The menace had been showing up repeatedly ever since she began battling for good shortly after her rebirth. He would usually ruin, or at least try to ruin, her attempts to save someone and he took immense pleasure in toying with her. Now, she was not in the mood to deal with him ... again.

Trying her best to sound unruffled, she countered, "Well, I would say it's great to see you, but we both know that it's not." With more bravado than she felt, Greylyn stepped out of the shade of the trees into full view of her opponent. "Any chance you could just go pester some other guardian angel? Not to sound ungrateful for the attention, but I believe we could use a break."

Her heart stopped a moment as she drank in the sight of him with his charming, yet cocky grin. She despised him for all the evil he had unleashed on the world and untold damage to humanity, but more so for the way he made her weak in the knees. With him around, Greylyn would have to be extra careful. Her head was never clear when he was near.

"Dare I ask what you are doing here aside from disturbing my vacation?" A waver in her voice betrayed her lack of confidence. Why did he always affect her so badly?

With a soft chuckle he emerged from the shadowed corner of the gazebo. Tall, dark, and sinfully handsome. His deep cognac eyes danced wickedly, alight with gold flecks that could hypnotize even the strongest mind. One minute they burned bright as topaz, the next they could darken to the shade of a tiger's eye gemstone. She discovered long ago that directly gazing into those seductive pools was more dangerous than teetering on the edge of a volcano. Although she was unsusceptible to regular demon thrall, the same did not apply to him.

He strode over to Greylyn, took her hand, and gently kissed it, his lips soft and warm against her skin. "Come sit with me, love."

Damn it!

An electrical surge raced through her entire body from the point of physical contact. Her breath caught in her chest. Every nerve ignited pinpricks of pleasure racing through her veins.

Trying to wrench her hand away, she steeled herself for any further interaction by digging her nails into her palms. Pain the only antidote to the physical influence he held over her. And sometimes, that did not work.

His chestnut brown hair, with a touch of auburn highlights, swept his forehead just above those brooding, dreamy eyes.

Get it together, girl! Stop looking into his eyes, for pity's sake!

"Love," he drawled, "we both know this is no vacation. Although I don't see why we can't have some fun together." The side of his mouth ticked up in one corner, showcasing his dimple.

"When Hell freezes over, Kael."

His soft chuckle washed over her. "Dear, dear, Greylyn. Why don't you save yourself the trouble? Go on a *real* vacation. The Shenandoah Mountains are lovely this time of year, and I know how much you enjoy hiking."

Now grasping both of her hands, his thumb traced a figure-eight pattern across her captured wrists. She would almost swear she saw sparks flying off her skin from his caress.

"No thanks, Kael. Tempting, but I'd rather kick your ass back to Hell." Brave words, but her tell kicked in as one hand shot up to absentmindedly clutch at the ring hanging from her neck. Gold flecks in his eyes sparked as the movement drew his attention away from her eyes to the small trinket. His smile faltered, but only for a second.

In her best low menacing voice, she asked, "Why don't you go enjoy the mountain trails and leave these poor people alone? Or we can just get this fight over with right now. That way I *can* enjoy my vacation while you rot in Hell."

His grin grew wider in apparent amusement. Despite her outward show of confidence, her insides felt like jelly. Even if she could overcome the distraction caused by his presence, he was a formidable opponent. He had bested her many times in battle, but she always managed to escape or gain the upper hand.

Good thing she texted Jasper already. He hated Kael even more than she did.

Kael's hand reached up and pushed a strand of her ebony hair behind her ear. "Now, love, I would never even consider leaving you. Perhaps, we can catch up, for old time's sake. Share war stories." Then to her surprise he added, "You remember that debacle in the Florida Everglades? I am dying to know how you beat my best swamp creature to save that group of lost Boy Scouts. I thought you were a goner. Thankfully, it was no match for you." He chuckled, "I wouldn't miss this for the world."

Strange. She did not recall seeing him during that little adventure. How did he know about the swamp creature?

Greylyn quipped, "First, cut the *love* crap. It's annoying. All this jibber jabber is boring me, Kael." She attempted to wrench her hand away from his grasp, but he held on tight. This encounter needed to end, and quickly. Already her insides quavered. It would not be long before her exterior followed suit. She had almost forgotten how intoxicating, and exasperating, he could be. Almost.

A dulcet Irish voice startled her. "Well, isn't that fantastic, the two of you have met. Sweetie, this is the handsome gentleman I was telling you about earlier. He is taking photographs for the wedding." Maureen winked at her.

Oh dear! Was she hoping to set the two of us up? Just terrific! Not going to happen, Maureen. No way. No how. Not a chance in Heaven or Hell.

Kael had the audacity to blush while flashing his dimpled grin.

"Actually, we were just introducing ourselves," Greylyn innocently stated with a coy smile in his direction. "So, you are photographing the wedding here? That's fantastic. How long have you been a wedding photographer, Mister ...? I'm sorry, what did you say your name was?"

"My deepest apologies for not introducing myself properly. I must have been carried away by your beauty." He placed his hand on his chest and bowed slightly. Unfortunately, Greylyn was not able to take her eyes away from the broad chest muscles evident underneath his thin, white button-down shirt.

He continued, "Kael O'Shea at your service. My photography business has just gotten started, but my dear friends Kelly and Matthew, asked me to do this favor for them. How could I refuse a request to contribute to their special day? It's the least I could do for them."

With a tilt of his head towards the innkeeper, he added, "Ms. Maureen allowed me the luxury of coming up a couple days in advance to take some pictures of the estate and surrounding countryside to add to my portfolio."

"Yes, Kael plans to create a photo brochure for the inn online so more people can discover us." Maureen practically beamed. "We could use the publicity." Greylyn detected a note of sadness.

"We'll put this place on the map, that's for sure. Don't you worry. As soon as I can get those pictures loaded up, everyone will want to visit here. You'll have to turn down guests." He had done his research, including getting in good with the happy couple, and charming the innkeeper. Kael knew what he was doing there. Up until a few minutes ago, Greylyn had blissfully thought she was on vacation.

"He is such a dear," the older woman gushed. "I didn't mean to interrupt, just thought you'd both like a glass of wine." With that, she carefully set the wine bottle and two delicate Heritage Irish Crystal glasses down on the side table in the gazebo. Without giving either of them an opportunity to protest that she was not joining them, Maureen briskly walked back to the main house, humming an Irish tune.

Kael smiled broadly and shrugged his shoulders. "What a kind lady! Remind me to let her live when this is over."

That snapped Greylyn out of her funk. She reached behind her back to withdraw her small, but deadly dagger. It had sent more hell-raisers back to the fiery pits than most exorcisms throughout the ages. Cold, pale iridescent light glimmered off its edge.

With lightning-fast speed, he grabbed her wrists. "Now don't ruin this romantic moment by introducing violence, unless that is how you get your thrills," Kael softly admonished. He applied pressure with his thumb to the area between her thumb and index finger, causing her hand to automatically open. The knife fell to the floor with a dull thud. "You know this is not the time or place."

The smug bastard sure appeared pleased with himself. Dammit! She had let him taunt her into losing control.

Slowly, he let go of her wrists, his fingertips grazing along the sensitive skin where her pulse beat wildly. Kael reached over and poured wine into both their glasses, handed one to her, and raised his glass in a toast. "To us! May this not be our last battle together, but may the best *man* win." With that, he clinked his glass against Greylyn's and took a long sip while never breaking eye contact. The butterflies in her stomach flew into a frenzy.

"Ah, French Beaujolais! This brand is divine! Mild, slightly fruity – more red currant and tart cherry than raspberry – with a smoky note finish." He tilted his glass towards her. "Perfect for a stormy afternoon. Please, drink up."

Taking a small sip of her wine to quench her parched mouth and stall for time to break free of his allure, she inwardly debated the best course of action. Slicing and dicing Kael in the gazebo was an option but would cause more trouble than not. How would she explain the dead wedding photographer to Maureen? No, it would be best to deal with him privately so as not to leave Gaelic Haven with a dead body and questions from the police that could never be answered.

After one more sip of wine for courage, she set the glass down, tucked her dagger back in its holster, and stood to leave. If she could not take him out now, and he was not going to reveal any helpful information, there was no point in sticking around. The creature may be handsome. He may make her still-human heart beat a little too fast – okay, more than a little too fast. All that added up to the fact that she needed to get away from him so she could clear her head. Jasper had been right. When faced with Kael, either kill him or run.

Why, oh why did he have to be the one to show up here? And why did he have that self- satisfied smug look on his face?

"Now, Greylyn, there's no reason we can't sit and enjoy some good wine and conversation. You don't want to disappoint your friend, do you? She has such high hopes for us. As soon as you called to say you were on your way, she didn't hesitate to kick me out of *your* room. The sweet old girl talked you up like you were a goddess ..." He winked. "... well, she was right about that." Pausing to pour another glass of wine for himself, Kael turned back to her. "Of course, Maureen asked plenty of nosy questions about my availability. She was thrilled to hear that I am currently unattached but looking out for that special someone." He chuckled softly.

Greylyn gaped at him. *What the hell?*

"Really, we should at least give her something to hope for and make it look good. Come on, love ... for Maureen. It'll be fun." His velvety voice made the offer tempting, but warning sirens were already screeching loudly in her head.

Run, Greylyn. Run.

A sigh of exasperation escaped her. Her inner smartass recovered from the fuzzy state of mind that afflicted her since stepping into the gazebo. "It's always fun and games with you, isn't it? Until I smack that smarmy grin off your face anyway."

His golden eyes twinkled mischievously, and his eyebrows arched slightly. "Love, you can do whatever you wish with me. But yes, I do enjoy our little games." He reclined against the wooden bench and crossed his feet at the ankles, all the while his gaze roved over her body. "Why not sit back and enjoy the storm rolling in? We don't even have to speak to each other. Just bask in the storm's energy."

Greylyn had not noticed how quickly the earlier storm clouds had moved in and how dramatically the wind had picked up. Kael had that effect on her. In his presence, she solely tuned into him and not to her surroundings. A fact that had been her downfall in earlier confrontations with him, more than once. She reprimanded herself to stay focused, while digging her nails harder into the palm of her left hand, piercing the tender flesh.

Rain pounded the metallic roof of the gazebo, like pennies from Heaven. A flash of bright light illuminated the tenebrous sky. Resounding thunder followed, shaking everything around them.

For a moment, Greylyn saw the lightning mirrored in his eyes. She shook her head to rid herself of the image.

Great! Now she was imagining things.

He warned, "It's too late to go running for cover. Let's just sit here and wait out the rain. Surely, there's something we can discuss ... in a civilized manner."

Greylyn felt a pair of cornflower blue eyes peering at the two of them from the manor's covered veranda. Maureen was watching. No killing Kael with an audience around.

After years of being subjected to his torment, she would have to endure the insufferable man for at least one more go-around. But that did not mean she had to loiter in a gazebo with him, pretending to be friendly. It was dangerous, in more ways than one. The gold flecks in his eyes beckoned her closer, not just to him but to the edge of her own sanity.

She drew in a long, refreshing breath to ease the ache in her lungs. Breathing out, a sliver of calm returned. "Rain doesn't frighten me, Kael. And neither do you. This little confab is over." Pivoting, she stepped out into the torrential storm.

Instantly soaked, she steeled herself to keep marching right back towards the house, away from him. She felt his eyes boring into her back. It was as if he reached across the distance to trail a finger lightly down her spine, leaving a delicious tingling sensation that raised goosebumps over her entire body.

Just as Greylyn cleared the grove, another, more powerful, surge of electricity pierced the air. She whipped around just in time for a lightning bolt to strike the ground a few yards away. The ground shook as the resulting thunder boomed and echoed through the valley. A flash of fire quickly quenched by the rain. The ground blackened in a loose oval pattern.

The charged air amplified her senses. Her heartbeat against her ribcage in frantic time to the raging rain. Adrenaline coursed through her body in waves. The smell of the singed grass tickled her nose. Every rain drop hitting the earth resounded loudly in her ears. Water washed over her head, down her body as if she stood directly under a waterfall. Everything seemed brighter, more vivid. Every detail of her surroundings accentuated.

Was it from the lightning strike or from the energy radiating from the being in the gazebo?

Greylyn could not be sure. It mirrored the energy surging between them. Her eyes locked with Kael's.

Rain pelted her body, and the wind whipped her hair around in all directions. But to her, everything stopped. All sound. All motion. Greylyn no longer felt a thing except his burning stare. It was achingly painful. Every molecule of her being hypnotized by his eyes. For that moment there was only Kael, everything else faded to black.

Another loud crack of thunder severed the invisible tie that bound her to him. Wrenching her gaze away, Greylyn turned back towards the main house. Her heart screamed to run, but her mind forced her feet to steadily retreat to a place of safety.

Kael sat back down on the bench, poured himself another glass of wine, and watched her go with a faint smile. He had watched her walk away many times. This would not be the last. But this time, he meant to have some real fun. This time was for keeps.

Chapter 4

The Reign of Terror

Back in her suite in the Carriage House, Greylyn shook with pent up fury...at herself for allowing the dark guardian to affect her. Again. She fought to recall all the horrors Kael had caused over the centuries. Doing so was her only hope to salvage the rage and redirect it towards the true enemy. She needed to keep the current situation in perspective and to prevent her feet from betraying her and running back out to the gazebo.

What the hell was wrong with her? Her heart hammered in her chest like the *My Generation* drum solo by Keith Moon from The Who. Back in 1967, the drummer had placed ten cherry bombs in the drum kit for added effect. Yep, that was what her heart felt like right now.

Come on, Grey. Think of the worst possible evil Kael has ever accomplished.

Well, it did not take much to recall that disaster ...

Paris, France – the City of Lights – was far from that on June 14, 1793.

A few months earlier, the French king had met a terrifying fate beneath the cold steel of the guillotine. His wife and son were currently awaiting their fate in the Conciergerie – formerly part of the royal palace, the Palais de la Cite, now the main penitentiary holding anyone accused of being a counterrevolutionary.

The country was in serious upheaval, with the stakes being the very survival of the French people. The radical Jacobins had just seized power from the more moderate Girondins at the National Convention. With their ascent, a ten-month period of horror commenced under the leadership of the charismatic Robespierre. Years later, this became known as *The Reign of Terror*, or "*La Terreur*".

Unfortunately for the French citizens, Robespierre had quite a lot of help from all the wrong people. His right-hand man, a tall, dark, mysterious man whose very presence caused men's hearts to quake in fear, and women to scream with desire, led the French leader down a destructive path that would almost end the very country he proclaimed he was meant to save.

Robespierre's greed and his unquenchable thirst for power opened the door to the very man who could give it to him: Kael O'Shea, known to the French people as Monsieur Kalman Ocaliot. It was rumored that Robespierre had not so much as blinked when he handed over his soul in exchange for political dominance.

A mob converged in the square to hear the latest proclamations from the draconian Committee of Public Safety headed by Robespierre himself. After instituting several radical measures to control the populace, today marked the day when Christianity was to be banned from the entire country. As a prelude to the announcement, the crowd awaited their new form of entertainment: the execution of twenty enemies of the revolution. The crime? Not agreeing with Robespierre and his compatriots.

On that oppressively humid day in the crumbling capital of Paris, Greylyn stood face to face with the evil guardian for probably the tenth time that century. He had been a pain in her neck for quite a while as he popped up from time to time causing mischief and worse. This, quite possibly, qualified as being the absolute most evil of them all.

Greylyn glared at the man she held responsible for it all. She and Jasper had arrived too late to stop the execution of the king or the takeover by the Jacobins. Of French royal blood, Jasper had been beside himself when the news reached them in England. The handsome guardian angel vowed to right the wrongs in his homeland. As his best friend, she had jumped at the chance to help him.

Electric pulses from the dark guardian's stare assailed her body. He stood above the square, looking quite debonair in his embroidered and beaded silk coat and matching knickers. Now, all she wanted to do was rip out his blackened heart, preferably in front of all these people. If the mob wanted blood, they should take his.

A slight tap on her shoulder alerted her that Jasper had arrived. What he had been up to while she waited for the bloody show to begin was a mystery. He insisted he had his own business to contend with; otherwise, she would have gladly sucker-punched him in the gut for making her wait.

Time was wasting. If they did not act soon, all those pathetic-looking people standing behind the executioner's platform would meet grisly fates. Most were formerly a part of the elite, or particularly devout Christians. With their finery tattered, smeared with their own blood from countless hours of torture, they did not even have the strength for tears or cries for mercy. The only thing standing between these sad souls and the razor-sharp edge of the guillotine blade were two guardian angels hidden in the throng of bystanders waiting for the main attraction.

Jasper leaned close to whisper in her ear. "Soon, mon cherie." Strangely, eyes still locked on Kael, Greylyn sensed the dark guardian's rising anger, a tightening in her chest. His fists clenched and flexed at his side. *How is that possible?*

She vowed that she would never get used to the way her body reacted to him, how she could feel his emotions without a word said between them. Based on Jasper's disgusted response whenever they were confronted with the fiend, she had chosen to not fill him in on this tiny matter. Never in their entire friendship had she kept a secret from him...except for this one thing. Most days she would not even admit it to herself. There was an inexplicable connection between herself and the dark guardian. Jasper would never understand, nor should he.

The plan? Well, there was no real plan to rescue the group of prisoners as their crimes against France were read aloud for everyone to hear. Perhaps Jasper had something in mind, but he was not sharing.

The low growl he uttered just behind her radiated from his chest and into her own. There could be only one reason for that. He saw the master of this diabolical catastrophe. It was his typical reaction to Kael sightings. Now that the sinister manipulator had invaded his country, there was no telling what Jasper would do to him. Come to think of it, Greylyn wanted a front row seat to that show.

Without taking his burnt-umber eyes off her, Kael spoke to the man beside him, the notorious Maximilien Robespierre, with his powdered wig making him appear several inches taller than he actually was. Decked out in the best French clothes suitable for an advocate for the poor and downtrodden, a cover for his more nefarious inclinations for political power, he was unmistakably the key to the success of the Jacobin ideology.

At first, Robespierre did not appear extremely comfortable with the scene before him. His face was screwed up in an anxious scowl, his lips thin, his complexion pale, and his hands fidgeted with the hems of his lacey sleeves. With just a few words from his very own devil's advocate, his countenance changed. He even smiled as the last names of the condemned were read out.

"Got a plan or are we just going to stand here like sheep?" she muttered under her breath to Jasper. The tall, elegant warrior for Heaven had the audacity to shush her.

"Just wait, darling. Just wait." She marveled at how he could be so stoic and composed at a time like this. He was usually much more of a hothead. The situation was usually reversed. When he had first heard the news of what was happening in his home country, he had torn apart an entire demonic brothel and laid a brutal beat-down on the humans enjoying the festivities that night. But she knew, any sense of calm he presented now only masked a pure, but controlled rage waiting to be unleashed.

As if to emphasize the severity of the situation, a ray of sun broke free of the heavy summer clouds to reflect menacingly off the guillotine blade. The glint distracted Greylyn momentarily from the stare-down contest with Kael.

Just as the first prisoner ascended the wooden stairs to the executioner's platform, a resounding boom like thunder filled the air, along with billowing black smoke.

"That's our cue." Jasper excitedly tugged her along towards the condemned group. Somehow, he had managed to find someone willing to besiege the event with cannon fire. He certainly was resourceful. As everyone in the square ran in a chaotic frenzy away from the center of the commotion, Greylyn and Jasper raced into the thick of the smoke.

Another boom rocketed overhead towards the spectator stands where the ruling class had just been overseeing their handiwork. The resulting explosion hit just to the left. If whoever was shooting did not fix his aim, the next cannonball might hit the prisoners!

As if hearing her thoughts, the very next earsplitting blast was followed by the crashing of wooden beams as the executioner's platform disintegrated into black, fiery smoke. Caught in the flames were the wretched executioner and the first of the prisoners in line for the guillotine.

The other prisoners were shackled together, unable to escape the inferno creeping towards them while the onlookers scurried away. All except for two – Robespierre and Kael.

Unmoved by the disaster playing out before his eyes, Kael had a lock hold on the human under his command. He would not allow the frightened political leader to escape despite the sheer panic etched in Robespierre's expression.

Greylyn could not imagine why they did not flee with the rest, other than that the stubborn devil enjoyed tormenting the man. Come to think of it, she was quite sure he enjoyed tormenting everyone possible. This scene was just his cup of tea.

Jasper and Greylyn reached the prisoners trapped on the other side of the platform, still chained to each other and to a thick wooden post. The wooden stage fueled the raging fire, blocking any escape. Several of their garments had already caught on fire, mostly the women's billowing skirts. Luckily, Greylyn had chosen to disguise herself as a young boy in tattered knickers instead. It made fighting easier.

Even with their combined guardian angel super strength, the iron constraints were difficult to break. Straining with everything she had, she finally yanked the post that held the group captive out of the ground. At least now they could run away from the fire if they ran together.

While she focused her attention on freeing the prisoners, Jasper sprinted towards Kael and Robespierre to unleash his own fury against those responsible for the destruction of his beloved homeland. Robespierre at one time may have had noble intentions for ridding France of an evil tyrant but selling out to the darkness led to where it always did: death and destruction. Now France suffered for it.

Kael sidestepped Jasper's assault, leaving the politician to fend for himself against the enraged guardian. He did not seem interested in protecting the man he used to cause this mess. He did not so much as lift a finger as Jasper pummeled him to a bloody pulp. Greylyn almost felt sorry for the man as she worked to unleash those he had intended to serve up to the guillotine's blade. Almost, but not quite.

She was a bit alarmed that Jasper might break his oath as a guardian angel. Killing humans, no matter how repulsive or nefarious they were, was strictly forbidden. At least that was what he preached to her from her first day as a guardian. Occasionally teaching them a lesson, while not killing them, was allowed – at least that was Jasper's excuse.

After freeing the last prisoner, she jumped into action, her anger fueling her body to face Kael. She preferred to take on the smirking, evil guardian by herself. He seemed happy to watch the carnage from the cannon assault, as well as Jasper's battering of the cowering Robespierre. First, she needed to pull her friend away from the human who was starting to look like a bruised banana in his yellow silk shirt and light brown knickers.

Her nemesis had other plans.

"Love," he added a tck-tck-tck noise while shaking his finger. "Let the boys play."

For a moment, he held her roughly by the upper arm while staring intently into her face, almost mesmerizing her with the way the flames reflected in his eyes, like topaz glinting in a furnace.

Attempting to clear her head, she shook it slightly. She hoped it came off as a firm "No" instead of what it really was, a sorry attempt to break the spell his gaze cast over her.

Thankfully, the mushrooming black smoke enveloped them both, making further eye contact impossible. Taking the opportunity, her fist flew out to find its mark square on Kael's chiseled chin. A normal man would have come away with a broken jaw, but he was far from normal. Instead, her fist throbbed from the impact. Her other fist immediately shot forward. This time it did not connect as he grabbed both her wrists to stop the assault. Unable to break free, she swept her foot out to take out his legs at the kneecaps. He staggered but did not fall.

Greylyn continued to rain down her own form of terror on the evil being in front of her while the fire raged around them. Despite her fierce onslaught of kicks, he refused to actively engage in the fight. He simply held a defensive stance, as well as a tight grip on her wrists. Not so much as a grimace of pain.

Another cannon blast obliterated the spectator stands behind them. Burning wood flew into the air. They both ducked down to avoid the main debris, but cinders fell over them like rain, catching Greylyn's clothes on fire. Thrashing only fueled the flames, incinerating the coarse material as it melted into the underlying skin. Kael kept his hold on her with one hand, while the other came down to tamp out the fire on her arms and then her legs. Her boy britches riddled with blackened holes now showed her burned and blistering skin underneath.

Defiant, her head shot up and instantly she stopped struggling. Kael's expression unnerved her. His eyes were wide with what appeared to be concern, even fear. He inspected her for further damage, his hands lightly patting her clothes. Once his gaze came back to her face, he stopped and heaved a huge sigh. A smile returned to his lips.

Not sure what to make of this side of her enemy, Greylyn stared. The ground shook underneath them as the podium threatened to give way. Kael's arms wrapped around her as they waited for the inevitable crash that never came.

The sounds of the pandemonium around them burst through to shock Greylyn back into the moment. Kael's hold on her tightened. Unable to break away, she realized a physical attack would not work. He was too strong. Her past dealings with Kael had not revealed any weakness for her to exploit. Her mind raced for a strategy that would.

Obviously, he had an investment in the politician a few yards behind him who now lay a blackened mess on the ground.

"Don't you need to check on your little plaything over there?" she asked with more than a hint of smarminess.

For a split second, his grip on her arms relaxed. It was enough for her to break free. With his focus temporarily on his prized human whose soul would certainly rot in hell soon enough, she shoved him with all her strength – right into the inferno that raged just behind him.

The sound of Kael's skin sizzling permeated the air and a howl erupted from the flames.

Must feel like home.

Not wasting a moment, she rushed over to Jasper to stop him from murdering Robespierre. It took every ounce of supernatural strength she could muster to pull her friend away. His brilliant ice-blue eyes flashed a wildness she had never witnessed in all her time serving alongside him.

However, the sight of Greylyn seemed to have the necessary effect of breaking through the rampaging wrath in his heart. Looking down at the battered, barely breathing body lying on the ground, he gave an exaggerated shrug. All he said was, "Oh well!" before spitting on the wounded man and walking away.

After the executions were halted and Robespierre assumed to be near death, Greylyn and Jasper hurriedly left France to return to their normal guardian angel duties. This trip had not been an assignment. This had been personal.

It was not until they were back in England when they heard the horrific news. They had not stopped Kael and his human puppet, Robespierre. Somehow, the politician recovered almost overnight from his beating. The fire failed to stop the dark guardian's quest to bring suffering, bloodshed, and chaos to the people of France.

As the French *Reign of Terror* played out a little later in June of that year, the rest of Europe looked the other way. The only positive news came in July of the following year when Robespierre was executed, and a more moderate political regime came into power.

Blame for all that destruction partly, if not mostly, belonged to Kalman Ocaliot, but the name would not even be recorded in the history books.

How and why could he still plague her over two centuries later? She did not know. But here she was...faced with her nemesis once again. They had nearly killed each other repeatedly, but neither one ever finished the job. She could fight him again and again, but it would not change the way her body thrilled at his presence. Despite knowing what she knew about him, her physical reaction to him was one of desire and passion. It would be her undoing one day. Of that fact, she was certain.

But it would not be today.

Chapter 5

Dinner Date with the Demon

Wiping the foggy mirror with her hand, the face looking back at her had worry lines etched into the forehead and around weary green eyes. For being an immortal, she did not look a day over twenty-two. Unfortunately, right now she felt every one of her four hundred-plus years.

She had not heard Kael come back to his suite in the Carriage House, directly above her own. Hopefully, he had gone somewhere far, far away and would not return. Did not care where, just elsewhere.

The writing on the wall could not be clearer. Evil planned something big this weekend.

Kael only showed up when the stakes were high with the potential for mass devastation. *Not going to happen, Kael. No way I will let you win. Not while there is breath in my body.*

Perhaps, subconsciously, she had been pulled to this place again by her guardian intuition after all. Trouble always did seem to find her.

But why couldn't she just get a damn vacation?

Time to get her game-face on. And that meant blocking out the image of Kael standing in the gazebo looking as provocative and menacing as the storm itself.

Easier said than done. A vision rose in her mind and replaced the face in the mirror with deep cognac eyes, strong masculine jawline with just a touch of stubble, and full, sensuous lips.

"Damn it!" She threw a hairbrush across the room. More than anything, she needed to punch something...hard. However, the last thing she wanted to do was have to explain a gigantic hole in the wall to Maureen.

Time to focus, girl. You have a job to do. Now, do it. Shut Kael out of your mind and do your damn job!

The storm had come and gone quickly as most southern storms do at the onset of summer. The smoky gray sky was still filled with a smattering of light clouds, but the welcoming breeze had disappeared. Stifling humidity hit her like a slap of wet laundry as she opened the door of the Carriage House. By the time she made it to the main house, perspiration had beaded up on her forehead and her Atlanta Braves tee shirt clung to her torso.

The delectable scent of shepherd's pie permeated the air as she entered the main house. Yum! Maureen had remembered her favorite. Not very capable in the kitchen herself, Greylyn took every opportunity to grab a home-cooked meal.

Peering into the kitchen to ask if she could help with anything, Greylyn nearly recoiled in horror. There stood Maureen with Kael, both decked out in clover-green chef aprons with the name *Gaelic Haven* spelled out in a florid print. He stirred something in a large pot while Maureen beamed with pride beside him.

She stepped back around the door quickly to avoid being spotted, but... "Come in, Greylyn! We are almost done making dinner. Kael here was sharing his family's secret recipes for shepherd's pie and bread pudding with me. I know how much you loved my pie last time you visited, but I have to say he has the culinary genius of a somewhat less flamboyant Emeril," she gushed.

Oh no. The dark guardian knew exactly what he was doing. The fastest way to Maureen's heart was a man who could cook. If he happened to specialize in Irish cuisine, all the better.

As she stepped fully into the kitchen, he even gave Greylyn a little sly wink. It was a good thing she had trimmed her fingernails. Otherwise, her palms would be bleeding again from piercing them. Not in a mood to play nice, she grimaced. With no other options at this point, she decided to suck it up and deal.

Greylyn strolled over to inspect the culinary creation and feign interest in his cooking skills. She just hoped she was enough of an actress to pull off this ad-lib performance for Maureen's benefit. There was no need to get her flustered by outright hostility towards her new favorite guest. "Anything I can do to help?" She forced a smile.

In a sly maneuver of her own, Maureen strategically stepped over to take the wooden spoon from her new apprentice, who had stopped stirring when Greylyn first entered the kitchen.

An uncomfortable electricity filled the air, causing the hairs on the back of her neck to rise. Kael stood completely still while staring at her with a goofy grin, and a mischievous gleam in his eyes. Her brain registered what he was doing. Obviously, he wanted Maureen to think he was smitten with her. It was a good plan. The woman was a hopeless romantic, after all.

Her body warmed under his gaze; her blood simmered under her skin. But it was all just a game to him. It only made her inwardly seethe more.

"No, no! It's too stuffy in here with the heat from the ovens. You two go relax and get to know each other better while I wrap up here." Maureen shooed them towards the door. "It's too humid to sit on the veranda just yet, so why don't we make use of the pub instead, if you prefer? Kael, choose a nice wine to go with our dinner, please."

If she knew just how well the two were already acquainted, Maureen would not have believed it. No one in their right mind would.

A bitter taste coated her tongue as Greylyn followed Kael out of the kitchen to the pub. He seemed right at home in the manor. Proving the point, he walked right up to the floor-to- ceiling wine rack and pulled out an awfully expensive bottle of 1975 French Bordeaux from Chateau Fonplegade.

Okay, so he also had excellent taste in wine.

"Well, you've made quite an impression on Maureen. You *must* be a good actor!" Greylyn smirked.

He did not acknowledge her barb as he took down three long-stemmed wine glasses and set them on the counter before turning to locate the corkscrew. Looking at his backside was just as disturbing as his front. His too-tight shirt did nothing to hide the muscles in his back as he reached up. Not to mention the snug jeans.

He turned towards her as he worked to extract the cork from the bottle.

His slightly smug smile prominently displayed his dimples.

Oh, dear Lord! He just caught me ogling his ass!

Riveted in place, she could not break away from his stare. Kael gave a soft chuckle, which thankfully broke the moment.

"It's so easy to fool good-hearted people. They always want to believe everyone else is as good as they are." He winked.

Greylyn winced. She may not like what he said, but she also knew it was mostly true. She struggled for an appropriate, yet snarky response. Nothing smartass came to mind. Being around him muddled her brain every time. The best she could do was so lame, she regretted the words before they passed her lips. "Kael, whatever it is you are planning with the wedding, know that I will stop you."

Before he could reply, Maureen entered the pub with a tray carrying three bowls of piping hot shepherd's pie and fresh oven-baked bread. Kael jumped up from his bar stool and rushed to assist her with the tray. It had the intended effect. Maureen beamed and gave Greylyn a quick wink as if to say, "See, isn't he a fine fellow?"

Greylyn fought the urge to roll her eyes at his pathetic play. "Smells delicious!" she reluctantly admitted. With a pointed look to Kael, she asked, "Is this an old family recipe? Do you hail directly from Ireland or did ancestry.com tell you that you were part Irish?"

Her flippant remark had an unusual effect. The smile stamped on his face did not match the serious, pained look or the nerve that twitched just under his left eye. Silence stretched out as if the entire house waited for his answer. "Actually, yes. Northern Ireland. But I came to the States so long ago, I'm afraid I've lost my accent."

Like a gentleman, he pulled out a chair for Maureen, which elicited a broad smile. Again, Greylyn struggled to resist the urge to roll her eyes.

Damn, why can't we just fight and get it over with? Playing nice was torture!

To avoid saying something she would regret, Greylyn picked up her spoon to dive into her food, but Maureen abruptly stopped her with a quick, reprimanding look. "Not before we say the blessing," she scolded Greylyn like a small child. "Kael, would you do the honors?"

Oh, now this will be funny. A demon saying the blessing over their dinner.

Priceless!

Surprisingly, he did not miss a beat. He stretched out his hands to both women as he began a rather elegant prayer over their food. The touch of his hand sent a shockwave up her arm as if she had touched a fork stuck in an electrical outlet. Not enough to set her hair standing straight up on top of her head, but enough that she had to resist the urge to jerk her hand back.

Seeming not to notice her reaction, he gave thanks for Maureen's hospitality and the opportunity to make new friends.

Shouldn't he be spontaneously combusting or something?

Curiosity got the better of her as she peered out from underneath her eyelashes as he continued. No smoke or flames billowing around him. Not even a look of pain as words of praise and gratitude to the Almighty passed his lips. She had at least expected boils. Something to indicate a battle within his unholy self at the words.

Nothing. His head was bowed slightly, but he was peeking right back at her with a stare that unsettled her even more than hearing a demon give thanks to God.

In a low solemn voice, Kael continued the prayer.

"Lord and Master, we give you thanks for this bountiful meal and the gracious hospitality of our hostess. We give thanks for all your gifts to us, your lowly servants in this world. Although, we are not worthy, you provide and sustain us. You guide us in our troubles and conquer those that wish us harm or endeavor to bring us down. Your glory shines on your people as we walk this Earth to serve you and worship you. We give thanks for your sustenance as we go forth to do Thy will."

Although, to the untrained ear, his prayer sounded elegantly simple and innocent, Greylyn heard the hidden meanings and innuendo in his choice of words.

Sly little devil!

He continued, "We give thanks for the people you purposefully put into our path to enrich our lives, and for the opportunities given to give and receive love regardless of our worthiness for love." After what seemed like an eternity, he ended with a simple "Amen."

He held onto her hand for a few moments after ending the prayer. Of course, Greylyn realized that she had not yanked her hand away either at the first possible moment. Their hostess certainly noticed as a sly smile crept up Maureen's face.

I need a friggin' drink.

Clumsily, Greylyn reached for her wine glass, nearly sloshing the wine over the worn wood table's surface. Kael deftly grabbed the glass before a drop escaped the delicate crystal goblet. He handed it back to her with a one-sided grin.

Luckily for her, and the wine, he avoided actual physical contact. She was sure the glass would go flying if he so much as grazed her hand with his. She looked up, embarrassed, to find Maureen repressing a giggle with a hand over her mouth. Well, at least someone was having a good time tonight.

Greylyn picked at her food, unsure if she should trust Kael had not poisoned the shepherd's pie. Maureen ate with gusto with no obvious ill effects and profusely complimented the chef in between bites. Kael's gaze rarely strayed from Greylyn, which only served to make her more flustered.

She raised the fork to her lips, taking a tiny bite. For a split second, the slight tastes of rosemary and cinnamon hit her with an overwhelming sense of déjà vu. Cinnamon? That seemed unusual, but it was quite delightful.

Wine... Wine was what she needed to calm her nerves. This time, she forced herself to concentrate on picking up her glass with a steady hand. Why did it take every ounce of her willpower to perform that one task?

As dinner progressed, Maureen and Kael carried most of the conversation. They talked about how he learned to cook from his dear grandmother.

"My Seanmhair took care of me while my parents worked all day. Even though, at the time, it was not considered manly to cook, she thought it was an important tool for anyone to learn. Without any sisters to carry on the family tradition, she taught me. Sadly, she passed away long ago."

Yeah, no kidding.

"I tried passing along the skill to someone once, but I wasn't so successful teaching." His tone was lighthearted and smooth as he flashed her a dimpled grin with one eyebrow arched. "How about you? Are you a good cook, Greylyn?"

A bite of carrot and beef stuck in her throat. After a brief coughing fit, she regained her composure, although unsure what about the question bothered her. "No, afraid not. I can barely boil water." To avoid further conversation, Greylyn gulped back more wine before plowing another spoonful into her mouth.

Kael and Maureen kept the conversation going, while Greylyn lost herself in her own ruminations. Kael. *What was he doing here, other than to torment her some more? Why did he also keep popping up over the centuries? Why couldn't he bother some other poor guardian angel? Oh yeah. There were only a handful of her kind left across the globe. Gee, how did she get so lucky? Her very own personal tormentor. Jasper would have a field day if he knew she was sitting at a table having a civilized dinner with their archenemy. Hell, she could not believe it herself.*

She was so deep in her thoughts it did not register for a few moments that both had stopped talking and were looking at her strangely.

Maureen cleared her throat. "Lassie, you look like you're someplace else entirely. You okay, hon?" While Maureen looked concerned and a bit perturbed, Kael's lips curled up in an amused smile.

Damn! It was as if he knew she was deep in thought about him.

"Sorry, Maureen. Guess I was more tired than I thought from the long drive. Feels like I haven't slept in days." Greylyn prayed she bought the lie. Actually, when was the last time she had slept?

"You're as pale as a ghost, sweetie. You're not sick, are you?" Maureen even went so far as to reach over to feel her guest's forehead as a mother would check her toddler for a fever. Oh, now this was a bit embarrassing!

To make matters worse, she added, "Kael, check her palms. Does she seem clammy to you?"

Horrified, Greylyn pushed away from the table. "No, that's okay. Probably too much wine is all." Looking down her glass was once again drained. "I'll just get some fresh air. Please continue without me." After promising to rejoin them later, she turned to go.

Kael immediately jumped up to walk her outside while the look on Maureen's face read like an open book. She was perturbed that her dreams of a love connection were not playing out like she wanted.

Greylyn protested, "No, No! I will be fine. I'll go splash some cool water on my face, and I will be right back. I promise."

To Kael, she muttered under her breath, "I can see myself out."

As soon as the backdoor swung shut, she bolted back to her suite in the Carriage House. Obviously, she was losing her touch, or her mind, or both. An encounter with Kael should not affect her so much. Of course, they usually just went straight to the fighting part. This congenial façade was exhausting. Time to regroup and get her emotions under control before delving back into that firestorm. The quicker, the better. She had a wedding to save, didn't she? What she wanted to do was jump back in her car and speed away, never to look back. But that was a coward's way out, and she was no coward. At least, she repeated that lie to herself from time to time.

There was only one person who could talk her down off the proverbial ledge. It certainly was not Jasper. If he knew Kael was here, she knew exactly what his advice would be...kill him. Not the best plan considering she would have to concoct some tale as to why she murdered Maureen's new favorite guest. And honestly, she did not know if she could kill him. She liked to believe she would gut him at the first opportunity. But if that were the case, why had she not done that by now. Besides, Greylyn needed a pep talk, not a directive.

She pulled out her phone and hit the number one button on her speed-dial.

Chapter 6

Calling in Backup

Carriage House

One ring. Two rings. Three rings. "Dammit! Where is he? Answer the damn phone, Thomas!!!"

Her heart sank into her stomach at the thought that he might not answer this time. It was not like she ever had good news to give him when she called. And he might still be slightly ticked that she left him in a lurch a month back when he needed help with a project. She had taken off to save someone else's bacon without so much as a good-bye.

The next ring she heard the most wonderful sound in the world. The deep, husky Australian accent of her buddy, confidant, and all-around great guy who knew everything about the supernatural, Thomas Moorefield the Third!

"Ow, How's me girl?"

"Well, it's about time you picked up the phone, Sparky!"

Inwardly she was so happy to hear his voice she almost cried with relief. Thomas was her "go-to" guy for *everything* she ever needed. Did not matter what ridiculous thing she asked of him – information about a particular monster, mythology surrounding a given species or situation – he delivered. And on occasion he served as her confessor. He was not an ordained priest or anything, just someone who did not second-guess her every move or pass judgment.

It also did not hurt that he had the sexiest voice on the planet. Not bad on the eyes either. "Nice to hear from you too, doll." Thomas chuckled.

She slumped against the antique dresser as relief washed over her.

"And what may I help my lil angel with tonight? Need some odd stubby?"

Oh shit! He better not be drinking again!

Thomas had come into her life eight years prior when she coaxed him back from alcoholism. She found the former rugby player passed out in the back of a shady establishment in Baltimore's inner harbor with a plethora of random prescription pain pills scattered on the tabletop along with an empty pint of rot gut whiskey. When he finally opened his blurry eyes, she had slapped him into sobriety – literally.

"Thomas ..."

Before she even got the dreaded words out to ask if he was drinking again, he stopped her.

"Just joking with ya, luv. Geez, can't even mention the stuff without you jumping down my throat!"

"Sorry, Tommy boy. It's been one of those days. You promise? No odd stubby or whatever you call that stuff?"

"Yes, what do ya want to pinky swear or something?" With a grateful sigh, Greylyn told him about her dilemma.

"I'm supposed to be on vacation," she whined. "Yet here I am having to deal with Evil's Number One Jerk!"

"Kael? Again? Someone needs to send that bugger packing back to the fiery depths." Greylyn could not agree more. "Guess you can't just slice and dice him and get it over with?"

A snicker escaped her lips. "It could raise a few unfortunate questions if I slaughtered the wedding photographer."

"I see your dilemma." There was a pause on the line with only the faint tapping of what she guessed was a pen or pencil against his chin. "Any indication why Kael's there? Sorry about your vacation but looks like you've been called in for duty."

"Yeah, seems that way, huh?" Greylyn sighed deeply. She filled him in on what little she did know. "... but I still have no idea what I'm up against. Hoping to find out more when the happy couple arrive. Until then ..."

"Until then, you got nothing. My suggestion stands...slice and dice until he squeals. In the meantime, I can run a background check on the bride and groom and any guests, if that'll help ya. Maybe see if any of my contacts have any information about the dark one's recent activities. Don't suppose he's been in a sharing mood and told ya anything?"

"Oh yeah, he spilled everything as soon as I arrived."

Thomas responded with a low guttural laugh. "I bet the bastard did. Doesn't he know by now not to mess with my lil angel girl? Just flash your mood eyes at him. That'll send him packing."

Greylyn giggled as she collapsed onto the bed now that she was relaxed. Yes, Thomas made it abundantly clear long ago that his favorite aspect of her appearance was her mood eyes. According to him, her usually emerald green eyes morphed bright blue whenever she was upset or angry. The angrier she was, the bluer her eyes glowed. She had never witnessed the transition, but it was a subject that Thomas and Jasper agreed on – if they saw blue, they knew to run...fast!

Thomas got down to business. "Any guardian angel insight that would assist my search? A gut feeling which way this thing is headed?"

"Just an obscure vision that didn't tell me too much. Bride silently screaming inside the manor. Most likely, she's the one in need of saving." From what was the question. What could Kael have planned? With him, it could be just about anything.

"Almost sounds too obvious though, darling. Kael is much more devious than that. He likes to come at you from odd angles, never directly from where you're expecting him. Can't rule out anybody or anything."

He had an excellent point. Thomas continued, "If you can, snag me the guest list."

This was exactly what she needed. Just moments ago, she had been too distracted to think straight. Something that was not acceptable since someone needed her help. Thomas's voice and no-nonsense approach set her mind back on track. The mission. That was what she needed to focus on. Not some sexy, infuriating dark guardian with gold-flecked eyes.

Stop thinking about the eyes!

Apparently, she had zoned out again as Thomas's voice took on a note of strain. "Earth to Grey! Ya there, doll? Come on! I know the sound of my sexy voice makes you weak at the knees and swoon, but seriously ... now is not the time to daydream about me in my knickers. There'll be time for that later."

A long overdue giggle burst out of her chest.

"Hey, Hey! I am not that funny! Seriously ... admit it! You were imagining me in my drawers, weren't you?" Greylyn could almost hear Thomas wink.

"Okay. Okay. Back to business. No more fantasies!"

"Good. Sorry to throw cold water on ya, luv, but I kinda got a date tonight so let's hurry this along." The tenor of his voice put her a little on edge. He was trying too hard to sound lighthearted. Besides, despite being a total Aussie hunk, he was also a recluse for the most part. He came out of his house to teach psychology and occult classes at the local college, but as far as she knew he had been dateless for most of the time she had known him.

"A date? Really?"

"Yes. A date! You know that thing where a man and woman go out, have a bit of dinner, make small talk, smooch for a while and then not call each other the next day or ever ... a date!"

"I am mildly familiar with the term, yes."

"Besides, I think I deserve a little time off. I am overworked and underpaid. Your buddy Jasper has been as annoying as ever. I curse the day you gave that jerk my number! He expects the impossible from me. Then, of course, there is the resurgence of wiccans thinking they are full blown witches. Had couple incidents here on campus just this week that ended with a burned building and one fatality." With a chuckle, he added, "I wish Hollywood producers would tone it down on the glorification of witches and warlocks. Every millennial and Gen Z-er across the country wants to be a *Charmed One* or fall in love with a vampire. Even zombies are making a comeback."

Greylyn understood his frustration. Two of her last assignments had dealt with that very thing. Seriously, how could anyone be attracted to a bloodsucker? And zombies? Just...yuck!

Thomas continued, "Maybe I should've stayed at Harvard, whiling my days away teaching philosophy and a bit of psychology to the under-informed. All I had to do was cut the occult crap from the class. At least those morons paid well. Working as an undervalued and underpaid parapsychology professor in this dump of a so-called college town while being angelic guardians' personal freelance research assistant can make a man cranky. Just need to feel loved, my dear. You understand. One date, that's all I'm asking for."

"Aha!" There it was. Greylyn recognized the tension in his voice and the reason he was being so snippy. He was nervous about his date.

With a smirk Greylyn could hear in his rough voice, he added, "However, I will pass on the university's new paralegal if you want to send me that little blonde bombshell friend of yours."

Laughter bubbled up again and she relaxed. The blonde bombshell was a case she worked six months ago. Candace, an up-and-coming model, had been tempted into the less glamorous side of the entertainment business to further her career. She had shown Thomas a picture of Candace after sending her ass back to Nebraska. He had relentlessly asked for her number.

"You know I love and adore ya, big guy!" she cooed over the phone and blew him a sloppy sounding kiss. "But Candace stays where she is. You're a smoking hot guy! Go on your date. Buy yourself a seltzer water and seduce her with that sexy accent and big puppy-dog eyes."

She received a gruff pfft in reply. "Can't blame a man for trying."

"Thanks for the help, Sparky. Enjoy your date. I want all the juicy details tomorrow morning. I better get back to the main house and see what I can find out. The devil should be finished with his dinner by now."

Before hanging up, she added, "Next time I get a good *business mixed with pleasure* locale like this one, you are coming along. We both deserve a real vacation."

"I will take you up on that, doll. But do not think that we'll be staying in separate rooms," he teased.

"Just if you bring the paralegal back to your place, don't scare her away by watching *Mystery Science Theater* all night, okay? At least get some heavy petting in or something. The research can wait until tomorrow morning."

"Research? Tomorrow? I'm done, kitten. Unlike some people, I can multitask. Pulled the files from the inn regarding guests for this weekend, so I have their names. Kelly and Matthew Ferguson. Northern Virginia address. Looks like only the newlyweds are staying there. No other rooms are booked. Even have the list of vendors for the wedding. I'll run background checks on everyone before I leave tonight. Already sent the files to your email."

"Damn! You are good." *How did he do that?*

"So, should I wear the scholarly button-down and sweater vest or the plaid flannel?"

Rolling her eyes, Greylyn knew he was kidding. At least, she hoped he was kidding. He would not really go on a first date dressed either way. Right?

"Stud muffin. Wear your skinny jeans and a too-small plain cotton tee that she can rip off you later. If you break out that sweater vest, I will burn it the next time I'm there." Seriously, Mister Rogers dressed more dapper than Thomas.

"Come on! All my students love the sweater vest." His tone was offended, but she did not believe that for a second.

"Have a good time and don't be too late, sweetie. And...thanks, Thomas. You're the best!"

"Well, of course, I am." After an uncomfortable pause, he added, "You know, a date wouldn't hurt you either..."

With a kiss to him over the phone, Greylyn laid on the bed for a few moments longer after hanging up. Twirling the chain with the metal band around her neck, she took deep, cleansing breaths. She already felt better about the potential for danger this weekend, but she refused to engage in another debate with Thomas about why guardians should not date. Besides the fact she would outlive anyone she possibly came to care about, which would cause tremendous pain, how could she endanger anyone else's life in that way? Just being in her orbit could mark that person with a death sentence from vengeful demons. Allowing Thomas into her life had not been her decision. The stubborn man had refused to take "no" for an answer. Perhaps he considered it a life debt after she had saved him from the bottle. Regardless, she worried some evil monster would discover her affiliation with him and use him against her.

The bull frogs from the small pond outside her window broke through her reverie. Armored with more confidence than she had felt since arriving at Gaelic Haven, she took one last look in the mirror to smooth back her wayward, raven hair before walking back out the door and into whatever lay ahead of her in the main house.

Back outside, she peered up at the window she had seen the vision in earlier. She pulled out her phone to check the files from Thomas. He had even attached pictures of the happy couple.

Handsome young man with a dark complexion and even darker chocolate eyes. Lovely woman with strawberry hair, freckles, and startling large hazel-green eyes. Yep, that was the woman from the vision. No doubt.

But something nagged at her. Greylyn could not place what it was. It was like a clue was staring her in the face, but she could not see it clearly enough. With a shrug, she put the phone back in her pocket and took a deep breath before opening the door to the main house. No way she would allow Kael to spoil the couple's joyous new life.

Chapter 7

After Dinner Drinks

Main House Pub

Celtic music drifted from the pub. "Bonny Portmore," sung by the refined soprano voice of Loreena McKennitt, elicited memories of profuse fields of green for as far as the eye could see sprang.

Believing the innkeeper to be in the kitchen cleaning up, she headed that way first. What she found was a shock – Kael up to his elbows in suds at the kitchen sink. Luckily, he did not see her, so she softly backpedaled away from the door and headed towards the pub.

She found Maureen relaxing in a lowboy chair sipping her wine. It was hauntingly beautiful. Her eyes were closed, and a smile played at the corners of her mouth. She may have only been at *Gaelic Haven* a short time on her first visit, but she could read her friend's expression clearly. Maureen was reminiscing about her late husband, Robert. Even if the widow could not see him, Greylyn sensed Robert's presence in the room – the light waft of a cigar.

Hating to disturb her, she quietly entered the pub. "Sorry about earlier," Greylyn started to apologize.

Maureen's eyes fluttered open. "Well, you look much better now. The color is back in your face."

Kael re-entered carrying a tray with three dessert bowls. "I hope it wasn't my cooking that caused you distress." *Still playing the charmer!* "Maureen, you did save enough room for my Seanmhair's bread pudding, didn't you?"

Maureen kept casting glances between the two young people. She even winked a couple of times at Greylyn. "It is so refreshing to have a young man around who can cook such delectable dishes. Don't you agree?"

Way to be subtle, Maureen.

As they ate, Greylyn attempted to steer the conversation to see if she could get some sort of intelligence about the wedding, and why Kael was really there. "What time will the bride and groom be arriving tomorrow, Maureen? I don't want to infringe on wedding preparations. I'll make myself scarce."

"Oh, dear. You couldn't possibly infringe on anything. Besides, all the arrangements have been made. Everything is set. The couple are coming up a day early to rest and relax for the big day."

Kael stood up to clear the table, despite Maureen's objections that it was her job after all. He insisted.

Good riddance!

His exit gave her the opening Greylyn needed to ask Maureen more specifics about the wedding. With a little wine in the innkeeper, she was quite talkative. Within a few minutes, she knew all sorts of minute details. Unfortunately, none that rung any alarm bells. The most concerning aspect, at least to Maureen, was the less-than-affable relationship between the groom's divorced parents. But nothing sparked supernatural concern.

"Matthew insisted ... those two aren't allowed in the same room, especially with the new stepmom." Shrugging, she added, "I got the feeling the couple preferred to elope just to avoid the potential family ruckus."

Maureen's words started to slur slightly, and her complexion glowed, sure signs she had imbibed a little too much. At least it made her talkative. "I can't wait for you to meet the happy couple. They are so lovely."

Giggling, she added, "They are smart. Insisted on privacy for their wedding night so no wedding guests will be staying here afterwards. Not so good for me. A booked inn is preferable, but I don't blame them." Greylyn did not blame the couple either.

The only issue with chatty Maureen was that she kept returning to the one topic she did not wish to discuss – Kael. She slightly stumbled over to the bar and picked up a folder, handing it to Greylyn.

"Kael showed me these pictures he's taken the last couple of days. He's even sketched out a brochure for the inn and says he will put it up on the internet for me. Isn't that sweet?"

Greylyn flipped through the stack while listening to the continuous lauding of the numerous talents of the wickedly handsome gentleman in the kitchen. The images were spectacular. He captured the simple authentic beauty of the estate in every shot. She was on the verge of saying as much, but Kael returned to the room.

Refusing to look at him, she glanced down at the next picture in the folder. She almost cried out in shock. It was a photograph of her as she had been sitting on the veranda that afternoon, before catching sight of the shadow in the gazebo. Her hair had been blowing from the gentle breeze before the storm and partly covered her eyes.

"Sorry. I hope you don't mind. Seeing such a beautiful woman so relaxed and at home in her surroundings was too great a temptation. I had to capture the moment."

Maureen sighed heavily. "How sweet."

"You were spying on me?" She fairly hissed at him.

It was enough to jolt Maureen out of her romantic daydreams. She stammered, "Greylyn, that's just silly."

Kael flashed a "Uh huh, I got you" smile. A moment later, he turned apologetic eyes towards Maureen before continuing. "No, really. I did not mean to intrude. I know better than to snap pictures of a subject without their consent. It's just that it would have been a crime to let such a vision escape. If you wish, you can have the picture. Tear it up if you want."

Maureen gasped. "Well, of course she won't tear it up. It's lovely."

Oh, I am losing this battle.

Greylyn turned on a faux smile. The folder still clasped in her hand, she refused to release it back to Kael. Silently, she continued to peruse it.

Another picture of her. This time, she had been resting on the patio outside her suite that overlooked the koi pond. She was soaked, with her hair clinging to the sides of her face and her white t-shirt turned transparent.

"Couldn't resist taking a picture of a woman in a wet t-shirt?"

His lips curled up along with his right eyebrow. Chuckling, "Like I said ... lovely view."

Her stomach curled into tight knots as blood thumped loudly in her ears from the rise in her blood pressure. She could hear Maureen in the background, barely audible, exclaiming how delightful the pictures were and how flattered Greylyn must feel.

She was not flattered. Far from it.

The remaining images were innocent ones of the grounds and the individual rooms.

Regardless, he had made himself crystal clear; he had her in his sights.

After taking a few moments to regain her composure by silently chanting "Om", Greylyn tersely complimented him through clenched jaws. It took all her will power not to lash out at him in front of their host. Kael at least had the sense to look a little ashamed, but that was an act too.

In no mood to deal with him any further, she racked her brain for a way to get rid of the troublemaker. She needed to talk with Maureen alone. His presence complicated things. As if reading her thoughts, he suddenly apologized to the ladies and said he needed to get back to his room. He needed to make a few business calls before calling it a night.

"And I'm sure you beautiful ladies could use some time together without a dude intruding on your conversation." Pausing as if waiting for someone to object to his departure, he reluctantly added, "So I will bid you both good night."

Maureen intervened. "Don't be silly, dear. I'm sure Greylyn would appreciate the company of another young person. I'm getting so old, I'm sure you two would find more to talk about and keep each other entertained."

Flashing her an "Oh, hell no, you don't" expression did nothing to dissuade Maureen.

"No, really I do need to attend to some business before calling it a night and I don't want to wear out my welcome." With that, he kissed Maureen's hand and walked away. As she heard the back door open and then close again, she visibly sighed in relief.

"Now you are such a strange lassie," Maureen chided Greylyn. "He's a fine catch."

Hearing it put that way, she could not help it as a giggle erupted out of her throat. The whole thing was just preposterous! It was inconceivable to explain precisely why they were the exact opposite of a match made in Heaven. But she had to offer some excuse, no matter how flimsy.

"Maureen, it's been so long since I've dated that I don't even know how to act anymore. I have found guys are just too much trouble with extraordinarily little payoff for my efforts. Besides, he's certainly charmed you. Maybe you should look in the mirror instead. Let's see. There is a term for an older woman with a young man. Cougar! That's it! You could be a cougar!" Greylyn teased. It had the intended effect. Maureen blushed the color of the Killarney rose.

The odor of her dead husband's cigar grew stronger. The widow was oblivious, but Greylyn sensed Robert was not happy with how she had maneuvered the conversation.

At last Maureen conceded temporary defeat on the topic of Kael.

Greylyn redirected the conversation quickly to that of the upcoming wedding. Did not do much good, though. There was not that much to tell. And nothing that screamed "Danger!"

Eventually, Maureen grew too tired and excused herself for the night, but not without one parting shot. "I bet that young gentleman is still awake though." With a sly grin, she yawned and retreated to her own room upstairs.

Draining her glass of wine, Greylyn let herself out the back door. The night air was cooler, refreshing. She had half a mind to confront Kael now. But she reluctantly admitted to herself, she was not at the top of her game. To face him in this condition, when she so desperately needed rest and a clear head, would be tantamount to suicide.

Still, what was to prevent him from harming Maureen during the night while a guardian angel snoozed close by?

She fished out a medallion from her back pocket. *Just in case of emergencies.* Too short to reach the top overhanging ledge of the door, instead Greylyn lifted the worn "Irish Welcome" door mat and placed it directly in the center. Would not keep Kael or anything else evil out of the house, but at least the resulting scream of agony from an evil creature crossing any threshold would wake her in time to run to the rescue. Just in case, she would sleep with the windows open.

Chapter 8

Shadow Dancing

Carriage House

Greylyn was too keyed up from her encounter with Kael to relax. She knew sleep was futile. Not to mention the nagging in the back of her mind about the woman in the vision. There was something she was missing. Something she was supposed to know, but that knowledge evaded her.

Parking herself in the cushioned rocking chair on the porch attached to her, she allowed the tension in her shoulders to release. The resident bull frogs were in rare form, drowning out any other noises. Strangely, she found the incessant croaking rather soothing.

Her thoughts drifted. She was blessed, a force for good. Kael was a power for evil. Immortal enemies. He was there to cause trouble. She was there to stop him. It was that simple. If she just knew what the trouble was.

The wine mixed with the sultry smells of lavender and the caressing cool breeze on her skin lulled her into a light doze. Images swirled across her eyelids. Golden eyes sparkling like a tiger tracking its prey. Sunlight glinting off auburn highlights accentuated by tendrils darker than chestnut. A wicked smile followed by a throaty laugh that set warmth racing through her veins. And muscle perfectly outlined underneath dark denim.

Long, thin, icy fingers curled around her neck. Her eyes shot wide open. There was nothing there. She bolted up out of the chair, but the invisible force threw her back down, tightening its grip. Her hands clutched at her throat...at nothing.

That was when she noticed the darkness surrounding her. Darker than the night. A shadow.

More precisely, a shadow demon.

She flailed around in an unsuccessful attempt to throw it off her. There was nothing for her to grab onto. Nothing to hit, punch, or kick. It was a shadow, a translucent demon without substance. Shadows were simply that ... shadows.

Dark fingers squeezed her throat shut like a vise. Her lungs burned. Her eyes searched desperately for a weapon. Nothing could fend off a shadow though. Nothing except light or water.

Clouds obliterated any illumination from the night sky. Still clutching at her own neck to remove the shadow's grip, Greylyn realized with dread it would have to be the water. Using all her energy, she pushed herself out of the rocking chair and stumbled towards the koi pond.

Though made of air, the shadow was strangely heavy, like a barbell weighted down with iron plates. It resisted her with uncanny strength, slowing her progress, at times jerking her backwards. All the while continuing to tighten its grip on her throat.

Her field of vision shrank into a tight tunnel. Deprived of oxygen, she'd soon black out. A fire burned in her chest. What she needed was enough momentum to fling them both into the murky pond.

Using the few precious seconds she may have left in this world, Greylyn centered herself to gather all her strength. Calling on her own inner light, she lumbered forward as an untapped well of energy burst open. One final push propelled her over the rocks and into the frigid, aphotic water. The instant her body broke the lily-pad-covered surface, the pressure on her throat released, followed by a shattering pain as her head struck a protruding rock. The relief was great, but she still could not take a breath to refill her lungs. The icy water shocked her senses like a defibrillator to her chest.

She was part angel, but her body was still human and would need oxygen soon. As if a vivid reminder of that fact, the fire in her chest flared. Her body convulsed with the necessity to open her mouth and gulp air but doing so would only flood her lungs with murky water.

Clinging to a slimy rock ledge just underneath the surface, her eyes peered up to see what the shadow was doing. All it had to do was wait for her to re-emerge, or simply let her drown. The black form hovered just at the edge of the pond, swaying as if blown by a turbulent breeze. It planned to wait her out.

Panic set in as seconds dragged into minutes. Silently she chided herself for not thinking through this particular course of action. The water? She chose the ice-cold, algae-infested water. Splendid idea! And yet, what else could she have done? Why had she not turned on the porch light when she came back to her room?

A lot of questions, and no good answers. Everything was in complete darkness. She had been so distracted by the playback reel in her head of Kael and his dreamy eyes, and his firm derriere, she had not sensed the inevitable danger of the pitch-black night, nor had she felt the shadow's presence until it was too late.

Looks like Kael will be the death of me.

Her vision narrowed further as she contemplated something she had seen on a cartoon once – the character used the stem of a lily pad to breathe while in the water. Somehow, she doubted that would work. All she needed was a one well-positioned ray of light and she could make a break for safety.

Another shadow appeared beside the creature. This one had more substance to it. Probably Kael checking on his pet, making sure it finished her off. Funny, she had always thought he would delight in being the one to finally succeed in killing her. Having a flunky do the job seemed a copout.

The inky blackness filled her vision completely. Her grip on the rocks slipped. Just before succumbing to the abyss something grabbed her hands and hauled her to the surface with brute force. Startled koi swam past. Strong muscular arms pulled her up and over the edge of the rocks lining the pond to lay her gently down in the grass.

After gulping in as much of the heavy, humid air as her lungs would hold, she pushed herself up to a sitting position with trembling arms. Covered in algae, with a stray lily pad wrapped around her leg, her eyes darted around for any sign of the shadow. It was nowhere to be found. Satisfied it had disappeared, she glared up at Kael.

He knelt beside her with what looked like a genuine expression of concern. She had seen that look before but would not allow herself to be fooled.

Silence spread like a virus. Not even the frogs croaked. She waited for him to spring his trap since she was in the perfect weakened position for him to take advantage. If he had been biding his time, waiting for his moment...this was it! The shadow had nearly drowned her. Now he could finish the job.

"Wish you had told me you liked moonlit swims, darling. I would've brought my swimsuit," he chuckled. "Second thought, skinny dipping would be more fun."

Ah, there is the smartass demon I know all too well.

"Seriously, though, could you please explain to me what you were thinking jumping into the koi pond to get rid of the shadow? It could've waited all night for you to re-emerge while you would've drowned in the meantime." After a pause, he asked, "So why didn't you simply swim away? With your speed, you could've stood a chance by climbing out the other side and running for the main house."

Gulping in more fresh air, she stared down at herself and unraveled the lily pad from her leg before answering...truthfully.

"I don't know how to swim."

Kael grabbed her chin, forcing her to look into his deep eyes. His voice filled with laughter and bewilderment. "You've been walking this Earth for 450 years and you still can't swim?"

Offended, she retorted, "Well, I've kinda been busy doing other things."

"You mean to tell me that you simply couldn't find the time to take a lesson or two at the local YMCA or something? Really? That's just so...you."

Her first impulse was to push herself up and stomp away. Too bad her knees buckled as she took her first step. She fell back, right into the strong upper body of her rescuer.

"Steady there, love," his amused voice whispered into her ear.

A minute ago, she was chilled to the bone from the pond, now a bolt of extreme heat scorched every place her body touched his. Unable to move, Greylyn's mind went foggy again. Kael stood up, carrying her body along with his own. His arms turned her around so they were face to face. Well, sort of...he was quite taller than her and had to hunch over to peer into her eyes.

She allowed him to guide her over to a wooden bench where they both sat down. Still, she could not look away. It was as if he held her in a trance. Perhaps he did. At the moment, she would have given anything to be able to discern what lay behind those swirling topaz pools. Had he just saved her or was this part of his game?

They sat on the bench, silent. Seemed like it could have been for seconds, or for hours. Their eyes remained locked until he moved to shrug off his shirt. Then her gaze fell to his smooth, ripped pectoral muscles and abs.

The tips of her fingers twitched as she fought the urge to reach up and trace the outline of his pectoral muscles, the smooth skin marred by a single scar running from just below his jugular notch to a point below his sternum. Without thinking, she raised her hand, on the verge of touching the jagged line. Kael dabbed at the blood dripping down her forehead with the shirt. She had completely forgotten she hit her head on the side of the pond. A blow to the head of that magnitude would have caused a human to lose consciousness, resulting in, at best, a bad concussion.

That's why I am acting so strangely. Must be a concussion.

But Greylyn knew better. She did not get concussions, and the gash in her forehead would heal by morning. There would be no evidence of the incident when she saw Maureen for breakfast.

As it was, she was certain the dizzy sensation she experienced was more from Kael's closeness than from the head injury. Not exactly a reassuring revelation.

She did not understand. A shadow creature had just attempted to kill her. It was perfectly reasonable to assume Kael had employed the shadow. But instead, his eyes were laser-focused on her, checking her for injuries like a parent tending a wounded child. Unsettling.

To make the situation worse, her body started shaking as if from severe cold. The temperature was not the problem. Of that, she was positive. His face was bare inches from her own as he inspected the cut on her forehead. His breath, as warm and soft as a caress from a tropical breeze, brushed against her cheek.

Satisfied the wound was healing, Kael began to briskly rub both her arms. "You could be cold in the Sahara Desert, I swear." The contact only caused her to tremble more violently. Not able to withstand the intensity any longer, she wrenched herself away.

The warmth evaporated instantly. Looking up, Greylyn saw his expression change. The grin he wore while teasing her transformed into something else she could not quite place. Hurt? No, that could not be it. Whatever it was, it spooked her out of her reverie and back to reality.

He was the bad guy. They were enemies. There was a strange comfort in the truth.

Clinging to that thought as if it were a life preserver in a raging storm at sea, she indignantly stood and marched back to her suite in the Carriage House without so much as a "thank you."

Watching her stomp away like a drunk, with her clothes sagging off her petite frame, Kael's soft, but deep chuckle reverberated in the night air as she slammed the door. Oh, how he adored that fiery Irish temper of hers. They had not spent this much time in proximity for centuries. It was...fun.

His brow furrowed with concern though.

What the bloody hell is up with a shadow creature making an appearance? And going after Greylyn?

Someone was going to have to answer for that flagrant misstep. If someone was after her, they had to come through him first.

Time was not on his side. Tomorrow, Kelly and Matthew would arrive. Then his job took precedence. Playing around with the angel would have to wait.

Chapter 9

Sunny Side Up

After a less than stellar night's sleep, Greylyn woke to stomping overhead from the upstairs occupant of the Carriage House.

Maybe it was the mass consumption of wine last night mixed with her near-drowning experience, but her head pounded in agony.

Seriously, does he have a herd of elephants up there?

Tenderly feeling the location of the head gash, she realized it had indeed healed already. Inhaling deeply, her lungs were free from the pond water. Yes, she could have easily drowned last night, but it would not have killed her. Not exactly. Recovery would have been a bitch and explaining how she was not dead after hours under water would have been impossible, but nevertheless she was alive. Too bad her angelic healing abilities did not encompass obliterating the effects of too much alcohol.

What she needed was coffee. Ah, coffee! Tall, strong, dark! Okay, so that also described Kael, but it was the beverage she yearned for at this moment.

Splashing cold water on her face, she took a long, analytical look at the woman gazing back at her in the small, oval bathroom mirror. Thankfully, neither the lack of sleep nor the head trauma from her midnight dive reflected back at her. The perks of being a guardian angel. Some days she would have preferred a paycheck and a 401K, but anti-aging, quick healing, and immortality were decent job benefits.

After pulling her hair back from her face with a cotton hairband and throwing on a faded, and well-worn, gray West Point t-shirt and jean shorts, she took a deep cleansing breath before opening the door to welcome the bright morning sun. Streaks of blinding pain shot through her skull.

Sunglasses would be nice about now.

As she glanced over at the koi pond, a shiver ran up her spine. It was not the recollection of the shadow creature shutting off her airway that bothered her. It was the image of Kael gently blotting the blood from her face with the shirt off his back. His expression had been tender.

No. No. No. Stop thinking like that, Grey. It was an act.

The balcony door of the second story suite creaked open. Casually, she turned to make her way into the main house. Kael cleared his throat. "Do a guy a favor and get your medallion from under the mat on your way inside, please."

Greylyn could not suppress a smirk. It would serve him right to keep it where it was and make his entry into the house painful. Instead, she knelt and removed the medallion from its hiding spot. Pocketing the item as she opened the back door to the inn, mouth-watering smells coming from the kitchen welcomed her. Bacon, eggs, biscuits, fried potatoes. With only two guests, their host had cooked up a breakfast feast! Good thing too. This guest was starving.

First things first, though. Coffee. Lots of it. She headed into the dining room where she knew there would already be a tall carafe of coffee waiting. Instead of dainty cups, large beer mugs were laid out on the counter. Greylyn chuckled as she filled two mugs up to the top and strolled towards the kitchen.

"Good morning, sunshine," she said as she rounded the corner into the large country kitchen where she found Maureen covered in flour. Her host smiled broadly as Greylyn set one of the coffee mugs down beside her on the counter.

"Thought you could use this after last night," she grinned. "I know I will need at least three refills to clear my head after all that wine."

Laughing, the innkeeper thanked her profusely. "My mum always said that the best cure for a hangover was caffeine, a large greasy breakfast, and Excedrin." By the looks of it, Maureen was preparing to cure the entire town. She nodded towards one of the kitchen cabinets. "Excedrin is in there, if you need it, lass."

"Exactly how much food do you think it will require to blast through our alcohol- muddled brains, Maureen?" Greylyn quipped as she reached into the cabinet for the bottle of painkillers.

"I haven't gone that overboard drinking in a long while, but it was so nice to relax and catch up with you, sweetie. Guess I should've kept a better eye on how much we imbibed. My head hasn't felt this bad since Robert took me to Las Vegas for our twentieth anniversary." She tried to laugh but grimaced at the pain it caused.

"Someone else has a little hangover?" a husky male voice asked from the doorway. Greylyn inwardly frowned but tossed him the bottle of Excedrin.

He nodded at the large beer mugs turned coffee cups and chuckled. "Yes, it does appear you two lovely ladies may also be suffering this morning if those coffee cups are any indication. If you don't mind, I think I'll avail myself of a tall mug as well."

With that, he walked back out to the dining room. As soon as he exited the room, she felt able to breathe again.

"Greylyn, would you be a dear and take some of the platters that I've already fixed into the dining room, so Kael won't need to wait for his food. You both go ahead and dive in. I'll join you as soon as the eggs are ready. Sunny-side up and just a little runny, right?" The innkeeper beamed.

It seemed Maureen still felt the need to play Cupid. Somewhat begrudgingly, Greylyn scooped up the platters and headed to the dining room where he waited patiently.

As she walked in, Kael put his newly poured coffee down on the table and came over to relieve her of one of the trays.

"Smells delicious, doesn't it?" he said as he gingerly set the food down on the buffet serving table. "Our hostess has outdone herself this morning. I've heard of feeling hungry enough to eat a horse, but I do believe she's fixed enough to equal that sentiment," he joked with a small chuckle. Moving next to her, he continued, his voice soft, "Although, my dear, you look and smell more delectable than this lavish feast."

He was a mere inch away, with his hands placed on both sides of her, trapping her in between the buffet table and himself. His warm breath caressed her face as she inwardly fought the urge to lean in closer.

"I trust you weren't plagued with any more nasty shadows last night and that you slept well. I know I certainly had sweet dreams."

With a deep, calming intake of breath, her eyes darted around for a way out that did not involve breaking his arms. The best she could do was to duck under his arms and casually stride over to the table to pick up her coffee mug.

Undeterred, he walked over to the table and pulled out a chair while gesturing for her to take a seat.

My, what a gentleman!

"So, have you figured it out yet?"

"Figured what out?" He really was becoming quite annoying.

"Why we are both here? Coincidence?" The way his eyes gleamed, she doubted coincidence had a damn thing to do with it.

"Not quite. So why not be a dear, cut the crap and tell me?"

He chuckled softly as he stood behind her chair, hands perched above her shoulders on the top of the high-backed chair. "Now, what fun would that be? Maybe I'm here to inflict catastrophic damage to the whole town? Maybe I enjoy disrupting weddings? Maybe I'm just here for you." For some reason, her heart skipped a couple beats at that last. "Or perhaps, I'm here to help."

Just as she was about to round on him, of course, their hostess chose that second to come into the dining room with the remainder of the breakfast feast. The woman's smile beamed from ear to ear. At least someone was enjoying herself this morning.

"Maureen, let me take that from you. Please sit down with us." He quickly swept the tray from her slender, yet sturdy arms before she had a chance to protest.

One look at her expression and it was clear that any hopes of disillusioning her friend of the gentleman's charms were long gone. However, this good-guy act wore on Greylyn's nerves.

After Maureen said a quick blessing over the bountiful breakfast, all three heartily dug into the bacon, biscuits, and eggs. The only sounds heard were those of silverware clinking on plates. Once plates were emptied, the threesome sat back in their chairs with full, satisfied bellies. Maureen excused herself to clear away the dishes. Both guests offered to help her clean up: Kael to play nice guy for the innkeeper, Greylyn as a ruse to get away from him. They were both scolded to remember their roles as guests, not as the help.

To avoid remaining alone in the dining room with the dark guardian, Greylyn begged the use of the inn's laundry room. She had been traveling for weeks without the convenience of a washer and dryer. She failed to mention the part about her soaking wet and koi pond filth-covered clothes.

Kael gave her a quick, wicked wink to tell her that he knew exactly why she needed to wash her clothes. Thankfully, he kept it to himself.

Maureen readily agreed, then swept out of the door to tend to the kitchen clean up and preparations for the arrival of her new guests. Quickly gulping down the rest of her coffee, Greylyn headed towards the exit to escape, but Kael grabbed her wrist. "Just think about it. Maybe I am here to help."

Sure, Kael. I will believe that when pigs fly.

If there was one thing clear from last night and this morning's encounters it was that Kael knew a lot more than he let on. Perhaps he was the key to discovering the information she needed. She was more determined than ever to find out what he was hiding. He was not here for the cordial company. He was not here to simply take wedding pictures. And he damn sure was not here to help.

Chapter 10

Discovery

Gaelic Haven and Surrounding Grounds

Checking that the protection spells were still in place around the windows, doors, and vents in her room to ward off any demons, or more specifically Kael, from encroaching on her space, Greylyn headed back into the main house with a pile of laundry in her arms.

Why do all old houses contain dreary, damp, cold basements? More importantly, why is that always the designated place for the washer and dryer?

The stairs to the basement creaked as she placed her weight on them. Tentatively, she put one foot in front of the other until she hit solid ground. She waved her hand in the middle of the room several times as she fumbled for the dangling string from the ceiling to switch on the lone light bulb.

Her breath hitched in her throat. Complete darkness. Confined space. A faint, pungent earthen odor. Just like...

Get over yourself, Grey! This is a basement, not a coffin.

After almost giving up, light finally invaded the room revealing a clean, tidy, and dry room. Nothing like a coffin.

She tossed her clothes into the washer, threw in a scoop of detergent, and set the machine to run before bounding up the stairs, two at a time.

When she had come back into the house, her excellent hearing picked up the muffled sound of the innkeeper milling around upstairs, probably tidying the bedrooms. She had also seen her nemesis walking towards town before she even poked her head out of her room.

Yeah, real brave, Grey. Avoidance was not a tactic Sun Tzu would approve.

Taking advantage of his absence, Greylyn decided to snoop around his suite, assuming it was not warded against angels.

Surprisingly, the door to the second-floor room above her own was not even locked. She suspected a trap, such as being electrocuted as she entered the door. She hesitated for a few seconds before taking a tentative step into the room and... Nothing.

Interesting. She stopped to visually inspect the room for signs of traps, but it appeared to be well-kept with everything in its proper place. There were no clothes on the floor or bags kept out in the open, unlike her own room, which was a mess.

She rummaged through the drawers of the lone nightstand first. Nothing but a copy of the Holy Bible, a local phone book, and a set of the ear plugs provided to all Carriage House guests. Under the bed? Nothing. Not even a dust ball.

Next, she checked the dresser drawers and closet. Just men's clothes tucked neatly away. Nice designer suit and shiny dress shoes. An assortment of ties hung neatly in the closet. Even his damp towel was perfectly folded and draped over the towel rack in the luxurious bathroom. No toothpaste spittle on the oval mirror above the sink. Just a hint of his signature scent – citrus and sandalwood.

After investigating the entire suite, behind mirrors and paintings, under drawers for false bottoms, she found nothing out of the ordinary. Nothing. He was just a super-tidy, handsome bachelor with everything in its place. *Jerk!*

She stood in the middle of the room, her balled fists on her hips.

If I were a dark guardian, where would I hide something of importance?

In the corner of the room next to the balcony door was a small writing desk with his photography equipment on top. The camera and equipment were expensive, high-quality gear. Kael must have been working on his photographer person for this job for a while, possibly months. Did not bode well for her then. She had been here less than twenty-four hours. He had quite the advantage.

Greylyn's fingers fumbled around under the desk. *Bingo!* Her fingers latched onto a folder taped under it. Not the sneakiest of hiding places.

Either the malicious demon was getting sloppy, or he wanted her to find it.

Greylyn pulled the folder out. More pictures. Some of the same ones from yesterday, but what she saw behind those made her knees go weak. She collapsed into a leather-bound vintage office chair in shock.

There were countless pictures of her and not just from her current visit to *Gaelic Haven*. Pictures of her guiding the Boy Scout troop out of the Everglades covered in blood from fighting off the swamp creature. Perhaps he had been there after all. How could she have missed him? Pictures of her in New York City smuggling young immigrant children out of a sweatshop run by demons to manufacture fake designer purses. That had been a particularly nasty encounter proven by the blood, gore, and icky pieces stuck to her clothes and in her hair.

Pictures of her posing as a swimsuit model wannabe in four-inch stilettos to save Candace from falling into the world of pornography. *Now that had been a humiliating experience!*

Another picture of her walking away from a burning ramshackle barn that had housed a group of vampires responsible for the deaths of several runaways. Yet another picture of her getting into her pride and joy, her 1968 Camaro, outside of a diner somewhere in the Midwest.

A photograph of her in a teal evening gown with matching lapis lazuli jewelry from a high society cotillion in the Hamptons. She had crashed it to exorcise a demon from an aspiring political candidate before he got in a position to do real damage. Maneuvering in that form-fitting dress to hold the man down while performing the ritual had been a disaster. At least it was easier to fight in than the taffeta gowns with the bone corsets and hoop skirts from colonial and pre-Civil War days.

More pictures of her from countless missions. A few of the depicted scenes were from times she remembered dealing with Kael. Others, he had not been around. At least, she had not seen him.

Soft padding of soled shoes coming up the stairs alerted her to Kael's return almost too late. No time to place the folder back in its hiding place so she threw it on the desk and bolted for the balcony door. Lithely, Greylyn jumped down to the ground outside her room without a sound. She quietly made her way back to the main house to retrieve her laundry.

She knew she could only avoid him for so long. Then she determined to get some real answers. First, she needed to clear her head...and then call Thomas. The bride and groom were expected to arrive soon, but she still had no idea what danger they were in.

The meeting with Jensen had not gone as planned. Kael's temperament suffered for it. He had been so wrapped up in his own angry thoughts, he had not capitalized on Greylyn snooping around in his room. It was logical she would investigate there while he was away. He had even left the door unlocked. But two seconds too late opening the door and she was gone, the thud of her feet hitting the ground outside his window the only evidence.

He grinned. There on the desk was the folder with the photographs. Good. She had discovered that. Maybe now she would start to question his repeated presence in her life. Of course, considering the evidence, maybe she would think he was merely a supernatural stalker.

Shrugging, he peeked out the window. Greylyn had already disappeared into the main house. Too bad, catching her in the act could have been fun. But for now, he had other concerns.

Damn Jensen! Kael recognized his handiwork with the shadow creature that assaulted Greylyn. The dark guardian had not been difficult to locate either, so he could not feign it was a coincidence he was in town. It had been over a century since they had been on the same continent, and if Jensen were lucky, it would be over a century before they encountered each other again.

After pummeling his pretty-boy face into an unrecognizable mass of flesh, blood, and tissue, Jensen had confessed. Their mutual boss had sent him. Orders were to maim the guardian angel, but not to kill. Odd considering their boss's stance on this particular guardian angel. Standing orders From Olivier were for her protection. No harm. He needed her alive and well. Now Lucifer was another story. That was what caused Kael more concern. Had the order come from Satan himself, it was business as usual. But no, Olivier pulled Jensen's strings.

As for the question of why Olivier changed course this late in the game...Jensen, as usual, knew nothing.

Kael cursed himself for not killing him outright, but deep down he knew the attack had been directed at Greylyn as a test for himself. Trouble was, there was no way to know whether he passed or failed.

Collecting the scattered photos and putting them back in the folder, Kael pondered the situation. "What the hell are you up to, Olivier?"

Surprisingly, Kael had not sought out Greylyn. She managed to throw her clothes back into her room and changed for a much-needed run. Running sucked. She never liked it but right now she needed the exercise, adrenaline, and space away from Gaelic Haven to clear her mind.

The sound of her sneakered feet against the pavement leading into town had a calming effect. After about a mile, adrenaline took over. The rest of her run was on physical autopilot as her brain began to process her findings.

There had to be at least a hundred or more pictures of her in that folder, all from various places over the years. One of the photos had even been an old black-and-white from a speakeasy in the 1920s. She smiled. Half the fun had been getting dolled up in that red-beaded flapper dress with the excessive black fringe and matching beaded headband. The lower heels had been easier to run in, too. And she had run a lot that night.

Her job made comfort more important than fashion, but occasionally, she enjoyed being fancy. That had been one of those times. The dance music had been incredibly loud, the prohibited alcohol had flowed freely, and the pack of sly werewolves running the joint had been easy to take down.

What are you up to, Kael?

Her feet pounded the pavement until she found herself at the top of a high hill looking down onto the Shenandoah River. The banks of the river were flooded from the recent storm. The roaring of muddy water rushed violently downstream and drowned out the sound of cars on the nearby interstate. Her leg muscles quivered as she made her way down to the edge of the water to rest on a fallen tree.

None of this makes sense.

True, Kael had appeared as her nemesis more times than she could recollect. He was the only one she had encountered more than once. He always seemed to enjoy tormenting her. Always a smile and a sarcastic quip, but he never tried to kill her outright. Something always held him back.

Wait! What?

The realization stunned her. Not once had he taken lethal action against her. He had beaten her bloody to the point she had wished for death, but he always stopped. Killing a guardian angel was difficult...damn near impossible...but Kael never delivered the fatal blow. Last night would have been the perfect way to finish her off. The shadow creature could not have taken her out. Not completely. You needed a better weapon than creepy black air to wipe her out. Still, the creature could have inflicted enough damage to put her out of the picture for a while. Instead, upon Kael's arrival at the koi pond, the shadow had vanished.

Why hadn't he taken advantage then? Instead, he had hauled her out of the water and essentially tended to the gash along her forehead. He could have easily swiped her own weapon from its holster at the small of her back, disabled her, and then ripped her heart out of her chest. Instead...

He saved me last night.

No, that was improbable. Maybe he just did not want the shadow to have all the fun, tormenting her as her lungs filled with pond scum.

The follow-up question plagued her even more.

Why haven't I tried to kill him either?

No answer.

Taking one last look at the muddy river water as it rushed past, Greylyn was startled to see a lone wolf directly across the river from her, staring with intent silver eyes. Its fur was unnaturally gray, like the color of refined steel. Something about the eyes seemed off. In addition to their unusual color, they conveyed more than the primal intelligence of an animal. It was as if the wolf were sizing her up as a human would evaluate a racehorse before placing a bet.

How long had it been watching her?

The wolf nodded as if answering an unspoken question, before it turned and raced back into the dense forest.

A little shaken, Greylyn high-tailed it back to the inn, sticking to the paved road. She did not even bother to put up a glamour so humans who witnessed her blur by at an unnatural speed would not see anything. Hopefully, she would at least get back before the bride and groom arrived.

Chapter 11

Here Come the Bride & Groom

J ust as Greylyn jogged back up the winding drive to the inn, she noted another car in the tiny parking lot to the side of the main house – the bride and groom had arrived, in an old, beat-up Chrysler LeBaron.

Due to her disheveled appearance – sweat-stained athletic wear and mud-covered sneakers – she did not wish to encounter the other guests yet. She skirted the main house by running around the tree line to the back. Luckily, there was no one in sight.

A quick, refreshing shower helped immensely. Droplets of water fell from her wet hair onto her small clothes sack as she pillaged it for something more presentable to wear.

Dammit! Only t-shirts!

She threw on a pair of wrinkled khaki shorts and her once-white-now-pink tank top. Another victim of her atrocious laundry skills.

A quick towel-dry of her hair, a smidgen of mascara and some peach-flavored lip balm and she was ready.

It was already past four in the afternoon when she quietly let herself into the main house. The sun glinted off the koi pond and metal roof making her squint up at the window where she had witnessed the vision yesterday. She planned to use the excuse of grabbing a quick glass of wine from the pub to relax before heading out to town for dinner. Not that she needed an excuse to be there. Maureen had made it clear last night that she did not expect her to stay hidden just because a wedding would be taking place. But she did not want to appear to be intruding on such a special occasion.

She found everyone convened in the pub area. A keg of Irish beer had been tapped for the men, while the young woman with short strawberry-blonde locks appeared to be sipping apple cider from a champagne flute. The innkeeper was apparently still nursing a slight hangover with no signs of an alcoholic beverage near her station at the bar, only a tall glass of ice water.

Maureen's face beamed with delight as she entered the pub. "Kelly, Matthew, this is the young woman I was just telling you about, Greylyn. She's staying in the Carriage House for a few days. Luckily, she has your handsome friend here to keep her company."

Maureen just could not let the Cupid thing go, could she? Graciously shaking hands with the couple, Greylyn tried not to blush too much as their smiles clearly indicated the potential love match had already been discussed openly with them.

Stepping over with his hand extended was a tall, broad-chested man with an olive complexion, jet black wavy hair and a sweet smile. "Nice to meet you, Greylyn. I'm Matthew and this lovely lady is my bride, Kelly." His handshake was firm and solid, not overdone like some chauvinistic jerks she had encountered, but not the "dead fish" handshake most people had sported since the 1990s. However, her guardian senses did not detect anything amiss. His aura was clean, radiant even.

Check the groom off the list.

The doe-eyed woman also stood and extended her hand in greeting. Giggling at Matthew's remarks, she added shyly, "Hi, please excuse my hubby-to-be. He's obsessed with only referring to me in terms such as *his bride, his forever love* ... you get the picture. It is a bit embarrassing, but ... I love it. We've already heard so much about you from Maureen and Kael. I was beginning to think you were a myth."

Kelly's voice was soft and sweet, with just the faintest Southern belle tinge. She was a happy bride, but there was something that bothered Greylyn from the moment she had walked in the room. A glimmer of gray hung over her like a cloud. When they shook hands, waves of energy spiked from Greylyn's hand all the way to her neck. Not painful, but more like the warmth of a cashmere blanket. Familiar, but foreign.

Greylyn's mind flashed back to the vision of the woman in white silently screaming in the window. Although the vision had been hazy, there was no doubt that Kelly had been the woman. For a split second, another image emerged. Glazed hazel green eyes, but the face was blurred. Again, the vision morphed to pitch darkness surrounding the woman in front of her, like acrid smoke billowing off a bonfire. But instead of the smoke floating away from the source, it encircled her.

Shrugging off the vision, Greylyn pointedly focused on Kelly and forced a smile. "Well, as I see it, Matthew has every right to brag about his beautiful bride, so let him. He should appreciate what he has and be proud to shout it to the world."

"Amen," Matthew and Kael agreed together.

"However, I am a bit worried what crazy stories Maureen and Kael are spreading about me. Do not believe everything you hear," she laughed before quickly turning the topic around to the wedding.

The group settled around the bar as Maureen refreshed drinks and poured a glass of Lusca for Greylyn. The conversation flowed easily as Matthew joked about most everything. He was a jovial soul. His orange aura radiated a good and generous heart, contentment, and optimism. Generally, it was the bride who glowed, but this groom exuded happiness in tidal waves.

All the while, Greylyn forced herself to avoid eye contact with Kael. From the moment she had entered the pub, the heat of his gaze seared her skin as if she had stepped too close to a furnace. After a while she was unable to resist the urge to look over. He was too quiet. He was smirking – a clear indication he knew full well she had been snooping around his room earlier. Just as she suspected, he not only knew but had planned for her to find exactly what she found. What game was he playing?

Trying to find out what she could about the couple, Greylyn turned the conversation to them. "So how did you two lovebirds meet?" The question was simple, but both groaned. Kael even rolled his eyes.

"Well, do you want the PG-rated version or the real deal?" Matthew laughed and Kelly blushed bright red.

"The full, unedited story, please. I love the juicy details."

"This is not a story for the weak of heart." Matthew's deep chocolate brown eyes, almost the exact color of a Hershey bar, shone with mischief.

As she moved over to their table, Kael pulled out the chair for her. His lips were turned up slightly as if to smile, but there was a dark glimmer in his eyes as if he just made a genius move on a chess board.

"Thank you," she whispered, but her mind said *My, how freaking gallant can that toad be?* He achieved his purpose. Everyone else in the room grinned broadly while exchanging knowing glances.

As she sipped her wine, the bride and groom bantered back and forth about the story of their first encounter.

"No, I absolutely did not come on to you first. You are the only man on the planet who would think a girl stabbing you in the hand with darts is a come-on technique."

"You did what?!" Greylyn was astounded.

"She stabbed me with darts. I stick to my theory that the darts were poisoned. They obviously were dipped into a love potion or something because...here we are. I've been head over heels ever since."

"Dude, hand it over." Kael held out his hand.

"Hand over what?"

"Your man-card, because you lost all rights to it with that cheesy declaration." The whole group laughed, including Matthew who pouted with feigned hurt.

Kelly added mischievously, "You never will know the truth about those darts."

These two were adorable. The way they teased each other, giving each other a hard time. They rarely took their eyes off each other. Normally, Greylyn would consider this kind of display off-putting and a charade. But no...they were the real deal.

"Can you believe she brought along a friend on our first date? Talk about throwing up obstacles!" Matthew rolled his eyes dramatically.

"Obviously not too much of an obstacle, as I recall," Kelly added. "The real obstacle was you not letting us inside your house so we could use the bathroom after drinking at the fair."

"It was a disaster! Come on, Kael. Back me up here. You've seen the inside of the house I shared with those guys. If she'd seen it that night, she would've blown out of there in a split second and never returned my calls."

Grinning broadly, Kael agreed. "A quarantine of that place is definitely in order. How did you survive living with such slobs?"

As the story continued to unfold, Greylyn could not shake the feeling that she knew Kelly from somewhere. However, she was more concerned about the dark vision she had had.

I may be wrong, but I think Kelly knows she's in trouble.

Then the young woman turned in her chair and Greylyn realized the truth. Kelly sported a slight baby bump. Not noticeable from a head-on vantage point, and barely evident from the side, but no mistaking it. There was even an electric white aura encircling her belly. How had she not seen that before?

Oh, no! I swear if Kael is after the baby, I will slice and dice him until he is stew meat.

"In conclusion, despite poison darts, third wheels, and messy roommates, it was very much lust at first sight," Kelly blushed.

Matthew corrected her. "Love at first sight, babe." He leaned across the small table and kissed his glowing bride full on the lips.

Greylyn had the decency to look away. Kael, however, seemed more interested in watching her reaction. He jokingly commented, "Hey guys, get a room, will ya? Wait, you have one already. Upstairs. Go!" He pointed up dramatically.

The lovebirds broke apart laughing. "Not yet, dude. She's making me wait until the wedding night. Seems silly, considering." Matthew delicately indicated his bride's small baby bump with pride.

"Besides," Kelly blushed, "I'm starving. Greylyn, you must join us for dinner. Please." She pressed her hands together in pleading.

"Well, we can't have both of you starving," Matthew joked with a wink. To Greylyn and Kael, he added, "I learned fast not to make a hungry pregnant woman wait for food. It isn't pretty!"

Gaelic Haven was a bed and breakfast inn, so dinners were not normally served. Last night's meal had been an exception. The last thing Greylyn wanted was to spend more time around Kael; however, she accepted the offer to keep an eye on the couple. They decided to walk a few blocks to a nice bistro.

Matthew and Kelly held hands as they walked in front. She had seen the curious and mischievous look in the other woman's eyes when Kael held the chair out for Greylyn. Kelly occasionally glanced behind them.

Oh no! Not her too.

She had enough dealing with Maureen's aspirations of playing Cupid.

Strangely enough, the usually smug dark guardian did not speak during the entire walk. She was not inclined to speak to him either, so they continued the trek in uncomfortable silence. Inwardly, she fumed about the possibility of him meaning to cause harm to Kelly and the baby. It would serve him right if she yanked him behind the next grove of magnolia trees and diced him to ribbons. Instead, she tucked that anger behind the façade of a shy smile. But only for the moment.

The late afternoon air had cooled, but the humidity was still heavy like they had just stepped out of a sauna. It was a relief to feel air conditioning again when they arrived at the restaurant a few minutes later.

The small town had little in the way of entertainment and cuisine. Regardless, the building was not crowded, and they were seated immediately in a cozy corner booth adjacent to the stage where a band would play later that evening. The sign at the entrance advertised a cover band playing that night. The name flashed in Greylyn's head as a memory emerged of a dimly lit bar bursting with co-eds from a small university in Alabama. If she recalled correctly, and if they were indeed the same band, this place should be rocking later. Too bad, she was not there for the entertainment.

The group found lots to discuss as they perused the menu and ordered their drinks. Kelly kept asking probing questions of Greylyn, trying to determine if she had a boyfriend, where she worked, how long she would be staying at the inn, etc. The woman was persistent in her quest for information. It became difficult to field all the questions thrown at her, but she did the best she could. "I travel a lot, so generally I'm not in any one place long enough to establish relationships. But I enjoy my work, so that's my life for now."

Matthew nudged Kael. "Dude, I have never, and I do mean never, seen you tongue-tied. What? You suddenly forgot how to talk to a pretty lady?"

Greylyn had thought it strange as well but not for the same reasons the others were thinking. It was an act, to make them believe he was interested in her. And he was convincing, but his silence had more of a brooding edge to it.

She plastered on a smile and redirected the conversation to the wedding. It would help her to know if any guests may also be added trouble. It would not be the first time demons used a family member to destroy someone. Inflicting pain at a special event, like a wedding, would be easy. Countless weddings and relationships had been eternally damaged that way.

"Oh, we're keeping things small and simple. Only immediate family and a few friends. My folks are coming up from Georgia but will stay at my townhouse closer to the city," Kelly stated. "Matthew's quite larger family will drive out tomorrow afternoon."

Nothing they relayed about the guests raised any red flags. Typical family dysfunction was all. But she would not put it past Kael to use family or friends as a weapon to inflict pain.

Kelly continued, "So, we are keeping it a small group. Only those that truly know and love us for ourselves. No co-workers or sorority sisters that I don't keep in contact with anymore."

"But you invited the *Sex and the City* girls," Matthew teased.

That caught Greylyn's attention. And Kael's apparently as he looked up with interest. "Well, I couldn't invite one without the others. However, I'll admit I'm glad Griffin is bringing his new girlfriend with him." Looking over at Greylyn, she explained. "He's been my best friend since college. My mom is still mad that we never got together romantically. But I wouldn't wish any of my friends on him. They are simply not worthy. It's best he's taken already."

With dinner over, the restaurant was starting to get more crowded as folks arrived for the musical entertainment. The guys seemed interested in staying as Matthew rocked back and forth to the music, but Kelly showed signs of fatigue. Her big, beautiful eyes could barely stay open.

Greylyn offered to see Kelly back safely to the inn. Meanwhile, the boys could indulge in a mini-bachelor party.

"Stay out of trouble," Kelly admonished as she planted a kiss on Matthew's cheek.

"No worries, babe. Just a few beers with the big guy here."

Kael chimed in, "I promise to keep him out of trouble. No bachelor party shenanigans." He had the audacity to cross his heart and point upwards to Heaven.

It was a short walk back, but they took it slow to make it less exhausting for the pregnant woman. Greylyn's eyes darted around for more shadow creatures, but nothing was amiss. A hint of magnolias hung in the air as they sauntered through the historic district towards the inn. The walk gave her a chance to try to gain more information from Kelly without arousing her suspicions. How do you ask a woman if there is anything demonic or even creepy about her family and friends?

The bride only wished to discuss one topic...Kael. More precisely, Greylyn's thoughts about her handsome friend. She used the subject to get Kelly to open up as to how they knew Kael, and for how long. Dark guardians did not normally spend large amounts of time cozying up to targets. It was obvious, Kael had been working the couple for a while.

"How did you guys meet Kael anyway? Seems you've known each other forever, but I believe he said he hadn't been in the area very long."

Kelly perked up at the question. Obviously, the girl took this as an indication that Greylyn was interested in the tall, dark gentleman.

"It's so funny. It has only been a few months, but it does feel like we've known him our whole lives. Matthew's company had a huge holiday party for New Year's at the Watergate Hotel. Very elegant. I love dressing up, but always feel so out of place at those soirees. Kael had been hired to take pictures there. He had just moved to the area, and apparently has a lot of gigs out of town because we don't see him around too often."

Kelly was starting to babble, so Greylyn tried to coax her into getting to the point a little faster since they were already close to the inn. "So, he was just walking around taking pictures at a party and now you're best buds?"

"Well, something like that, I guess. He kept coming around, trying to get me to smile. It was our last big evening out before I discovered I was pregnant, so I was drinking. Didn't have a lot, but for some reason I was light-headed. He suggested Matthew take me out on the balcony for some fresh air and followed us out there to make sure I was okay. We ended up talking the night away. Weird. I don't remember ever being cold."

Well, being around Kael can do that to a girl.

Kelly continued to ramble about how wonderful he was, and how he and Matthew had immediately connected over fishing stories and fixing up classic cars. "So, Kael is such an incredible photographer. We are so lucky he offered to take pictures for the wedding...for free. I don't think we could have afforded another professional. He's a real life saver. Have you had a chance to see any of his portfolio?"

And on and on for the entire walk. By the time they arrived back at the inn, Greylyn had heard quite enough of Kael's numerous virtues.

Oh, if this poor girl just knew the truth about the fiend!

Just as Kelly was about to walk up the stairs to her suite, Greylyn nearly jumped when an image of a younger Kelly sprang into her mind. Those beautiful eyes glossed over from alcohol barely concealed the emotional pain she was suffering. Kenny Chesney music playing in the background. "Kelly, did you by chance go to college in Tennessee or Arkansas?"

Kelly stopped on the stairs with one hand on the railing, her expression of shock clear. "Why, yes. Rhodes College in Memphis."

"Ever hang out at a joint called *Dueling Hearts* in West Memphis?"

Kelly's eyes grew wide. "All the time. Not that I'm exactly proud of that fact. How did you guess?"

"Oh, it's just that you looked familiar."

After Kelly retired up to her room, Greylyn placed a call to an immensely perturbed Aussie.

"Doll, I am not your beck and call boy. I expect some level of consideration. I left a ton of messages. Where the bloody devil have you been all day?"

"Sorry, Thomas. Really, I am. Thought I was giving you time to recover after your big date last night. How'd that go, by the way?"

"It went about the way you'd bloody think it would. She drank an entire bottle of awfully expensive wine while I nursed a damn soda all night. By the time we got back to her place, she was snockered. Passed out on the sofa with her blouse halfway unbuttoned. I left. Not planning on calling either."

"Sorry, pal. You win some, you lose some."

"Yeah, I'd like a fifty-fifty shot, but I'm batting zero for a hundred here."

"Stop it. You haven't been on one hundred dates since you sobered up. Give it time, Sparky."

Once he finally piped down about his dating woes, she gave him all the information she had discovered along with the names of the wedding guests for him to check out. The news that the bride was pregnant caused him concern. "Are you sure it's her? You don't think Kael would be after the baby?"

"No, I'm certain it's Kelly. But anything that threatens her also threatens the child." Greylyn left out the part about finding a folder of photographs of herself in the dark guardian's room. She needed him focused on their mission. The more personal stuff could wait. Besides, the last thing she needed was him raising the alarm to Jasper.

"How did the evil dude get so chummy with the couple in the first place?"

She let out an exasperated sigh as she sunk down onto the worn velvet trimmed chair next to her bed. "Get this. He conveniently stopped Kelly from drinking too much one night before she found out she was pregnant. Sounds fishy to me."

"No kidding."

"The funny thing is, he hasn't shown any signs of aggression or ill intent. Being around them all night, he acts like he's genuinely enjoying himself and that he adores Matthew and Kelly."

"Well, he's a bloody good actor then!"

"Yes, I know. It's just I can usually sniff these things out. Remember the Bolshevik Revolution? It looked as if he was going to take down the tsar using a few political enemies of the Romanov's. I figured he would target the family friend and physician, Rasputin. Kael was the one who introduced Rasputin to the tsarina in the first place, but he was also the one who lured Rasputin out that night to be slaughtered by those sympathetic to keeping the tsar and his family in power."

"I remember you telling me about it, and it's in my archives somewhere. But the family all died, even after Rasputin was done away with and after they were promised safety."

"Well, maybe not everyone died."

"Okay, you definitely didn't tell me the entire story. You owe me, darling."

After promising a full recounting of all horror stories related to Kael, Greylyn lamented that the dark guardian was always innovative and a real genius when it came to manipulating humans. "You should hear Kelly go on and on about how wonderful he is. Makes me nauseous."

Thomas did not have much more information on Kelly and Matthew than she did. "However, I did uncover one little nugget about Kael that was of interest. Seems our boy is on the rise politically. He's always shown a penchant for getting in with the political types, like Rasputin and Robespierre, and there are some that suggest he influenced Mao, but there's no literature to back it up. But it's enough to consider it a trend of his over the centuries."

He added with a snark, "His appearance in the DC metro area a few years back coincided with a new low in national politics that led to a particularly nasty scandal. Any guesses?"

"Okay, I get the gist. What does this have to do with the here and now?"

Clearing his throat as if to make a big announcement, Thomas continued, "Apparently, Kael is on the ascent in the supernatural political ranks as well."

Seriously? Why am I surprised?

"Two years ago, he was photographed meeting with a much higher-level demon. Higher level in that the being was a fallen angel. Not the infamous Lucifer, but just as scary and lethal. How someone managed to get the picture and live was a miracle. If Kael is working with that guy, then all bets are off. This apparently small-time wedding could be something more catastrophic."

Oh, great! My vacation has turned into the apocalypse.

A sick feeling surfaced as she hung up the phone, after promising to touch base with Thomas in the morning. So, Kael had made friends in extremely low places? This was getting worse.

Greylyn marched back to the main house. She wanted to be around when the two boys came back from the festivities in town. She and Kael needed to have a little chat.

Just as her hand touched the doorknob, an eerie howl broke through the quiet of the night – a lone wolf from the sound of it. Then silence. Not so much as a cricket chirp. Not even the bull frogs dared to croak.

Chapter 12

A Bride's Confession

Gaelic Haven Main House

The back door creaked softly as she re-entered the main house. Maureen was sitting in the front parlor with a romance novel in hand, reading glasses adorning her face.

"Did you have a good time, dear? I did not expect you back so soon. Why don't you grab yourself a drink?" That was the best idea she had heard all day.

As soon as she returned with a glass of wine, Maureen started in. "You haven't answered my question. Did you enjoy your time with the soon-to-be newlyweds and *Kael*?"

"Sorry to disappoint you but there's nothing happening in that department so please stop playing Cupid," Greylyn practically begged. She explained that she escorted Kelly back to the inn while the groom enjoyed one last boys' night out as a bachelor.

Thankfully, Maureen let the topic drop and the conversation turned to more benign subjects, such as the innkeeper's ideas for remodeling the kitchen and whether to take a couple weeks' vacation to travel back to Ireland or to some other part of the world.

They were so engrossed in the pros and cons of international travel that they did not hear footsteps coming down the stairs until Kelly padded into the room in her slippers.

She was decked out in ivory silk pajamas, which drew more attention to her baby bump as it strained the fabric buttons. However, Kelly's expression seemed almost sad. Her eyes glistened with unshed tears and the tip of her nose was tinged pink. It tugged at Greylyn's heart. Marveling at how connected she seemed to be to Kelly, worry crept up at the sight of shadowy bags under her eyes, which now showed subtle blue tones instead of hazel green.

Maureen fussed and fretted over her. "Dearie, come over here and have a seat. What can I get for you?"

Kelly flashed a timid, embarrassed smile. "Guess I just couldn't sleep with all the excitement about tomorrow."

Maureen offered, "Let me fix you a cup of warm milk to help you sleep, dear."

"Does that really work?" Greylyn was skeptical.

After she returned with the cup, the ladies chatted for a while about nothing in particular until the innkeeper began yawning. Maureen excused herself for the evening. "Don't stay up too much longer. The lassie needs her rest."

Strangely, Kelly's expression quickly changed to one of nervousness after the innkeeper left. The blue in her eyes deepened with uncertainty and flicked around the room. Faint worry lines became visible on her forehead. The gray outline in her aura grew more pronounced, so much so that it appeared as if a thundercloud had ensconced the poor girl. Something was bothering her greatly, and Greylyn did not think it was the wedding.

"Kelly, is everything okay? Not to be nosy, but you seem disconcerted. Is there something else weighing on you than just the wedding?" She knew that as a guardian angel people felt unusually free to discuss their problems with her, even if they did not realize why.

The young woman's face relaxed and her eyes grew wide as teacup saucers. After taking a couple of deep breaths, Kelly began, "I know we don't know each other...yet, but I feel calmer with you close by. Like I could tell you anything. Does that sound strange or what?" Greylyn nodded in agreement. "If I'm making you uncomfortable, just let me know and I'll shut up." She rolled her eyes to the ceiling before continuing. "It must seem odd having a complete stranger wanting to unload their worries on you."

With what she hoped came off as a comforting smile, Greylyn encouraged her to talk about whatever was weighing on her mind.

Relief washed over her features as Kelly began her story and her shoulders visibly relaxed.

"You probably guessed from our love story retelling earlier that when Matthew and I first met, our relationship was – and still is – deeply passionate. From the beginning, we couldn't keep our hands off each other."

Okay, definitely TMI.

"A few weeks after we met, I discovered that I was pregnant. According to my doctors that was impossible. Years ago, I was diagnosed with ovarian failure after a severe bout of endometrioses. Imagine my shock when I saw the two blue lines!"

Kelly uttered a nervous laugh while shrugging. Greylyn nodded as encouragement to continue.

"I have always known I wanted to be a mother. When the doctors told me that I would never conceive on my own, I was devastated. Then ... WHAM ... what was impossible had become possible."

Yes, it did seem rather miraculous. Oddly miraculous.

"How did Matthew take the news?"

A big grin broke out on Kelly's face. "Like a champ. Seriously, I thought he'd run out and never return when I told him. But he was so happy about it. Excited. Even though we had only been together a short time, he knew this was it. We were that *forever* type of love. Having a baby was a blessing in his eyes."

Greylyn felt a twinge of jealousy at the mere idea of a *forever* love. That was something she would never know. Destined to walk the Earth for eternity, but never free to enjoy the gift of loving someone and being loved in return. She had accepted it long ago, but this glaringly obvious case of all-encompassing love stung just a little.

"Wow, that's amazing. You are so lucky. But ..." She hated to speak the words. Greylyn could tell by the sadness in Kelly's face that *that* pregnancy was not *this* pregnancy.

A lone tear streamed down the young woman's freckled face. She looked down to her lap where her fingers were twisting the edge of her pajama top.

"I lost the baby at the beginning of the second trimester, just as soon as I finally got up the courage to go public with the news."

"Oh, no!" Greylyn's heart ached for Kelly. The loss of a child, whether already born or not, was a soul-wrenching experience that she believed no one should endure. Undoubtedly, the loss had impacted Kelly deeply.

"Matthew was so supportive. He was sad, too, but he kept his focus on cheering me up. Promising that we would have more children. If I got pregnant once, surely I would again."

"But you had doubts?"

Nodding, Kelly eyes were downcast as she continued. "I honestly believed that my one shot at becoming a mother had been ripped away. I was depressed and angry and…a train wreck. I thought I was being punished for something, just didn't know what. Perhaps I had sinned too much that God would refuse to bless me with a child. Considering the things I've done, maybe I wasn't worthy of being a mother."

No, no she could not believe that.

"Didn't help when my parents threw scripture in my face when I told them about the pregnancy and then after the miscarriage. Well, that certainly did not improve my state of mind. Just reaffirmed that God was punishing me." Kelly would no longer look Greylyn in the eyes. She stared at the floor as she hesitated to finish the story.

Oh, strict religious upbringing sometimes did more psychological harm than good when misinterpreted and misused. The knots in Greylyn's stomach grew tighter. Kelly was still holding something back. "What happened after that?"

Kelly kept wringing the material of her pajama top with her fingers into a thin cone. The silence permeated the small room. Finally, after nearly a minute or more passed, the young woman took a long, haggard breath and stuttered hastily. "I wanted answers. Needed answers. Did God…did He hate me? Would I ever have a child? No amount of praying seemed to help, so I sought answers from another source." Again, Kelly paused as if struggling to utter the exact words. "A psychic to be exact."

Oh.

In her experience, a fair percentage of psychics were quacks who took people's money while telling them what they thought the person wanted to hear. Others had the gift but were incompetent, meaning to do good things but having the opposite effect. A true medium who had firm control over his or her talents was rare.

Was this the cause of the darkness surrounding the young woman? Had the psychic done something to rain down evil on her? Or was it merely Kelly's own limited beliefs from the way she was raised that now caused panic?

She said a quick, silent prayer that Kelly's psychic friend was not using black magic to *help* her. If she received supernatural assistance in conceiving, that could lead to all sorts of cosmic ramifications. She had witnessed it enough over the centuries, especially with European nobility desperate for a male heir. Her stomach coiled in knots at the prospect this was what had a dark hold on Kelly. "That's interesting," was all Greylyn could say.

"I know. Sounds corny, but visiting this woman was such a comfort to me. She was extremely sweet and encouraging. Said I would be a mother someday, which made me incredibly happy. She even offered to say blessings over me to help ease my mind."

Greylyn cringed inwardly, digging her nails into her palms to keep herself calm so as not to show signs of concern. No need to alarm the poor girl. Blessings? Or dark magic?

"After the blessings, I felt happy and light, as if all that despair from losing the baby was easing up. Then, a few months later, I got sick to my stomach. Couldn't keep anything down for days. It took over a week for me to figure it out and buy a pregnancy test." Kelly took a deep breath. "Before I even told Matthew, I booked it over to the psychic's apartment. I thought she could tell me if I would miscarry again. The thought of losing another baby scared the hell out of me."

"What did the woman say? Did her blessings have anything to do with the quick pregnancy?"

Kelly shook her head. "She was just as shocked as I was, so I don't think so. She practically fell over when she let me in the apartment. I wasn't even showing yet, just a few weeks along. But she knew as soon as she saw me." Her knuckles were white from wringing the corner of her pajama top so tightly.

"The woman could tell you were pregnant before you told her?" Kelly nodded. "And she was surprised?" Again, an affirmative nod.

"Sofia, that's the lady's name, picked up on my insecurities about carrying the child to full-term after the first miscarriage, so she offered to have more blessings said over both of us to ensure a healthy pregnancy, safe birth, and strong child." Kelly paused; her eyes rolled slightly upward. "Actually, she had said *son,* which I thought was odd. Of course, I said yes. Couldn't hurt to have blessings said over the child, could it?"

The anxious look on her face belied the truth. No, Kelly was worried about the psychic's involvement. But why? Knowing the potential for disaster if things were not as they seemed, Greylyn was more than concerned.

"So that's when you told Matthew?"

"Oh, he was over the moon about the prospect of becoming a father. He proposed that we move up the wedding date. We went back and forth about it. I didn't want to wed while pregnant, afraid of jinxing the pregnancy, especially during the first trimester. Not to mention the horror of a protruding belly in my wedding photos." Kelly patted her baby bump as her lips turned up in a sweet smile. "Matthew, however, insisted we be married before the baby's birth. Eventually, we compromised and settled on a wedding date after the completion of the first trimester, which happened to correspond with our two-year anniversary of meeting. Romantic, huh?" An uncertain smile crossed her face briefly before her lips turned down again in worry.

"Well, that is romantic. And you make a lovely bride, baby bump or not." Greylyn could tell Kelly needed reassurances with the big day less than twenty-four hours away. But she knew better than to believe that was the entire issue. Kelly's frown lines deepened after admitting about the psychic – a clear sign there was more to the story. Greylyn prodded her a bit more. "But that's not what is bothering you, is it?"

"The thing is I never told Matthew or ... anyone. About the psychic anyway, or the blessings. Don't get me wrong. He's very open-minded, but I am not sure how he would react to a psychic. He usually makes fun of all that hocus pocus. You should have heard all his quips during our ghost tour of Charleston. He clearly does not believe."

Greylyn chuckled and nodded. Yes, that was a common reaction.

"But it's not really Matthew's reaction that concerns me." Kelly's words started to flow faster as the crux of her stress came pouring out. Finally, she was about to spit out the true problem.

"I grew up in a deeply religious household. Sundays were for church, as were Wednesday nights. Even taught Sunday School to the kindergarten class, as well as Vacation Bible School every summer. It's just that … psychics are rather taboo, forbidden, and … sinful. If my family knew I consulted a psychic they'd freak even more than my obvious pre-marriage fornication." Her half-hearted attempt at a laugh fell empty. "Now I'm afraid that by consulting one that I may have invited evil into my life, and the life of my child." Her hand came up as if to ward off any objections. "I don't think Sofia is evil or anything, but if I messed with God's plans by seeking one out…" The woman was on the verge of breaking down as her voice quaked to quote a Bible verse, "Turn ye not unto them that have familiar spirits, nor unto the wizards …"

"No, no. Kelly, no. You can't believe that." She had to stop the poor girl from beating herself up, particularly because of scripture that had been misconstrued so often.

"I know. It sounds ridiculous. Maybe it's my pregnancy brain. Hormones and such making me second-guess everything. But the idea has really been bothering me lately. Guess I just needed someone to tell me that I didn't commit an atrocious sin. Saying the words out loud makes it sound so silly!" Kelly sighed heavily as if she had just confessed to the Valentine's Day Massacre. "Wow, I am so sorry for unloading on you like that."

The psychic's blessing worried Greylyn. Also, if the conception were helped along by the medium's interventions…that could spell heartache and disaster. She needed to check into that ASAP, but she did not want to frighten the young woman by running out the door. The bride's confession had not diminished the gray tinge around her. If it had, that would have been more reassuring.

Smiling, Greylyn held out her hand to clasp Kelly's. A comforting squeeze and a white light surrounded the bride, obliterating the gray aura. Although Kelly did not see it, she visibly relaxed and even smiled.

The first thing Greylyn needed to do was to dissuade Kelly of her limited belief that consulting a psychic (if a true psychic) was evil and she should be punished for it. Also, she needed to reassure her that she had had not wittingly invited evil into their lives.

Although, in reality, she may have.

"Kelly, consulting a person of vision," she had to choose her words carefully, "is not a sin. I firmly believe God grants people these gifts for a purpose. It is what they do with their gifts that makes them good or bad. This woman sounds delightful so I don't think speaking with her could possibly cause any negative effects for you or the baby. But thinking that way can lead to emotional distress for you and that is not good for either of you." Greylyn hoped she came off as comforting and the message got through to the distraught woman. Mental and emotional anguish, whether regarding something real or not, could cause all sorts of spiritual damage. Kelly needed to believe, to know, that she had not committed some horrific sin and God would not strike her down for it.

She patted Kelly's hands reassuringly and smiled. "I'm so glad you found answers with this woman. Consider it a blessing she was able to assuage your fear." Sitting back in her chair, she watched as the white energy wrapped around Kelly. Her shoulders relaxed noticeably. A tentative smile upturned her lips as she deeply sighed with relief.

Greylyn continued to prod with more questions so she could check on the psychic personally. "What was her name? I have always wanted to visit a psychic. With my track record with men and pretty much everything else, I could use some guidance myself."

Kelly beamed as she relayed contact information for the psychic, Sofia. Luckily, she lived in nearby Washington, D.C. Just close enough for a late-night visit. "Perhaps you could ask her if she sees a future for you with Kael ..."

Greylyn's arms stopped in the middle of an exaggerated yawn and stretch. How had this turned back to Kael? She groaned. "What is it with you and Maureen pushing your friend on me? Do I look desperate or something?"

Both women yawned. Greylyn's was more for show so she could leave to pursue the psychic angle, but with Kelly's apprehension relieved, sheer exhaustion had set in. She and the baby needed sleep.

In a move unnatural to her, she reached over and hugged Kelly. One hand came up to stroke the woman's silky strawberry-blonde hair as a mother would comfort a small child. A few strands clung to her fingers as they stepped apart.

Her retreat was halted as the boys came stumbling back in. Matthew looked happily drunk, but not slobbering drunk as she had witnessed in many a prospective groom after his bachelor party. His eyes were glazed over, but at least he was still coherent.

Kael was as bright-eyed as ever but was doing a good job of pretending to be intoxicated. He was a decent actor, showcasing just the slightest slur in his speech. However, his eyes gave him away. They conveyed wicked intelligence not the least bit dimmed by alcohol.

Of course, both gentlemen were surprised to find the bride not tucked away snug in her bed.

"I'm fine, silly. Just couldn't sleep until my Prince Charming was safely back."

Seriously, these two are just too cute together. I can't take it.

She and Kael both rolled their eyes and groaned. With that, the couple headed up the stairs, giggling. Kelly called out, "Good night, you two." She lowered her head to peer at them over the railing and winked.

Greylyn did not respond, just turned away, anxious to get on the road, but Kael put his hand out to stop her.

Impatience welled up inside her. Impatience to get to the psychic and determine if the woman had anything to do with the current predicament Kelly was in. Impatience to smack Kael across his smug face for bringing evil anywhere near the beautiful couple. And impatience for her vacation being interrupted.

Her jaw clenched with an effort not to aggravate the problem by sucker punching Kael. She needed every possible moment to get to Kelly's psychic friend to determine the extent of the problem. The last thing she needed was to tangle again with this egomaniac devil. It was a waste of time...for now. Once she learned what, if any, of the psychic's dealings had inflicted the danger Kelly was in now, she would be more prepared to thwart his plans.

She flung his hand off her forearm. "I may not know what your plan is, but you will not...repeat...will not harm a hair on Kelly's head. I won't allow it."

Almond-shaped topaz eyes glistened in the dim light of the parlor. "I have no intention ..." Without waiting for his entire *I am innocent* speech, she roughly pulled him out the back door.

"Now, stay away Kael, or I will kill you." She fished out the medallion and placed it back under the door mat and added a quick incantation in

Latin to bolster its effect. The amplified protection spell would keep the dark guardian out of the house while she was away at least.

"Greylyn, don't you think we should talk?" Kael called after her.

"Oh, we'll talk soon enough." She did not even turn around but sprinted to her car parked a few yards away and was squealing out of the lot before he had a chance to object.

Chapter 13

Discovery Road

Interstate 66

Gravel flew up into the air as the '68 Camaro raced down the winding driveway. Greylyn dialed Thomas. Voicemail. Ugh! It was after midnight, but she needed him now more than ever. She hit the redial button, cursing the phone until he finally picked up.

"What is it now, Grey?" His voice was groggy. She shared the news about Kelly and the psychic's blessings over the unborn baby. That seemed to break through his fog of sleep. In seconds, she heard the clicking of his fingers on his computer as he searched for something.

"Okay, now things are starting to make some sense," he declared.

"Huh?"

Thomas started to explain his new theory, but first she needed him to look up the psychic's address. Kelly had given her a general idea where the woman was located, but she needed an exact address...pronto. And considering she was driving and talking on the phone at the same time, it was best to not complicate matters by attempting an internet search too.

It took a few minutes, but he came back with the information she needed. Interstate 66 towards Washington, DC soared by as he related his theory.

"There isn't a lot of lore regarding humans becoming guardian angels and most of what has been published is malarkey. Unless, you are hiding an amazing set of wings, can fly, and land on someone's shoulder to whisper in their ears, then no one past or present has a clue about your kind."

Greylyn giggled. Yes, that was a common misconception. "I also don't carry a magic wand and turn pumpkins into carriages or anything like that. Although, I could probably make a lot of money if I did."

Thomas ignored her. "And there is less known about dark guardians. Until you told me about Kael, I had never heard of them either. In hindsight it makes sense there would be the good angel on one shoulder and the bad devil on the other shoulder vying for a person's attention to make the right or wrong decisions. I researched everything I could on dark guardians but found close to nothing."

"Sparky, you're rambling here. What's your point?" Her earlier impatience had only sharpened.

"The one prevailing thought is that guardians are chosen long before they are born. Now, whether or not the person becomes a guardian for good or evil depends on a lot of factors both before and after the birth." He continued, "Both sides are aware of who is chosen and seek to influence them from the beginning." He took a long, drawn out breath. "At least that's the theory."

"What does this have to do with Kelly and her child?" Greylyn swerved around a particularly slow tractor trailer, almost colliding with a large silver-maned animal that sprinted off a split second before the Camaro would have struck it. "Dammit!"

He uttered an exasperated sigh. "The child *may* be destined to be a guardian. Perhaps Hell found a way to identify potential guardians in vitro and they've zeroed in on this one?" He paused, waiting for the words to sink in. The headlights coming towards her became starbursts as the ramifications of what Thomas said swirled in her mind.

Well, that could explain Kael's interest in Kelly and possibly her unborn child. Getting in a little early to influence a potential guardian though. The kid was not even born yet. Regardless, there was no way Greylyn would allow him near the child. If she finally had to destroy Kael to protect the baby, she would.

"Well, Doctor Moorefield, how do we stop the bad guy?" How did one protect an unborn child from the devil? Even if she managed to defeat Kael, there would be more dark guardians in his wake eager to take up the challenge.

"I'd imagine..." Thomas paused as his brain ran through all the possible scenarios to land on the most logical. "To begin with, the child needs to be blessed while still in the womb. Later, baptized or otherwise dedicated in their faith while still an infant. It is tricky to get the blessing right, though, so it holds up against the hosts of Hell. This should work at least until the child reaches maturity as long as the parents teach the kid right from wrong, basic moral principles, and aren't satanic worshippers ... they aren't, are they?"

"No. Absolutely not. The poor woman feels so much guilt for visiting a psychic in the first place due to her religious upbringing. I don't think that is something we need to worry about."

Greylyn did not want to think about what could happen once the child reached the age of maturity. No amount of angelic protection could prevent an adult from making a catastrophic bad decision. As a guardian, she could only offer advice and try to sway humans to choose the right path, but nothing was guaranteed. Free will and all.

Thomas cleared his throat. "If this psychic is legit and truly blessed the child, that's a good start. But if the blessing was not really a blessing but an evil incantation, then it is going to be much harder to protect the child. Think *Rosemary's Baby*." A shiver ran through Greylyn's body. That would indeed be bad, unbelievably bad.

"Worse yet, the psychic could have intended good blessings and protection for the child, but if she didn't know what she was doing, it could have the opposite effect or unintended consequences."

That was exactly what Greylyn feared. It was the very reason her stomach was knotted so painfully and the nerve under her left eye throbbed.

In a worried tone, he continued, "Not just simple protection spells either. Specific ones: otherwise, the whole effort would be wasted."

If Hell were already interested in Kelly or her child, even the smallest weakness could be exploited for their gain. They needed a little amped-up angelic protection.

"What if it's not the baby at all, but Kelly they are after?" Despite all the horrors Kael had committed over the centuries, Greylyn found it difficult to believe he would target a child.

"Well, that's a bit different. Obviously, the blessings cover Kelly as well, but she's an adult. From what you've told me, she may not be squeaky clean. That would not explain Kael's interest right now though, unless ..."

That pause scared her because she knew what it meant. "... unless she's about to die."

Well, I will have to make sure that does not happen.

Hanging up the phone, she glanced down at the speedometer. 110 miles per hour! It was a good thing she had already placed a glamour on the car as she raced undetected by police scanners.

The miles passed quickly as the city lights came into view. At this time of night, even the nation's capital seemed like a ghost town. As her Camaro passed over the Roosevelt Bridge, on the right was the famous Kennedy Center, submerged in darkness. There were still a few bars and restaurants open, but otherwise, the streets were deserted.

Pale moonlight cast an eerie glow over familiar monuments. A few blocks up, she made a sharp turn onto 14th Street and ran more than a few red lights. Again, she was grateful for the cloaking glamour as the speed and red-light cameras were placed at every intersection of the city. Thankfully, her car would not show up on their video footage. Speeding along, she guided the car towards U Street.

A few blocks away from her intended destination she parked at the side of the street, sandwiched between a dilapidated flower delivery truck and a rusted-out coupe with the driver's side window shattered. It was the closest she dared in case there were any surprises waiting for her. She would walk the rest of the way. The streets were vacant, at least of humans. The only sound was a vehicle's theft alarm in the distance.

Nearing the address, she took to the shadows to veil her approach. She regretted not changing into darker clothes for camouflage. Her pale pink tank top seemed to glow in the inky black night.

In her experience, the homes of psychics – or mediums, or whatever they liked to be called – were surrounded by spirits vying for attention. Those that truly had *the gift* gave off an inviting glow in the spirit world that attracted beings from hundreds of miles away. These always included evil spirits. She needed to avoid those at all costs. If the psychic was a fraud, the coast should be completely clear.

Her game plan was simple: get in and back out quickly. As she rounded the corner, she saw the building and, as expected, shadows and spirits on all sides. To most, the scene would appear to be nothing more than an old red brick building in the heart of a rundown neighborhood. Stray newspapers blew across the street on a brisk breeze. A streetlamp buzzed with electricity. But something was missing...no sounds of organic life, not even the chirping of crickets or a lone dog barking to warn of her approach.

What Greylyn saw stopped her heart mid-beat. A nearly black, ominous grouping of clouds blocked her path. Grotesque forms were silhouetted in the dense fog. Such a crowd of evil entities was disturbing. Some she could chalk up to the normal spirits attracted to the energy the psychic emitted. But there was no denying that there were a lot of sinister spirits intermingled with the rest, along with demons in more corporeal forms. Getting past that mass was not only dangerous, but close to suicide.

Guess this makes it official ... the woman is a true psychic.

She drew her dagger out from behind her back, letting its reassuring coolness and energy spread from her palm throughout the rest of her body. Greylyn took a deep breath, burying deep down any fear or trepidation.

There was no sound of her feet as they hit the broken pavement at a sprint. No more than a hundred yards from the building, she penetrated the black mist. Like a swarm, they descended on her.

She sliced her way past a dozen or more entities. There were a few iridescent puffs of mist that were simply spirits that got caught in the crossfire. For that, Greylyn was regretful. Most spirits were well-meaning, or just looking for answers to their own afterlife. But tonight, they were collateral damage in her fight through the more malevolent creatures standing between her and the human medium in that building.

Interspersed in the fog of spirits were a variety of monsters, some she had never encountered before tonight. She whirled amongst the throng of evil forces standing between her and the building entrance, slashing with her dagger. More creatures filled the void, collapsing in on her. A banshee flashed before her with its fairy's face contorted as it wailed for impending death. Well, this banshee was not going to be around long enough to claim another life. The jagged edges of Greylyn's blade slit the hag's crinkled neck before she turned to fight off a horde of Jinn who continuously changed form. Some stayed invisible until just before they struck out at her. Others, both corporeal and not, Greylyn used her intuition to track, stabbing and cutting as she raced for the building.

The splintered wooden door was just within her reach when a large Vilkacis, a nasty werewolf hybrid, yanked her away by grabbing her ponytail. Intense pain flashed down her spine as a shriek escaped her lips. Her dagger slashed out, slicing its hand off. Free, she burst through the door.

Finally, inside the building, blood trickled down her face from a gash along her cheek. The demonic squad outside did not follow her in. At least the building was under full supernatural protection. She swiped at the blood with her forearm and continued up the darkened stairwell. Grimacing against the agonizing pain shooting through her side with each step, Greylyn climbed the stairs to apartment 207.

Chapter 14

Sofia the Psychic

Apartment 207

Sprinting up the unlit stairwell to the second floor, Greylyn encountered more spirits, but they posed no threat. Mostly they were lost souls desperate for attention. Her chest constricted and dusty air caught in her throat as she passed through one midway up the stairs. Apparently, the medium had done a decent job of warding off the demonic entities since none had made it inside the building. That was a comforting thought.

A red door at the end of the hallway had a faded sign, *Psychic Readings by Sofia*. Greylyn loudly rapped on the door until she heard a raspy woman's voice from within. "Hold on, hold on. I'm coming."

The woman cracked the door open, her near-black eyes narrowed in suspicion.

Guess she did not sense I was coming for a visit.

"Sorry to bother you so late, but I have an urgent need to consult with you." Despite how horrific she knew she looked with the torn clothes and dripping blood, and the fact she was banging on the woman's door in the dead of night, Greylyn still did not want to frighten her.

Shoving the door open, she entered the apartment while the elderly lady looked on in mild shock and fear. The front room was decked out in stereotypical psychic fashion. It was small and poorly lit, with red velvet wallpaper and multiple religious symbols throughout. An antique 1920s-era round glass table stood in the middle of the room with a large opaque crystal ball dominating it.

Greylyn gazed upon the elderly woman, probably in her seventies or even eighties, with long white hair pulled behind her head in a tidy bun and deep olive skin that was so thin and wrinkled it gave the appearance of crepe paper. Her eyes were deep brown, almost black, with the telltale signs of advancing eye degeneration; spotty clouds had begun to cover the iris of her right eye. More importantly, her eyes and expression reflected more surprise than terror despite the presence of a blood-covered young woman who had burst into her apartment uninvited.

Geez! I could have given the poor woman a heart attack!

Opening her mouth to apologize for the abrupt intrusion, the old woman shushed her and motioned for her to follow into the main living room. She gestured for Greylyn to take a seat on a faded, gold brocade sofa.

After a moment of contemplative silence, the psychic spoke with a voice crackled by age, but honeyed with wisdom.

"The spirits told me that I would be visited by an angel of ethereal beauty and immense strength. Regardless of everything these old eyes have seen, and ears have heard, I honestly did not believe them this time. It appears that I was mistaken."

The woman's gaze moved up and down as if assessing Greylyn from head to toe. "My name is Sofia Romani. How may I help you, dear? Are you in need of medical assistance?"

Covered in blood and other gory bits and pieces, Greylyn knew she looked frightful. Pain ricocheted through her body from several wounds over her body, but she would heal soon.

"No, thanks. I'll be fine shortly."

Sofia's aura surrounding her physical body glowed like a glittering violet orb, indicative of intuition and attunement with one's self and the spiritual world. Her eyes and warm smile reflected kindness.

Just to verify her preliminary perceptions, the guardian angel reached out a hand to clasp her hand – a traditional handshake, but for Greylyn, it was how she got to know a person's thoughts or intentions almost instantly.

Visions flashed in her mind of a young, beautiful Romani girl transforming into a highly acclaimed spirit medium. Her upbringing had been difficult as her family had been unsupportive of her gifts, demanding she hide them away. Still, she had kept her own counsel, and had braved her life mostly alone with only a handful of people worthy enough to be called family. No husband. No children. Just lost souls looking for answers and the comfort of acceptance.

There was also a vibrant hum like a child singing a happy nursery rhyme. Greylyn's lips twitched up in a playful smile. The tune was familiar, yet she could not place it. With the music came images of brilliant stars above in a cloudless sky and the warmth of raging fire against one side of her face, while the other was chilled by a brisk breeze.

Deepening the connection, she saw a carefree child who must have been Sofia years ago. But the time period did not seem to fit, unless the woman was several centuries old as well. The child smiled up at her in the vision and nodded as waves of light rushed towards her.

Greylyn jerked back from the woman, releasing her hand. Yes, this psychic appeared to be the real deal. Hopefully, that meant that the blessing she performed for Kelly and the baby were indeed good and fully functional protection spells.

With a deep breath to start, she shook off the vision and proceeded to let the whole story spill out. Sofia listened with keen interest. Her eyes widened in horror at the news that the child she hoped to protect was being stalked by evil. At the end of the story, she sat silently for a few moments, followed by a short coughing fit.

Twisting her wrinkled and weathered hands, the psychic's eyes filled with tears. "Kelly is a beautiful, sweet young woman. She was heartbroken by the loss of her first child. I did not tell her this, it would have upset her too much, but the miscarriage was no accident at all. Evil had caused it, not some dysfunction of DNA or bad timing. What she needed was closure... reassurance that things would be different this time. Knowing what happened with the first child, I insisted on having the blessings said over them both."

Greylyn's heart ached for Kelly. "Were you able to discern why?" Surprisingly, Sofia started the story years before the first pregnancy.

"It was true that Kelly couldn't get pregnant, at least according to the doctors who examined her when she was twenty years old. With what you say is happening now, it is my belief this was by some nefarious design for the news distressed her greatly. She did not handle it very well. To deal with her grief…well, let's just say she lived a rather wild life for a while."

Greylyn understood. The one thing she regretted the most about her own life was that, as a guardian angel, she would never become a mother. To have that hope ripped away must have been devastating.

Sofia continued, "All that changed when she met Matthew. He was her knight in shining armor. Saved her from going deeper down a very dark path. Miraculously, Kelly became pregnant almost immediately into the relationship. She was completely shocked!"

The woman paused for a sip of water. "I'm not sure what the catalyst was for the conception. I suspected supernatural interference but could not discover why or how. All I saw in her readings was a giant steel door guarded by a gray mist." Shaking her head, Sofia sighed. "Not to toot my own horn, but it takes a lot to hide something from me."

This story was taking longer than expected and Greylyn's impatience began to emerge again. She tapped her toes against the worn foot of the sofa. She needed to know what she was supposed to protect Kelly and the baby from. What kind of attack should she expect? Some actionable intelligence. "What happened with the first pregnancy?"

"Everything appeared to be fine with Kelly and the baby. Not a lot of morning sickness, nothing unusual. Then she visited a friend in California before taking a side trip back to Georgia to tell her parents about the unplanned pregnancy. When Kelly returned, she quickly became ill with a remarkably high fever. Dangerously high. At her next routine ultrasound, the baby's heart was no longer beating."

Sofia's eyes closed and her hands visibly trembled. "Kelly was devastated! All her hopes and dreams blew up that day."

Greylyn prompted, "But you said evil forces caused the baby's death?"

Nodding, Sofia's eyes narrowed. "Something didn't seem right to me about the miscarriage. Call it nagging intuition. I tried everything to find out more, but the only thing that was clear was that darkness surrounded the first child almost from the very beginning. I'm not sure how they got to the baby, but the truth remains that evil was responsible for the miscarriage."

Her voice was so stern that Greylyn would not have dared to contradict the woman's assertion. Besides, her own intuition agreed one hundred percent.

"Did something happen to her while she was in California or Georgia? You don't think her parents ..."

"No. No. Nothing like that. Her parents weren't thrilled, but they would never have brought down such devastation on their own daughter." Sofia's eyes crinkled. "Good instincts, though. Kelly asked the same thing. Her strict religious upbringing had her doubting her own parents' love for her. Of course, it also made her feel enormous guilt when she was blameless. A child conceived in love is never a mistake."

Still, Greylyn intended to do a thorough auric sweep of Kelly's parents before allowing them near their daughter again. Just in case.

The question remained. Why would evil forces want to harm Kelly's first child and what exactly were their intentions for the second?

Greylyn had never witnessed an instance where one woman's children were targeted like this. She had never heard of it happening either. Could it be because Kelly's child was destined to be a guardian? If so, why kill the first one? They would have had years to get to the child before it was determined if he or she would be a guardian for good or evil. But why go after both?

Unless the point was to drive the grieving woman to desperation and make her spiritually weak so evil could influence Kelly.

That theory was starting to hold more substance now. If evil could make the potential guardian turn dark, the plan certainly seemed to be working. But Greylyn was not about to let it come to fruition.

Again, the question bugged her – was Kelly the target or her child?

The old woman took Greylyn's hands in her own and looked her squarely in the eyes. The intensity that shone from them startled her, like a cosmic ray beaming straight into her soul. "Until tonight, I didn't know guardian angels actually existed even though I've been blessed with insight into the spirit world since I was a young child. Guess you are never too old to learn something new." She chuckled softly which brought on another coughing fit. "When Kelly first came to me there was a soft white glow around her, almost like an aura, but it seemed different somehow. I knew she was special but not why. There was also a tinge of gray, almost invisible but I saw it right away."

This agreed with what Greylyn herself witnessed upon meeting Kelly. But the gray tinge had grown immensely and dimmed the white light.

The woman's words came more quickly now as her thoughts outpaced her own tongue. "Kelly came to me after she found out she was pregnant again. She was so frightened at the possibility of losing another child. Unfortunately, the spirits are so in awe of this child that they will not speak about him. Not a peep!" Sofia sighed sadly before continuing, "I had multiple blessings said for the child and mother, as well as several protection spells performed. Thought it would be enough. I guess not if you are here now on their behalf."

The psychic's face crinkled in concern. Greylyn wished she could provide her some comfort. But she did not like to lie. Things were not looking good right now.

She decided to press her for assistance now that they were on the same page about protecting the young woman and her child. "Help me make things right...for Kelly and the baby. I need to see the blessings and any other spells you utilized." Sofia stood up gingerly. Hunched over a wooden cane with a labradorite crystal ball on the tip, she shuffled over to a corner table for a piece of paper and a pen. Trying not to let her impatience get the best of her, Greylyn nervously tapped her toes against the worn wooden leg.

Sofia handed her a stack of worn and partially torn lined paper. Upon a quick review of the list, she found one glaring error. The Babylonian protection spell specific to the unborn was lacking a key ingredient that made the spell inclusive of the mother carrying the child. Without that part, the mother could still be harmed, which would undo the protection of the baby.

Thankfully, the other spells had acted as a deterrent to any harm Kael or others wanted to deal out, but they were not completely foolproof. Regardless, evil was still lurking around them, waiting. It needed to be eliminated permanently.

Informing her of the error, tears brimmed in Sofia's eyes and threatened to spill down her wrinkled cheek. Greylyn reached over to pat her trembling hands to reassure her.

"It's going to be okay. There's a real easy fix – well, sort of an easy fix – and we can ensure Kelly and the child are protected fully. But we must do this now. I cannot stress enough how critical time is for them." Greylyn resisted the urge to explain that Kelly was within fifty yards of a dark guardian at this exact moment. Causing the psychic to panic could only lead to mistakes.

"Anything you need to remedy this situation as soon as possible...absolutely anything," Sofia vowed while straightening her hunched shoulders with determination.

Dialing Thomas, Greylyn conferred with him over the specifics needed for the spell she thought would provide the most coverage. She quickly jotted down the ingredients, words, and processes that were necessary to fix this particular incantation. She had used it before. Only once, but it had worked.

The old woman's eyes grew wide as she read the list. Nodding, Greylyn thought she recognized admiration.

"Looks like you know your stuff, young lady. Or at least the young man on the other end of the phone does." Her thin lips quirked up in a toothy smile. "Come this way then. I'll take you to where the magic happens," Sofia said with renewed energy. "I think you'll be surprised we have the missing secret ingredient."

The old woman shuffled faster than before, leading Greylyn to a back room where multi- colored lights peeked out from under the door. A gentle hum came from the room, almost like a distant echo. Sofia pulled out a skeleton key to unlock the door.

The room could not have been larger than a ten by ten-foot guest bedroom. Greylyn was surprised to find it jammed with people. She had not heard anyone else in the seemingly tiny apartment when she entered. Had not sensed anyone else in the apartment either. Either she was getting sloppy or Sofia had a kickass cloaking spell.

It was lit only by the ethereal glow of thousands of candles casting a rainbow of colors against the walls, ceiling, and floor. Various symbols from a plethora of religions adorned the walls. Altars were set up at the four corners, each manned by at least one human who was praying or chanting, sometimes with incense and sometimes with songs, some even in languages that had not been heard in centuries. Several symbols were posted at the door and above the blacked-out windows to protect the space against demons. She suspected that Sofia had these symbols strategically placed throughout the apartment, just not as overtly as in this room.

In the middle of the room was a large circle of women and a few men of varying ages and ethnicities holding hands and chanting in Aramaic, the ancient tongue of the Jews. From what she could discern, they were praying for strength and bravery, probably for one of Sofia's clients.

The gray-haired psychic turned to Greylyn and then motioned to all the activity in the room. "This is what I call the work," she whispered with a wry smile.

Greylyn grew impatient as they waited for "the work" to finish their incantations. To intrude in the middle of a prayer or a spell could mess up the whole thing, especially for the person it was designed to help.

Several minutes passed as she leaned against a bare spot on the paint-less wall, careful not to touch any symbols or relics. The ceiling was painted light blue as if it were the sky. She had seen ceilings like this before in antebellum homes in the Deep South. It was old folklore that ceilings should be the color of the sky so ghosts would not dwell in houses or be trapped under covered porches. This was most likely the reason Sofia's work room had the same ceiling motif. Probably the same reason there was not even one mirror in the small apartment. Spirits used them to latch onto the physical world to avoid going into the afterlife.

The eerie humming from the various chants dwindled away. Sofia took her hand and led her to the group in the center. Introductions were made and Greylyn quickly filled them in on the situation.

One woman wore a sour facial expression. The way she glowered darts at Greylyn, it did not take guardian angel senses to feel the animosity radiating off her. The middle-aged woman with graying chestnut brown hair, a too-thin face with pronounced cheekbones, and bulging eyes addressed Sofia and the group in another language, probably to conceal her criticisms of the unwelcome newcomer. Her words were sharp and spoken in such a rushed manner that it took Greylyn a moment to recognize the old Armenian dialect. Luckily, being an angel allowed her expert knowledge of most languages, including ones that had long since faded into non- existence.

"This woman is a stranger and an interloper. Clearly, she knows nothing of the esoteric arts. There is no way my spell was anything less than immaculate. I am from a long line of spiritual sensitives that goes back centuries. This little tart," she glared over at Greylyn, "knows nothing."

She threw a few more demeaning remarks towards Greylyn, so vehemently that she inadvertently spit in the face of a meek looking young lady with her ashy blonde hair tied back with a ribbon. The poor girl recoiled as if bitten by a snake.

"Isabel, you know not what you say." Sofia reprimanded the woman. "You must not underestimate the powers of our young guest."

Greylyn was grateful that Sofia did not enlighten the group that she was a guardian angel. It was apparent that if Isabel were indeed spiritually gifted as she claimed, she would have readily discerned the truth. She had been told more than once by persons with special abilities that there was an incandescent aura surrounding her that signified her status as more than a human, more than a light worker.

Even if Isabel did not understand that the woman before her was an angel, she should have been able to *see* that there was something different, something special about her. Her lack of sight was a strong indication as to why the spell had not worked.

This lady has no clue what she's doing. She is a fraud.

The group looked on in respectful silence. A few averted their gaze from Greylyn, almost as if they were fearful of her or unable to comprehend what they were seeing. When she addressed them in the extinct Armenian dialect that Isabel just used, several turned to look directly at her with interest.

"I do not wish to insult the work of the group, but in this particular case, it was faulty. The mother and child are still in peril. Only by rectifying the spell can we help them."

Isabel glared at each member of the group in turn before facing Sofia who gave her an ultimatum. "You can either help or you can leave. Now."

The candles flickered as Isabel stormed out of the room. Moments later, the front door slammed shut loudly and with such force that the entire apartment rattled.

Oh well, guess we will just have to go on without that one. What a shame!

The woman's sudden departure left the group looking startled and confused, but a few snickered. Greylyn was glad to see her go, but a nagging feeling crept into her gut.

If Isabel was responsible for the faulty spell, was it simply an accident, an oversight? Or was it on purpose?

Honestly, it did not matter now. What was done was done. All she could do was to fix the problem. Putting the woman out of her mind, Greylyn hurriedly instructed the rest of the group in what they needed to do. Sunrise was mere hours away. They needed to work fast.

The group quickly assented to the revised plan. Within half an hour the room was prepared to facilitate the incantation. Greylyn had been sure to snag a couple stray hairs off Kelly's pajama top when she hugged her at the inn. Having a physical attribute of the person intended to benefit from the spell only amplified its chances of success. She was proud of herself for having such foresight.

This time, the spell would not just cover the pregnancy, but would continue over the course of the mother, the child's, and any future siblings' lives. That had not been part of the initial spell, but Thomas had suggested it during their phone call earlier. Greylyn knew the necessary steps and ingredients to add that on.

If everything worked according to plan, all of Kelly and Matthew's children would be the most blessed and protected children in the world. Not in a showy way, like the next Einstein or Joe Montana or Babe Ruth. But blessed in gifts of love, family, intelligence, strength, and spiritual clarity...and of course, protection from the evils of this world. That was the main focus after all.

Everyone in the workroom joined in the circle to pray for the safety and fortification of Kelly and her child. Sofia entered the center of the circle where she lit a couple sage leaves and dripped holy water over the obsidian sphere placed on the new makeshift altar. In front of the sphere were two white ceramic figurines – a mother and child in a cradle, most likely replicas of Mary and Baby Jesus from someone's nativity set.

As the group joined hands, they began their prayers in earnest. Within moments, the hum was back as each person said his or her part. Sofia took a small, serrated kitchen knife and cut a cross-shaped incision diagonally on the inside of her right wrist while a young man with long blond hair pulled into a ponytail carved the Star of David into his left wrist. With their other hands, they both squeezed their arms to propel the blood to fall onto the figurines: Sofia's blood onto the Virgin Mary and the young man's blood onto the child statue.

Greylyn hoped he was still a virgin because it was male virgin blood that had been missing from the earlier spell, as well as some vital words of blessing over both mother and child. The blood of a male virgin was such a rare commodity, it was not surprising that Isabel skipped that part. But Sofia had insisted she had all the ingredients, so she was just going to have to trust her on that. For a moment, sadness gripped Greylyn's heart. If Sofia was providing the female blood for the spell, that meant she was also … the truth was too sad to dwell on.

The chanting continued for the better part of the next hour. Voices raised and lowered in praise as they beseeched assistance from Above and Beyond.

Finally, Greylyn stepped forward to the altar to offer up her own prayers for the health, happiness, and safety for the body, mind, and spirit of Kelly's child and any future children she may have. She stared at the obsidian sphere as she recited the ancient Aramaic words.

"…and the evil spells and the one who sends…" Greylyn continued, "…the evils from those afflicted and the people of that house…," and "…a day and from now unto forever."

Candle flames reflected in the sphere, dancing like swirling ballerinas. The sage smoke wafted around the group until she could no longer see the others in the room. Her vision blurred. The sphere became the one point of focus. Everything else disappeared from her view until an unnaturally bright cerulean glow rose from the black stone. If anyone else in the circle noticed, they showed no outward surprise.

As she finished, the candles flickered wildly as if a window had been opened with a giant gust of hurricane-force wind. The others were clearly amazed, but Greylyn knew it was a small indication that the spell had been successful. All the candles, except the one burning behind the obsidian sphere, were extinguished. The flame from the lone candle flickered higher, changing colors as it grew and then receded to its natural color, shape, and size. A calming peace settled over everyone in the room.

Greylyn turned to Sofia with a smile of satisfaction.

Chapter 15

Sunrise

T he antique Grandfather clock in the foyer chimed five times. Greylyn hastily took her leave of the psychic and her circle, promising to contact Sofia soon.

Before she left, they performed a quick incantation to remove the dangerous entities hovering outside the building. It was unfortunate the spell had not been invoked earlier. "I felt the evil surrounding us for the last few days and could see the dense fog of spirits. We have never experienced anything quite like it so we put extra protections on the building, and I would not allow anyone to leave. But I must admit I was curious why they were all congregating here so I didn't obliterate them. Guessing you're the cause." She winked at Greylyn before pulling her into a grandmotherly embrace.

Intelligent black eyes squinted up at her, unsettling Greylyn's temporary feeling of ease. "Something else is wrong, isn't there?"

Sofia smiled weakly and patted the top of her hands. "I don't know quite what to make of it, but the spirits are in a turmoil, but not over Kelly. Seems they desperately want to tell you something, warn you, but they cannot. The lamentations swirling in my head are chaotic, and don't make any sense to me." Her body trembled so much that a couple of her friends took her arms, urging her to sit. She refused.

Greylyn's heart seized. Sofia was indeed a legitimate medium. Anything she said could be taken as truth. This news did not bode well, but she was accustomed to always being in danger. "Anything specific you can tell me?"

Sofia shook her head sadly. "I will have blessings and protection spells cast for you. God speed, lovely one." Greylyn turned to walk away but was stopped again when the woman's eyes lit up as if in a trance. Her normal dark eyes shone stark white.

"There's a dark entity circling you. You believe him to be a threat, but he is not. At least not now. He is not what you need fear for a greater evil holds you both in his grasp." Suddenly, Sofia collapsed, but Greylyn caught her frail body before she hit the floor. A couple other women from the group ran over to tend to their matriarch by laying her on the ragged couch.

After making sure she was okay, Greylyn left her in the care of her friends. She trusted Sofia was in good hands. The woman's entire life had been devoid of a loving, supportive family, but she felt a strong bond between them already. Like the grandmother she had never had, or at least, did not remember having.

The front door of the building was splintered, but still mostly intact. Perhaps she had used too much force on it when trying to escape the mix-matched demonic army earlier. Pushing it open, it thudded against something soft, but solid. Dread rose like bile in her throat. Looking down, she saw the mangled body of Isabel, barely recognizable and covered in her own blood. There were too many wounds to count, some deep cuts, others where something had impaled her entire body. A wave of guilt slammed into Greylyn. No one deserved to die like this. Her conscience weighed heavy because she had not thought to protect the woman when she left. Her focus had been completely on Kelly and the child. Admittedly, she had also been highly annoyed at the woman for all the nasty names she had called her.

Perhaps the banshee from earlier had been sent to signal Isabel's impending death.

Greylyn knelt beside the body and whispered, "Through this holy anointing may the Lord in his love and mercy help you with the grace of the Holy Spirit. May the Lord who frees you from sin save you and raise you up."

She moved to scoop up Isabel's body, but a couple of the gentlemen from Sofia's group had followed her outside. Without a word, they motioned for her to go. Making an effort to put aside her sadness, she forced herself not to dwell on the loss. There would always be casualties in the war between good and evil. And quite frankly, she was not sure which side of the equation Isabel had been on. Sadly, she could not protect them all.

But I knew a demon army was outside the building and I just let her go. Her death is on me.

The walk back to her car was long. By the time she slid behind the driver's seat, a sharp pain radiated from her side. It would be gone in no time, she knew. Probably before she arrived back at the inn.

Being up all night started to take its toll as she turned the Camaro back west onto Interstate 66. At this time of the morning, the vibrant nation's capital and the surrounding metropolitan area were still and quiet. Her eyelids drooped so she cranked up her radio. AC/DC on full blast would have to do the trick.

Even though the sun had already started its ascent into the sky, the thickening cloud cover gave the illusion of a dismal night. With the world bathed in a relentless violet hue, Greylyn pressed the gas pedal to the floor. The windows were down, and her hair whipped about her face as she raced over the Roosevelt Bridge. The music changed and through the antiquated stereo system blared Motley Crue's "Primal Scream." She could certainly use "Dr. Feelgood" about now.

A stinging sensation from a slash across her face irked her. It would heal soon. Strange that it had not already. However, the ripping agony in her side only increased as she drove. Adrenaline had kicked in during the fight and while casting the spell, so she had not paid much attention to the pain or the still seeping blood until now. Besides, she never had to worry about such superficial wounds before. It was odd that they had not started to heal yet. Very unusual.

She hoped she could get inside her room at the Carriage House before anyone else woke up and glimpsed her in this state, looking like something from *Night of the Living Dead*.

A large silver form streaked across four lanes of highway and disappeared down a deep gully. Jerking the wheel to one side, the Camaro skidded off the road slightly. Deer were abundant in the Shenandoah, but *that* had not been a deer.

Damn! Was that the wolf? Again?

She scanned the deserted highway. Nothing. Shrugging the incident off, Greylyn edged the car back onto the road. A little more slowly this time in case more animals were waiting for their kamikaze runs.

Moments later, she was lost in her own thoughts. Still too many questions. Still not enough answers. Well, at least Kelly and the child were thoroughly protected...for the time being.

Sofia had said that she could feel the energy and power exuding from the unborn baby, even months ago, when Kelly just found out she was pregnant. That certainly coincided with what Greylyn felt when she first met the young woman. Wouldn't that indicate something more powerful going on with this little one? The psychic also said that she felt or saw a similar, but not as powerful, aura from Kelly herself. Something had made her first child a target for evil. Perhaps the point was to drive Kelly to forsake good for evil by taking away the one thing she so desperately wanted – children.

But then why would the unborn baby have such a strong aura himself? Would all of Kelly's children be as strong as this one? Was there something in her bloodline that led to this situation?

Greylyn had heard of ancient bloodlines of prophets or saints carrying into modern times. Persons from those bloodlines were blessed above others with special gifts, all for the betterment of man and the glory of God. Perhaps this was the case. If so, Kelly was oblivious to it.

The dawn sky edged on full morning. Greylyn called Thomas to report on the evening's events and ask him to continue researching. Of course, he was sleeping so she left a message.

Her brain was too muddled to figure out this mystery right now. The past twenty-four hours played out in jumbled video clips in her mind. She was so distracted by her thoughts that she nearly missed her exit off the main highway. Swerving over to the right to make the turn, the tires skidded. The return trip had been made in record time. She did not even remember the drive. Only a couple more minutes to Gaelic Haven.

Please let everyone still be asleep when I get there.

All she wanted was to get a steaming shower and curl up in the comfy, queen-size bed. It would be a long day tomorrow, but Greylyn still had to make sure Kael, or any other evil creature, did no harm. She wanted confirmation that Kelly and her child were indeed safe now after the revived protection spell.

Just as a small ray of early morning sun peeked between the slate-gray clouds, the shadowy outline of Gaelic Haven came into view. There were no lights on in either building. Breathing a sigh of relief, she tiptoed from the car to the Carriage House and opened the foyer door without so much as a creak.

"Didn't realize you were such a partier, Greylyn. If I had known you wanted to party all night, I could've joined you."

She froze in place. Despite the sarcasm, there was an underlying tension behind his words, more clipped than usual. Greylyn did not know what to make of it and was too tired to care. Ignoring him, she reached for the door to her room.

The shadow at the top of the stairs pounced like a preying tiger to stand between her and the door. The little light that was available in the foyer from a small tabletop lantern reflected the gold in his eyes. No matter how she tried, there was no looking away.

How could she be this exhausted and still be so affected by his closeness?

Without warning, his hand came up to her face. She flinched. Instead of striking as she expected, his hand caressed the place just below her eye where she had been sliced earlier. His fingers softly moved over the now dried and crusted blood. Her skin warmed, as if she had stepped too close to a bonfire.

His eyes strayed back to her own. The pupils enlarged, registering alarm and something else she could not place. In a strained, gruff voice, he whispered through clenched teeth, "Who or what did this to you?"

It was difficult to think, much less speak, with Kael this close to her. His hand, still cupping her face, paralyzed her. Silently, in her head, she repeated, "This is the enemy. This is the enemy," in an effort to free herself from his hypnotic gaze. It did not work.

The best she could manage was to say, "What's the big deal? Worried that someone else might kill me before you've had your chance?"

She had wanted to sound sarcastic. Instead, her words came out more like a breathy whisper that ended with a pitiful squeak.

He leaned in closer, a mere inch or two from her face, his eyes locked on her own. "I don't want to kill you, Greylyn. I would never allow anyone else to hurt you either. Haven't you figured that out by now?"

The raw emotion in his voice brooked no argument. She could not comprehend how a dark guardian could even utter those words with a straight face. They were mortal enemies, but something deep inside her wanted to believe him. Needed to believe him. No, that would be too dangerous.

Mustering all her inner strength, she broke their eye contact. "Kael, it's been a long night..." she started to sidestep around him to open the door. He could not get into her room due to the warding spells she had placed upon her arrival at the inn. Inside, she would be safe from him. Safe from what exactly, she did not have a clue. Safe from harm or safe from the longing desire she felt whenever he was near. At the moment, they were way too close. If she did not distance herself from him, Greylyn feared she would lose her resolve.

She reached for the doorknob and turned away from him.

He hissed, "What is that?" He grabbed her upper arm to keep her from escaping.

Following his stare, Greylyn looked down to see a large, crimson red stain along the side of her shirt.

Oh yeah, that...

She remembered the piercing pain as something stabbed her while she made a mad dash to Sofia's apartment building. It had returned with a vengeance as she drove back along the interstate, but Kael's presence had made her forget the pain, the exhaustion, everything.

A strong hand pinned her firmly against the wall while the other yanked her shirt up. Cursing under his breath, he took her arm to lead her upstairs.

She wrenched free of his grip and rushed to get past him to her room.

"Greylyn, you are seriously injured. Better let me check it out and bandage you up. Do you want to bleed out here in the foyer for Maureen to find you before breakfast?"

Attempting to laugh off his concern caused the pain in her side to flare and she doubled over. "In case you have forgotten, I heal rather quickly without medical attention. Thanks, Doctor, but I'll be fine."

Still, it was curious that the wound was still bleeding so profusely. And the pain!

Eyes that shimmered like two tiger's eye gems fixated on her face, questioned if she really believed that statement. His voice was laden with tension, and something else – concern. "Apparently, you don't heal as quickly as you think you do. Otherwise, you wouldn't be covered in so much blood. It's not even dried blood. It's still flowing freely. Don't you find that odd? Think maybe you should have it checked out?"

"So what? You think I should go to the emergency room?"

His eyes narrowed and he ignored her statement. "Now, we both know your room is warded so I can't help you in there. You will have to come to my suite. Don't even think of arguing with me on this."

Instead of waiting for a reply, he scooped her in his arms to carry her up the stairs. Shocked, she found she could not even scream.

He pushed against the door to his suite with his foot, walked into the room, and deposited her unceremoniously onto the queen-sized bed.

"Ouch! Do you mind? That hurt!"

Without a word he went to the bathroom and brought back several towels. He grabbed an open bottle of bourbon from a small nightstand on the far side of the bed. Any other time, she would have bolted out of the door as soon as he stepped away, or grabbed the lamp on the nightstand to bash his head in.

Handing her the bottle, he knelt beside her. Gingerly this time, he lifted her shirt to investigate the source of the bleeding. A shockwave of warmth radiated along her skin everywhere his fingers touched, followed by renewed pain.

She was dumbfounded. Why would he want to help her at all? This was just too bizarre. The loss of blood and the closeness of his body had her paralyzed by shock. All she could do was stare.

It was nice to be taken care of, she thought guiltily. She remembered Isabel's body, broken and bloody on the street. She had died alone, in pain and terror. Greylyn was being ministered to by a dark guardian. The world made no sense. But she could do nothing but hope and pray Kael really did mean to help her; otherwise, she was lost. All he had to do was extract her own weapon from its holster at the base of her spine and drive it into her heart. There was nothing she could do to stop him.

"What's gotten into you? Turning into a regular Nurse Nightingale, aren't you? Or are you more the Doctor Kevorkian type?"

He ignored the comment. After a few moments, Kael ripped her shirt from its hem upward to move the material away from the open cut. Sitting there, with most of her top gone, she suddenly became shy. She crossed her arms over her chest to cover herself.

"Stop being such a prude, I'm not going to ravish you," he muttered irritably. Strangely enough, Greylyn realized she was disappointed that he did not have other ideas.

"Maybe you should take a swig or two of the bourbon. I need to probe the wound. Seems like there's something still in there that is not allowing it to heal. This could hurt...a lot," he said, almost tenderly.

She looked up, surprised to see worry written on his beautiful face. His usual happy-go- lucky and sarcastic demeanor had vanished. Too fatigued to fight, she acquiesced. The dark amber liquid burned down her throat and lit a fire in her belly immediately, but it did little to reduce the pain when Kael started feeling around in the cut. Greylyn had been injured many times before. Injuries that would have killed anyone else. She had even had bullets dug out of her body, but this onslaught of pain pulsated outward like an explosion.

In desperation, she fought not to scream, knowing the ruckus it would cause if someone in the main house heard her. He stopped long enough for her to swig more of the bourbon. He then rolled a small hand towel and gave it to her to bite on. It was better than nothing. Would not stop the pain but at least her screams would be muffled. Before returning to poke around the inside of her waist and lower back, he gave her a look of sympathy.

He stroked her cheek softly and whispered, "It's going to be okay."

Subconsciously, her fingers reached up to grasp an old iron ring hanging from a platinum chain around her neck while her other held tightly onto the towel. She had found it in a pocket of the dress she was wearing when she had been resurrected. It was the only remnant of her past life, one that she did not remember, but it always gave her a sense of comfort when she needed it. Greylyn clutched the ring like it was her last chance of survival.

Kael's gaze lifted from her injured side and locked onto the tiny trinket. She saw something flash behind his eyes, something...but another shock of excruciating pain from her side blurred her vision, erasing all other conscious thought.

"Definitely not the diamonds and pearls type of girl, are you?" One corner of his mouth curled up with amusement.

Incapable of speaking, Greylyn rolled her eyes as if to say, "Not now."

As he continued to poke and prod her side, the severity of the situation hit her. Normally, she could go nine rounds with Mike Tyson and look like a model off the cover of *Cosmo* in less than an hour. Something was not right here. Quite frankly, it frightened her. What if she was not as immortal as she thought?

Another burst of blistering pain and the bourbon was not enough anymore. Without the strength to maintain the fight, Greylyn allowed the darkness to overwhelm her and carry her away into the comforting abyss.

Luckily, it was at that moment that Kael fished out the jagged tip of a black claw from her side. He took the bourbon from her now limp hand and poured some of the brown liquid into the gash in lieu of alcohol for sterilizing.

With a smile of satisfaction, he noticed that the wound immediately started to heal. The torn skin melded back together. An angry red puckering scar appeared, then faded almost to nothing. Within an hour or two, Greylyn should be perfectly fine without so much as a scar to mark the ordeal. In the meantime, he would allow his little patient to rest and recover.

Kael cleaned up the bloodied towels. He was even so bold as to remove her ruined shirt and redress her in one of his own button-down flannel shirts. His fingers yearned to linger on her soft skin, but even he would not take advantage of an unconscious woman.

He leaned over and planted a kiss on her forehead, his lips barely brushing her pale skin. He inhaled her sweaty scent that even now contained the slightest hint of jasmine.

She would wake up mad, of course, but at least she would wake up.

A Tenju? A Japanese demon and harbinger of war. Why would Greylyn be tussling with one of those nasty creatures? The last time he saw one of the monstrous birds who could morph into human forms when needed, it was hiding deep within the Ishigaki Island Limestone Cave. The demons preferred to remain out of sight and only came out to steal young boys from the countryside during lunar eclipses. Why would one even be in the United

States?

This was the second time since her arrival at Gaelic Haven she had been attacked and injured. He had been reassured no harm would come to her, but it had. Someone owed him answers.

Chapter 16

In the Light of Day

Carriage House

Greylyn woke from a sound, dreamless slumber. The luxurious cotton sheets and heavy comforter cocooned her in warmth and peace. Stretching out like a cat, it took a couple of moments for the fog of sleep to depart. Her eyes blinked back the sudden onslaught of sunshine filtering into the room.

She shot up in horror. Kael's room. On the bed, and ...

Where the hell are my clothes?

The old-fashioned clock hanging above the nightstand read 9 AM.

Unholy fires of hell! What happened?

Gingerly moving to swing her legs off the bed, her muscles protested slightly, and her spine cracked when she stretched. Overall, not too bad. A little sore, as if she had completed the IRONMAN triathlon in record time, but otherwise, okay.

A soft husky chuckle caught her attention. Blinking a few more times to clear her vision, a tall form came into full, vivid focus. Kael stood just inside the doorway, carrying a tray of food and a tall carafe of coffee. There was even a Killarney rose draped over a cloth napkin.

"Good morning, Sunshine!" Kael chuckled again as he lay the tray beside her on the plush comforter.

Oh! Her favorite breakfast dish—Eggs Benedict with creamy hollandaise sauce, two slices of Canadian bacon, a small bowl of cantaloupe and honeydew melon balls, and fresh English muffins. The bold, aromatic coffee from a tall steaming carafe was heaven to her groggy senses. The meal presentation was exquisite with a tall mug with the Celtic Trinity Knot, or Triquetra, embossed along the sides, and a silver canter of sweet cream.

The breakfast of champions.

Embarrassingly, her stomach betrayed her by letting out a huge growl. "Guess we better feed that tiger," he snickered.

He reached behind her to grab a couple of pillows to prop her up against the headboard. Still weak and paralyzed by a sudden onset of shyness, her elbows buckled underneath her, and she fell back to the bed. Without a word, but with a devilish grin, Kael lifted her from under her arms and gently helped her to sit up. Her eyes roved over his chest where his muscles strained against the fabric of his snug shirt. Damn, even in her weakened condition, her body betrayed her.

Kael, with a slightly comical flourish, placed an ivory linen napkin across her chest and the tray of food on her lap. He poured sweet cream into the mug followed by the robust coffee, exactly the way she fixed her own.

Why hadn't he taken advantage of her weakened state to kill her? Twice, in as many days, he had helped her instead of killing her. She was not sure what to make of this new version of dark guardian.

Her tummy spoke up again. Rather than overanalyze the situation, she dove into the feast set before her. If he had wanted to kill her, he would have done it already. Not waited to poison her over breakfast.

After taking a few bites of the eggs and draining the coffee mug, she looked up to find that he had pulled a chair over to the bed. The gold flecks in his eyes danced as his mouth curved up on one side, emphasizing his dimples.

"Okay, what's so funny?" Handing him the mug for a refill, she took another heaping bite of the delectable eggs. Sauce ran down her chin. A chuckle escaped Kael's lips.

"What's not funny about this entire situation?" he asked as he threw another napkin at her. "I just served breakfast *in bed* to a bloody guardian angel, who, by the way, wears my shirt better than I do. Always wanted to know what you looked like the morning after." There was more than a hint of humor in his voice.

The fork clanged onto the plate as his innuendo struck her. What had happened after she passed out? Greylyn glanced down. Definitely not her formerly white-now-pink tank top. Instead, a soft yellow button-down shirt covered her arms and torso, mostly unbuttoned. At least her pants were still on.

"Relax, your virtue is still intact. I may be on the darker side of the afterlife, but I would never take advantage of an unconscious woman. Particularly one with the ability to retaliate in a most vicious manner, which I'm sure you would." His wicked smile made her heart stop for a beat.

An evil guardian with a sense of chivalry? Odd.

Hoping her hair covered enough of her face to hide the encroaching blush creeping into her cheeks, Greylyn turned the conversation back to a safer topic. "Where's your breakfast? Sorry, when it comes to Maureen's Eggs Benedict, I'm not really the sharing type. But you're welcome to what's left of the fruit."

"Thank you for the offer, but I already had breakfast at the main house with Matthew and Kelly. They were asking about you. Maureen also seemed concerned, particularly because she fixed your favorite."

The way his lips curled up on one side, outlining a dimple, caused her heart to skip a beat or two again. If he kept smiling that way, in all likelihood her heart would stop completely.

Focus Grey! Control yourself.

"So, if you already ate breakfast," she inquired, "how did you explain bringing another complete meal back to your room? Everyone must think you have quite the appetite. Wait! How did you get inside the house? The medallion..."

"Oh, that little thing. Piece of cake." His lips twisted into a full, perfect smile. "Painful. Excruciatingly painful. But easy enough to move away from the entrance with a well-placed stick. Although, you may want to reposition the welcome mat when you do go over to the house later."

Well, the plan had not been foolproof anyway, but it was reassuring to hear that everyone was alive and well at breakfast. She would have to find another method of keeping him out of the house in case she had to leave again. He may have saved her life, but that did not mean she trusted him.

Kael continued as she scooped an oversized bite of cantaloupe into her mouth. "Well, I didn't exactly say that the food and coffee were for me. I do have a healthy appetite, for a great number of things." His eyebrows rose provocatively.

Heat crept up Greylyn's neck.

"I simply asked Maureen if I could have a tray to bring breakfast over to you. She was more than happy to comply. The rose, however, was my own idea."

His "appetite for a great number of things" comment riled up the fluttering butterflies in her belly. She almost choked on the juicy bite of cantaloupe. He laughed as she coughed uncontrollably, explaining that when the others had questioned Greylyn's absence from breakfast, he alluded that she was probably still asleep ... in his room.

"I explained that we talked until the wee hours of the morning. Nothing more. When I awoke with your lovely ebony hair on my shoulder," he sighed dramatically, "you looked so angelic that I did not have the heart to wake you, so I moved you to the bed before going to grab breakfast."

The clatter of her fork against the delicate china echoed as she dropped it again. No sarcastic retorts came to mind despite her desperate need to fling one at him.

"You should have seen the looks on their faces. Maureen, in particular, was practically glowing at the news."

Greylyn glared at him. Hoping the fire in her belly reflected in her eyes, "How could you lead them on like that? You know Maureen already has crazy notions in her head. Encouraging it is not a good thing. I'll never hear the end of this!"

"Oh, stop acting like such a prude! It was only a cover story, an interesting one that perhaps is more convenient than the truth. At least, if she thinks we are together, she will give us some quality time alone."

Plopping the tray aside, Greylyn threw off the covers. "Well, I thank you for the yummy breakfast ... and for taking care of my wounds ..." She paused as the realization hit her hard like a punch to the stomach. Here she was having breakfast in bed with her lifetime enemy instead of them both attempting to kill each other. "Wait a second! Why? Shouldn't you be trying to kill me? None of this makes sense!"

With a finger wagging frantically, first pointing to him and then to herself, she raved, "Our kind do not play well together. If we had a job description, I am quite sure it would say to destroy the other at whatever cost. So why exactly are you going off script here?"

The tenor in her voice rose in alarm as she fired questions at him. So much for playing it cool. Instead, she was a stark-raving mad lunatic.

Steadily placing his cup on the nightstand, he stepped over to the bed. Greylyn had stood up at the onset of her diatribe with every intention of leaving, but he eased her back down.

"I know you have a lot of questions, and I promise to answer them all...eventually. Right now, though, you need to chill and let me check those wounds to make sure they are healing and that you didn't just rip that gash open again." His matter of fact, Dr. Know-It-All tone grated on her nerves.

"No, you are going to answer my questions. Now, Kael!" Sofia's last words flashed in her mind, but she pushed them back. She needed to be angry. She needed to believe Kael was the enemy, because if he was not...

"I will answer one question, and only one, and then you will let me check your wound. After that ... we'll see." He stepped back from the bed.

She ignored the second part of what he said.

"Okay, then. Why are you helping me? Isn't it your job to *not* help me? After everything we've *done* to each other over the years ... why would you do that?"

He waggled a finger at her. "Listen to directions better next time. I said one question." She hissed at him.

Kael sighed deeply. "But I'll answer them. First: As much as I would like to be seen as the hero of this piece, I cannot claim such noble intentions. I helped you simply because I can, and I see no downside to doing so. To gloat while you drowned in the koi pond isn't my style either. You are much too attractive for me to want to see you bloated and pale from inhaling rancid pond water. Yes, you would not actually die that way, but it wouldn't be a pretty picture."

She nodded for him to continue.

"Second: Having you die a rather nasty death, even for an angel, because you couldn't heal properly with a broken talon of a Tenju still inside you isn't my style either. By the way, I do expect an explanation for how you came to be in that condition in the first place. Tenjus are not known to come out and play whenever they desire, so you must have stirred up quite the hornet's nest.

Hell, they aren't even known to frequent the United States."

A what? Tenju? What the hell was that?

With a slight half-smile, he added, "However, I believe the important point to take away from all of this is that we have both had plenty of opportunities to vanquish the other over the last couple of centuries or more, but *we haven't*. It's something interesting to ponder, don't you think?" He paused for her answer but continued when she simply stared at him silently with her mouth wide open in shock. "Ultimately, I don't wish to end our relationship here and now. We have many more years to enjoy thwarting each other."

Greylyn's head swam with this information. He did not want to kill her, at least not yet.

"Besides, if I want you dead, I'll do the deed myself. No one else gets that pleasure. No one." His tone was teasing, but she suspected it was the underlying truth.

Strong, firm arms eased her back into a reclining position against the pillow-lined headboard as he pulled her shirt up. "Now, please be still so I can check this out."

Greylyn slumped back onto the bed. His fingers lightly traced from her waist halfway to her spine where the gash had been, leaving behind a blazing trail of heat. It also did not help that he was leaning in so close she felt his warm breath and smelled the aroma of dark-brewed coffee.

Goose bumps raised the tiny hairs on her arms. All sound was blocked out except the thud, thud, thud of her own heart. As her eyes closed involuntarily, Greylyn uttered a soft sigh.

As if in response, she heard his breath catch and become more ragged. Even though there was not even a scar left to mark where the Tenju had sliced her, his fingers continued their path from her waist, dipping to graze over her hip bone, and then coming to rest on her abdomen. She was helpless to stop him.

His other hand came up to caress the side of her face and pulled a stray tendril of hair to tuck behind her ear. Greylyn half-opened her eyes. Kael had lost his usual cocky half-smile and was looking at her with a smoldering intensity that left no doubt what was on his mind. It was exactly what she was feeling.

Riveted in place, all she could do was take in every perfect detail of his face – his almond-shaped eyes that lured her in, the way his eyebrows arched ever so slightly as if in expectation, the wave of auburn highlights in his hair as it fell over his forehead in a roguish way. But those lips...

She had not realized she was holding her breath until he removed his hand from her hip to cup the other side of her face. An involuntary gasp escaped her lips.

He broke their eye lock to glance at her cheek where she had sustained another gash last night. It had most likely disappeared, but that did not stop him from caressing the side of her face with his thumb. The heat was so intense from the contact that Greylyn half expected to see flames spring from her skin or a trail of burnt skin branding her as his.

She leaned her face into his palm and closed her eyes. It felt right, and so natural.

Excitement revved up every nerve in her body, but somehow it was also a comforting feeling. Yet a small voice in the back of her mind screamed for her to run, to save herself from...from what she did not know. Even in this state, she recognized the jeopardy she was in. It was just that her body did not seem to care about the danger. It only yearned for him to continue touching her. The need was too powerful to ignore.

Opening her eyes, they were so close she could count the gold flecks in his eyes, but her brain was too muddled to remember how to count. As if of its own accord, her hand came up to touch his face, stubble scrapping against the pads of her fingertips. Kael's eyes closed. A low exhale, almost a moan, pressed through his lips. The entire world had vanished. There was only Kael. There was only the desperate need to melt into him.

A shrill ringing penetrated through to interrupt the sweet torture. At first the sound was soft as if coming from another room, another place, another time. But it continued, demanding attention.

Greylyn pushed herself away just as her lips had been a hair's breadth from his.

Disappointment curdled in her stomach, something she could not explain away. There was no denying what she had just felt. There was no explanation for it. But logic won the day.

Cursing, Kael broke away to brusquely answer the call. Pacing back and forth as far as he could with the attached cord, he raked his fingers through his lustrous locks of hair. His voice was low and Greylyn's senses had not yet recovered enough for her to overhear the conversation. Suddenly, the invisible force that paralyzed her moments ago lifted. She was free.

Before her body betrayed her again, she jumped up, grabbed her things, and bolted from the room as if Hell itself was on her heels.

Chapter 17

An Unexpected Invitation

Greylyn burst through the door to her suite as if trying to escape the devil himself.

What have I done?

Collapsing against the door, her lungs ached as she gasped for breath. What she needed was an ice-cold shower. Bone-chilling, hypothermia-inducing burst of cold water. She would gladly bathe in a glacial pool if it would help tame her traitorous body.

How could she have allowed herself to be captured by her own desire for someone so... forbidden?

She stomped into the bathroom. A clatter on the tile floor jarred her attention. Glancing down, there was her cell phone. It must have fallen from the pile of her clothes she still clutched to her chest.

As much as I drop this thing, I really should invest in a protective case for it. Just peachy! Dead battery.

She turned back around to plug the phone into the outlet by the antique desk and stumbled over her own feet.

As it beeped back to life, she viewed the call log and voicemails. Five messages. Three from Thomas, one from Jasper, and one from Sofia.

She called Thomas and reassured him that things were fine. Without letting on everything that had occurred after her return last night, she did ask him to check why a Tenju would be guarding the psychic's building.

"Tenju? Jinn? A banshee? Did you happen upon the Cirque du Soleil of demonic entities or what?" Disbelief carried in his voice. "Hon, Tenju aren't even supposed to be in the continental United States, much less the nation's capital."

She laughed nervously before hanging up the phone. The creatures had been the least of her worries last night.

Listening to Jasper's voicemail soothed her frazzled nerves. That is, until he said, "I finished up early here in Indiana. Wasn't much for me to do anyway. Boring case. Thought I'd swing by there. You did say there was a wedding this weekend, right? I love crashing weddings."

Oh, no! Jasper, no! He will murder Kael.

Wait! Shouldn't that be what she wanted too?

Then again, I can just sit back and watch Jasper beat the bloody hell out of the dark guardian. That could be satisfying.

As usual, Jasper did not answer her return call, so she left him a message saying all was cool and to *please* not show up. The potential for public violence would quadruple if he and Kael faced off, and that was not something she wanted to explain to Maureen or the other guests.

The last message sent trepidation zipping down her spine. It was from Sofia. The elderly woman sounded distraught. She said that the blessings and protection spells were complete; however, after consulting her spiritual contacts, she learned there was still danger, something about a prophecy.

Well, of course! There's always more danger.

And prophecies were rarely good things either.

Sofia did not leave specifics on the voicemail, but her tone gave Greylyn a sinking feeling. She hit the "Call back" button. A trilling note came over the line as it rang and rang. Finally, the antiquated answering machine picked up. After leaving a message for Sofia to call her back as soon as possible, she ended the call. However, her stomach was queasy now. The word "prophecy" hung in the air like a hot air balloon ready to pop and plummet to the earth.

In the shower, ice cold water cascaded over her skin. So cold each droplet stung. A not- so-gentle reminder to keep her body under control from here on. Jasmine-scented body wash coaxed the remnants of dried blood from her body and eased her chaotic mind. Her fingers traced where the Tenju had sliced her. A faint line of skin lighter than the rest, but even that would fade away completely with time.

Refreshed, Greylyn emerged from the shower, her skin a pale shade of blue spattered with goosebumps.

Back to work. Not going to get the job done turning yourself into a popsicle.

Toweling off, she brusquely rubbed the plush cotton towel against her skin to revive her circulation. Then quickly brushed her teeth and donned a faded pair of jeans and a v- neck white t-shirt. Before heading out of the room, she tried calling Sofia one more time. Still no answer. Hopefully, whatever had the psychic spooked would be easy enough to combat without advance knowledge. Not likely if anyone was batting around the term "prophecy."

Kael's discarded shirt on the back of the desk chair caught her eye on the way out the door. She had ripped it off her body so quickly, a couple buttons had popped off. Well, she did not intend to give the shirt back to him anyway. She grimaced at the memory of their close encounter less than an hour ago. The warmth of his body so close to hers, the fragrance of coffee on his breath...

Well, THAT will not happen again.

Unconvinced, she marched over to the main house in search of more coffee. Before opening the door, she stooped down to readjust the mat and look for the malfunctioning medallion that was still underneath it. Apparently, it just was not an effective deterrent to Kael. Damn! She picked it up and examined it for defects. Nothing. It was still in perfect condition. Useless for keeping dark guardians at bay, at least this one. With a sigh she pocketed the coin.

Weaving her way through the throng of extra help hired for the day's event, Greylyn found Maureen in the dining room, clearing the breakfast dishes.

The smile on the woman's face when she laid eyes on Greylyn was enormous.

Looks like the cat that swallowed the canary. Glad she is enjoying my torture.

With an effort to appear light-hearted and unconcerned, she strode over to the antique mahogany sideboard where the coffee carafe was still warm. Right now, the best cure for her ills was a tall cup of that black rejuvenating liquid.

"There's more in the kitchen, along with some leftover fruit if you're still hungry," Maureen said with a quick wink. "Sit down and drink your coffee, sweetie, and tell me about your ... um ... evening ... morning. Did you enjoy yourself?"

Greylyn could not help but smile at the obvious attempt to prod her into revealing details about last night's interlude. While lounging in a side chair, she wove a tale of how much fun it was to go out to dinner with the others and to relax for a while. All very innocent and mundane details.

What the inquisitive innkeeper wanted to know had to do with only one thing – the gorgeous photographer staying in the upper story suite of the Carriage House. Kael's play that morning sealed her fate. Everyone believed them to be in the throes of budding romance. No amount of contradiction would dissuade Maureen now.

"Okay. Okay. You want to know about Kael. Fine. But I hate to disappoint you. Nothing happened."

The frown on Maureen's face was priceless. With a hand over her mouth, Greylyn suppressed a laugh.

Thankfully, she was saved from further inquiry by the entrance of the young bride in a summery white sundress and sandals. Her hair was still damp and wavy, and she only wore the most minimal of make-up. Large hazel green eyes sparkled.

A glowing bride if Greylyn had ever seen one.

Kelly wasted no time. "So, um, how are you feeling this morning? I hope you enjoyed your late breakfast." She winked at Maureen as if they shared in a conspiracy.

Greylyn stared into her coffee mug, fighting the urge to hide her face. "Fine, thanks, but I think the real question here is how is the lovely bride this morning?"

Thankfully, the ploy worked, and the Kael inquiries stopped. As the two discussed preparations, Maureen left them alone to finish cleaning up before the other guests arrived.

"Actually, I was hoping to find you," Kelly said with a touch of shyness as a faint blush crept up her neck and onto her cheeks. "We haven't known each other long. Okay, we've known each other less than a day. And I did rather unload all my deep, dark secrets on you last night. But...I have a huge favor to ask."

Wow! This was working out better than she had hoped. The bride needed a favor from her. That gave her a legitimate excuse to stay close in case something happened.

"Of course. What can I do for you?"

Kelly's aura glowed brightly. Not all the gray tinge was gone, but it had receded quite a bit. A good indication that last night's blessings worked.

"I, well Matthew and I, would love it if you would agree to attend our wedding ceremony and reception."

Jackpot! Guardian angel security detail reporting for duty.

"We realize you don't know us very well, and you may have other plans altogether, but we really enjoyed your company last night. It's strange how it feels like we're old friends already."

Kelly continued selling her on the idea. With a hopeful smile as she chewed her bottom lip. Greylyn could not resist a conspiratorial wink. "How much of this has to do with you and Maureen's designs for Kael?"

"Busted, aren't I?"

Both laughed. Regardless of the intent, Greylyn planned to take full advantage of the opportunity. If allowing everyone to believe she and Kael were becoming romantically linked gave her a chance to stick around to protect Kelly...well, even she could pretend to crush on the handsome devil.

Who's pretending, Grey?

"Of course, I would be thrilled to be a part of your big day. I just hope it's not that you feel sorry for the poor lonely lady staying here while everyone else is celebrating love and family. I hope I don't look *that* desperate."

With a giggle, Kelly assured her that was not the case.

Uh oh!

Realization slammed into her. With a hitch in her voice, Greylyn admitted a most embarrassing truth. "Actually, I may not be able to attend after all. Unless the wedding is super-casual. I only brought jeans and t-shirts to hike and laze around in all weekend."

"Well...it's not exactly Cinderella at the castle, but it's not *that* casual a ceremony." What was she going to do without a proper dress to wear? "I would offer you something of mine to wear. I way over-packed, but I don't think we're the same size."

After some contemplation, Kelly brightened at the thought that they could go shopping. At about that time, Maureen came back around the corner and Kelly asked about local stores. With her rosy cheeks practically glowing in delight, the innkeeper drew a rough map on a napkin detailing how to find the town's only clothing store that would be open on a Saturday.

"Otherwise, the closest store is about a thirty-minute drive away."

Greylyn tried persuading Kelly to stay at the inn so she could rest before the big event and greet her guests, but the stubborn bride would not hear of it.

"If I don't get out of here and away from all this craziness, my head is going to explode. Please, let me come with you. I could really use the distraction."

"Again, how can I say 'no' to that? Alright, let's go."

Chapter 18

Guests Arrive

Gaelic Haven Main House

After returning from their quick shopping trip into town, the bride went upstairs to rest before the guests started to arrive. Greylyn had to admit she had enjoyed shopping with Kelly, even though shopping was at the bottom of her favorite-things-to-do list.

They had talked about many subjects, but Kelly always brought the conversation back to one topic: Kael. How no one else saw the evil in him made her blood boil.

Not paying attention to where she was going, Greylyn collided with the man himself in the entrance to the Carriage House. His eyes twinkled, with the gold flecks seeming to flash like a fireworks display. "Shopping, I see. I was under the impression you weren't a real fashionista. Every time I see you, you are always wearing the same thing. Jeans and t-shirts. However, may I suggest that you look amazing in a man's button-down shirt, with just a few buttons undone at the top?" He casually stroked the side of her face where the gash had been before walking away towards the main house.

"Ugh!" She stormed into the Carriage House, angry at herself as her body had ignited once again at his merest touch.

This would be so much easier if I could just kill him already.

Back in her suite, Greylyn hung up the dress and checked her messages. Still nothing from Sofia, which was concerning.

Thomas left a disappointing message. "Sorry. Nothing to report on last night's demon siege. Psychics tend to attract all sorts of spirits, but that many demons and outright monsters indicate something far more troubling is up. Do you think Kael called in the demonic mod squad when he saw you leave last night?"

Greylyn did not think that was possible. Even if he did guess where she had been going, it was unlikely he could have convened such a multitude of evil entities on such short notice. It seemed more likely that the battalion had been stationed there as a pre-emptive measure. Either way, the increased presence of demons to keep anyone else away from Sofia made her nervous.

Tires crunched on the gravel driveway. Her best chance to discover if anything else was amiss that could threaten Kelly and her child would be to mingle with the guests before the wedding, or to beat it out of Kael.

Now, that is the best idea I have had all day. Why hadn't I thought of that before?

Prophecy or not, she had no intention of allowing anyone or anything to spoil Kelly's big day.

One more try to reach Sofia before heading out was unsuccessful. Still no answer. She called Thomas back to request he keep trying the number.

Finally, on the fifth ring, an obviously irritated Thomas answered. "What now, Greylie? Bit busy here, darling."

Without apology for adding to his workload, she explained the situation with Sofia and gave him the contact information. After just a bit of playful pleading, he readily agreed to pursue locating the psychic.

"I'll give my contacts in DC a buzz," he assured her.

She was not sure how he knew so many people, but he *always* knew someone, no matter where she was located. Feeling better with Thomas on the case, she sweetly begged him to call her as soon as he learned anything. "And thank you. You're the best."

"Damn well better believe that."

She paused before hanging up. "Sparky?"

"Yeah, babe? What else is bothering you?" His voice dipped tiredly.

"Sofia's message said something about a prophecy..."

The loud inhale of breath indicated Thomas knew just how dangerous that word could be.

She continued, "...and that the dark entity currently surrounding me isn't the real danger. You don't think she means Kael, do you?"

Silence greeted her question. After several seconds, she grew concerned when he did not respond. "Thomas?"

"First off," he sighed, "prophecies are not my area of expertise. I know enough to cringe when I hear there's one. I have yet to hear of a prophecy, at least in the last two thousand years, that was a good thing." He cleared his throat before continuing. "As for Kael? Are you kidding me? Of course, he's dangerous. To you. To everyone. How could you dare to imagine otherwise?"

Yeah, how could she think that was a possibility? This was Kael we were talking about. "I know. It was just ... oh, never mind. I claim temporary insanity."

With that, she quickly ended the call. More disappointment coiled in her gut. She had not realized how much she had wanted to believe it was true that Kael was not the real enemy.

Greylyn took one last glance in the standalone, full-length mirror next to the closet. In her new lavender linen sundress and strappy silver low-heel sandals, her skin practically glowed. Her raven hair shone like a swatch of fine silk, and the mascara accentuated her large emerald eyes. Combined with her flawless complexion, she looked as magical as she was, and she could not help feeling happy about that. Although vanity was not particularly an angelic virtue. A spritz of jasmine perfume, and she was ready.

She walked into the sitting room just as Matthew was demonstrating the size of a fish he almost caught on his and Kelly's recent trip to the Outer Banks. Apparently, it was *this BIG!*"

As he finished his story, Matthew noticed her entrance. With a big smile, he waved his arms to beckon her to join them. "Hey, everyone, here is someone I would like you all to meet. We just met last night, but Kelly and I both adore her already. This is Greylyn. She has kindly agreed to join us for the wedding, even though I'm sure that wasn't her intention in coming to Gaelic Haven this weekend. But we managed to rope her into it somehow." His eyes glinted mischievously. Perhaps he had the same romantic notions about her and Kael that the ladies did.

He then made the round of introductions of his family and future-in-laws. His parents, Luke and Janice, were divorced but acted amicably enough despite last night's dire predictions to the contrary. His stepmother, standing on the other side of her husband, looked highly uncomfortable. The rest of family cast nervous glances between the two ladies.

When she shook hands with everyone, Greylyn did not get that special tingling feeling whenever evil was around or someone was thinking of doing anything malicious.

All good so far.

Greylyn racked her brain to remember what Matthew had said about the rest of his family but could not recall. At the time they were discussing his siblings last night over dinner, Kael's leg had brushed up against hers. All coherent thought had flown out the window. She did not start listening again until Kelly busted her on her lack of attention. That had been embarrassing.

The round of handshakes revealed no malevolent intentions, despite a sense of unease Greylyn felt from Matthew's sister-in-law with the too-sugary sweet voice. His sister's incessant giggling triggered minor annoyance, but no concern.

An elderly silver-headed gentleman in a light gray, three-piece suit stood up to introduce himself. It was easy to surmise this was Kelly's father, a proper Southern gentleman with a most refreshing Southern accent straight out of *The Andy Griffith Show*. Father and daughter had the same honest, hazel eyes and heart-shaped face. His skin was leathery and seamed, his eyes tired. Nothing but peace and an encompassing sense of love radiated when she shook his hand. Instantly, she felt a familiar connection to him. Must be because Kelly seemed most like him.

Kelly's mother was a petite woman in her late fifties with short, mostly gray hair and a kind smile. She was decked out in the pinkest floral outfit Greylyn had ever seen. Honestly, the woman was so obviously Southern and adorable that she belonged in the middle of a Fannie Flagg novel. She even smelled like a rose garden. Again, the handshake was soft and Greylyn felt only love and a deep sense of home.

So far, so good. All guests passed guardian angel inspection.

After the round of introductions was over, she glanced over to the corner of the crowded room where Kael stood ever watchful. He had been silent the entire time, but she had felt his presence with every fiber of her being, as if his eyes could send out invisible waves through the air to touch her. The groom noticed the direction of her gaze and let out a huge laugh.

"Kael, dude! Cat got your tongue ... again? A gorgeous woman walks in the room, and you just stand there like a dunce? Dude, snap out of it or the pretty lady will get away."

At that, even Greylyn giggled, gleefully watching a flush creep up his neck to his freshly shaven, smooth cheeks.

Just then, a waiter came into the room, carrying a silver tray with champagne flutes filled with sparkling cider, while another server brought in a tray of canapés.

As the guests indulged in the refreshments and conversation, Greylyn performed reconnaissance on the staff. All checked out fine. There was the one waiter whose leering aggravated her, but nothing demonic. Just as she completed her task, the doorbell rang. Deciding to be helpful, Greylyn answered the door.

More guests. This time a small group of young ladies dressed to the nines with large gift bags. Kelly had told Greylyn about her girlfriends last night – the *Sex and the City* girls. All attractive twenty-somethings looking for love in mostly all the wrong places.

Luckily, all passed the handshake test though.

Hey, this may all work out after all.

A renewed sense of confidence filled her. Greylyn escorted the ladies to the sitting room. The buxom blonde, her skin-tight dress with ample cleavage revealed by a near-waist cut V-neckline, where nothing was left to the imagination, made a beeline for Kael. She did not even acknowledge anyone else in the room. The fact that he looked so uncomfortable brought a smile to her lips, but also a little nagging thought in the corner of her mind made it clear that she was not exactly happy with the situation either. Shaking off the negativity radiating from her mind towards the innocent woman, Greylyn decided to leave Kael to her.

Instead, she left the scene with the excuse of checking on Kelly who was in her suite resting before the ceremony. First, she found Maureen at the back of the house ushering in the floral arrangements that had just arrived. Beautiful, large calla lily bouquets! Callas had always been a favorite flower of hers. She found it amazing that she and Kelly shared a lot of the same likes and dislikes. They both loved Callas, the Eagles (the band, not the football team), Atlanta Braves baseball, and they despised the color pink.

She climbed the stairs to the second floor and found Kelly in a separate seating area from the bedroom of her suite with her feet up on the ottoman trying to paint her toenails with several small spongy rollers dangling from her head. Kelly looked up from her toes in exasperation. Tears brimmed in the young woman's eyes and her mascara was smudged underneath her large now blue-green eyes.

"What's wrong?"

The bride had been so happy just a short while ago. She had been all smiles and laughing as they had strolled through the aisles of dresses at the boutique shop. What had caused the turnaround?

Half-laughing and half-sobbing, Kelly rolled her eyes.

"I can't reach my toenails anymore and now it looks as if my feet are bleeding frosty mauve!"

After a slight pause, both ladies burst out laughing hysterically. The tension in Greylyn's shoulders relaxed. Thank heavens, it was not anything serious.

Regaining her composure, Greylyn took the nail polish out of Kelly's hand. Sitting across from her on an antique Victorian settee, she grabbed a couple of cotton balls, soaked them in nail polish remover, and started cleaning up the pink mess. The acrid alcohol smell of the remover stung her nostrils, making her crinkle her nose. Once all traces of the polish were removed from the bride's feet, she commenced giving the poor girl a proper pedicure for her big day.

"I'm so sorry for being melodramatic about something as asinine as my toenails. You know the funny part? I'm wearing closed-toe shoes! Why am I freaking out about my toenails?"

Both howled. Tears of laughter cascaded down Greylyn's face. "It's better that your freak-out was due to nail polish instead of something more serious."

The pedicure continued as they talked about other brides and their irrational hysterics on their wedding day. She related a story about a bride she knew who went berserk when she found out that one of the groomsmen had not cut his '80s rocker style hair before showing up for the wedding. "Of course, the guy in question was actually a member of a '80s rock band."

By the time the full pedicure was finished, both were laughing uncontrollably, when the bride's mother entered the room with a stern expression.

"It's about time to fix your hair, sweetie."

Kelly's face dropped. A faint voice came through Greylyn's mind. "Oh, this will be a disaster. Why can't she just let me get myself ready? I don't want to look like a beauty pageant contestant on my wedding day."

Greylyn wished she could spare Kelly, but the best she could do was offer to bring up some refreshments for them.

"Tequila would be perfect ... alas," Kelly indicated the baby bump, "I guess ice water with a slice of lemon will have to do instead." They both grinned. By the narrowing of her eyes and the fists on her hips, Mrs. Calendar appeared on the verge of a full sermon. Kelly had said she came from a strict religious upbringing, so she should not be surprised.

Greylyn really liked this young woman. She had become attached to her assignments before, but she felt a particularly strong draw to Kelly. Her resolve was heightened to protect her.

Perhaps it was time she and Kael had a little chat to make sure he understood that as well.

Chapter 19

The Justice of the Peace

The talk would have to wait ... again. The doorbell rang as she descended the stairs. When she answered the door there stood the smallest, most colorful little old lady Greylyn had ever seen, and she had seen thousands of colorful little old ladies in her time. With a mass of snow-white hair and bright fuchsia lipstick to match her dress and shoes, the elderly woman was all smiles as she introduced herself as Edith Smith, the justice of the peace.

She looked perfectly harmless, like a character from the movie *Steel Magnolias*. However, the hot-poker sizzle shooting up Greylyn's arm from her handshake said otherwise.

Oh no! Not the little old lady!

The hunched over, but otherwise healthy-looking woman was possessed!

Mrs. Smith shuffled into the house. Her gray eyes darted around wildly, and her nose crinkled as she sniffed the air. She visibly recoiled from the stairs where Greylyn had secretly stashed another protection medallion under the carpet runner on the third step.

"I'd like to see the bride and groom as soon as possible. Got paperwork for them to sign before getting them hitched and need to go over what they should expect from the ceremony."

No way I'm letting you anywhere near Kelly.

It was doubtful that the woman usually gave off demonic shock waves, this was most likely a recent possession. That did not bode well for Mrs. Smith, as demons never left their human vessels in good shape when they finished using them.

Now, how do I perform an exorcism quietly in a house full of guests?

Guiding Mrs. Smith towards the back of the house, and away from Kelly, Greylyn contemplated between the cellar door and the back exit. She doubted the cellar was soundproof. She would have to get the old lady out to the Carriage House.

Matthew appeared in the hallway, coming from the direction of the pub. With a grin, he raised his glass to salute them. "Hello, you must be the justice of the peace." Indicating his glass again, "I've had about enough apple cider for a lifetime. This occasion calls for something a bit stronger."

Mrs. Smith introduced herself to the groom. It was rather creepy how the woman's crinkly eyes roved up and down Matthew like he was a piece of meat. He did not seem to notice.

"Why don't we go into the dining room so we can take care of business? I'll run upstairs to get Kelly."

Greylyn needed to deter him quickly. "I think you're forgetting one of the most important fundamentals of a wedding. The groom cannot see the bride in her wedding dress. We do not want an incident on our hands. You absolutely, positively, cannot see Kelly."

Laughing, he agreed. "I guess you're right, but ... we haven't done anything the traditional route yet," he joked with a playful twinkle in his eyes.

Relief flooded her body. She fought the desire to audibly sigh. An overly exuberant groom could have put Kelly and the baby in jeopardy. Thankfully, Matthew was easily distracted in his quest to get a stronger drink.

Leaving Matthew in the clutches of the possessed magistrate did not leave a warm and fuzzy feeling in Greylyn's stomach, but she was certain Matthew was not the one in the most danger. "I'll let Kelly know you're here," she assured them. Instead, she stepped back into the hallway to eavesdrop. Even with all the noise coming from the sitting room, her angelic hearing allowed her to listen in on their conversation.

"Now, all I need are your signatures on this form, so this marriage is considered legitimate by the commonwealth."

He scribbled his name everywhere she indicated without bothering to read the document. "And, you must know before we proceed that this is a very simple ceremony, complete with the usual 'do you take this man/

woman' and the 'I do' parts, but there will be no religious references."

Somehow that did not surprise Greylyn. As Mrs. Edith Smith was currently sharing her body with a demon, the evil creature could not utter any religious references without severe pain.

However, the next words from the groom caused Greylyn to cover her mouth with shock. "That's fine."

Damn it, Matthew! With Kelly's parents so religious, she had just assumed the ceremony would be as well. If for no other reason than to appease them. Well, this wedding was going down as a disaster! A wedding ceremony conducted by a demon with no religious references to the holy covenant of marriage! Not that all weddings with the religious references made for perfect marriages, but it was an added layer of protection.

What God has joined together, let no man put asunder...

In biblical times, the wording had been more inclusive of supernatural forces ... *let no man nor evil put asunder* ... but the phrases had been cut out when people stopped believing demons really existed. There was a quote from movie she remembered that pretty well summed it up. *"The greatest trick the devil ever pulled was convincing the world he didn't exist."* That was the truest statement she had ever heard.

The muffled sound of a door opening alerted Greylyn that Kelly was on her way downstairs. She had only a minute or less to avoid a catastrophe. The demonic justice of the peace could attempt to possess the bride or otherwise cause her harm. With the protection spells, she had thought everything was fine, but once Sofia mentioned a prophecy, all bets were off. The mere thought of Kelly being in the same room with a demon sent a shiver of anxiety down her spine.

Greylyn popped back into the room and did the most convenient thing she could think to do in the situation. She lied. "Kelly will be here in just a couple of minutes, so Matthew you need to make yourself scarce. Why don't you fetch Mrs. Smith a glass of cider or water?"

The possessed woman piped up, "Scotch on the rocks, please."

Matthew shrugged in surprise, excused himself and headed off to the kitchen, leaving her alone with the demon.

Thankfully, Kelly chose to go down the front staircase. With the dining room towards the back of the house, it would take her longer to get there.

Not wasting a second, Greylyn grabbed the elderly lady's arm and escorted her out the back of the building.

"Mrs. Smith, there's something I'd like to add to the ceremony as a surprise for the bride and groom, but I wanted to run it by you first. Would you mind coming with me so I can show you what I'm talking about?" All the while she forced a smile on her face, pretending all was well.

The way Mrs. Smith's arm tensed, and she faltered a step, the demon within clearly suspected something was amiss.

Exiting the main house, a cool drizzle fell from the gray sky, a light mist so subtle that a person would not even realize it until looking down at the tiny droplets forming on the skin. It was soothing and reminded Greylyn of the way the dense fog in Scotland would roll in and leave everything damp as if it had rained for hours. She had spent hours after daily training sessions with Jasper just gazing out over the lakes, allowing her skin and clothes to become soaked by the mist. That had been the last time she had felt true peace. If not for the demon at her side, perhaps she could have experienced that again here.

Greylyn tightened her grip on Mrs. Smith's arm as she pulled her over to the Carriage House. All she had to do was get the woman inside her room, which was fully protected from just about every known evil entity. The warding spells would take care of the demon, hopefully leaving Mrs. Smith intact.

The risk was that the demon would just find a new victim amongst the crowd of guests. To avoid this scenario, Greylyn determined to eradicate this one before all hell broke loose.

Flinging the door to the Carriage House open, she roughly shoved the little old lady inside. "I know *what* you are and why you are here. I'm sorry, but your services will not be needed today or any day for that matter."

The foyer was tiny, not a lot of space to maneuver. The area was sparsely furnished with an antique Grand Marquis console table and a vintage table lamp. There was barely enough room to stand between the door and the table. Greylyn needed to get Mrs. Smith inside her suite but keeping a hold on the squirming demon was proving difficult in the cramped quarters.

The ideal plan included getting Mrs. Smith inside her own room where the warding spells would dispel the demon. She could not risk the woman breaking free and escaping upstairs to Kael's room. If the two were in cahoots with each other, and they probably were, then he might have warded his room against angels after her abrupt exit this morning.

Despite being in the body of an eighty-something-year-old lady, the demon was strong and resisted as it flailed around to jerk free. Light gray eyes filled with the deep maroon color of blood.

Unable to let go of the woman to open the door, Greylyn executed Plan B. Wrenching the woman's arm behind her back, Greylyn began muttering an exorcism in Latin.

Exorcizamus te,
omnis Immndus spiritus,
omnis Satanica potestas,
omnis Incursio infernalis Adversarii omnis legio,
Omnis congregatio et secta diabolica

Greylyn repeated the words several times. All the while, the old lady seethed and spat obscenities at her. Her arm screamed in pain as the demon woman's grip burned claw-like marks into her forearm. The old lady thrashed about as the exorcism started to take effect, but not quickly enough. Something more was needed to speed up the process before someone came looking for them and discovered the ruckus.

Grabbing the vase off the foyer table, Greylyn yanked the flowers out. The demon took the opportunity of being held by only one hand to strike out with her long sharp nails. Pain erupted across her neck and chest as the woman's nails sliced superficial wounds. Involuntarily, her arm flew out of its own accord and smashed into Mrs. Smith's overly made-up face.

Her fingers fumbled in her dress pocket for the platinum cross she always carried and dropped it into the vase. Already blessed, the crucifix transformed the regular water into holy water instantly.

One final verse in Latin.

Ergo, draco maiedicte,
Ecciesiam, tuam securi tibi
Facias iibertate servire,
Te rogamus.
Audi Nos!

Trapping the woman's arm behind her, Greylyn held her still with one arm wrapped around her chest. Prying her mouth open, she poured the holy water down her throat. The demon gagged and tried to spit the water out. But she clamped the woman's jaws together before slamming her against the wall to force the being to swallow.

The justice of the peace's body convulsed violently. Unable to scream, sizzling sounds erupted as the holy water burned out the evil entity. The red in her eyes faded away until her eyes rolled back in her head completely. Finally, Mrs. Smith crumpled to the floor.

Please do not be dead!

Greylyn knelt to check the woman's pulse. A very faint thumping. At least the experience had not killed her outright. Mrs. Smith must have been made of sturdy stuff to withstand such supernatural violence at her age.

Struggling with remorse that Mrs. Smith suffered bodily injuries, Greylyn forced the guilt back down. Once the demon possessed the woman's body, she had had no other option but to perform the dangerous exorcism.

The foyer was a mess. The justice of the peace was barely hanging on to dear life. And Greylyn was covered in cuts and burns.

Now, how am I going to explain this?

Pulling out her cell phone from her dress pocket, she dialed 911 and tried to straighten the place up and remove any signs that would indicate a struggle.

She could explain away most things. The bruises suffered by the woman could be due to her fall, which could have been caused by a seizure. The marks on her arms and neck could be the result of the woman flailing about before she ultimately collapsed.

With assistance now on its way, she would have to inform the others in the house of what had transpired.

She unleashed her best 'slasher-movie-actress' scream for help.

Chapter 20

The Show Must Go On

Kael had been the first one to the scene, followed by everyone else wearing confused looks. Now that poor Mrs. Smith had been whisked away by the ambulance, the dour expressions of every member of the wedding party matched the overcast sky.

Maureen assured the group that her long-time friend, Mrs. Smith, would not want her unfortunate condition to destroy the couple's happy day.

Sure, the human Mrs. Edith Smith would not want that.

Greylyn worried that the lady would not fully recover from this fiasco and whether she would have any memory of what transpired. The doctors would certainly commit her to the psychiatric ward if she told them the truth.

One of the late arrivals, the groom's friend, Tony, who certainly did not win any awards for couth, had to be the one to state the obvious …

"Unless someone's an ordained minister or a magistrate, this wedding won't happen."

Maureen offered to make a few calls to local clergy to see if anyone was available. With it being a Saturday, the odds were slim. However, Greylyn had an answer, but she did not know how well it would go over.

"Kelly and Matthew, can I speak with you both privately?"

They readily agreed and followed her to the kitchen. Luckily, the bride was still in her pre-wedding attire, so the groom had not seen her wedding gown. However, worry clouded the young woman's facial expression and a glimmer of blue speckles shone in her hazel eyes. Even Matthew's usual carefree smile had faded.

After sitting down at a small kitchen table, Greylyn explained her proposition. "It's a long story, but the gist of it is that a friend requested that I conduct his wedding ceremony a few years ago to a lovely woman he met in Guatemala while working for Doctors without Borders."

She did not mention that she had saved him from drug addiction or that he had had an unbelievably bad experience with the minister of the church he had grown up in. All Luke had needed was some divine healing and a good therapist.

"So, technically...I'm ordained to perform weddings."

The bride's eyes lit up like fireworks. Kelly jumped up and embraced Greylyn in a warm hug. "God must have sent you here this weekend! You are truly a miracle!"

She does not realize just how close to the truth she is.

Matthew called Maureen into the kitchen to share the good news. Greylyn hurried back to the Carriage House to call Thomas in private. She hoped he could find her ordained minister certificate from Old Dominion University.

Thomas was slightly taken aback. "I'm not your personal secretary, toots! If you recall, I am a bit backlogged with all your other requests. Something about protecting a bride and unborn baby ... checking on recent trends in demon army recruitment ... Tenju ... Kael's political aspirations ... oh, and a prophecy. Not to mention I have seventy-five research papers to read before Monday morning's class."

Greylyn realized she probably was asking him for way too much. She usually did. Perhaps she should not have come to depend on him as much as she had. Utilizing her best, most flirtatious voice, she begged him to be quick about it and to call her back ASAP before blowing a loud kiss over the phone. Inwardly, she swore to make it up to him soon and to show him more appreciation.

At the completion of the call, there was a stiff knock on the door of her suite. Opening the door, she found a handsome devil with an intense look of curiosity. Her heart skipped a beat.

Damn him! I have enough to deal with right now.

In his stylish slate-gray designer suit, cream-colored button-down shirt with French cuffs and dazzling pearl cuff links and a plum-colored tie, Kael reminded her of a young Laurence Olivier with his rakish smile. Even standing a few feet apart from him, her knees went weak and her breath caught in her throat.

"I would invite you in, Kael, but we both know that's not possible."

"Perhaps you would do me the honor of joining me on the covered porch outside your room then. Unless your warding spells extended to the outdoors as well."

He was right, of course. The porch was open territory. Without responding, she shut the door in his face and strode over to the French doors. Kael was already sitting in the cushioned loveseat, patting the place next to him. Reluctantly, she acquiesced.

Trying to appear nonchalant, Greylyn asked, "So how may I help you, sir?" All the while she fought the way her traitorous body nearly hummed in response to his closeness. Maybe there was an inoculation she could get when this was over to counter the hold he seemed to have on her. Surely, someone in the pharmaceutical world had an interest in supernatural medicine and could cure this.

Leaning in close, his breath warmed her face. However, it was not the temperature that caused heat to creep up her neck to flush over her cheeks. "Just curious as to what happened earlier and if you're okay. Seems to me you have had a very *eventful* vacation."

"Funny, I thought if anyone knew what has been happening lately, it would be you. Don't tell me that you weren't apprised of the Hail Mary plan to get at Kelly and her baby." Although she whispered the words to avoid being overheard by anyone in or around the house, it contained all the force of a scream.

His eyes narrowed and creases formed over his usually smooth forehead. "I knew nothing about Mrs. Smith. She certainly was not working for me. Don't you think a simple demon possession would be beneath my talents anyway?" A perfectly full eyebrow shot up quizzically. "Why don't you explain what happened to cause the old lady to collapse earlier?"

Greylyn quickly explained her demon radar going off and how Mrs. Smith developed the ability to change her eye color to blood red.

"I tried to make sure she didn't suffer any injuries, but you know how exorcisms go."

Kael sat back against the cushioned love seat. For several awkward minutes, silence ensued while a vein throbbed across the bridge of his nose. Biting his lower lip in contemplation, which riveted her attention, he began to explain.

"There's a lot going on with this particular situation that you cannot possibly be aware of."

Apparently.

"Hell, I don't even know as much as I should." Pausing, he added with emphasis, "But at no time have I attempted to hurt Kelly or her child, nor would I."

Stunned, Greylyn nearly swung her arm to slap him for telling such lies. "What? Do you think I was reborn yesterday? Give me a break!" How was she to believe a dark guardian was not present to bring forth something evil?

"Please, let me finish. There are factions that have sought to kill off Kelly and Matthew's potential lineage, and they have their reasons. I don't know what they are. I don't ask. There are others high up the power chain who have ordered that they not be touched. Period. Instead, they are to be protected at any cost. They were *very* adamant about it. Again, I do not know why. I don't ask. They don't tell."

His expression, in addition to his words, sounded sincere, but demons were always good at lying. However, Greylyn was impeccably good at reading people's true thoughts and intentions by the look in their eyes. It was one of her special gifts as a guardian angel. But then, perhaps she was not at the top of her game whenever Kael was around.

His warm eyes glimmered with his signature flecks of gold giving them a look akin to topaz. They held an expression of veritable disquiet, but also honesty. If he were human, she would swear he was being one hundred percent truthful. But the fact was...he was not human.

"Run that by me again. Someone in Hell has ordered that Kelly and her child not be touched, but others are looking to destroy them?"

He nodded. "Yep, that about covers it."

"What about Kelly's first miscarriage? I have it on good authority that evil played a significant part in that. Forgive me if I do not buy into the idea that the bad guys are actually the good guys in this scenario. I've been in this line of work way too long."

She was not ready to believe Kael's story yet, although it would explain a couple of things. There was a peculiar urge in her to believe him, though. Thinking back, he had never been a part of any schemes that harmed children or babies. Okay, minus the Boy Scouts in the Everglades incident, but the target had been the scout leader who had taken the boys out into the wilderness with nefarious ideas in his head. The swamp monster had done her a huge favor by eliminating him, but she still had to get the children back to safety before it or other dangerous critters – alligators, snakes – killed them. Perhaps she could question him about that incident later since he seemed to have some insight into that fiasco.

Right now, she needed full disclosure about why Kelly and the baby were under such a deliberate and vile attack and from whom exactly. Why was Hell itself interested in protecting anyone, especially a child? Seemed contrary to the nature of demons. Greylyn's head spun with the possible ramifications. None were good.

A now familiar electric shock coursed through her veins as Kael placed his hand on top of hers. Maybe the touch was meant to be reassuring, but it was far from it. It only caused her heart to race more and her thoughts to blur. She felt his gaze on her, imploring her to look up into his face, but fear kept her head bowed.

I am not afraid of anything. What the hell, Grey?

Moments passed until he apparently decided he had been patient enough. With one hand, he cupped her chin and guided her face up until their eyes locked. Both sat unmoving. Finally, with a deep sigh and visible shake to break the connection between them, he commenced his story of how he became involved in the lives of Matthew and Kelly.

According to Kael, there were those in power in the underworld who were fascinated with a long-foretold story. "I don't like to use the word prophecy because there is little indication that it's true, but the phrase has been bantered around a lot lately. No one knows the story's origins. Something about an ancient line of half humans/half angels, otherwise known as Nephilim."

There was that word again ... prophecy.

Greylyn had heard of Nephilim before, but had never come across one –

the offspring of sons of God and human women. The Bible mentioned them briefly in Genesis, before Noah's Ark:

"The Nephilim were in the earth in those days, and also after that, when the sons of God came in unto the daughters of men, and they bore children to them; the same were the mighty men that were of old, the men of renown."

But what did that have to do with the here and now?

"I thought they had been eradicated long ago, killed off by both Heaven and Hell as abominations. With both sides against them, there's no way their kind would've survived all this time." She thought back to other religious texts outside of the Bible for mention of Nephilim. "According to Enoch, the real purpose of the flood was to kill them off."

Kael nodded his agreement. "I believed so, too. Wasn't until recently I learned that one line was preordained to survive for all time. Offspring from that particular descendant have played important roles in the continuous shifting in the balance of good versus evil from the very beginning. The Nephilim were known to be revered and holy men, but prone to temptation and falling into wickedness. But right now, I'd say evil is ahead of the game, so a survivor from this line would be ripe for Hell to mold into a force great enough to complete the conquering of mankind." His college professor's tone annoyed her.

She could not argue with that. Thomas's theory about Hell wanting to lay claim to a powerful supernatural being was looking to be the most plausible. But instead of influencing a future guardian, this one could be much more powerful if he was a Nephilim.

"Recently, it came to light that a young woman in Virginia might be the descendant of this ancient pedigree of Nephilim. More importantly, she was the last of her lineage. There are no others. With outright control of her and any offspring, Hell would continue to reign supreme."

At his words, prickles of tensions arose in her shoulders. That would definitely be a bad thing.

Greylyn countered, "But there's an equal chance that she and her children will be more inclined to be servants for good."

He nodded. "Agreed. Their mere existence would tip the scales back in favor of good. The effects could last for centuries, maybe even longer. Certainly would benefit mankind as Nephilim were considered to be superheroes in ancient times."

Leaning in closer, as if they were conspirators in some crime, Kael added, "Some contingents believe that striking them down before they could be born would eliminate the threat to Hell's dominance over the planet. Hence, the miscarriage, I suspect." That was the most probably theory yet.

"However, there are others in the ruling class that do not hold this belief. They contend that the reward for seducing the last of the Nephilim to their side is too enticing to pass up. They see it as their way to further increase their power on Earth. How any of this relates to some prophecy, I have no idea."

Greylyn sat still as a whirlwind of thoughts raced through her mind with this information. The entire situation was much more volatile than she had imagined. There was far more at stake than saving a single woman's life and soul. Sofia had been right to worry if her spirit guides were foretelling of a prophecy.

Kael paused, as if expecting her to interrupt. She nodded to encourage him to continue. "Now all this is based on conjecture and rumor. I could be completely off base on the real reason one part of Hell wants her dead, and the other part wants her alive. I happen to agree with the rationale to keep her and the child alive. It certainly could not hurt matters. So, I was sent on this mission to, for once, save someone rather than destroy them. Quite ironic, isn't it?"

All this was a bit too much for her to comprehend. Of course, he could just be saying that to get on her good side. Kael working for good? Impossible.

If Kelly was Nephilim, she was most likely unaware of it. If she did know, she did a good job of hiding it. But that would explain the inner light surrounding her, which would befit one of such a heritage.

"I've sensed a brilliant power coming from the baby in her womb. It is quite remarkable. If the story is indeed a valid prophecy, there's little doubt that Kelly and her family were the ones spoken of." After a moment's pause, he interjected, "All that power wrapped up in such a tiny package! Imagine the possibilities!"

So, Kael is convinced Kelly is Nephilim? And he is not trying to kill her?

Shaking her head as if that would make her jumbled thoughts coalesce, Greylyn asked, "So, what's your role in all this? Hell sent you as a bodyguard?"

"I guess if you put it that way...yes. I was ordered to keep watch over them until the imminent danger passed. That is why I befriended Kelly and Matthew months ago. There have been several threats during a short amount of time. Not one has gotten by me to lay a finger on her." His eyes begged her to believe him. "Based on the new light surrounding Kelly, which I imagine you had something to do with, they're both safe ... for now. I will also check in on them from time to time for the next few years until this whole situation plays itself out."

Greylyn's mind ran over all the scenarios. Once Kelly and Matthew were wed, and under Heaven's protection, courtesy of the psychic's efforts, the child and any subsequent children should be safe until adulthood when they would have to carve their own paths in life. It would be their choices as adults that determined the course of their lives, for good or for evil. Kelly was an adult already, but Greylyn was confident she would stay strong...for herself and for her children. But her offspring...had she been sent there to save them now, only to have them face down Hell later?

She needed to know more about this so-called prophecy. Perhaps this was all a bunch of hoopla for nothing. It was worth noting that those in power were convinced enough to go to such extremes. To her knowledge, this was the first time Hell wanted to protect someone.

Staring off into the distance, her mind barely acknowledged the beauty around her – the summer flowers, the flourishing green mountains in the distance. Her gut was telling her that, contrary to his nature as an evil being, Kael was telling the truth. But how could she possibly trust him? That ran against every fiber of her being ... trusting a dark guardian! She almost laughed.

Wrapped up in her thoughts, she failed to sense him moving closer until his face was a mere centimeter from her own. His palm tenderly cupped her chin as he lightly rubbed his thumb over her cheekbone to her ear then back down to linger at the edge of her mouth.

The caress sent a flood of pleasurable sensations throughout her body, like a gentle waterfall cascading over her. Incapable of moving away and no longer able to think about anything else, she found herself welcoming his touch. They were eye to eye, nose to nose. She would simply have to lean forward the slightest bit, and their lips would meet. Full, sensual lips, slightly parted, served as an invisible force that tugged her forward.

No. No. No.

Exerting the full strength of her will, she pulled back instead. Incapable of words, she shook her head.

Disappointment in his eyes cut her soul like a jagged knife. Instinct raised her hand toward his face, anything to alleviate that pain, but he sat back and closed his eyes.

Immediately the temperature chilled. Still only inches apart, Greylyn felt the vast emptiness, as if a depthless black abyss now stretched between them. Strangely, the distance caused her pain.

Her heart ached as it struggled not to burst out of her chest. His brooding expression seemed to convey the same inner torment.

To recollect herself, she started talking, much too fast. Nervous habit.

"So, you expect me to believe you are here to protect Kelly and the baby? That will be a first! In effect, we have the same purpose here. That's why you have been helping me? That makes zero sense. You've done nothing but work against me since I can remember. Not to mention the somewhat veiled threats you spouted when we met under the gazebo just two days ago."

Agitated, she stood up abruptly and started to pace the small covered porch, nearly tripping over his long, outstretched legs.

"Supposedly, the Hell Powers That Be are at odds as to how to handle a *possible* Nephilim descendant? They don't even know for sure!"

Continuing to rant, Greylyn repeated his story out loud as if by saying the words she could discern the facts from fiction. Kael stood and grabbed her hands, halting her pacing.

"As difficult as it may be to believe, I am telling you the truth." His eyes locked on her own as if the legitimacy of his words could be conveyed through them. "Actually, if you think about it, I may be the only person who has never lied to you."

What? Never lied to me? Ha!

She fidgeted to get away from him, but he held her hands so firmly her body stilled. "I am here to protect Kelly and the child from any rogue elements that were sent to kill her before she could give birth and raise her little family of possible Nephilim."

Sternly, as if making a point to a small child, he concluded by saying, "So, yes, in essence, my mission here is the same as yours, so we might as well work together."

Her head spun. Such news would shellshock anyone familiar with guardian angels and their demonic counterparts. Too dumbfounded to speak, Greylyn allowed her hands to remain entwined with Kael's. They stood there, silent, hands locked as energy flowed between them in an infinite circle. The last shred of her belief system frayed – Kael was not the villain, at least not in this scenario.

Matthew cleared his throat to gain their attention, ripping her out of her reverie. She turned towards him knowing her face was as red as a cherry tomato.

A big grin plastered itself on his face as he said, "Sorry to interrupt, but I thought you'd want to know that the email came in with Greylyn's certificate so the wedding can continue. Kelly requested a half hour to finish re-doing her hair for the fifteenth time. She's upstairs arguing with her mother about whether it should be up or down, curled or straight." He threw his hands up in the air. "I gave up trying to intervene in that battle. But as soon as my bride's hair is in place, then we are all set for the main event!"

His apparent joy showed itself as his aura radiated pink and yellow for love and happiness. It was hard not to share in his enthusiasm. It certainly was a welcome diversion from the fiery incalescence that racked her small frame, originating from where her small, slender hands were still trapped between Kael's larger, sinewy ones. Looking down, she noticed the dramatic contrast in their skin tones. Her seamless ivory versus his golden tan color, but somehow, they just looked right together.

Laughing, Greylyn extracted her hand from Kael's grasp and gave Matthew a tight salute. "Ready to report for duty, sir. Give me a second to gather up my materials and refresh my memory on the order of things. It has been a while since my last wedding, and I certainly don't want to screw this up. Please excuse me."

With that, she hurriedly walked back into her room via the patio French doors. Their dress shoes crunched on the pebbled path. Each step Kael took away eased her frazzled mind and body. Peeking out the window, Greylyn saw him turn around slightly for one last look back at the Carriage House.

The salacious devil had the audacity to wink.

Chapter 21

Wedding Crasher

Greylyn searched her worn leather-bound bible for the appropriate wedding passages, but her head jerked up at the sound of tires crunching on the long gravel driveway along with the distinct roar of a high-performance sports car. All the guests were present and accounted for. But a familiar twinge at the back of her mind let her know exactly who had arrived.

Oh no, he could ruin everything!

She raced to the window in time to see an incredibly tall, well-dressed man slam the door of a shiny black Mercedes coupe. His jet-black hair matched the car and shimmered like silk despite there being no sun to cast light on it. His all-too-familiar voice rang out crystal clear, with just the slightest French accent, as he addressed the group gathered in the gazebo.

"Good day! I'm so sorry to interrupt what looks to be quite a party, but could someone point me in the direction of a gorgeous little brunette that goes by the name of Greylyn?"

His usual husky baritone made anything he said sound sultry and alluring. In addition to Jasper Moreau's exotic good looks and dazzlingly perfect smile, he could easily undress a room of women with just his voice. It draped over you like a mink coat on a cold winter's day, like a warm caress of a Caribbean breeze. If the ice-blue eyes set in his dark, handsome face did not leave women panting, just a few words from his angelic lips worked their own black magic. She could not help but grin at the collective feminine gasp from the gazebo.

Although he had often tried to use his wiles on her, she had always insisted they keep things platonic. Not that she had not been tempted. After all, 450 years was a long time to be alone. But it just had never seemed right somehow. Besides, she knew how desperately she depended on him. Romance would only complicate things.

On any other occasion, she would have run out to him and flung her arms around him in relief. He was her best friend. The one person who knew all her secrets...well, almost all.

But this time was the exception. His presence could do more harm than good. Aside from spoiling the façade of a blooming relationship between herself and Kael, the contentious history between Jasper and Kael...well, they could never be accused of playing well together.

Jasper despised Kael even more than she did, or at least more than she thought she had before this weekend. Although not fully aware of their history before she met the dark guardian, she knew Kael was at the top of Jasper's Most Hated List. It was also clear, that the feeling was mutual. Keeping these two hotheaded men apart was imperative if there was to be any chance for a peaceful wedding. The last time Jasper and Kael were in the same location, the damage to a full- mile radius of downtown Tel Aviv had been ruled a terrorist disaster.

Praying that Kael, Matthew, and Kelly were still in the main house, her mind raced to adjust her story. She had not calculated Jasper into this scenario. How had she forgotten his voicemail about crashing the wedding? Any chance to Kael not going full dark and demonic would evaporate if those two came face to face. The best thing she could do was to get rid of him immediately.

Ha! Convince Jasper to leave? Yeah, good luck with that.

The tall, Adonis-like guardian had an incredible stubborn streak. With Kael present, it would be damn near impossible. She had not even told him about the dark guardian's presence here for a reason.

Cowboy boots crunched on the pebble pathway, indicating he was heading in the direction of the Carriage House. Jasper did not go anywhere without his boots and he did not put them on unless they were as shiny as stars in the midnight sky. They were as much a part of him as her jeans and worn-out tee-shirts were to her. The sad thing was the male guardian angel was a much snazzier dresser than she would ever be.

Before he even knocked, she threw the door open and yanked him inside – slamming the door behind them. He was a century, or more, older than herself, but Jasper appeared to be in his late twenties, early thirties. Tall and muscular, long ebony hair pulled back in a sophisticated ponytail. Smiling from ear to ear and decked out in a fashionable suit, he could have been the cover model for every romance novel ever written. In fact, he had been on the cover of one years ago. She still had a copy of the book in the Camaro's glovebox.

Jasper's exquisite eyes, the color of a glacial lake, glinted with glee at her, along with his self-satisfied smile.

"Hello, darling! How is my beautiful angel?"

Any other given day, she would have welcomed his presence, his help. But today just was not one of those days.

"Miss me, darling?"

She backed away from his embrace, biting her lower lip in contemplation of how to break the news to him that he had to go.

"What? What's wrong?" His lips had already taken on a pretty pout.

With an elaborate eye roll, she took a deep breath and tried unsuccessfully to stifle a return smile. She could no more stay irritated with Jasper than she could deny the sky was blue and the grass was green.

Quickly, she explained what was going on with the couple, the wedding, Kael, etc.

Jasper's features automatically grimaced at the mention of their nemesis. "So, you see ... I need you to leave. The sooner the better."

The ceremony was to start soon, so she did not have time for a full discussion of the matter. He had to go! Now!

Astonishment would be an understatement to describe the play of emotions on Jasper's face. As she divulged her tale, his eyes grew wide with shock and dismay. Mostly dismay, then morphed into outright anger.

Good thing I left out the juicy parts.

"I know this is difficult to believe, but I'm sort of working with Kael on this one." Those last words pained her immensely. She waited for the lightning of Jasper's fury to zap her. He stood silently for a few moments. The usual happy-go-lucky glint in his eyes churned until his irises were almost iridescent. Jasper was never silent. That worried her more.

Suddenly, he grabbed her arms roughly and whisper-screamed, "What in the unholy fires of hell are you thinking? Kael? Working with Kael? That creature ..." pure venom dripped off his tongue at that word, "... needs to be destroyed!"

No, he was not buying her story any more than she was, and she had not told him the worst of it. As if to prove his point, he reached behind his back and yanked out his own dagger, almost identical to her own except for the symbol carved into his hilt was of a French design. A bright red gem sparkled in the handle; brighter than any ruby she had ever seen. Hers held what looked to be a small black opal embedded in a Celtic symbol on one side, with a lighter opal on the other side.

"We do not work with that low-life scum ... ever!"

That last word was said so loudly, along with a string of French curse words, that she was sure those outside heard. Shoving her away from him, Jasper stalked towards the door. It was clear that he had one thing on his mind ... to kill Kael. Now.

Greylyn jumped in front of him, blocking his access to the door. "Quiet down, or the entire wedding party will hear you."

Peering up at him with what she hoped conveyed contrition, she attempted to explain the situation in a way he would accept. An impossible task, but she had to try.

"It's not exactly on the top of my list of favorite things to do ... cavort with the enemy, but right now, it's the best course of action. It got me close to the bride and groom. It got me invited to the wedding, and now I'm even performing the ceremony in place of a recently possessed justice of the peace." She put her hands on her hips. "Do you think I made the decision to work with a dark guardian lightly?"

She paused to see if her speech was having any effect. His expression was clear ... it was not working at all. Long-instilled hatred clouded his judgment.

"The charade has served my purposes so far. When this is over, I will *take care* of Kael, but right now I need him."

Did I just say that? More importantly, did I mean it or was that a lie too?

Jasper stomped angrily around the small room while ranting to himself in French again and waving his arms dramatically. At least he was not bolting over to the main house to decapitate Kael, which would be the best alternative under normal circumstances. Today, however, not so much.

In mid-rant, her cell phone rang. Checking the caller ID, she hurriedly answered to Thomas's rugged Australian accent. It was a welcome relief from the French cursing.

Unfortunately, he did not have good news. His contacts in the district had found Sofia's apartment building.

"Darling, the protection spell they had placed over the building is holding for now, but a large demon army has taken up residence around the place. A good quarter mile radius is nothing but demon-city. All electricity and communications to the building have mysteriously been severed. The rest of the neighborhood appears as if it was a normal Saturday in the heart of DC, but there is a large contingent of Hell holding an almost invisible siege on the building. No one enters. No one leaves."

Greylyn's stomach plummeted. It was worse than she had imagined.

He continued, "Doesn't appear to be as diverse of a group as what you encountered last night." He explained that his friends had some cool new toy that allowed them to see the battalion of demonic creatures which ordinarily would have been cloaked, but Greylyn was not interested in the exact specs of the technology at the moment. "These new guys are warriors geared up for battle, not a ragtag demon boy band."

Thomas's cohorts were not outfitted to deal with such an evil force. No one was. Rescuing Sofia and her friends would require extra help ... angelic help.

She had to be here for the wedding. Kelly was her priority. Quite possibly this was a diversion to lure her away. Why else would an otherwise innocent psychic and her friends be targeted for a Hell siege?

Looking hopefully over at Jasper who had apparently overheard her conversation, he mouthed the words, "I'll go," with a resigned sigh.

Relief flooded her body, all the way to her soul. Once again, Jasper came through for her. They may have gotten a rocky start on that long ago cold, winter's morning, but he always came through for her even if he was pissed. She quickly relayed the message to Thomas that help was on its way.

With the call over, Jasper shrugged. "So, where exactly am I going now, darling?" It was obvious, he would rather spend his time slaughtering Kael, but there was work to be done. Guardians did not get the luxury of picking their own battles. He knew she had to be at the inn. He did not have to like her methods, but it was her assignment. Her responsibility. Besides, Greylyn had a feeling he would hold the favor over her head until just the right moment for payback.

She gave Jasper the address and a quick assessment of the situation. "Call Thomas on the way. He can brief you more fully."

Now how to explain Jasper's arrival and abrupt departure? She had peeked out the window while she was on the phone. Everyone was assembled under the gazebo except for the bride and her father, the groom ... and Kael. They had all seen him come inside her suite.

"Act like we're arguing but trying to be quiet about it. I'll explain that you're an ex- boyfriend making a last-ditch attempt to win me back and I've sent you packing again."

Jasper's eyebrows raised inquisitively. "Now who in their right mind is going to believe that? I mean," he pointed to himself, "just look at me."

The crowd under the gazebo was oddly quiet as Greylyn walked Jasper to his car. No one even tried to feign disinterest.

Taking his cue, Jasper began to gesture wildly with a pleading look on his face. Greylyn, in turn, pretended to speak softly, but firmly, hands on her hips for effect along with an occasional dramatic wave of her hands and shake of her head. They must have been convincing because her sensitive hearing picked up the shocked comments from the young ladies of the wedding party. The buxom blonde was more than dismayed that the hunk appeared to be leaving.

"Oh, what is wrong with that girl? He's divine!"

Jasper even audaciously glanced over at the woman and gave her a wink. Sure enough, it gained him what his ego wanted to hear, a soft gasp as she was drawn into his orbit without him even needing to take a step closer. The woman looked as if she would swoon any second now. One of her friends reached out to grab her by the elbow.

Yes, Jasper had yet another female under his thrall.

"Works every time," he breathlessly whispered as they reached the car.

Just as he turned to give Greylyn a quick kiss on the cheek, the back door to the main house swung open. Every fiber of her being screamed. The way the little hairs stood up on the nape of her neck and her body temperature rose by ten degrees or more, she knew. Kael.

He despised Jasper as much as the male guardian angel hated him. She sent up a silent prayer that he did not pick this moment to unleash his dark guardian wrath.

Jasper clenched his jaws together so tightly she heard his teeth grinding. "You sure, hon? I can stay and kick his ass for you." Greylyn shook her head. "Your loss" He sunk into the leather seat of his sleek sports car, gave her a reassuring pat on the hand, and revved the engine to life.

"Hey, by the way, what happened to the Harley?" The Mercedes was new.

"Trying to show-off for the crowd. Didn't think a hog would be appropriate for a wedding." With that, he slammed the door. For show, he gunned the car down the driveway. Tires screeched as he veered sharply onto the main street.

At this point, she breathed a sigh of relief that the two male guardians had not bloodied each other in full sight of everyone. No one in the gazebo uttered a sound.

As she turned back towards the Carriage House, her eyes met Kael's. An icy chill crawled down her spine. Everyone else was watching her or trying to appear that they were not. If they turned around, they would be faced with an inexplicable picture ... his normally warm, seductive eyes blazed a deep crimson hue. He was enraged. So much so, he did not have control over the one trait that could visibly identify him as something other than human. The eyes. It was always the eyes.

The back door to the inn opened again as Matthew came out to join the group under the gazebo. As the door shut, Kael blinked, his eye color returning to a dark topaz. Thankfully, no one witnessed the maroon-eyed demon. However, the scowl he still wore would have frightened any creature, human or otherwise. The groom slapped him good-naturedly on the back, oblivious to the tension, and dashed to the gazebo as rain started to fall.

Without taking his gaze off her, he nodded towards the Carriage House to indicate they should convene there – now.

Every step he took toward her deepened the pit in her stomach. Still trying to play the part of the gentleman, Kael held the door open for her as they arrived at the Carriage House simultaneously. White-hot fury radiated from his body in shock waves so strong, it slammed into her chest.

With a look back towards Matthew, he raised a finger to indicate, *Give me a minute.*

As soon as the door closed behind them, he pinned Greylyn against the wall. He leaned in so close that she could smell the wine on his warm breath. He seethed between clenched jaws, "What was *he* doing here? Please tell me that you don't allow that poor puppy dog excuse for a man to ... to ... to touch you."

Flames ignited in his eyes as he continued. "If he so much as lays a finger on you, *I will kill him!*"

Oh yeah, enraged was an understatement.

Greylyn did not like the possessive tone he used. But then again, a small part of her did. What she did know was that she needed to calm him down quickly. The situation could rapidly escalate into something ugly. They were here to protect Kelly and her child, not ruin everything with a lovers' quarrel.

Trying to maintain a soothing, placating tone, she faced him down. "Please just listen to me. You are acting irrationally!"

Based on the way his eyes narrowed at her, she guessed her approach needed some adjustment.

"You know as well as I do that we are not a romantic item, so in private you can stop the mummer's farce. We need to play nice together ... for Kelly and Matthew. Remember. This is not about you and Jasper in the grudge match of the millennia. This is about protecting Kelly and the baby."

His tense scowl relaxed a fraction, but he did not let up on his grip.

"It was your brilliant idea that we work together on this. Focus on the endgame, Kael. Jasper is gone, so let's get past this. Please. I need you ..."

Staring into his eyes, every ounce of her willed him to see reason. It took a moment for her words to sink in, but he eventually backed off and let go of her arms. There were red marks on her biceps where his fingers had dug into her skin. His breathing slowed as he paced the tiny foyer, all the while raking his hands through his thick chestnut locks. The way his auburn highlights glinted as his hair fell back in place just above his right eye riveted her attention. Resisting the urge to reach up and comb that hair with her fingers, Greylyn mentally thrashed herself for not focusing on the task at hand. Again, Kael got to her in a way no one else had, could, or ever would.

Now that he was calmer, she explained Jasper's presence and that she had sent him away because of her little pact with him.

"Jasper Moreau would never voluntarily leave you here with me," he smirked. "I bet he loved being told to take a hike."

Yes, Kael was gloating. The good guardian had been forced to leave, while the evil one remained. Score one for the bad guy!

Strands of soft piano music drifted into the room, indicating it was time for a wedding. A full explanation would have to wait. She needed him on board ... now.

"Fine. He was not happy about it but agreed it was best if he left under the circumstances. If I had not needed him elsewhere, I'm sure things would've gotten nasty around here."

Too late, she realized she had said too much. Kael did not miss a beat.

"What circumstances? Where did he go?"

Glancing out the window, she saw everyone in their places under the gazebo. All except for the ordained minister performing the ceremony and the photographer. In exasperation, she begged more with her eyes than with words. "Please, we can discuss all this later when we have the luxury of time. Right now, there's a wedding ceremony on hold until we get out there." She jerked her chin towards the window.

With a look of resignation, a deep sigh, and a slight roll of her eyes, she added, "I can't believe I'm saying this, but I need your ... help."

He was still steamed from seeing Jasper and eager to enact some form of violence on his nemesis, that was evident, but she also saw the turmoil reflected in his cognac eyes. Then a slight twinkle slowly returned. Finally, as she held her breath, he silently nodded.

"You need me. I like the sound of that." He raised his hand to caress her cheek. "It's just the idea of that bastard touching you ..." his voice trailed off without finishing the sentence.

Something important remained unspoken between them. If they emerged from this adventure unscathed, she needed to seriously contemplate what all this meant.

Their bodies were so close she could feel the heat emanating from him. She tried to move away but found her back against the door to her suite. He leaned in close, pulling back a strand of hair that had fallen over her eyes. His lips turned up, showcasing his dimples, and mouthed "You. Need. Me."

A rapping on the outer door startled them both, but Kael refused to move away.

Matthew's voice rang out. "Hey, guys, we have a wedding going on here. We kinda need you two in place before my blushing bride can make her entrance. Do you think you two can control yourselves long enough to get me hitched?"

They both laughed, but just before Kael opened the door he leaned in close to her ear. "You. Need. Me." His lips brushed against her hairline.

What have I gotten myself into?

Chapter 22

The Wedding

Gazebo

The unfaltering rain continued, but the couple decided they still wanted the ceremony outside in the gazebo, overlooking the quaint koi pond with the majestic Shenandoah Mountains in the background. Greylyn did not blame them. Even with the rain, the view was spectacular! The gray color surrounding the gazebo and landscape contrasted sharply with the colorful attire of the guests. At first glance, the gazebo appeared to be an oasis from the dreariness brought by the early summer shower.

All that was needed was for the bride to make her appearance. The processional was to start with a song special to Matthew and Kelly in lieu of "The Bridal March." The groom impatiently waited with frequent expectant glances to the back door of the inn for that particular song from a specially made playlist to start.

Piano notes twinkled as "At the Beginning" by Richard Marx and Donna Lewis began to play. Everyone turned toward the main house, waiting for Kelly and her father to emerge. But the door did not open. About midway into the song, the door still had not opened. Matthew shifted from one foot to the other, eyes glued to the back door. Even the mother of the bride looked disconcerted, with worry lines creasing her forehead, as the second verse of the song began.

Finally, Tony, the tall, robust best man with lots of salt and pepper hair (unusual for someone in their twenties), paused the song and bolted into the house like a firefighter seeking someone to rescue.

No one spoke, except for the future sister-in-law, Andrea. In a barely concealed whisper to her boyfriend, she stated, "Guess that means I win the bet."

A nasty look from everyone else, especially her brothers, shut her up quickly enough.

Good thing too, because Greylyn was not inclined to put up with such callous negativity regarding such a sacred event, especially when it involved Kelly.

The groom's face was etched with worry, and a tinge of fear. Greylyn softly touched Matthew's arm, hoping to convey reassurance. Just a simple touch from a guardian angel could assuage anyone's anxiety. Besides, she knew there was no way Kelly was not coming out that door to marry her soulmate.

Momentarily, she allowed the question to float through her mind. What was keeping Kelly? Tiny hairs on the back of her neck raised as she imagined the worst. Had a demon infiltrated the manor while she was acting ridiculous with Kael or playing peacekeeper between the good and the bad guardians? But there were no alarms going off inside her head. No faint tingling behind her eyes. Could she be wrong?

No sooner had she convinced herself that Kelly was again in danger, Tony raced back out the door. Laughing, he explained, "It's the *next* song!" With a shrug, he said, "She is very insistent that it *has to be* that particular song."

Everyone laughed at the misunderstanding, except Matthew. Both future sisters-in-law rolled their eyes, irritating Greylyn further. Instead of letting the song finish, the flustered groom reached over to the stereo and pushed the button to skip to the next song and increased the volume. Apparently, he had waited long enough.

A Jim Brickman piano melody filled the air: "Angel Eyes." Almost instantly, the back door to the inn opened, and the radiant bride and her somewhat nervous father emerged with a giant gold and white golf umbrella to keep the bride dry for the short walk to the gazebo.

Greylyn glanced over at Matthew. His expression was priceless, a gigantic smile and eyes glistening with happy tears. Looking back to Kelly, she saw the most glowing, joyous bride with her eyes locked onto her groom and the sweetest, shy smile. Neither could tear their eyes away from each other. It was as if there was no one else there. Just the two of them.

It was a bittersweet moment for Greylyn, as she knew she would never experience a love like that. If she had during her human lifetime, she had no memories to cling to. She had long ago accepted that truth, but sometimes it still haunted her lonely heart. Like an invisible hole that desperately yearned to heal. Seeing them so happy though, she could not help but smile. There was no purpose in dwelling on things that could not be changed anyway. Instead, she rejoiced for them.

Almost as if in defiance of the rain, the bride shone brilliantly in an ivory chiffon dress with an empire waist to hide the budding baby belly. Her lovely, light auburn hair was held back from her glowing face by a matching hair band covered in pearls. Apparently, Kelly had won the argument to avoid the up-do and her hair brushed her shoulders in natural wavy cascades. A simple pearl necklace and pearl-drop earrings were her only adornments.

Kelly's short journey from the main house to the gazebo ended, and she now stood face- to-face with her expectant groom. So enraptured by the beautiful couple, it took the sound of Kael clearing his throat to signal that it was Greylyn's turn to speak. Giving him an appreciative half-grin, she proceeded.

"Dearly beloved, we have gathered here today, in the sight of God, to witness the joining together of this man and this woman in holy matrimony; which is an honorable estate, instituted in the necessities of our being, and dedicated to the happiness of mankind; an estate not by any to be entered into unadvisedly or lightly, but reverently, discreetly, soberly, and in all sincerity. To be true, this outward form must be a symbol of that which is inner and real, a sacred personal union, which a church may solemnize, and a state make legal, but which only love can create and mutually fulfill."

Shifting her eyes to Kelly's father, she asked, "Who gives this woman to be married to this man?"

Mr. Calendar, with tears streaming down his face, answered, "Her mother and I do." Slightly trembling, he presented Kelly's hand to Matthew and with some hesitation took a step back to join his wife.

Greylyn continued, "I would like to commence this ceremony with a marriage prayer to bless this union of Matthew and Kelly." As everyone in attendance bowed their heads for the prayer, she glanced sidelong at Kael to witness his reaction. Surprisingly, he nodded in affirmation and bowed his head.

Well, he is certainly full of surprises.

"Father in Heaven, You ordained marriage for your children, and you gave us love. We present to You, Matthew and Kelly, who come this day to be married. May the covenant of love they make be blessed with true devotion and spiritual commitment. We ask that You, God, will give them the ability to keep the covenant they have made. When selfishness shows itself, grant generosity; when mistrust is a temptation, give moral strength; when there is misunderstanding, give patience and gentleness; if suffering becomes a part of their lives, give them a strong faith and an abiding love. Amen."

Everyone, including Kael, reiterated, "Amen" and took their seats in the white plastic patio chairs provided, except for the couple who turned their rapt faces to Greylyn.

Even though she had not explicitly informed the couple that the ceremony would follow full Christian rites, in contrast to the demon-possessed elderly magistrate's approach, neither appeared offended as she continued.

Of course, since they were so attuned to each other, she could have said, "*Yabba Dabba Do*" and they would not have noticed.

"Matthew and Kelly, our God of love has established marriage as the symbol of Christ's perfect relationship to His Body, the Church. We have come to bring you as one before Him."

She cast a quick glance at them both to see if they were taken aback by the religious ceremony. Both were smiling, practically beaming. With a cleansing breath, she continued. "God will lead you into such situations as will bless you and develop your characters as you walk together. He will give you enough tears to keep you tender, enough hurts to keep you compassionate, enough failure to keep your hands clenched tightly in His, and enough success to make sure you walk with Him. May you never take each other's love for granted, but always experience that wonder that exclaims, 'Out of all this world you have chosen me.' When life is done, may you be found then as now, hand in hand, still thanking God for each other.

May you ever serve Him happily, faithfully, together until you return to glory or until at last one shall lay the other into His arms."

So far, so good.

Before resuming the ceremony, she hazarded a glimpse of Kael, who was standing just off to the side with his camera snapping photographs. He caught her look and lowered his camera for a second, gave her a wicked wink, and raised the camera to take a picture of her. Assured, she continued. Tomorrow she would consider why she found Kael's presence a comfort.

Raindrops pinged on the metallic roof of the gazebo as vows were exchanged. "Matthew, will you have this woman to be your wife, to live together in the sacred estate of marriage. Will you love her, comfort her, honor and keep her, in sickness and in health, in sorrow and in joy, and be faithful to her, as long as you both shall live?"

Matthew turned to his blushing bride and readily replied with the requisite "I will." She giggled lightly in response.

After Greylyn reiterated the question to Kelly, the bride enthusiastically responded, "I will." Her chin quivered as her voice trembled. A single teardrop slid down her radiant face.

As the couple, each in turn, repeated his and her "to have and to hold" vows, neither could hold back their happy tears. Matthew lifted his hand to stroke away a stray tear as it ran down her cheek, followed by another.

There was not a dry eye under the gazebo either as evidenced by several sobs. Tears were threatening to fall from Greylyn's eyes as well as an intense unfamiliar emotion brimmed within her chest. Being around for so many years, she had witnessed many weddings. Never once had a tear escaped her eyes. Somehow, this wedding was different.

There were no songs to be sung or poems to be read so the ceremony proceeded rather quickly.

"Inasmuch as Matthew and Kelly have consented together in marriage, and have witnessed the same before you, and thereto have pledged their faith to each other, and have declared the same by joining hands and giving and receiving of rings, I, by the authority invested in me by God and by the Commonwealth of Virginia, pronounce that they are husband and wife."

With a raspy breath, tears brimming in her own eyes, she added, "May the grace of Christ attend you; the love of God surround you, and the Holy

Spirit keep you that you may grow in love, find delight in each other always, and remain faithful until your life's end. Go now in great joy, in the name of the Father, the Son, and the Holy Spirit."

Greylyn ended with, "Matthew, you may now kiss your lovely bride."

No one had to tell him twice. As they embraced and kissed, the wedding guests cheered. With a sigh of relief, she closed her bible, congratulated the newlyweds, and then quickly made way for the rest of the wedding guests to give their best wishes to the couple as well.

Someone turned the music back on and "From This Moment On" by Shania Twain and Bryan White played in the background.

Kael busily snapped pictures. She took a moment to just watch him work, mesmerized by how easily he solicited genuine smiles from each person. Even the toddler cooperated with him – a small miracle in itself.

Not realizing she was staring, Greylyn suddenly found herself embroiled by dark eyes locked with her own as Kael lowered his camera. Shaking herself out of her stupor, she retreated to her suite.

The ceremony had taken an enormous emotional toll on her. There was no reason for it, but Greylyn felt it just the same as if she had just been party to a wedding for a close relative whose happiness in and of itself meant everything to her. Relief mixed with a bittersweet sense of something she could see, could not fathom, and would never experience herself.

Chapter 23

Should I Stay or Should I Go?

Soft strands of piano music threaded in from the courtyard as the door to her suite shut behind her. The rain had slacked off during the ceremony, and a few rays of sunshine peeked out from the clouds to brighten the newlyweds' day. Drawing the curtains to block out the sights and sounds from outside, she picked up her phone to check for messages.

Please let there be good news.

Two messages. One from Thomas saying he had not heard back from Jasper or his other contacts since he briefed the other guardian on his way to the psychic's apartment building.

The other was a terse and to-the-point message from Jasper, "Call me back now!" Chills streaked down her spine. Her guardian angel mentor had never sounded frazzled. Never. Not even in the midst of battle. She clicked the call return icon. It took two rings and then she heard his familiar husky voice, breathless and agitated.

"It's about time! Enjoying yourself, I hope. All Hell is about to break loose here, darling. Get your sweet ass to DC now!" He quipped without his usual humor.

He quickly filled her in on what had transpired while she had been officiating the wedding. The building was on a complete supernatural lockdown. No one and nothing could get in or out. There was no power to the building; all communications were dead.

"Everything looks normal around the building but is far from it."

He explained that everyday life was going on in the streets. The humans outside could not ascertain anything out of the ordinary. However, with his angelic visionary powers, he could see the pulsing glow of a demonic force field enclosing a score or more of monsters. They appeared to be waiting. What they were waiting for was anyone's guess. After her last trip to DC, Greylyn figured they were waiting for her again.

"There's been exactly one time that I'm aware of that anything like this has ever been seen. It was horrific!" his voice quaked. "A couple of Thomas's pals approached the building unawares before I arrived. Apparently, they had yet to use their high-tech goggles that would have allowed them to see the supernatural activity. One poor bastard was electrocuted. It must've looked like a heart attack because someone called 911, but it was too late."

Taking a ragged breath, he explained, "Now that they are aware of the dangers of approaching the building, none are eager to do so. I told them to hang back and simply watch." He sighed deeply. "I don't think they are going to be able to help much."

"Anything to indicate why they are besieging the building?" Greylyn guessed the why did not really matter at this point. Demons did not ever really need logic.

"Darling, I have no idea what they want. So far, they've done nothing except keep those inside Sofia's building in and all others out."

A knock at the door to her suite startled her – so much so that she almost dropped the phone. After asking Jasper to hold that thought for just a moment, much to his chagrin, she opened the door to find the bride's father, Mr. John Calendar.

Rather surprised, she greeted the gentleman with a friendly smile and a "Hello." In a quaint southern drawl easily indicative of Georgia roots, he informed her that her presence was requested for a few last pictures before everyone reconvened in the main house for dinner. "Miss, we are just so grateful to you today. You single-handedly saved the wedding! We insist you join us. The party cannot go on without you." His blue-gray eyes beseeched her.

"Really, it was the least I could do."

"Well then, it's the least we can do to offer you a good meal and maybe some dancing later."

As much as she argued that it was nothing and they should continue with the celebrations without her, he would not take "no" for an answer. The sweet, mannered Southern gentleman also had a stubborn streak.

Although she appreciated the gesture, she was needed in DC. Politely begging for their forgiveness, she heard Jasper's voice over the phone calling her name. She quickly put the phone back up to her ear and walked further into the room so Mr. Calendar could not overhear their conversation.

"Listen, Grey. I have no clue what is going on here. But what if this is all a ploy to divert your attention." He advised. "You know I'd rather have you here beside me, darling ..."

"But you just ordered me to ... how did you put it? Get my sweet ass to DC now!" He must really be flustered if he was already contradicting himself.

A loud, annoyed sigh came over the phone. "My genius brain is a screaming roller coaster, babe! Try to keep up."

"Genius?" For being around half a millennium or more, he was brilliant, but genius?

"Well, if it is a ploy to get your attention, then you would be walking into a trap if you showed up. We'll wait and if nothing happens because you don't show up ... score one for the good guys!"

"And what if my missed appearance just pisses them off and they destroy everything in a two-mile radius?" Innocent people could die. She was not willing to take that chance.

"If it looks like the situation is heating up, we'll make a move here and I'll call you in. But I really don't see how handing you over to a demon army would be a wise choice." There it was ... the truth. Jasper was more worried about her than anyone else at risk, including everyone in the besieged building. "My gut says for you to stay put, for now at least. And my gut is never wrong."

Normally, she would argue the point, especially since she knew of more than one occasion when "his gut" had not only been wrong but had gotten them in far more trouble.

"Well, there was that time in Belgrade," she began before he rudely shut down the conversation.

"Stay there, for now anyway. If things get dicey here, I'll call." Reluctantly, she agreed. Putting him on hold once more, she thanked Mr.

Calendar for the invitation and promised to be right back out once she finished her phone call.

Happy to have completed his errand, the bride's father opened the door and hollered, "She's coming back!"

As the door shut behind him, Greylyn gave strict instructions for Jasper to call her the second any nefarious activity began. As soon as she could ascertain that the danger for Kelly, Matthew, and the baby was over, she planned to extricate herself from the festivities and join him in DC. After all Sofia and her friends had done to help, she was not about to leave them to the mercy of a demon squad.

He ended the call with "I can't believe you brought up Belgrade. That's low."

Before heading back out to the gazebo she glanced in the mirror. Worry was stamped on her every feature – lines appeared in her forehead, blue dots grew in her irises, and she had chewed off the last of the peach color on her lips. Determined not to let on to the others that something was amiss, she applied a fresh coat of lip balm and prayerfully meditated for a couple of minutes.

I walk upon heaven and earth.
I walk through hell with ease.
All is suffering, all is love.
I embrace it all with serenity,
When my heart is at peace.

As an afterthought, she rifled through her overnight bag and found an ancient Gaelic blessing coin that she had held onto ever since leaving the country a long, long time ago. It was the Irish Portrait coinage of Henry VIII with the king's portrait on the obverse side and a cross and pellets on the reverse side. Even though it had long been decommissioned when she left Ireland, it had been among the effects in her dress pocket when she first woke up in the coffin. It had not become blessed until some years later by a wise woman recluse living in the hills of northern England, just outside of Newcastle.

Greylyn kept it with her always. The old woman had said that one day she would know when it was time to pass along the coin and to whom. Now she did, as it vibrated softly in her palm. It had never done that before.

With the coin tucked away in a pocket of the dress, along with her phone, she took a deep breath and walked back out the door to rejoin the wedding festivities.

A lively crowd greeted her return. The rain had stopped but continued cloud cover foretold more showers, perhaps a storm later. The bride and groom were glowing, with eyes only for each other. Everyone else could have disappeared into thin air and they probably would not notice.

Kael snapped the last pictures of the couple with the koi pond and the majestic Shenandoah Mountains in the background. If he were as good a photographer as his early photos indicated, Kelly and Matthew would have an incredible wedding album.

He blatantly winked at her return before hustling everyone around to the front of the main house for a few shots from the porch to showcase the manor. They decided to go through the house since everyone might get a bit muddy walking in the grass.

Inside everything was set for a cozy, but elegant dinner. Soft orchestra music played over speakers set up throughout the main floor. All overhead lighting had been dimmed, and fragrant candles flickered on every table surface, along with delicate crystal vases containing yellow and purple calla lilies. Crème colored lace tablecloths covered the tables. The innkeeper truly had outdone herself prepping the inn for the reception. It truly felt as if she had stepped back in time.

As the group filed out the front door onto the covered porch, Kael waited for Greylyn to pass and gently touched her arm to get her attention. She read the quizzical look in his eyes. He sensed something else was wrong. At this point, she could not be sure if she could trust him with that information. Quite honestly, she was not certain that he was not involved in the whole debacle. Maybe it was his idea to divert her attention away from Kelly and Matthew by besieging Sofia's apartment building. He had lulled her into believing he was there to be helpful.

She smiled up at him and mouthed the word "Later." With a slight nod, he let go of her arm, and they both exited the inn as swaths of sunshine streaked between thin slits in the clouds. However, tremendous heat still simmered over her skin where they had touched.

With Kael back in photographer mode, she was able to observe him in action. He was all business, but charming, even when the groom's errant niece kept wandering off to pull flowers out of their pots. Overhearing the child's mother and grandmother talking, Greylyn realized she had missed the child's earlier near swan dive into the koi pond. Somehow, Kael had managed to grab the tyke just in time.

Guess he likes playing the hero.

Standing a little away from the crowd, she found it entertaining to eavesdrop on the bride's single lady friends whispering amongst themselves about the hunky photographer. Apparently, there was a contest brewing for who could snag him for the night, or even longer. The buxom blonde appeared to be the frontrunner as she batted Hollywood starlet long eye lashes at him, pursed her lips, and used every opportunity to bend over so her cleavage showed even more. "He's mine. One of you so much as winks in his direction, you can ..."

Disgusted, Greylyn tuned her out. Strangely enough, a twinge of jealousy flared upon hearing their various designs on Kael. Reflecting on the situation without bias, she admitted that if she had a bet, she would have put her money on the busty blonde as well. Certainly, all the men at the wedding had taken notice. The best man cast glances her way every few seconds, but she ignored him. Too bad, he seemed like a nice guy. Even though Kelly had worried about her college bestie, Griffin, getting snared, he was happily occupied by his super-model tall girlfriend.

Then she heard the oddest thing. The brunette friend commented, "Personally, I think none of us have a chance. He's hooked on the minister, or is she a justice of the peace? Whatever she is ... He couldn't take his eyes off her the entire ceremony. I should know because I didn't take my eyes off him."

Greylyn tried her best not to laugh. It made her stomach hurt to stifle the giggle. The entire idea was absurd.

After a lengthy photo shoot, the wedding party moved inside for a scrumptious traditional Irish dinner. Kael was still busy taking pictures while everyone else ate their meal, but Maureen made sure he had an open seat sandwiched between Greylyn and the groom's sister.

In between snapping pictures, he would come by for a quick bite of food, sip of wine, and a quick smile or wink at her. This apparently upset the blonde – Greylyn tried to recall her name, maybe Kayla – whose mood deteriorated each time Kael came near her. Between the irate looks her way and the melodramatic pouting, the young woman was not very subtle.

Everyone else appeared in high spirits, especially the exultant bride and groom. It did not take guardian angel senses to realize that the happy couple were looking forward to the guests departing so they could be alone.

Her angelic hearing also caught Kelly's whisper to her new husband, "Would it be rude to ask them to leave?" as they held hands.

The dinner party eventually broke up, and everyone retreated to the gazebo for some music. In lieu of the usual DJ party club dancing found at most weddings, the couple opted to keep things simple, to play soft music while the guests mingled, but have the gazebo area available if anyone really wanted to dance. Considering how much the happy couple wanted to be alone, it was a good strategy not to provide too much entertainment to prolong the party.

Greylyn's cell phone rang with Jasper's rock-and-roll song ringtone as she exited the main house. She excused herself to take the call, but Kael followed her into the foyer of the Carriage House.

Annoyed, she ignored him while she listened to Jasper detailing what had been happening at the psychic's apartment building. As night overcame the city, the local shops had closed, and human traffic had come to a halt. Mysteriously, there was not one human on the streets. An entire five-block radius had turned into a ghost town in a matter of minutes. The demon battalion had kept under cover in the daylight but was now out in force.

"Even more arrived at dusk. Some creatures I've never even seen before. They're prepping for something big, but I have no idea what. But something bad is brewing and they are ready to unleash Hell, so back to my original statement … Get your sweet ass here now!"

Greylyn groaned, partly in frustration because she had let him talk her into staying at the inn earlier instead of racing out to DC and partly because Kael was overhearing the conversation as he stepped up directly behind her.

"Time to stop partying and get back to your real job, darling," he insisted. "There are no other guardians close enough to call for backup and these humans are not equipped for a fight of this caliber."

Sometimes Greylyn and Jasper shared a mental connection. She could see what he was seeing even if they were hundreds of miles apart. It was rare when she could tap into this gift, but now was as good a time as any to try. Closing her eyes and taking three cleansing breaths, she stretched her mind out to him. Her entire body shook from the effort with no success. Either their connection had weakened, which she doubted, or her psychic tie to Jasper was being purposefully blocked – and not by him.

"Damn," she muttered to herself. Unable to assess the situation from Gaelic Haven, she reassured Jasper that she was on her way there. "Don't do anything stupid till I get there." Jasper's resulting laugh was not reassuring.

Opening the door to her room, she intended to close it behind her so she could quickly change into something more suitable for a fight. Kael put a hand up to block the door.

"Kael, I don't have time to play games with you. Get back to the party and make some excuse for me." After a second, she added, "Please." The annoyed look he shot her spoke volumes.

"Not until you tell me what is going on, Greylyn. Remember, we are working *together* to protect Kelly and the baby? Why are you jetting off to help that lousy excuse for a guardian angel?" he said with more than a touch of ire.

Irritated, but trying not to alarm him, she took a reassuring tone. "We can discuss all this when I get back, but I have to go. Now!" She hoped he took her words at face value and let her leave without a lot of drama, that just maybe he would realize the gravity of the situation and let her go.

He continued to hold the door open, staring intently at her. His large, muscular arms strained against the fine fabric of his dress shirt. He had ditched the suit jacket long ago. Those same muscles twitched. She could tell he was fighting the urge to reach into the room and grab her, knowing a huge electric shock and perhaps more awaited him if he did since she had gone overboard on protection spells for her room.

"Why does Jasper need you anyway? He's a big boy. Apparently, he was acing this guardian angel gig long before you showed up. Or is this his way to get you away from me?"

Greylyn's eyes closed in aggravation. She did not need his jealous tripe right now. "The situation calls for an extra guardian. Okay? That is all you need to know."

The nerve in his jaw twitched and a crimson film washed over his eyes for just a moment before fading away. "Does this have anything to do with why you came back last night all cut up and bleeding? You never did explain what happened. I think I deserve some answers after all the help I've provided."

His tone was urgent and demanding. He had no intentions of letting her go anywhere without an explanation, especially if it meant she was joining Jasper.

With an exasperated sigh and melodramatic eye roll, Greylyn tried to think of the quickest way to appease him so she could get going. Time was not in her favor.

"Kael, I am sorry there is no time right now. I promise when I return you will get all your questions answered. But if I don't leave right now an enormous tragedy could befall innocents, and I can't allow that." He stared at her blankly. "Okay, yes. It does have something to do with where I was last night. Actually, it's the same place. Perhaps my appearance there alerted a local demon squad or something. But I will not allow the people there to be killed. I have to go."

She hoped he would accept that answer for now, but the look in his eyes did not promise luck in that department. Eyelids narrowed to mere slits like a snake. His shoulders squared. One fist rested on his hip.

As an afterthought she again added, "Please."

Ashamed to employ such tactics, she even looked up at him through her thick, curly eyelashes in what she hoped came off as flirtatious pleading. If Kayla could pull off the look, certainly she could too. There it was again, a jealous twinge in her chest. What the hell was wrong with her?

His response surprised her. "Well, I will just have to go with you then." With a wicked grin he continued, "Can't have you bleeding out somewhere without me to save you."

Not the response she hoped for, but perhaps she could work this angle if he were in the mood to be so helpful.

"Kael, don't think I don't appreciate your ... umm ... offer of assistance, but the truth is that I do need your help. It's just that I need your help – here."

She could not believe she was requesting assistance from a dark guardian. Not just any dark guardian, but this one. The same one that helped kick-start the bloodshed during the French Revolution. The same dark guardian that beat her near senseless the night of her first guardian assignment. The very same one that leveled an entire mile radius of farmland setting off the Dust Bowl during the 1930s. Her brain could not even conjure up all the horrific things he had been responsible for and now here she was asking for his help!

Good thing there was not a performance evaluation for guardian angels because she was fairly sure this would cause her to fail.

He gave her a look that clearly stated, "I'm not buying it."

Frazzled, she continued, "I can't be sure this isn't an attempt to distract me from my primary purpose, which is here, to protect Kelly and her baby. But I cannot allow the assassination of innocent humans who have also worked diligently for the same purpose. If Jasper says the situation is that dire, then I trust his assessment, and I must go. But, if this is a distraction, someone needs to be here to maintain watch over Kelly." Pausing, she looked up into his face.

The next words out of her mouth stunned even her. "Truth is I can't go and help the others unless I have backup here that I can ... trust." She stuttered on that last word.

If she honestly analyzed the situation, she would have realized that she did trust him in this one thing. Against all logic and good reason, she trusted him. However, if he betrayed her, well ... there would be literal hell to pay.

The proclamation seemed to shock him as well, as his eyes rounded. After a moment, his stern, determined facial expression morphed into a sly, but pleased look.

"Wow, who would've thought?" he replied with a grin.

The muscles in his face relaxed as he pondered the situation and then with a more serious scowl, nodded.

"If I agree to stay behind, you must agree to two conditions: First, you CANNOT get hurt like that again. You may be immortal, but you are not invincible."

"Fine." She had no intention of being injured again, but if it made him feel better, she would agree.

"Second," he continued, with the gold flecks in his eyes practically lighting up at what he was about to say. "You owe me a dance."

Huh?

Now that was not what she expected to hear. Just to hurry things along, though, she agreed. "Okay, okay. I agree. But I have one counter-condition for you. If anything bad happens to anyone here, particularly Kelly and the baby, I will know you played me false, and I will spend the rest of eternity making you pay for it," she replied, trying to portray real malice with one hand fisted on her hip and the other pulling out her dagger from where she had taped it to her leg, barely concealed by the soft fabric of her new dress.

"I mean it, Kael, if so much as a hair on anyone's head is out of place I will hunt you down like a hell hound."

Somberly he raised his right hand like a Boy Scout, "I promise to do everything in my power to protect these humans and to earn your trust in this matter. Nothing evil will befall any innocent human here, *particularly* the newlyweds and the baby." He raised one finger. "However, I cannot make any promises to not toss any of those girls into the pond to cool them off. Their constant staring and giggling frays my last nerve. If the blonde one bends over any steeper, all her assets are going to fall right out. I appreciate a good feminine physique as much as the next guy, but ... come on, have some decency."

Greylyn doubled over in a fit of laughter, nearly dropping her blade in the process.

His solemn declaration turned to a coy grin as he suggested, "How about we seal our bargain with a kiss?"

Not even bothering to answer, she stalked back to the door and shut it in his face. She heard him chuckle and call out, "I'll take that as no for now, but maybe later." The foyer door thudded closed as he left to rejoin the wedding party.

A silent, fervent prayer went up. This was a first for her. Placing her trust in a dark guardian. Deep down in her soul she knew he would not betray her, but her mind screamed that this was incredibly dangerous territory. Shaking off her doubts, Greylyn hurriedly changed and added a prayer that she would make it in time to save Sofia and her friends.

Chapter 24

Battle Zone DC

Sofia the Psychic's Apartment Building

Greylyn invoked a glamour rendering her vehicle invisible to cops between the Virginia bed and breakfast and Washington, DC. As a guardian angel, she did not possess abilities to alter time and space to facilitate a quicker trip like pure blood angels. They could simply think of where they needed to go and immediately transport there. At least, that was what she had heard. She had never actually met one before.

The cloaking spell had served her well over the years, as her lead foot would have gotten her countless tickets otherwise. There had been one time she just forgot to utilize the spell. State troopers in Montana clocked her at 140 miles per hour. Since they could not catch her, there had been a Wanted poster of her car across the state for the next decade. Needless to say, she avoided Montana for a while.

To not alert the demons that might be patrolling the area to her presence before she was ready, Greylyn parked a few blocks southwest of the neighborhood. Jasper had not exaggerated the case. The night air was charged with foreboding and fear. The place was deserted. Not even the faintest sounds of life. No lights. No music. No voices. No car engines. She did not even hear the rumbling Metro underneath the ground.

Calming her mind, she telepathically located Jasper. She found him, along with three humans, paranormal investigators turned demon hunters, hiding out in a back alley beside a mom-and-pop sandwich shop with a clear view of the front entrance of Sofia's apartment building.

The stench from the industrial size garbage containers served to mask the scent of humans from the demons surrounding the building. At least something was working in their favor, even if it was the putrefied odor of rotting lunch meat.

Jasper quickly filled her in on the events that had transpired as the sun went down and the demon army converged on the tiny land parcel in the middle of the nation's capital city. During the daylight hours, some demons had masked themselves as humans or even animals to blend in with their surroundings. Others had stayed back in the shadows out of sight. Those invisible to human eyes stood guard around the building. "This isn't just a demon convention. Every species I recognize are vicious soldiers, built for nothing but annihilation. They do not take prisoners and they show no mercy."

"Any Malphas legions?" The second in command in Hell, Malphas, commanded up to forty legions of Hell's army. She had never personally encountered them, but guardian angel urban legend told of mass destruction and horrific ends for all involved in the battle against them. They had shown up in Vietnam, and there were rumors of their presence in the Middle East. Greylyn prayed they were not part of this army.

Jasper shook his head, and they both breathed deep sighs of relief. "No, they're a mish-mash of demons, mostly mercenaries, but highly organized. Malphas keeps his soldiers all the same species."

One of the demon hunters, looking more like a WWE wrestler, relayed how their numbers seemed to swell just as the sun began to set. With bloodshot eyes as round as the top of a beer can, he fidgeted with a large, jagged knife in his hand. His gaze shifted from her to the alley entrance to the ground at his feet and repeated the cycle. "Since the sun went down, more creatures kept showing up, like cockroaches. Never seen anything like it." The tremor in his voice belied the truth ... he did not want to see anything like this, did not want anything to do with this situation, and most certainly regretted the demon hunter life for the moment. "This neighborhood isn't exactly the safest part of town, so most people wisely vacated the area as soon as nightfall approached, except for a few local thug types. Those poor bastards didn't stand a chance."

The way the man said it made it clear that the humans had not been asked nicely to leave.

Jasper and the others had callously deemed it unsafe to intervene. If she had been present, she probably would have blown their cover to save the miscreants. That was just how she was. No human should have to suffer at the hands of a monster. Her strategic mind acknowledged that the gentlemen had made the right call, though.

Instead of a small battalion to fight off, they were facing an army of more than one hundred. This was going to take some ingenuity on their part, as well as a foolproof battle plan.

With a deep sigh, she asked the obvious, "So what's the plan?"

All four men looked at her with vacant stares and shrugged shoulders.

"Well, that's fantastic! No one has any ideas? Jasper, come on! You're the military genius or so you are always saying." Actually, he was, and she knew it. He was the guardian angel military general equal to Patton, Alexander the Great, and Attila the Hun with the splash of Sun Tzu for added brilliance. At this moment, she needed him to be all the above.

"Hey, I am a genius, but this goes far beyond anything I've ever encountered. I was less nervous on D Day." After she flashed him a shocked look, he added, "Okay, I wasn't nervous then, but I am now."

Her fingers twitched as she paced the cramped alley. *Think, Grey, think!*

"What I need is a spy camera to get a closer look." It was a start. Without hesitation, she pulled out her phone and speed-dialed Thomas.

In a hushed tone she conveyed to Thomas what she needed: satellite surveillance of an entire five-block radius. Lucky for her, he had contacts up the food chain over at the NSA. "I don't know what to tell you, Grey. Not sure they'll come through. That is a tall order." She begged him to at least try. Otherwise, this was nothing but a suicide mission and everyone in the alley knew it.

While they waited for Thomas to call back, she silently climbed to the roof of the sandwich shop to take a look. Greylyn did not need night-vision goggles to see the nightmare before them. There were twenty demons of various factions guarding each entrance into the building. Some wore heavy armor while others wore nothing at all. The one thing they all had in common was the pure evil radiating off them, casting a hellish glow around the building. The streetlamp at the corner facing the east side of the building flickered, allowing shadow demons more mobility in that vicinity. There appeared to be only four of those, for which Greylyn was grateful, but they were the best at hiding so she fully expected more.

Congregating around a park bench on the front, southern side of the building were human-looking demons that could only be shape-shifters. They were well equipped with military-grade armor and weapons and could easily pass as a SWAT team. But as long as someone had a silver knife, those could be easily disposed of, but it would be messy. Upon death, their bodies congealed into a bloody cottage-cheese-looking substance before melting into the ground. They were at the bottom of the list of her favorite monsters to fight giving the goriness of their deaths.

Her vantage point did not allow her visual access to the northern side and only an abbreviated view of the western side of the building. She guessed from the growling noises that there were at least a few more feral beasts lurking in those areas, possibly werewolves since it was a full moon, even if clouds covered most of the night sky. But werewolves were not known for active military duty. Gang-style fighting for their pack, yes. Not this type of situation.

Within fifty yards of the building, there was a mishmash of other sinister entities that appeared as a secondary line of attack. The place was surrounded, and she still did not know what lay in wait on the far side of the building.

Thomas, don't let me down. I need you, buddy.

Just as she was about to descend back to her comrades in the alley, something highly unusual caught her eye. Coming out from behind the northern face of the building was a freakishly tall, hulking figure of a man. He seemed to be barking out orders to the rest.

So, there is a general leading this siege.

Now if she only had binocular vision along with night vision, she could figure out who exactly this was. Based on his size and obvious leadership capacity, she surmised he was higher up the chain than a mere demonic entity. If not Malphas himself, this was likely one of the most notorious demons around … a full-fledged, pure blood fallen angel. They were rumored to be the worst of the worst.

She had encountered a couple over her lifetime as a guardian, but never defeated one outright. They always managed to get the best of her. Perhaps, if they could eliminate the general, the rest of this little army would fall apart. Unfortunately, she was too far away to get a good look at the guy. If this was indeed a fallen one, their job had just gotten a lot more difficult and dangerous.

She scrambled down the side of the building to ask if anyone had thought to bring binoculars. None that were handy anyway. They had the fancy demon-vision goggles, but no binoculars.

The shorter, thirty-something man with shaggy dirty-blond hair, looking more like a drummer of some backroad bar cover band had some. Unfortunately, he left them in his truck several blocks away.

Things just were not looking up for this tactical unit. Greylyn and Jasper both had excellent sight, but neither could see through buildings. This could be an unmitigated disaster if they charged in without knowing what lay on the other side.

Just then her phone buzzed softly.

"Hey, doll. You know never to doubt the Wizard!" Thomas boasted. "Considering I had to promise the moon and stars to get this information, you owe me – like huge! I was thinking a Caribbean vacation – just the two of us ..."

"Yeah, yeah! Put it on my account, will ya?" she snapped.

Unaffected by her ill humor, Thomas described what he saw. His contact had agreed to allow Thomas to see the imagery, but no one else. "Dude says he'd be court-martialed and thrown into a tiny five by five jail cell underground in some godforsaken country for the rest of his life if someone finds out. Considering it's their job to track every single call, text, and email throughout the world, he is reluctant to provide a visual of the satellite pictures. However, my communication channels are so tough, even the NSA can't break in." A soft chuckle came over the phone speaker.

After a moment when she did not reply, Thomas got down to business. "Each side of the building is heavily guarded, but there are fewer guards on the north. There is a secondary line of attack in the adjacent alleyways covering a one-block radius. The troops appear to be tightening ranks around the derelict building. There's a lot of them, doll."

Thomas paused, clearing his throat. "There's something else."

"Well, what is it?" Greylyn gritted between clenched teeth. Her nerves were already frayed like live power lines after a hurricane.

"The image isn't too clear, seems to be a haze cast over it so we can't see it clearly. Whatever it is, it is well over seven feet tall, and weighs 250 pounds or more. Normally, their imagery could make out the smallest polka dot, but not this time. Fred is freaking out thinking that his software's on the fritz. I don't think that's the problem though."

"Well, any ideas what I'm dealing with?" Greylyn's heart raced as she held her breath waiting. This had to be the hulking figure she just saw.

"Nothing good. That's a certainty. The best I can make of the image, besides the size of it, is long, white hair. Seriously though, this thing's size alone makes Thor look like a tyke."

"Oh, shit!" Everyone in the alley turned to stare at her, waiting for the bad news.

"What, doll? You have an idea who or what this is?" The Thor reference was all she needed.

Olivier!

Bile rose in her throat. Olivier was a notoriously evil archangel who took the mere existence of humans as a personal affront to himself and all angels. Rumor had it that he was the one who whispered evil tidings into Lucifer's ears just prior to the *Fall*. The story was never proven, but it was never disproven either.

"Ever heard of Olivier?" she asked.

A sharp intake of breath heard from the other end of the line affirmed that Thomas had most definitely heard of him. "Apparently, there's volumes of books on this dude, but I have to say I'm not up to speed on the particulars of fallen angels. But this guy's name stands out. Seems he has a particularly nasty side when it comes to dealing with guardian angels. There aren't many ways to kill a guardian angel, but he seems to specialize in it."

Wow! How'd I get so lucky?

"Wait! How did I miss that?"

"What is it, Sparky?"

Tapping her foot nervously against a pile of broken bricks, she awaited his response. "You know I told you about Kael being photographed with a high-ranking power of Hell?"

The pregnant pause that followed the question left her breathless. A painful knot formed in the pit of her belly.

It was Olivier. Greylyn's heart stopped. *Dammit, Kael!*

Dread rose in her very soul at the possibility she would have to confront one of the most heinous fallen archangels in history. If he were in cahoots with Kael, she had just left Kelly defenseless against the enemy.

What had she done? Furious at herself for allowing Kael to worm his way into her good graces to the point she would trust him, an image of driving her dagger into his blackened heart and watching blood ooze out his eyes flickered before her mind.

"I've read plenty of tales of encounters with fallen angels. Most of the lore on the subject is false. But this guy ..." Thomas's voice trailed off.

Not wanting to alarm him further, Greylyn calmly thanked him for the information and hung up the phone before he could ask any questions to which she did not want to answer.

The four men looked at her for reassurance. They expected her to have the answers. Sadly, she had none to give them. Even Jasper was at a loss for words, evidenced by the way he chewed on the edge of a fingernail with downcast eyes.

Silently, she paced the cramped alleyway for an agonizing couple of minutes, as she struggled to come up with a solution that did not border on suicide.

This must be what the Spartans felt like before Thermopylae.

Realizing her options were limited if she wanted to keep casualties to a minimum, a plan formed in her mind. Not a good one, but her options were lacking.

This was her mess to clean up. She would not allow the others to pay for her fatal mistake of trusting a dark guardian. Finally determined on a path, the only thing she said before marching off towards the apartment building was, "Wait here. Do nothing."

Jasper opened his mouth to argue, but one blazing look silenced him.

If Jasper did something stupid – of course, he would do something stupid – the whole situation could easily blow up in their faces. The residents of DC could wake up to the equivalent of the aftermath of an atomic bomb going off in the middle of their city.

"Please, Jasper," Greylyn prayed, "do as I say, not as I do. Stay put." Telepathically, she begged him, "If I don't make it back, hurry to the inn and make sure everyone is okay."

"What the bloody hell are you doing, Greylyn?"

As a precaution, she quickly chanted an imprisonment spell to keep them locked safely behind the deli. It would not hold long, but she hoped long enough for her to do what she had to do. Before Jasper could question or curse her insanity, either by voice or his mind, she shut down all avenues of communication between them.

She detoured through more connecting alleyways to disguise where she had come from. Within minutes, she emerged from the unlit alley immediately in front of the besieged apartment building.

Out in the open, she stood there, completely still, waiting for the demons guarding the building to attack. Her heart hammered so loudly in her ears she was deaf to all else.

Nothing. They did nothing. It was not as if they did not see her. She was in plain sight. A few snarled and growled in her direction, but not one of them moved towards her. If they wanted her, well here she was.

Now that cannot be good.

Her lungs burned with the need for oxygen, but she just could not force herself to breathe. Chewing on her lower lip, she waited. After a few moments and still no reaction from the demon platoon, she marched forward to the building's front entrance where the giant fallen angel waited with a smug grin.

The demon soldiers moved aside to let her pass without challenge, for the most part. One ugly creature with pointed teeth, looking as if its face was turned inside out, lashed out at her. Without hesitation, Greylyn sliced its arm off at the elbow. The demonic being retreated into the horde with an ear-splitting howl that echoed down the deserted city streets.

Upon closer inspection of the group, it was quite the mixed primordial soup of creatures. How Olivier managed to coerce such a large range of monsters into his own little army surprised even her. Most of these creatures did not get along with each other. Several so-called natural disasters over the years had really been the various clans of monsters going after each other in gangland-style skirmishes. She could not imagine what would unite such a hideous group. The situation must be much bigger than anyone could comprehend to have elicited such a profound turnout of Hell's most wanted.

She approached the front of the building where Olivier waited with a self-satisfied smarmy smile and a chuckle.

With his gigantic hand outstretched towards her, in an elegant British accent he intoned, "Good evening, Greylyn. As you can see," his over arm indicated the army surrounding them, "I've been waiting for you."

Chapter 25

Olivier

Well, if those words did not strike fear into a guardian angel's heart, nothing would.

Greylyn steeled herself against the panic flooding her entire body. The thumping of blood pounding through her brain drowned out all else for just a moment as her heart fought to break free of her ribcage.

She did not question why Olivier would stoop to know the identity of a guardian so far down on the angelic totem pole. The mere fact that he did was enough to instill terror, evidenced by the uncontrollable trembling in her limbs as her knees threatened to give way. But there were people inside the dilapidated brick building that could die horrible deaths if she did not step up to defend them. Even if that meant facing off against the next worst thing to Lucifer himself.

Taking a few deep but ragged breaths, she craned her neck to look Olivier in the face. "How nice of you to go all out with the welcoming committee, but really, you shouldn't have gone to so much trouble." She heard the tremor in her own voice.

A wide smile overcame Olivier's face. "Nothing is too good for you, my dear. I have been waiting to meet you officially for some centuries now. Just never had the *right* opportunity."

Greylyn took in his seven-foot, muscular frame, long flowing platinum blond hair, and nearly glowing aquamarine eyes. Yes, the Thor description was right on...if Thor was also a giant. Olivier certainly looked more the part of the fair-featured demi-god than a villain. Excellent façade for someone so purely diabolical.

He was dressed all in black – a stylish and expensive business suit with a red power tie and shiny black dress shoes. Olivier looked like he was headed to the opera, not to a battlefield.

"Nice suit," she quipped in an attempt at bravado. "Hope you know a good dry cleaner." His soft chuckle filled the air. His laughter was hypnotic, almost flirty. Something about Olivier invisibly tugged her closer to him. Unable to fight it, she found herself staring up into his neon orbs with barely an inch between their bodies.

He took her arm in the crook of his own and led her to a small wooden bench just outside the entrance to the apartment building. Greylyn had never felt pure, unadulterated evil before now. No doubt, she had gone up against various forms of evil over the centuries, but this was overwhelmingly different. Her skin felt like she was tied to a spit over the fiery pit of Hell, while her insides roasted, and the oppressive smoke choked her lungs.

Olivier gestured for her to take a seat. Unable to share the small bench with her, he pulled up a lawn chair that someone must have left behind. She was surprised when the chair did not collapse under his massive frame. Inwardly she was grateful for even the short distance. The air cooled instantly.

For several minutes he looked her over as if he were surveying a piece of artwork. She could almost swear that he was peering into her very soul, reading her every thought and emotion. It did not feel intimate, though; she felt violated.

Unable to stand his scrutiny any longer, Greylyn broke the silence before her nerves got the best of her. "To what do I owe this privilege of a face-to-face meeting with one of the most notorious fallen archangels in existence?" Damn, there was still a slight tremor in her voice. "If I had known in advance, I would've dressed up a bit more. Her hand indicated his designer suit and then her torn jeans, tee-shirt, and sneakers. "Next time you wish for a meeting be sure to indicate cocktail attire on the invitation."

A loud guffaw echoed across the empty streets and alleyways. Looking around, she noticed that the demon army had drawn back. Olivier seemed deep in thought as he continued his inspection of her. His eyes had narrowed to slits and a wry smile played on his lips. Clearing her throat, she hoped to break the uncomfortable silence.

His perfect teeth displayed in a wide smile. "For such a tiny thing you certainly have caused a lot of trouble. How have you survived all these years?" Without bothering to wait for her answer, he continued, "By listening to all the tales from those you have defeated, the ones who lived to tell the tale anyway, I would have thought you'd be more the Pink Power Ranger type. I didn't expect to meet such a wisp of a creature."

Was that a compliment?

After a slight pause, he added, "Not that I'm complaining. You are quite extraordinarily lovely. I would wager Aphrodite herself would pale in comparison. She is taller though." A perfectly manicured hand reached out to stroke her flushed cheek, causing searing tremors to race over her body, and not in a good way.

"I may be a wisp, but I can still pack quite a punch." The terse tone of her voice conveyed more bravery than she felt.

"You misunderstand. I am highly impressed. Perhaps your size led others to underestimate you but be sure I won't make that mistake." To emphasize his point, he leaned over to pat her knee as if she were an errant child.

She jerked away. "At the risk of being impolite, how about we discuss *why* we are meeting and under these circumstances. Apparently, you were expecting me, but I have to say that I was not expecting you." Greylyn clasped her hands to keep them from shaking.

"Not at all, dear. As a matter of fact, we *should* discuss our situation. It is a most unfortunate one ... for you and those innocent humans in the building anyway. However, we could possibly come to an arrangement to benefit all parties involved and avoid an unfortunate and ugly incident altogether."

The way he raised his platinum eyebrows did not instill confidence he truly meant his words. His neon green eyes flashed crimson for a split second. With a flick of his wrist, the building exploded outward, fireballs shooting in all directions. The force of the blast obliterated everything in a two-block radius, except for Olivier, herself, and the now howling demon soldiers.

Shrieking, Greylyn fell to her knees. Her ears rang from the thunderous sonic boom and tears poured down her cheeks. "No!"

Just as quickly, the building came back into focus. Still standing. Intact.

Unharmed. "It *can* be over with that quickly."

Giving her a second to recover from the shock of the realistic, but thankfully faux, explosion, Olivier continued. "Several months ago, this lovely young lady came to visit the old psychic woman. Sofia, isn't it? The reports from this particular visit were highly interesting since the lady in question had already been in our sights for many years. Since birth actually."

Chills ran down her spine at his words. He was talking about Kelly.

He stopped for a moment, peering into her eyes to ascertain her reaction to the news. Try as she might to remain inscrutable, she felt a nerve jumping in the corner of her left eye.

"You see, she's much more important than you could possibly imagine."

Pinpricks of pain stabbed her lower abdomen as Olivier continued his tale. "Kelly has been fun to play with over the years. But I have grown bored with the game. It's time to take things up a notch."

His glowing eyes lit up the darkness around them as he beamed with playful glee.

"You see, Kelly was playing right into my hands until the *love of her life* waltzed in to give her hope." His sneer clearly expressed what he thought of love. "WHAM! She's pregnant! It's a bloody miracle!"

Olivier laughed. The look in his eyes was one of fury, not jest.

"Oh, things could've been just lovely – for me anyway – but early indications were that the child lacked a certain *quality*. Sadly, in walks Abyzou to sit beside her on a plane, and ... the game continues." Abyzou was an infertile female demon who reportedly inflicted miscarriages to compensate for her own jealousy of not being able to have her own child.

Unthinking, she jumped up to strike at the smug bastard. Out of nowhere, strong hands knocked her back so hard she toppled over the bench. She had not even seen the movement. He was that fast.

"Now, now, dear, sit down and let me finish. It's rude to interrupt in the middle of a story."

He held out a manicured hand, the same one he just utilized to shove her, to help her off the ground. Her palm burned as if she had touched a hot grill. Once she was settled back on the bench, he began again.

"Kelly was devastated beyond belief, poor thing. She blamed God. She blamed herself. She blamed everyone but us. Big win for me." His smile faded into a deep scowl. "I underestimated true love."

Trying to sound calmer than she really felt, Greylyn swallowed the saliva that had built up at the base of her throat. "So why not just admit defeat and move on? I'm sure your kind have bigger issues than a tiny woman trying to start a family."

She hoped he would give her an indication, any indication, of what made Kelly so important. Was it because she was Nephilim? A guardian angel in waiting? Both? Neither?

"Oh, darling," he emitted a deep-throated, sinister chuckle. "Kelly is, shall we say, vital to my plans. If not Kelly, then most definitely the child she now carries. Come on, I know you have felt the power emanating from the baby in her womb. It's extraordinary!" His incandescent eyes gleamed in the darkness.

He was not wrong. Greylyn had sensed its light even though Kelly was barely in the second trimester. But quite frankly, she had not given it much thought, she had been too wrapped up in saving them both from a mysterious evil that she had not pondered what it meant.

She decided to agitate him on the issue to see if he would reveal anything. "So, why the monster army besieging innocents? You cannot expect me to believe that the great and mighty Olivier has nothing better to do than scare humans on a Saturday night. Shouldn't you be overseeing a new torture chamber in the west wing of Hell or something?"

He let out another guffaw. Leaning forward, patting her knee again, Olivier positioned his face mere inches from her own. His eyes, sparkling like the Dead Sea in the middle of a raging storm, peered with steel into her own as he uttered his next words. "Kelly and all those supposed innocents in the building behind us were just the pawns to get to you, darling."

Huh?

He allowed his words to sink in. Her stomach convulsed. Sofia had been right. This was more about her than anything. The others were in danger because of her. Kelly and the baby were simply a ploy. She did not know if she should be relieved or not.

"You see, this game started with you centuries ago. You disappointed me. Took your game piece off the chess board, so to speak. And now others may pay the price for your failure."

She had disappointed him. How? At no point of time did she recall ever encountering Olivier.

Trying to keep her wits about her, she barely squeaked out, "So now here I am. You can leave them alone. However, if you wanted a face-to-face chat, all you had to do was ask."

With a devious grin, Olivier stood up and motioned for Greylyn to join him. He took her arm in his again, causing nausea and a headache to surge.

A huge uproar from the demonic army surrounding them pierced the otherwise quiet night. A banshee howled in the distance mixing with the screams from the rest of the monsters encamped around them. Jasper must have broken the imprisonment spell.

Dammit!

Sure enough, several yards away Greylyn saw Jasper and the others slashing and stabbing their way through Olivier's minions. All the while, he screamed for Olivier to unhand her. She would have laughed at his hero machismo if the situation had not been so deadly.

The overbearing fallen archangel grasped her arm in a steel-rod grip causing intense pressure and pain to shoot down into her fingertips and up to the base of her skull.

Knowing, despite Jasper's skill, he and the hunters had no chance against this army of demonic thugs, she turned to face Olivier. "Let them walk away. They have nothing to do with this."

"Oh, dear. This is just starting to be fun." Flames danced in his eyes.

As if to make the point for her, one of the men, the trucker with the stained flannel shirt and beer breath, let out a screech no human should ever make. The roar of a small group of demons to the far right signaled they had delivered a death blow. Snarls permeated the air, as the victors descended on their prey, along with the repulsive noises of a feeding frenzy.

Flailing her arms and legs around with all her strength, Greylyn struggled to break free of Olivier's clutches to no avail. His grip only tightened, as the bones in her arm crackled near the breaking point.

"Please, stop this now and I'll do whatever it is you need." Tears ran down her face as she waited for his response to her desperate plea.

With a mischievous gleam in his eyes, he bellowed, "Cease!"

On command, every demon stopped in its tracks. Never had she witnessed such absolute control as Olivier wielded over his minions. Never. It was like watching an army of robots when the off switch flipped. Malphas would be envious.

"Bring them to me." His sinister tone, despite the elegant accent, sent a new wave of fear shuddering through her.

Neither Jasper nor the remaining hunters came willingly. They fought and struggled, but in vain. Bloody but alive, they were brought before Olivier. The humans were clearly terrified. Jasper was just pissed. Even as blood gushed down his handsome face from a cut above his eye, he glared down the fallen archangel as if he were nothing more than a low-level demon rat.

Greylyn almost laughed when he spit a mouthful of saliva and blood onto Olivier's fancy dress shoes.

"Hello," the archangel hissed. "Now what shall I do with you? The one and only Jasper Moreau. It's a pleasure."

With his fist raised to throw a deadly blow straight to Jasper's face, Greylyn jumped in front of Olivier to stop him. The way he smiled at her caused new waves of nausea to assault her body. He had gotten the reaction he wanted from her.

She uttered one word, "Unharmed."

With more than a hint of annoyance, he finally spat out, "Fine!"

A sharp snap of his fingers resounded in the air. Jasper and the others fell to the ground unconscious as if they were simply rag dolls. "That should take care of them for a while. Long enough for us to conduct our business anyway." With one last glance back at his army, he snarled, "Hands off." Again, he took her arm and led her around the little park in front of the apartment building.

"So, what exactly is it that you need from me?" She no longer tried to quell the tremor in her voice. The effort was pointless anyway.

"Darling Greylyn. Sofia and the other occupants of this decaying hulk of a building are in fear for their lives merely because, after Kelly's visit a few months ago, we knew that you would eventually end up here."

"Wow! Didn't realize I was so popular that you had your personal paparazzi following me as well." The reference to Kael went unacknowledged.

"To entice you back – an invitation, as it were – I noticeably increased the number of soldiers and ratcheted up the threat."

He paused and turned to face her, with a sneer blemishing his otherwise perfect features. "My dear, the lives of those in the building are nothing to me. Kelly and her child are none of my concern." He paused as if in consideration of his last words. "Well, not really. They are secondary players, but players nonetheless if you do not cooperate. Everyone can walk away from this freely if the price is right."

Afraid to ask but knowing she had to, she heard herself in a near whisper say, "And what exactly is the right price?"

Olivier patted her hand sending searing pain up her arm. "I knew you would be reasonable." He was well assured of himself. To save lives, Greylyn would do anything. He must have known that from the beginning.

With a lump in her throat, she was barely able to ask, "Why me?"

"Ah, yes. The ever-useless question of 'why'. It doesn't matter, but if you insist." He took on the posture and tone of a snobby college professor as if lecturing a particularly trying group of students. His arms crossed over his thick chest as his eyes rolled upward. "Before you were made into a guardian angel, you were human. Well, sort of human. Your heritage is much more profound than that of a mere mortal. This guardian angel business is beneath your talents and *bloodline*."

The way he said *bloodline* so condescendingly raised the tiny hairs at the nape of her neck. What could he mean?

"So, Kelly and the child were a diversion to get to me? Why all the theatrics then? You could've just sent me an invitation in the mail or something," she said.

Olivier threw his head back and let out a loud, guttural laugh that sent shivers down her spine and out to her extremities.

"Well, my dear. The answer to your question is not quite so simple. It is both *yes* and *no*. Yes, you are the primary target. Yes, using Kelly and her unborn child was a means to get to you, but ... No, that was not the only reason. You see, they are my fallback if you fail to accomplish your mission."

That knot in her stomach grew as she realized they were in jeopardy because of her, no matter what she did right now.

"We've been waiting for a time when another would be born to fulfill a prophecy I'm intrigued by. The person had to be from the right bloodline and all sorts of other factors had to line up, making it nearly impossible." Clearly, this fact aggravated him as his eyes narrowed to small slits. "With only one Nephilim bloodline still in existence, the odds were against us."

Did he just say Nephilim? That word kept popping up, along with prophecy.

Trying to digest all this information, she racked her brain to recall what Kael had said about them. He was tasked to protect Kelly because they thought she was Nephilim.

Olivier continued, "Not every descendent possesses the talents and power needed for this particular task. So, we waited and watched. Kelly was brought to our attention as a possibility. She has the inner fire just below the surface so it's harder to detect. And unimaginable gifts if she'd just access that part of her being." He shook out his long platinum mane. "The child ... well, he's extraordinary beyond even my expectations. But ..." he looked deep into Greylyn's eyes before he concluded, "there's no substitute for the original."

Stunned silent, her breath caught in her throat, Olivier's words shot through her mind. Nephilim. Prophecy. What did this have to do with her?

After a moment he leaned in closer, so close that the heat from his breath nearly suffocated her. "You see, my dear, I am a traditionalist. I like simplicity. Elegance. That is my preference and always has been. To have the original main character play her prescribed role, not some understudy. Well, it is destiny. Your destiny."

Was he saying she was supposed to help fulfill this mysterious prophecy, but if she didn't, Kelly or the child could? That would mean they would stay in danger.

Olivier's eyes sparkled in the moonless night. "In the meantime, the alternate contestants will remain under my *protection* until they are needed, or not. For their sake, it's your job to make sure I don't require their services."

The archangel stepped back a few inches, leaving the air much cooler and breathable again.

One word kept flashing in her mind – Nephilim.

And then his words punched her in the gut: "... it's your destiny ..."

No, none of this could be right. Everything she had ever heard, up until today, had been that Nephilim were extinct. They had been hunted down and slaughtered by angels and demons because they were abominations.

But now the word "Nephilim" was bantered around as if it were the latest trendy mantra on everyone's lips.

Greylyn's mind spun madly, trying to make sense of it all. Nephilim or not, the fact remained, she had to do whatever was necessary to keep Kelly and her child safely away from Olivier. She knew her protectiveness of them surpassed the normal guardian angel job description. It was deeper and more personal.

The once sweltering and humid summer air had turned oddly cool during Olivier's remarks as goosebumps prickled her skin. Silently chiding herself for allowing fear to dominate her, Greylyn took a deep breath before staring directly into Olivier's eyes. She hoped to convey resolve and fearlessness. Willing her voice not to tremble, she finally asked the obvious question. "What exactly is it you want me to do? You can have my cooperation, but you and your minions will leave Kelly and her family *alone*. So much as a hair on their heads is harmed, and all bets are off." She inwardly cringed. She knew her statements sounded more like a bratty child giving an adult an ultimatum with no way to possibly retaliate if she did not get her way.

With a soft chuckle, Olivier broke eye contact and stepped away to slowly pace. "My dear, what fun would it be if I told you everything? Watching you squirm will be so delightful."

This was just peachy! She was left to do all the grunt work without knowing what she was even supposed to accomplish!

"Can't help you if I don't know what it is you want. Not going to help you if you continue to threaten Kelly and her child." Her fear was finally morphing into a more appropriate emotion … anger.

"Oh, don't fret. I have given my solemn promise to protect Kelly and the child, even from other less savory entities. I have gone to great lengths to keep them safe thus far. If you fulfill your end of the bargain, they will live rich and full lives, none the wiser to the danger they are in. If you do not," he paused for a more menacing effect, "then I will need them. So, either way, they will remain safe. With your easy willingness to cooperate, I am feeling generous. To sweeten the pot, I will even guarantee no other children of hers will be touched. Deal?"

He flashed a wide, perfect, smarmy smile. Despite his angelic good looks, she had never met a viler creature than this one, and that was saying something. She had met plenty of nasty monsters that would send the most courageous human into a permanent catatonic state of terror.

"Well, I need something to go on if I'm to do whatever it is you think I'm supposed to do." Pausing she decided to reveal her cards just a bit. "So, this has something to do with a prophecy. Based on your interest in me, I'm assuming you are in favor of this thing being fulfilled." He nodded smugly as if she were a rookie reporter asking a seasoned politician about whether he smoked weed in college.

"It may or may not have to do with Nephilim."

Olivier frowned and rolled his eyes. "Yes, only a Nephilim can do the work. And that is you." He shoved a perfectly manicured finger into her chest so hard she nearly toppled over.

Aside from not being sold on labeling herself as a Nephilim, Greylyn let the comment slip for the time being.

Regaining her balance, she glared at him. "So, what does this prophecy entail exactly?"

Another question popped up in her mind. She doubted he would answer, but it was worth a shot. "Also, you have yet to inform me how this supposed prophecy profits you."

Clearing his throat, Olivier strode back over to where she now stood with her hand placed on her right hip, less than an inch from where her dagger was hidden under her shirt. Her fingers itched with the need to pull it out and thrust it into Olivier's giant form. He noticed the miniscule twitch of her fingers and laughed.

"Really, my dear. You must know I'd rip your heart out and have it for a snack before you could wrap your fingers around the hilt of that paltry blade."

Her hands fell back to her sides. He was right, but the thought had been exhilarating.

"Now back to the issue at hand. Even if I wished to lay out the entire prophecy in front of you, I simply cannot. The written form of the prophecy was considered much too dangerous by my heavenly brothers."

Too dangerous to be written? That was bad, very bad.

Olivier rolled his eyes extravagantly upward and held up his hands to the sky. "They decided that it should remain unwritten. *Completely* unwritten. They went overboard trying to hide its existence, but Lucifer knew of it. He was there when it was foretold by another archangel. Even the host of Heaven could not bypass the prophecy, written or not. So shall it be written – or not – so it shall be done." Shrugging, he added, "Something like that anyway."

So, if he does not even know what it is, why does he want it done so badly?

To be honest, she did not want to know. If the angels thought it was too dangerous, that was enough to convince her.

"So, if it is not written, how am I supposed to find out what it says? Maybe it foretells how to kill you." Her lips curved up in a wry smile at the delicious thought.

"Well, my dear," Olivier's tone was all business, "that's up to you. I am interested in seeing its fulfillment. And no, I have no reason to believe it entails my demise. If it is what I imagine it to be, it could be the answer to everything I've ever imagined."

"Damn. Can't blame a girl for dreaming."

"You, my dear, are simply the means to an end. If anyone can discover the what, why, where, and how, that would be you. From what Lucifer has said, it all lies with you. He believes that our brothers left clues to be found, but only you could find them. Believe me, I've looked for millennia."

Well, that was not very reassuring. Being on Lucifer's radar terrified her more than anything. It was bad enough being accosted by Olivier.

"The original time for the achievement of the prophecy passed, due to your untimely death. Agents of Heaven and Hell thought that was the end of it, but I knew better." His smarmy grin grew wider. "However, with the lucky circumstance of your resurrection and the proper alignment of the stars, or something to that effect, it appears the prophecy has been rekindled. So, let's strike up the band and start this party."

With any luck, Greylyn hoped to crash that party.

"Just remember, with the power radiating from Kelly and the child, either would serve as a proper substitute if you fail." Goosebumps erupted over her entire body at his menacing tone.

Her head pulsated again as Olivier leaned in close to plant a soft kiss on her forehead. White-hot pain ricocheted through her skull as if she had been shot at point blank range.

"It's your job to make sure we don't have to pull them back in," every word punctuated with malice.

All this ruckus over a prophecy, and he was not even going to tell her what it was or how she supposedly played into it.

Olivier's mouth widened into a smug, fearsome-looking smile that did not make her feel any better about the situation. "Oh, one last thing you should know. I can guarantee that you will meet lots of resistance from both Heaven and Hell. Those above have no desire for this event to ever transpire. If the angels are so adamantly against it, things must not bode well for them if this thing comes to pass." His smile faded. "Surprisingly, there are those in Hell that wish to keep things as they are. Even Lucifer is against seeing the prophecy to fruition."

"You mean to tell me that Satan himself is against this thing? Man, your chances are not looking so good," she said with amusement.

"Actually, that means your chances aren't so good for surviving. It will be your pretty little ass on the line, so I advise you to tread carefully. Lucifer, as well as every angel in Heaven, will be looking to stop you. They did so once. They can do it again. But they should know by now that it is pointless. A prophecy is inevitable." He stared down at her. "This time we have to be smart. Last time you knew nothing. You were a hapless human with your full potential unrealized. Now, have an advantage. Becoming a guardian angel may have been foretold as well, so maybe we had to suffer that setback to get to where we are."

All this "we" stuff made bile rise in the back of her throat.

"After your human death, I have done everything in my power to protect those involved, including Kelly and her child. It's purely for personal, selfish reasons, but then I am a purely selfish being."

No kidding.

He continued in a stern, guttural voice. "Let me be clear. You are the one chosen thousands of years ago to fulfill this prophecy. You will do so, or I will seek out the young newlywed, soon-to-be mother, or her child as alternatives. They will not be given such preferential treatment as I am giving you now. In addition, the other innocents you seek to save will pay a high price for your refusal or failure to deliver what it is that I want." He raised his hand again as if to flick his wrist as he had done before when she saw the building explode and then return to normal.

With a pointed look behind him to the derelict apartment building in the center of the demonic siege, he ended with, "It is your choice, Greylyn. I urge you to choose wisely and quickly. My patience runs thin and my soldiers are thirsty for blood."

With his last statement, a fearsome howl came from the demonic army behind them. He gestured to where Jasper and the humans lay splayed out helpless on the ground. Even passed out on the asphalt, Jasper still had a cocky grin on his face. The same grin he wore all the time, whether he was seducing a room of ladies or lopping off some demonic creature's head with a machete.

The visual was a much-needed reality check as she fought the primal desire to slit Olivier's thick throat with her dagger. On second thought, sawing through his spinal cord slowly appealed to her inner sense of vengeance too.

But there was no other choice. She had to buy herself time. If she could keep Kelly and her family safe, it was worth it. To keep Jasper alive, she would give anything. He was her best friend and only person in the world who understood her life. And poor, frightened Sofia and her friends trapped inside the building, Greylyn knew she could not allow Olivier to unleash a demon army on them either.

No longer able to speak, she nodded. This is what personal attachments cost, the same reason she had tried, and obviously failed, to limit them.

With a self-satisfied smile, Olivier barked something to an oversized werewolf-looking creature in a language Greylyn did not understand, and she was fluent in hundreds of dialects. The being nodded his elongated head and turned around to deliver the same message to the rest of the beings circling the building. In an instant and in complete unison, the battalion of grisly creatures retreated, with some vanishing from sight immediately.

Olivier turned back to her with a fearsome glint in his eyes. His styled eyebrows raised. "Oh, I almost forgot. We need to seal our agreement."

Greylyn did not like the sound of that at all. Frozen in horror, she watched as Olivier stretched out his arm. The index finger of his right hand grew a long pointy fingernail in the span of a couple of seconds. With the razor-sharp nail he carved an unfamiliar symbol into his other palm. A blackish, but glowing liquid oozed out. He then caught her wrist and cut her palm in a swirling motion, like an infinity symbol.

Before she could react, Olivier clasped their bleeding palms together while saying words in another language. What was that? Enochian? Aramaic? Something else? So overcome by the moment, her blood thumping in her eardrums, Greylyn did not hear the words, just a low, guttural mumble.

The intermingling of their blood sent an explosion starting in her hand and then burning up her arm and throughout her body. The painful sensation ended in her heart where the heat flared briefly, then cooled, leaving behind something akin to a lump of coal.

Doubtful that she had made the right decision, but not seeing an alternative, Greylyn accepted her fate with abject terror coursing through her veins. She was now tied to one of the deadliest fallen angels next to Lucifer himself.

Olivier raised her hand to his lips. As they brushed against her skin, he vanished into a thunderous funnel cloud. In a matter of seconds, he was gone.

Chapter 26

The Aftermath

Sofia's Apartment

With Olivier's departure, the surrounding air returned to hot and miserably humid. Sweat broke out all over Greylyn's body as she rushed to Jasper's side.

"Wake up, wake up!" Shaking him violently, his eyes slowly blinked open. The others took a little longer to come around.

"What the hell?" was all Jasper could say.

Looking around at the now vacant neighborhood streets, Greylyn confirmed that every last demonic creature was gone. Not one remained. Even the illusive shadow creatures had vanished. The streets were empty. The streetlights buzzed back to life and crickets chirped once again.

Reassured that Jasper was not permanently damaged, she had to take a moment to gather her wits. The whole experience had been surreal and terrifying. Now that it was over, her stomach roiled. Hands on her knees, Greylyn took several deep breaths to ease the nausea. The cut on her hand had sealed shut, but still burned. She suspected there would be a scar to mark her deal with the devil. No angelic healing would cure that.

She turned to stare at the building. The evil energy that surrounded it slowly dissipated as the blackness faded back to the electric blue force field Sofia had put in place. The foyer light fixture began to hum as it returned to life. She pushed the heavy door open as if it weighed nothing, and then sprinted up the stairs to Sofia's apartment. Along the way there were sounds from the residents of other apartments. She wondered if they had even noticed the demon siege or if they had been blissfully ignorant of it all.

There was no need to knock on the door; it swung open. The psychic and her friends began to slowly emerge from the back workroom. Shell-shocked expressions greeted her – some with reddened eyes and others pale as cheesecloth. Only Sofia smiled with gleaming eyes when she caught sight of Greylyn in the doorway.

Each person looked to her with a question in their eyes that did not need to be asked: "Is it all over?" That was all that was important.

She gave the biggest smile she could muster and hoped it was enough to reassure them as they filed out of the apartment and to their respective homes. All except Sofia. Surprisingly, the ordeal did not appear to have scathed the elderly woman as she softly padded into her kitchen and motioned for Greylyn to follow.

The lights flickered back on, and Sofia fired up the outdated gas stove to put a tea kettle on to boil water. She shuffled around the room, humming softly while opening and closing cupboards and arranging a small snack tray of crackers and peanut butter. She then set about cutting apple slices as if she were hosting a tea party for a friend instead of having just survived a demon siege.

Every muscle in Greylyn's body cried out in weariness as she collapsed in a vinyl chair at the small round 1970's style Formica-topped dinette table and laid her head down on her crossed arms. It was so quiet in the apartment now that both women jumped slightly as the kettle started to sing on the stove. They both uttered small giggles. After the events of the evening, a tea kettle seemed innocent enough.

Sofia poured the light brown liquid into tiny teacups with faded and scratched painted daisies on the sides. The two women sat silently for a few more minutes as they tentatively sipped their beverages and nibbled on the crackers. The tea was fragrant with hints of chamomile. The ritual soothed Greylyn's frayed nerves.

How was she supposed to explain what had happened to this sweet woman? She knew the truth would be difficult to believe, if not impossible, even for a medium as powerful as Sofia. Anything less than the truth would be a disservice to her newfound friend. Besides, Greylyn knew she would understand her dilemma.

After taking another sip of her tea, she pushed her teacup aside and began her tale. "First, how are you, Sofia? Really? I am so sorry you and your friends had to endure something so awful." Greylyn continued to explain what transpired outside the building, including Olivier's ultimatum.

Sofia listened intently as she sipped her tea, her gaze never leaving Greylyn's face. Deep- rooted concern showed in her weary eyes. Occasionally, she would utter a soft "*tch, tch*" noise or would nod or shake her head.

"And there you have it. I'm now in cahoots with a notorious fallen archangel."

The psychic bowed her silver head as if in prayer. After a few moments, she looked back up with a smile and placed her wrinkled, arthritic hands over Greylyn's as a sign of reassurance. "My child," she began, "you did the only thing you could do under the circumstances. And now we know more than we did yesterday." She absently picked at a slice of cheese while contemplating the tale. "I knew when Kelly first came into my apartment that she and the child were special but could not ascertain how or why. We can continue to work to keep them protected, but they are no longer my greatest concern. It seems that this has all been some elaborate ploy to get to you, my dear. I fear for your safety."

Before she could respond, Jasper and his cohorts burst through the apartment door. Blood soaked their clothes and dripped onto the carpet. No deep, fatal wounds as far as Greylyn could tell, which was remarkable. The only casualty lay slain in the middle of the street in pieces. Sadly, the tall, rotund trucker turned demon hunter had hunted his last.

Now back to his full, vibrant self, Jasper stepped into the kitchen. When he saw her sitting calmly at the tiny table, he stopped in his tracks and let out a string of curses. "What the hell, Greylyn? Mon Dieu! Putain! You could've been ..."

He caught sight of the elderly woman sitting across from her with a delicate teacup poised just inches from her face. Flashing her a contrite smile, he quickly apologized for his foul language.

Recovered from his injuries, Jasper ran over and picked up Greylyn in a bear hug then tenderly set her back down on her feet. Without letting her go he proclaimed, "That is absolutely the *last* time you charge in alone! What were you thinking? That imprisonment spell?"

Giving her a stern look, he asked the obvious. "How are you not dead?"

With a soft laugh, both women chimed in, "Sit down." Greylyn added, "You're going to hyperventilate if you don't calm down."

To give the two guardians much needed time alone, Sofia escorted the wounded men towards the bathroom where she could attend to their injuries. It was best not to let more people in on this little secret.

Motioning for Jasper to join her at the table, Greylyn explained in brief detail about what had transpired. It was the talking points version, minus a few key details.

One: she did not want to completely freak him out so soon after he was almost killed by a fallen archangel.

Two: she needed time to process everything that transpired without her bestie having a full-blown fit. She had confided in Sofia because she knew the woman would not overreact and do something to make matters worse. Jasper ... well, his easily inflamed temper was not what she needed to deal with at the moment.

Three: she did not want the others to overhear the particulars. Nothing good ever came of feeding the hunters' grapevine of gossip. Best to keep the important stuff to herself for a while. She fully intended to fill in Jasper later, except possibly for the crucial part where she agreed to be Olivier's go-to girl.

Jasper had been there for her since the first moment she emerged from the grave. Albeit their first meeting was not the greatest. She had remained mad at him for some time for leaving her to dig her own way out. He also had been slow to fully explain her situation. But he had proven himself a true friend. After four centuries together, he had more than earned her trust.

To recall all they had experienced together would be impossible. To recount the adventures, remember the conversations, and to understand how watching the march of history, so many lives and so many deaths, had changed them in similar and dissimilar ways ... was beyond her. But their connection filled her soul and made her eternal lonely existence more bearable.

Jasper had remained with her for many years just to help her acclimate to her new life and teach her the ropes. He even set up a bank account for her with his own money so she would not have to live a destitute life as she wandered the world. Even when they did not work together, he always checked in after each assignment. He was the one constant in her life. She owed him and respected him. More than anything, she despised keeping secrets from him. If anyone could help her, it would be Jasper. He would not count the cost, but she would. The weight of the pain of keeping him in the dark pressed down on her like a stack of mason bricks. It saddened her deeply to know that she was on her own now. She refused to pull her best friend into this debacle. He had been so close to death at Olivier's hands, she just could not accept putting him back in to the fallen angel's path.

After securing the building, the other demon hunters left with profuse thanks to Sofia for her hospitality and incredible fortitude under such extreme circumstances. They had to hurry to care for the remains of their friend before someone else found him and called the police.

She looked up at the clock. It was nearly 3 AM!

For all her calmness and strength throughout the grueling events of the day and evening, even Sofia showed signs of fatigue. It was remarkable the elderly woman had held up so well. Jasper even commented how impressed he was. "Sofia, you are quite a feisty lady. I wish everyone we saved had nerves of steel like you."

Unsuccessfully stifling a yawn, Sofia admitted, "I believe I've reached my limit of excitement for one day. Time for sleep. Please stay and rest yourselves."

Grateful for the invitation, Greylyn knew she had to return to Gaelic Haven. After all, leaving Kael to guard Kelly had been one of the dumbest decisions she had ever made.

Jasper was less than enthusiastic about the plan. "Come on, Grey! You do not seriously intend to go back there. Let me handle that dirtbag for you." His desire to do so gleamed in his icy eyes.

"Absolutely not! This is my mess. Besides, I need to see Kelly one last time. Make sure she is really okay." Biting her lower lip, she paused. "However, I do need one last favor."

"One last favor? Ha! It's never one and it's never the last but shoot." He flashed his signature smile.

"Would you stay here, at least tonight ... *just in case*? It would make me feel so much better." Of course, she did not admit that if he stayed here, he could not kill Kael.

Batting his thick, long, luscious lashes at her, "Come on, that lovely brocade sofa looks comfy and big enough for two."

She was used to his flirty theatrics but always laughed them off. Sometimes she suspected he was not joking, but she never allowed the thought to linger. It made her inexplicably nervous.

They remained at the small dinette table for another half hour or so as she filled him in on the details she had skipped when the hunters were present. When he heard that Olivier had intentionally lured her there, and was the source of all this torment, Jasper's usual light-heartedness turned to profound concern. He was more than painfully aware of the damage that one fallen angel could dish out, much less a fallen archangel. She had never seen her friend so out of sorts before, and that was saying something considering all they had been through.

"All this, just to set up a meeting with you. Seems a bit overdone. What does he want with you?"

Oh, the dreaded question. And the one she could not fully answer just yet.

"Doesn't matter. Maybe that is how he gets his kicks. Thought he would frighten a little guardian angel. What's done is done. All that matters is Kelly and the baby are safe."

He stared at her across the table. His long, dark hair falling over to obscure one of his iridescent blue eyes. Jasper was not buying her act. She was a terrible actor, she knew it. The trouble with knowing someone for such a long time was that person could tell when one was lying. Jasper's anxiety was obvious as he rubbed the bridge of his nose.

More than anything, Greylyn wanted to throw herself into his reassuring arms, sobbing and blurting out the entire horrid story. She wanted nothing more than to break down and let Jasper soothe her and tell her that everything was going to be okay. He would take care of everything. Just as he had done several times in the past. Instead, she dug her nails into the palms of her clenched fists to fight the urge to confess.

For the first time in her afterlife, Greylyn lied to her best friend about something more important than her attraction to a dark guardian. It went against her very soul to do so, but she had no illusions it was for the best. She would not allow Jasper to risk it all for her.

"Jasper, who really knows what Olivier's motives are? He wanted Kelly and her child. With all the work Sofia and I have done, he realized he could not break the protection barriers to get at them. He wasn't happy about it, so he lured me here. I do not believe for a second that this is the last we will see of him. And I don't believe Kelly is completely out of danger."

Hoping that she sounded convincing, she continued. "Apparently, I pissed him off enough to warrant a face-to-face meeting, so he arranged the siege on this place. He didn't try to hurt me, though, which is odd."

With those words, she clasped her hands together, hoping Jasper did not see the dried blood on her palm from her altercation with Olivier.

"Just warned me that this wasn't over yet."

"Greylyn, his type doesn't issue warnings. Hundreds of creatures were stalking the building for hours. I watched you waltz through an entire battalion of demonic creatures and you come out unscathed. Not even a bruise or broken bone."

He leaned over and tugged a stray strand of raven hair away from her eyes and tucked it behind her ear. All so she could not shield the truth from him. He could read everything through her eyes. They were that connected.

Nose to nose, eyes locked on hers. "Tell me the truth, hon. I cannot protect you if I do not know what is going on, and I *will* protect you always. I am not going to allow some over- achieving fallen angel to threaten so much as a hair on your head. Please. Just tell me."

Averting her gaze, she bowed her head. They sat together in the quaint, dimly lit kitchen with their foreheads touching for a few minutes in complete silence. With more strength than she believed she had; she lifted her face to his. The hardest thing she had ever had to do was to stare into those crystal eyes and tell him less than the truth and be convincing while doing it.

Her stare shifted between the worn Formica tabletop and Jasper's face as she attempted to reassure him. "I promise you that I am telling you everything I can for *now*. The important thing is that everyone is safe for the time being, including me, so please don't worry. If and when the situation changes, you will be the first to know."

His expression fell and a nerve twitched in his jaw. With a sigh, he reached across the table, pressing his lips to her forehead. Leaning back in the rickety chair that was much too small for his tall, muscular frame, the chair let out a muffled groan under the burden of his full weight.

He abruptly stood up and started rifling the kitchen cabinets. A genuine smile crept up the corners of Greylyn's lips as she realized what he was doing. "I got it." She made her way to the liquor cabinet she had noticed her first night here that was tucked away in a corner of the hallway. In a few moments she was back with her trophy, a half-empty bottle of potato vodka and two small shot glasses with engravings of seashells, sand dollars, and the words, "Sunning at the Seaside," apparent purchases from a long-ago beach vacation.

After filling the tiny glasses to the brim, she pushed one over to Jasper while she raised her own glass in a salute. Without a word, they both lifted the glasses to their lips and chugged back the clear liquid. It burned going down, but the heat was welcoming and soothing.

Jasper started to refill the glasses. Greylyn anxiously eyed the clock again. She needed to get back to Gaelic Haven to check on her charges before claiming a temporary victory. It was not a victory at all, just a lull in the fighting. For now, she needed a check mark in the win column.

Her stomach muscles clenched though. She knew there was something else important she had to deal with ... Kael. How exactly was he involved in this demonic endeavor? How much did he know? Had he kept his promise and protected Kelly, or had he laughed when she had left at her gullibility.

It was agreed that Jasper would stay there the rest of the night to keep watch on Sofia. Walking her to the door, he uncharacteristically crushed her in a big bear hug and squeezed her so tight she could not inhale. He had always shown affection before but something about this time seemed unusual. He enclosed her in his embrace as if truly afraid to let go.

As the grandfather clock in the foyer struck 5 AM, she reluctantly pulled away from him. Turning to leave, Jasper whispered in her ear, "You will tell me when you're ready to talk, right? I couldn't stand it if something bad happened to you when I could stop it."

Without answering, she turned to leave. It was not until she was out the front entrance of the building that she heard him close the door and her unshed tears scorched down her cheeks.

Chapter 27

Last Dance

Gaelic Haven

The Camaro made record time getting back to the inn. To avoid being distracted from the road by all the chaotic thoughts running around in her mind, a Def Leppard playlist blasted through the speakers the entire ride back. There was nothing like eardrum-splitting decibels of rock-n-roll music to eradicate all negative thoughts. The highway scenery blurred as she gunned the gas pedal all the way to the floor. With the glamour still intact to shield her speeding muscle car from the police, she arrived in less than an hour.

Creeping up the long gravel driveway in an attempt to not wake anyone, Greylyn caught a glimpse of a human-shaped shadow on top of the metallic roof of the main house. Without having to glance twice, she knew that it was Kael. How long he had been up there she could only imagine. At least he had taken his assignment of watching *over* everyone seriously.

Now her only hope was that he had been honest with her when he said he was there to keep Kelly and her child safe. If he was working with Olivier, of all foul miscreants, she needed to know. If he was working for other Hellish forces that did not maintain the same objective of keeping them safe, she needed to know that too.

A deep, hollow pit seemed to open in her gut as regret washed over her like a tsunami wave for having placed her faith in him. At the time she had not seen another choice available. He had lulled her into a strange sense of security. It was time to find out the truth.

After parking the car, she quietly tip-toed over to the main house and soundlessly climbed up to the roof using the smallest edges around the brick exterior. In the past, she had scaled more perilous heights, but not with her heart racing like this.

Their newfound intimacy unnerved her. She was grateful that they had never interacted so closely with each other in previous encounters considering all the rotten decisions she had made this weekend.

Despite the ordeals of the last couple of days, and extreme fatigue setting in, Greylyn knew she had one last loose end to wrap up before she could rest. It just so happened that loose end was an insanely sexy, yet infuriating, dark guardian. As stealthily as possible, she hauled herself up and over the edge of the forest-green roof and came face to face with the eyes of a tiger.

Kael's rich, husky voice whispered, "Well, it's about time you returned. Where in hell have you been?"

"Actually, you answered your own question. Hell, or close to it."

He reached out to pull her closer, but the electric shock of his touch made her flinch and tumble back over the side of the roof. As she clutched at the roof tiles with her legs dangling in the air, strong hands wrapped around her wrists to haul her to safety.

"Damn, Greylyn! You are such a klutz," Kael cursed without letting go of her wrists.

Recovering her footing, she shrugged in agreement. They looked at each other for an awkward moment then burst out laughing. For the third time this weekend, he had saved her. No wonder she was so confused. With a wicked grin, Kael motioned for them to climb down where they could talk without the risk of falling.

Once back on solid earth, he reached for her hand again. This time every nerve in her hand pulsated with energy. He led her over to the gazebo by the koi pond. Just a few short hours ago, she had performed a wedding ceremony there. There had been joy and laughter and love. So much had happened since the wedding.

All evidence of the celebration had been cleared away except a pair of wireless speakers and two champagne flutes perched beside a vase of yellow and purple calla lilies – quite the romantic setting.

Oh no! This does not look good. Time to bail.

"Listen, it's been a long day ..." She edged towards the Carriage House. "I ... I appreciate your ... your help, but ..."

When she turned, Greylyn ran into a wall made of Kael, eye level with his broad chest muscles, rippling through his thin cotton shirt.

How did he move around me so fast?

"Considering all the assistance I've provided you this weekend, the least I deserve is an update on what you've been up to all evening. Not to mention you owe me a dance." He reached for the champagne bottle and filled the flutes with the golden bubbly liquid. Once filled to overflowing, he handed her one and then raised his own, clinking the two together.

"Here's to enemies turned allies. Even if it is just this once."

She watched with fascination as he raised the flute to his lips and took a long sip, draining the glass. Acknowledging the toast by slightly raising her flute with a half-smile and an exaggerated roll of the eyes, she did not take a sip. Instead, she walked over to the small brick wall of the gazebo and placed the glass down.

"Thanks, but after my night I was thinking of something much stronger than this stuff. As for an update on tonight's events ... let's just say that things are settled ... for now anyway. All is taken care of, and you can go back to your evil ways as soon as you vacate the premises. However, I'll have to give you a rain check on that dance."

Her mind was already fogging up just being near him. She had arrived with a clear mind and purpose, but now struggled to remember what that was. It clawed at the back of her brain, like a cat on a scratching post. All she could see was Kael. All she felt was the overpowering need to lift her hands to his chiseled face and bring his lips down to hers. One last flicker of sanity reared up before she fell victim to her own desire. Just that one second of clarity rang loudly like an alarm bell ... *Get away from him as fast as you can ... or gut him now.*

Never throughout their countless encounters had she dared to think of him as anything but evil. Insanely attractive ... yes, but evil, nonetheless. Being thrown together like this had taken its toll on her. She could not deny the attraction any longer. The burden would weigh on her for the rest of her existence. Deprived of the luxury of a romantic personal connection to anyone for centuries, and here she had fallen for a dark guardian. She could not mess up any more horrifically than that.

Greylyn knew any future meetings with him would be much more dangerous. His mere presence muddled her brain. He made her weak. And the worst part was that he knew it too.

Even as she tried walking away, a live wire sizzled inside her, waiting for that one small touch to set off a spark. That spark could incinerate her. If anything, this weekend had shown her how deep-seated her vulnerability to him was. She did not trust herself anywhere near him anymore.

What faint hope she had of simply walking away faded in an instant. Before she took a step, Kael's hand reached out and grabbed her wrist to stop her retreat. All resistance fled as she blindly allowed him to lead her over to a small stone bench.

Bowing over her hand, planting a soft kiss on her palm. "Well then, let me assist you one last time. I'll run into the house and grab us some stronger drinks. Wait here." His tone was gentle yet firm. His message clear. He was not going to take *no* for an answer. Sheer exhaustion and lack of will kept her from doing the reasonable thing: leave immediately, hide in her room. She was certain if she did, he would knock down the door to get to her, regardless of the pain it would cause.

Resigned, Greylyn looked out over the horizon as the moon continued its descent. It was not even until that moment that she realized the cloud cover had dissipated completely, and the sky was a magnificent scene of dazzling stars and a nearly iridescent full moon. Sunrise could not be far away as the sky had already begun to fade to a deep purple hue.

A sense of peace washed over her mind and body as she listened to the bull frogs' song intermingled with the fainter symphony of crickets and other nocturnal creatures. A soft breeze rustled tendrils of her hair. A fish jumped in the pond. Her gaze fell to the water where she stared in fascination at the smooth ripples along the surface before turning up her face again to the masterpiece above.

Unsure how long she had been gazing up at the stars, the moment of tranquility vanished when a soft crunch on the gravel path announced Kael's return.

"Here you go. One extra strong beverage as ordered by the lovely little angel." Giving her a mock bow, he handed her a leaden glass tumbler of deep amber liquid.

She took the glass and nodded her thanks but waited to see if he would drink from his tumbler first. With a provocative wink, he held out his free hand.

"Here. Give me your glass."

He then proceeded to take a sip from his glass and then hers as if to prove his innocence. "Happy, now?"

Accepting her tumbler back with a small, embarrassed laugh, Greylyn took a long swig. The amber liquid tasted bitter yet with just enough sweetness. It had been years since she had an honest to goodness "Godfather," half scotch whiskey, half amaretto. Based on the smoothness of the beverage, he had used the good stuff too. Just what she needed after the ordeal of the last couple days. Too bad he had not brought the liquor bottles out with him. She was sure she was going to need another.

How had he known the perfect drink for her? The question lingered for just a second before she gave up caring about the answer.

An awkward silence settled between them as they sat and enjoyed the warmth of the scotch. She realized that this was probably the first time, and maybe the last as well, when two such opponents would be this close without trying to kill each other. A quiet giggle escaped.

Kael raised an eyebrow in question.

"Oh, come on. This is a rather hysterical historical moment that sounds more like a bad bar joke. 'A guardian angel and a dark guardian walk into a bar ...'"

They both burst out laughing, startling the bull frogs into silence.

She was certain that no one she knew would see the hilarity of the situation. Jasper's reaction alone ... oh, she did not even want to consider that right now. There was no way he would ever understand or condone this behavior. He would expect her to slice and dice Kael to ribbons, not this.

Honestly, she could not even think about Jasper right now, or anyone or anything else for that matter. Kael's closeness shut out all thoughts, particularly those of common sense. She had had a purpose when she arrived. To ask him something. To pummel him into a bloody pulp for something. Nothing registered in her brain.

When his arm brushed up against hers, heat radiated outward, warming her entire body. Blood pounded like a bass drum in her ears. Everything else blurred.

As they continued to sit in silence, the sky lightened to a dusty purple haze, and the glittering stars faded away. The bull frogs did not take up their chorus again and the crickets fell silent.

Even as the whiskey took effect and eased the built-up tension in her body, a figment of sanity flared. That inner spark deep within would not shut off the danger alarm.

Downing the remainder of the beverage in one long gulp, she stood up to leave. With what she hoped came off as a nonchalant tone, Greylyn briefly turned to face her nemesis with her own stoic mask in place.

"Thanks for the drink, but I really need some rest. It's been a hard couple of days." Even Greylyn realized how trite she sounded. Her hopes of an easy escape went up in flames as he stood up lightning fast and caught her elbow.

"Not so fast, little one. You owe me a little more than a mere, 'Thank you.' At the very least I deserve to know what you've been up to away from here, especially since you sustained such injuries last night. I'm simply happy you returned in one piece this time." As if to hold her in place, his large hands rubbed up and down her arms.

His golden eyes darkened to a burnt umber hue, radiating intensity and determination with those words but glinted with mischievousness the next second. "Besides, you are crazy if you think you're leaving without a dance."

Before she had a chance to object, he pulled her over to the cover of the gazebo. Without another word, he pressed a button on his phone. Soft piano music began to play from the wireless speakers. With a giggle, she recognized the song ... a Jim Brickman piece called "Partners in Crime." Obviously fitting to mark the occasion when two enemies came together for a common purpose.

Taking advantage of her moment of mirth, he pulled her close. She opened her mouth to object, but the formidable look he flashed silenced the words on her tongue.

Unable to look away, Greylyn was vividly aware of everything about the moment and the man. The soft musk fragrance of his cologne – citrus and sandalwood. The warmth emanating from his body through his clothes.

The glint of the auburn highlights in his hair as the moon melted over the horizon and the sun peaked up from its slumber. There was no sound except for the tinkling of piano keys from the tiny speaker that were almost drowned out by the thudding of her own heart as it threatened to break free of her chest.

She was incapable of pulling away from what was the most dangerous situation of her life. Greylyn had just faced down a fallen archangel, but she was much more frightened now. Her sanity hung by a thin fraying thread the longer she stayed nestled in his arms. She did not know if the music still played or not as she allowed Kael to hold her and gracefully move around the gazebo floor in small side-to-side steps.

Her skin warmed as if with a faint sunburn wherever their bodies touched. There was not a fiber of her being that was not completely attuned to the way his muscles moved underneath his thin, button-down shirt and twill dress pants. Blazing heat emanated from his hands as he traced invisible designs on the small of her back while they danced. His warm breath tickled the side of her neck causing goosebumps to break out all over her body.

Never had she experienced such a sense of physical awareness combined with such an inability for coherent thought. Somewhere in the far recesses of her mind, she knew there was something she needed to ask him. The reason she had sought him out in the first place but could not remember in the moment. Something ...

Eventually, the side-to-side steps melted into a gentle swaying. Firm fingertips came up to cup her chin and forced her to look at him. His stare seared through her. Oblivious to all else, Greylyn could do nothing but return his gaze.

They remained that way for how long, she could not tell. Her body hummed in tune with his. Without conscious thought, she raised up on her tiptoes, just enough to where she had only to lean in the slightest and their lips would touch. More than anything she wanted to know what those sensual lips felt like. Her need to find out how he tasted overwhelmed her good sense. Kael lowered his own head to cross the insurmountable distance between them.

A jolt of electricity sparked as their lips finally touched. Not painful, but an exhilarating rush spread throughout her body. Strange, but oddly familiar sensations raged as her own mind shut down and she gave all control over to her traitorous body.

Timidly at first, her fingers splayed out on his chest to bask in the feel of his muscles underneath them. A moan escaped her lips, but Kael only deepened the kiss and pulled her closer as if they could melt into each other.

Lost in the moment, lost in the way his tongue expertly parted her lips to play with her own tongue, lost in the surge of desire welling up in her body.

A lonely howl pierced the dawn. It was just enough to shock Greylyn out of her hypnotic state.

What have I done?

She jerked away. A long dormant part of her reached out to him even as Greylyn willed her body to cooperate, to escape. Overcome by an indescribable yearning to collapse into his arms and meld every inch of her body with his, uncontrollable tears sprung into her eyes. Never had she felt such searing pain as what accosted her when she disengaged from Kael. An invisible knife stabbed into her chest and ripped her heart out of her ribcage.

Backing away from him, she realized that her inner fear and turmoil must be evident in her face. There was no way to hide this level of distress. Fresh tears blurred her vision before cascading down her face.

His own expression mirrored her own unsatisfied desire and longing, but also a deep sadness. Immediately, his hand darted up to stop her escape, but ceased midway with his dark golden eyes showing anguished resignation.

Desperately she wanted to say something to soothe his turmoil, as well as her own. Somehow to put words to the feelings rampaging through her heart, mind, and soul. But no words were adequate. The only word that came out was a raspy, "No."

If pain could be embodied in a glance, she recognized it in his eyes. Without another word, she abruptly turned on her heel and retreated to her room, every step a debilitating agony, leaving Kael alone to welcome the day.

Chapter 28

Never Say Good-Bye

What the hell, Grey? The longest, coldest shower in the world could not alleviate the pain scorching her body since she pulled away from Kael. Still, she let the stinging water assault her skin. Her mind raced. Not on the evening's revelations with Olivier and her deal with the devil. That memory receded. The only images scouring her mind were of Kael and how it felt having his arms around her. How right it felt, like the one necessity she had been deprived of her entire life. And she had ripped herself away. But the pain was far from being just physical. It ran much deeper.

Shivering, she stepped out of the shower. A look in the mirror revealed slightly blue lips and dark circles under bloodshot eyes that shone electric blue.

Sleep should have been impossible. Drawing the plush covers over her, Greylyn closed her eyes and prayed for oblivion. Surprisingly, darkness enveloped her exhausted mind almost immediately.

Thankfully, her sleep was dreamless. Nothing but a pitch-black welcoming abyss.

An annoying buzzing infiltrated the darkness. The buzzing morphed into a muffled chorus of "Back in Black" (her ring tone for Jasper).

No. No. Just five more minutes, please.

Again, another soft buzzing broke through, followed by strands of "Honky Tonk Women" (her ring tone for Thomas).

Oh, for goodness sakes. Leave me alone, people.

Eyes scrunched closed, she reached out a leaden arm and smacked around the nightstand for the phone. Somehow, it remained elusive. The damn song finally stopped, but it had already ripped the veil of sleep away.

Memories blocked during sleep reared their ugly heads as soon as Greylyn opened her eyes. Kissing Kael. His heat penetrating every fiber of her being. The shocking way she responded to him. Then running away like a frightened squirrel.

Oh, and something about a prophecy.

As if the memories were not enough, she grunted when she saw the image reflected in the mirror. Bad hair. Her mop of raven strands was teased up like a frazzled beehive.

Another shower. This time scalding hot, with a glop of jasmine-scented conditioner. To block all thoughts, she turned the volume up on her phone so nothing but AC/DC infiltrated her mind during her shower. Greylyn emerged with pink skin and silky-smooth hair.

She wrapped herself in a plush cotton towel before snatching the phone from the vanity counter. Caller ID showed two missed calls from Jasper and one from Thomas.

Oh yeah, that was what woke her up in the first place.

Jasper wanted to know one thing. "Have you taken care of Kael yet?" His second message was more relaxed. "All is fine here with Sofia. No signs of trouble. You missed a lovely breakfast. However, I'm off to Kansas. Some rodeo clown needs saving."

He always gets the fun assignments!

He ended the message with, "Hope you dispatched that damn dark guardian this time."

Yeah, not so much, Jasper.

Thomas wanted to check in and make sure she survived the night. He sounded rather frantic. "Darling, you still alive? Call me. Jasper won't tell me anything."

Splashing some cold water on her face, she then stared at her own sad reflection evidenced by dark circles under her eyes.

I haven't looked this bad since Nebraska 1988.

She shrugged. No use in fretting over her appearance. Throwing on a pair of faded Levi jeans and an equally faded West Point gray tee-shirt, Greylyn paused at the door to her suite. Her heart pounded against her ribcage and a bead of sweat broke out on her forehead.

Courage, Grey. You can do this. You can face down Kael again.

The back door creaked loudly as she entered the main house. Maureen's alto voice floated down the hall from the kitchen, humming an old Frank Sinatra tune. Poking her head into the kitchen, she eyed the petite woman at the sink up to her elbows in suds.

"Well, good morning, sleepyhead! We were getting worried about you. You must have had quite the adventurous evening." She winked. "Tried to call you earlier, but there was no answer in *your room*." Another wink.

"Sorry, Maureen. You know how much I adore your food. Any chance there's anything left over? I'm starving!"

Great, she probably thinks I was in Kael's room all night. Again. One last time.

"Why, certainly. Grab yourself some coffee in the dining room and I'll whip up something fresh for you."

With her heart pounding like a bongo drum, Greylyn cautiously moved into the dining room. After last night's encounter, she knew to the depths of her soul that she was not prepared to face Kael again ... not yet. No amount of sleep would bolster her courage enough to undo the damage from last night's weakness.

Taking a tentative step around the corner, she breathed a sigh of relief. The room was empty. Why, then, did she feel disappointed?

A tall mug of silky black coffee with a splash of vanilla cream beckoned her. Walking out to the covered front porch, realization hit. Despite the glorious beauty of the Gaelic Haven landscape and her wish to stay, she would have to leave. She had promised Maureen that she would stay a day or two more. But not with Kael around. She needed space away from him. Lots and lots of space. Preferably a continent or two.

Who are you fooling, girl? Certainly, not yourself. A shuttle ride to the moon is not going to help.

Kael was owed an explanation about the events of last night. He had stepped up to watch over Kelly and Matthew for her. Or was he doing it strictly for Olivier? Had their truce been real or just a trick?

At least, she should relay the parts related to saving Sofia and her friends. She would like to confirm if he were working with the fallen archangel,

Olivier, or Satan himself.

A sudden murmuring in the back of her brain alerted her to someone else needing her help. Greylyn could not afford to delay if the intensity of the buzz was any indication.

Besides, since when did she share information with a dark guardian? That was ridiculous, right? There was no way she trusted Kael with the knowledge of some prophecy. If he did not already know from Olivier himself, then he did not need to know. If he did know …

I just can't. I cannot face him again.

His recent help did not erase the fact that Kael was still an evil creature under the command of Hell. He was still her enemy. End of story.

At least it should be.

Maureen called to her from the dining room. "Breakfast."

After re-entering the inn, she saw Matthew trudging down the stairs with the couple's suitcases. He beamed with joy.

"Good morning." As she shoved bites of cheesy eggs with crushed up bacon into her mouth, Matthew teased her about missing breakfast again. "We appreciate all the privacy, but really … you both didn't have to skip breakfast on our account."

Huh?

"Kael missed breakfast?"

"Yeah, haven't seen him since last night after he fled from Kayla's incessant attention." He squinted at her. "Funny. After hearing the music coming from the gazebo in the wee morning hours, I kinda thought you two may have …"

The soft padding of sneakered feet on the front staircase saved them from further embarrassment. The epitome of the glowing bride, Kelly walked over to her new husband and sat on his lap.

"Okay, the cuteness factor is getting a bit much with you two lovebirds. Knock it off!" They giggled and Kelly smirked at her, without moving.

"So," Kelly began with a mischievous smile, "what have you done with our friend, Mr. O'Shea?"

Matthew piped up. "Apparently, the hoodlum stood us all up. Probably sleeping off a hangover. I haven't seen any man drink that much and still be able to stand. The alcohol just caught up to him. Or … perhaps your friend

Kayla popped back over for a visit."

Kelly playfully hit his shoulder. "Shut your mouth! I have half a mind to stomp over there and check. But the way he was avoiding her," she winked at Greylyn, "I'm confident he's alone. No. Best to let him sleep it off."

Greylyn changed the subject quickly by asking about what she missed after she left.

"Oh, not too much," Kelly began, "I'm sure you don't want to be bored with all our wedding talk. Now about ..."

Interrupting her, Matthew saved the discussion from returning to Kael. "Come on, don't forget to tell her the good stuff. When Kelly went to throw the bridal bouquet, there was such a mad scramble that Amy twisted her ankle in the attempt to snag the flowers. Luckily, she had Tony to help her get home." Greylyn smiled. Those two would make a delightful couple.

"The best part was watching Kael fight off all the girls, though. They were throwing themselves at him." Kelly winked at Greylyn again. "Kael had zero interest in them."

Greylyn forced herself to not roll her eyes. Instead, she took another long draught of her coffee. She was saved from further embarrassment when Maureen walked back into the dining room, checking on her guests.

Matthew and Kelly regaled Greylyn with funny stories from the wedding and the reception. Maureen added a bit of good news.

"I called the hospital this morning. Edith is recovering nicely but seems to have a bad case of amnesia. She doesn't remember a thing from the last two days. The doctor says that is common with a stroke."

An hour and another cup of coffee later, Matthew rose to leave. They both thanked Maureen again for the gorgeous wedding and reception. "The wedding was everything we ever dreamed of. Really, it was perfect."

Kelly turned to Greylyn with tears springing up in her eyes and threw her arms around her. Squeezing her back, she realized something.

If what Olivier said was true, if Kelly were Nephilim and if she was Nephilim, and there was only one descendant line of Nephilim still in existence then ... was Kelly her family?

Tears burned her eyelids. For centuries she had felt a great void in her life because she did not remember her human life, her family, or friends. She had forced the desire for such connections behind a steel door in her heart.

The mere idea of family ... a sob threatened to erupt from her soul at the revelation.

Reluctantly, she pulled away from the embrace. "Oh, I almost forgot something. Wait right here." Greylyn sprinted to her suite for the gift she had forgotten about yesterday amidst all the drama.

Grabbing the blessed medallion, she raced back to the main house and placed the item in Kelly's palm as she explained its significance. "It's a portrait coin from the time of King Henry VIII, but it's also a Gaelic blessing and protection medal."

In Gaelic, Greylyn recited the blessing for them:

Mi\le fa\ilte dhuit le d'bhre/id, Fad do re/ gun robh thu sla\n. Mo/ran la\ithean dhuit is si\th, Le d'mhaitheas is le d'ni\ bhi fa\s.

"It means, A thousand welcomes to you with your marriage kerchief, may you be healthy all your days. May you be blessed with long life and peace, may you grow old with goodness, and with riches. It's from Reverend Donald MacLeod from Scotland in 1760. It is traditionally passed on as a blessing to all friends and family upon their marriage and beginning of a new family."

Tears free flowed down Kelly's freckled cheeks and the tip of her nose turned a soft pink hue. Even Matthew looked ready to cry. Shifting from one foot to the other, somewhat uncomfortable with all this show of emotion, Greylyn cracked a joke about most Irish blessings being coined by drunkards.

Greylyn and Maureen waved while the couple drove down the winding driveway. An unfamiliar feeling knotted and twisted inside her.

So much for the guardian angel mantra of not getting too close to your charges.

Maureen sighed. "Still want to stay a little longer?" Greylyn sadly shook her head. "Next time, I promise."

The innkeeper wrapped her in a giant, warm embrace, then retreated inside the manor. Greylyn retired to her room to pack up, weary, but determined. Hours had passed since she had woken up.

Still no sign of Kael. A vast emptiness opened in her heart. Her rational side knew she could not face him again. Not now. But another part of her wanted to see him desperately. To have him take her hand and pull her into his embrace. Frustrated at her own lack of sense, she threw the rest of her clothes into her bag.

Somehow, she felt him drawing closer. It was a sensation like no other. She had experienced it many times before but was just now recognizing it for what it was – a telepathic connection of some sort between them. She desperately wanted to escape before he returned.

With a couple additions of the inn's complimentary signature spa shampoo and conditioner thrown into her overnight bag, now slung across the passenger's seat, Greylyn gunned the Camaro down the winding driveway. A deep, pulsating sensation rose in her chest, as she passed the turn-off to the Shenandoah River. Something pulled her towards the water's edge, exactly where she had stood just the day before, pondering all the troubles facing her quest.

Kael.

The temptation to turn down the broken path was immense, almost over-powering. The desire to see him again, to feel the electricity between them, threatened to overcome her good sense. The memory of that kiss blinded her as she fought for control over herself.

You are stronger than this, Grey. Actually, no I am not.

Cranking up the radio to ear-splitting decibels, she raced onto the ramp to Interstate 66 West towards her next assignment. Someone in Louisville, Kentucky, called out silently for help. She had less than a day to reach the young man she pictured poised atop an old country bridge overlooking the rapids below.

On the muddy riverbanks of the Shenandoah, Kael felt Greylyn's approach. His thudding heart would not lie. She was near. He had waited for this moment for ages. The moment they could finally meet, no longer enemies. Their chance to explore what once was, what could be. Time to reclaim each other.

Too quickly, his stomach plummeted like he had reached the crest of a roller coaster and had just plunged over the other side at breakneck speed. She was gone. Just like that ... gone. Greylyn had slipped out of his grasp again.

His knees buckled and he collapsed into the squishy red clay of the

Shenandoah riverbank. Angry, bitter tears formed at the edge of his eyes, blurred his sight, but the drops refused to fall. Lifting his face to the cloud-covered sky, a roar rose from within and released his agonizing frustration to the world. The trees shook. Nesting birds scattered in all directions, squawking in fearful protest.

After all he did for her this weekend, all he had done for her in the past, she was still just out of his reach. An unattainable, priceless treasure ripped from his arms. Perhaps they were cursed to remain apart. Wasn't that what Hell was for? Eternal torment.

No, he refused to admit defeat, despite the facts flashing through his brain – he was an evil guardian whose sole purpose is death and destruction; she was a guardian angel meant to save humanity from the likes of him. Despite what he had become, he could not let go of her, not completely.

For centuries, he hungered for her. The way her emerald eyes lit up, even when they sparkled like sapphires when she was angry, haunted him. Her scent – jasmine intermixed with lavender – enchanted him. Even when she was not around, he would catch a whiff of her fragrance as if a phantom of long ago. The sound of her laughter rang in his ears like a lullaby. The mere thought of her soothed the monster he struggled to keep buried deep down.

He had waited. Every year, every month, every day a hellish torture. He knew he could not be patient much longer.

Kael's superiors concealed many things from him. This weekend's events were just as obscured. A big secret that he was not privy to. The family, Matthew and Kelly and their baby, were important in a grand scheme, but he did not know how. He did not care. All he knew was that everything traced back to Greylyn.

For centuries, his boss had kept a tight leash on him when it came to Greylyn. Each time he encountered her, someone always observed him, ready to report any signs of disloyalty. Every instance was analyzed for signs of another rebellion. He had suffered decades of hellish torture for protecting her. All the pain was worth it, had to be. There had to be an end in sight.

He would have her. Just a little while longer, he would wait. He would play Olivier's game, if it meant being close to her again. His chance, their chance, would come.

Fists clenched tightly, he swore, "Next time, Greylyn. Next time, we do things my way."

To Be Continued

For book release updates and more paranormal shenanigans from KC Freeman, follow the author on Facebook at @KCFreemanAuthor[1] or her Amazon page https://www.amazon.com/ KC-Freeman/e/B07QDTJD19 or subscribe to her newsletter at https://sendfox.com/ kvcfreeman5.

The Greylyn the Guardian Angel series is completed with Book 2, "Revelations" and Book 3, "Redemption," published.

---

1. *https://www.facebook.com/KCFreemanAuthor*

For a sneak peek at Book 2

Greylyn The Guardian Angel Series
Revelations

Please turn the page.

Chapter 1 – Dante's Inferno

Washington, DC

Modern Times

T he windows of the three-story building in the heart of Adams Morgan, an eclectic suburb in Washington, D.C., visibly pulsed with a shimmering kaleidoscope of neon colors. Had it only been three months since Greylyn had been in the nation's capital? Only three months since she had performed the wedding ceremony for Kelly and Matthew? Only three months since she allowed Kael to kiss her under the gazebo at Gaelic Haven, as if they were a normal man and woman in love?

She had not expected to return for some time. Quite frankly, with everything going on with Olivier's threats and her search for clues to this prophecy, she did not relish being back.

Yet, she still had to do her job as a guardian angel – saving innocent humans from their own inner demons or the more nefarious real ones. Too bad that was now secondary on her list of priorities. At the top was discovering what the prophecy entailed that Olivier wanted fulfilled. Just three months ago, a few short blocks from here, he had given her an ultimatum – fulfill the prophecy or he would use Kelly and her child to do it. Not wanting to put innocent lives at risk, she had accepted his deal.

A deal with a devil; one who was possibly worse than Lucifer himself.

But now she had guardian angel business that required her attention. Shaking the memories out of her head, Greylyn pushed her way through the line and into the club. *Dante's Inferno,* a popular nightclub, was packed for a weeknight. Its three floors catered to different musical genres to draw larger crowds. The basement belted out country music. The main floor boomed with hits from the '80 and '90s, and the top floor played modern dance and hip-hop tunes. There was something for everyone.

Greylyn squeezed through the crowd on the second level toward the small corner bar; the walls reverberating from the loud music and the air carrying the stench of sweat and stale beer as bodies gyrated to the beat on the dance floor. Some patrons sported decade-themed attire, but most did not. However, the guy with the Richard Simmons hair and the Brett Michael spandex pants caught her attention. A couple of *Flashdance* girls bounced around with mismatched legwarmers, spilling their beers everywhere. If nothing else, the comedic entertainment factor would be worth the trip. Maybe it could take her mind off other more pressing matters for a short while.

Screaming for a whiskey shot over the high-pitched sound of Toni Basil cheering on some boy named "Mickey", Greylyn surveilled the room. There was no sign of Jasper.

Where the hell is he?

His call a couple of nights ago had brought her back to DC, post-haste. He rarely requested assistance, so she felt compelled to join him. Besides, guilt had gnawed at her gut. She had yet to fill him in on the entire prophecy deal with a fallen archangel. In all of their time together, she had never kept a secret from him, except for the "Kael" thing. She could never tell him that.

Jasper had not provided a lot of information during the call. There was a suspected clutch of vampires targeting young couples at this club. A little research uncovered that, so far, five couples were missing. One couple had been found unceremoniously dumped in a water drainage pond close to the city zoo, a few blocks away, with signature puncture wounds in their necks.

The theory was simple. Vampires lured unsuspecting couples in with promises of eternal life spent with their true love. If the couple agreed, they were turned and became bloodsuckers themselves. More importantly, they *shared* the love amongst the group.

Gross. Blood-sucking swingers!

The watered-down whiskey did little to tame the ball of nerves in her stomach. She half-expected Olivier to appear out of thin air and scold her for not making enough progress on the prophecy. Or, worse yet...Kael reappearing just to torment her.

The last time that she had seen him was still etched into her brain. The scene played out in her dreams, both sleeping and awake; the way that gold flecks danced in his dreamy eyes like sparkling topaz. Goosebumps erupted across her skin, as she remembered how he trailed his fingertips along the base of her spine as they had danced in the moonlight. The sweet taste of his lips...

Warm breath fanned the base of her neck and a large hand snaked around her waist. For a second, Greylyn allowed herself to relish the sensation as part of her imagination before a familiar feeling washed over her like a warm blanket on a cold night. The memory of Kael shattered into slivers of glass. Instead, she turned to gaze up into Jasper's ice-blue eyes.

"Hello, darling. Glad you could make it," he grinned.

Unexpectedly he planted a kiss on her mouth. His firm lips grazed her own before he playfully nipped her lower lip. Something like that should earn him a smack across the face, but it was Jasper. Besides, it felt...nice.

Reaching up to encircle her arms around his neck, Greylyn whispered in his ear. "Spotted any vamps yet or are you just getting your thrills?"

A killer smile was his answer. "Aw, can't I have just a little fun?"

She shook her head in mock protest while wagging her finger at him. With a disappointed roll of his eyes and sultry pout of his full lips, Jasper filled her in on the case. He did not drop the lusty couple act, though. His nose nuzzled her neck. One stray hand dropped to cop a feel of her derriere.

"It's hard to make out who's alive and who's not in this lighting, but if I were a vampire looking to increase my clan of undead swingers, I'd target...that couple in the middle of the dance floor." Jasper's icy eyes shifted toward the couple in question.

Greylyn followed his gaze. A waif-thin blonde with glitter make-up clung desperately to a mass of muscles in denim just a few yards away. Yes, they fit the profile; at least she did. Nothing but pure adoration poured from the woman's glassy eyes. The man seemed to be enjoying himself immensely, if the bulge in his crotch was any indication. Everyone else on the overcrowded dance floor appeared to be just looking for a good time, while drinking their cares away.

Jasper snatched a couple Jell-O shots from a passing server while Greylyn surveilled the couple. She was a pretty good reader of people, even from a distance. To really see into someone's psyche, she had to touch the person. But she suspected that Jasper's instincts were right on this point.

Yes, the girl looked desperately in love with the guy. Her eyes never left him. Her hands continuously roved up and down his body seductively, but almost too clingy, as though she was trying too hard. She would easily agree to anything in order to be with him forever, in the very literal sense. However, the object of her affection did not ooze the same devotion. He pawed at her while they danced, but his eyes canvassed the room for other quarry.

Slinging back the shot, Greylyn took Jasper's hand off her ass and led him toward the dance floor. Bodies writhed all around in rhythm to an upbeat tempo – something about "Funky Cold Medina." They squeezed through the tightly packed crowd. It would be easier to get the Titanic through a crack in the iceberg than to maneuver to the spot that she wanted next to the couple. More than once she felt someone grab her ass. Someone even had the nerve to slide a hand around to the other side, but Jasper's audible growl sent the owner of the hand scurrying away fast. The last poor soul that tried to cop a feel of her in his presence had come away with a broken arm and a black eye. It would have been worse if she had not stepped in to stop him.

I hate clubbing.

As they reached the couple, Jasper suddenly turned Greylyn around so that her back was against his chest. He gyrated to the beat. Or was it called twerking now? The last time she cared to know what a dance move was called had been during the swing era.

Kissing her neck, he whispered, "Over in the corner." With her guardian senses heightened, she was still barely able to hear him over the thumping music. There was no way a human could have caught what he said.

Greylyn immediately noticed the group of attractive, and uniquely pale, young men and women. They were not dancing, just watching. Watching with such feral intensity that it was not difficult to deduce to the trained observer that they were a vampire clutch. Their collective eyes were riveted on the young couple next to them. They blended into the background so effortlessly, that none of the other bar patrons paid them any heed. It was as if they were invisible.

"Time to step up the action, sweetheart, if we're going to out-do the X-rated display next to us," Jasper muttered against the nape of her neck. Yes, they would have to up their game. With the blonde rubbing up against her man in that fashion, they would be full on having sex on the dance floor in minutes.

Normally, she would shy away from acting like a harlot, but the situation called for drastic measures. However, after upping the ante with flagrant PDA and rocking her hips against Jasper in rhythm to the beat of the music, heat crept up Greylyn's neck. Unbidden thoughts arose of someone else's body molded against her own. Her head fell back. Her eyes closed as smooth lips caressed her neck.

Thankfully, the moves did the trick. Sure enough, it only took until the middle of the second song for Greylyn to feel the eyes of the vampires trained on them – a change in the energy around them like standing too close to an overcharged electric fence. They certainly were not subtle. Glancing over, every undead eye was glued on her and Jasper. For good measure, she cast a few *come-hither* glances their way.

Moments later, a wave of revulsion swept over her, threatening to bring the Jell-O shot back up, as one vamp boldly pressed his pelvis against her butt while moving through the throng of dancers. Another one trailed sharpened fingernails across the exposed part of her lower back, lingering on the low-waist hem of her jeans.

An unnatural chill permeated the air as the vampires enclosed them in a circle. She pretended to be oblivious to anyone but her dance partner and the sensual beat of a new song she did not recognize. With a couple of seductive glances their way, however, she noticed that they would occasionally look in the direction of the other couple. Deciding more needed to be done to get and keep the vamps' full, undivided attention, Greylyn raised up on her tiptoes to lock lips with Jasper.

As their lips parted and their tongues stroked each other, he unexpectedly deepened the kiss with a guttural moan.

Oh, no. Hope he does not enjoy this too much.

To her amazement, she found herself savoring the feeling of his soft, sensual lips on hers and the way he possessively held her to his body with his hands on her hips. There was a pleasant tingle that spread downward and out, but not the raging inferno that consumed her when she had locked lips with Kael.

Dammit! Stop thinking about him!

Jasper reached down and lifted her petite body off the ground while cupping her bottom with only one hand. The other hand latched onto the back of her neck, fisting his fingers into the tendrils of hair that had escaped the ponytail holder. Greylyn's legs wrapped around his waist. Her hands roved over his powerful shoulders and downward to trace the chiseled biceps that bulged beneath the tight cotton t-shirt that did little to hide his muscular perfection. Proof of his excitement pressed against her. No longer dancing, they instead put on an erotic public display more suitable for cable television than a dance floor.

Someone muttered, "Get a room."

Jasper answered with a raspy chuckle. "Oh, I plan to. Indeed, I fully intend..."

A familiar jolt rocked through her body suddenly as if she had been zapped with a taser. Her tongue ceased its trail up Jasper's neck. Every muscle locked. Every nerve sizzled. She did not have to look around to know that a pair of intense cognac-colored eyes studded with flecks of gold watched her. More importantly, the owner of those eyes was far from happy at what he saw. Turbulent waves of red-hot fury blasted Greylyn's body. She had felt that before, the last time being three months ago.

Kael.

All thoughts of Jasper or the endangered couple obliterated from her mind. Guilt pervaded every pore; guilt for every lustful action that she had just taken. The very question as to why she should feel guilty for making out with someone else vaguely floated across her consciousness. It was wrong; a simple innate truth. The heart knew, but the mind lacked understanding.

In every way unable to continue a public make-out session with Jasper, she unraveled her legs from around his waist and jumped down. His hands came up to draw her back to him, but instinct pushed him away with enough force to make him stumble backward. His eyebrows furrowed together with confusion; his eyes lightened to the pale blue of glacial ice.

"Sorry," she stammered, craning her neck to peer up at him with what she hoped came off as a sincere apology. Going with the lamest excuse, but the only one that she could articulate in the moment, "Bathroom." She pivoted, almost knocking into a vamp in too-tight black denim and too much eyeliner.

The DJ's announcement that it was "last call for alcohol" barely registered in her ears. She felt more than saw Jasper dramatically shrug before sauntering over to the bar while Greylyn practically sprinted for the ladies' room on the floor below. With every step her head stayed rigidly focused in front of her, not freeing her eyes to roam around the room, making every effort to not look in a certain direction.

Dealing with Kael right now would be dangerous given the right situation, but considering what he had just witnessed, she knew better than to believe that they could be civilized about it. Worst-case scenario, he would pick a fight with Jasper and they would bludgeon each other to near death, maybe even succeed in killing each other. Best case, Kael would wait to confront her personally and would entirely ignore Jasper. In turn, Jasper would not even know his nemesis was there.

The big empty abyss opening in her stomach knew that the first scenario was more likely. Regardless, she needed two minutes to calm herself, and to get her own emotions in check. If a portal to another dimension appeared in front of her right at that second, she would gladly dive through it.

Luckily, the blonde female that the vampires had originally targeted rushed past Greylyn into the bathroom. At least she could keep an eye on the girl, just in case.

The restroom was not crowded, despite the throng of partygoers and the late hour. Splashing cold water on her face and neck from the filthy pink ceramic sink, wild emerald eyes stared back at her from the fractured mirror. With her little finger, she wiped at the black smudges under her eyes. Her lips were swollen and now devoid of the ruby lipstick, which she had so carefully applied earlier. Absentmindedly, Greylyn pulled what remained of her hair out of the scrunchie to allow her ebony locks to cascade down her back in unruly waves.

How does he affect me like this? More importantly, why do I allow him to affect me like this?

If she lived a thousand more years, she would never understand it. Kael had no right to be angry at her...well, other than they were immortal enemies. With she being a guardian angel and he being a dark guardian, the battle lines were pretty much drawn right there. But Kael being angry about the thing with Jasper...that was none of his damn business!

The young woman came out of the tiny bathroom stall to wash her hands in the sink next to Greylyn. On closer inspection in the harsh LED light, she was attractive and in her mid-twenties, with long blonde hair, average height, and a waif-like physique. Sweat coated her body, causing her gossamer top to cling to her thin frame. Greylyn locked eyes with her in the mirror as she reapplied a peach-colored lip gloss, and then patted her chest and neck with a damp paper towel. "Crazy night, huh?"

Greylyn cringed at her own inept attempt at small talk, but the glassy-eyed woman simply nodded with a small smile before adding, "Yeah, I can't wait to get home. Alone with my man, if you get my drift."

Oh, my word! Does this girl think I'm coming on to her? Had she not witnessed her display of affection on the dance floor with Jasper?

Heat crept up Greylyn's neck. Since when did a simple greeting come off as a come-on?

"Me too. Can't get out of here fast enough." Hopefully that cleared up the awkward confusion.

Just as the woman turned away to exit the bathroom, with her hand extended to grab the door handle, the door flew open and a couple of the vampire women stalked into the room. Instinct kicked in to protect the blonde as Greylyn lunged forward to stand between her and the vamps. Her eyes darted around. There was no other escape route, not even a tiny utility window. Too bad a tall, pale, nearly six-foot tall redhead with candy-apple red lipstick and nails blocked their only escape path.

The unsuspecting blonde did not realize that anything was amiss, as she tried to slide by Greylyn's arm and then by the overbearing woman in her haste to get back to her boyfriend. A long, slender hand reached out to snarl around her wrist.

It took every fiber of her being not to rip the vamp's arm away or punch their way out of the tiny bathroom. She did not want to alert them of her own true nature; not yet, anyway. Sometimes demons could sniff out a guardian, but other monsters, such as vamps, lacked the special sense to do so. That one fact alone had saved her hide several times.

Trying to play things cool, she slurred her speech like she had had too much to drink. "Excuse us. Just trying to get back to our guys." She grabbed the other woman's hand in her own and made for the door again.

Unfazed, the redhead piped up, "In time. Your gentlemen can wait.

There's someone else who wants to meet you both." Her tone brooked no dissent. By their stone-cold stares and thin-lipped smiles, Greylyn knew that this was not a request, but the young woman was still oblivious. She tried to wrench her arm free from the vampire, but nails sharpened into lethal daggers which dug into the delicate skin of the girl's wrist eliciting an exclamation of "Ouch, bitch!"

With a sneer, the other vampire, with pixie-cut, platinum blonde hair, and a little less gaudy lipstick, made a grab for Greylyn. Trying not to blow her cover as a hapless human, she allowed the vampire to latch onto her upper arm and put up the appearance of a struggle. "Hey! Hey! What's the deal? Ladies, we already have dates and clearly we do not *swing* your way, so let's just walk away calmly."

That earned her a resounding slap across her cheek, leaving a thin bloody scratch. The blonde vamp leaned over and licked the blood off her face.

Yuck!

Of all the grotesque things that she had encountered, a vampire running its tongue along her face creeped her out the most. Even a shifter shedding its skin – blood, skin, and slimy tissue – did not make her stomach hurl as much as that.

The redhead grinned wickedly at the sight. "I said your men can wait. We have a friend who wishes to meet you. NOW." She whipped the human girl around and clasped a rag over her mouth. There was not much of a struggle. Already slow from all the alcohol that she had consumed, in addition to not realizing what she was up against in the first place, the chloroform overcame her. A bundle of blonde hair and long thin limbs slumped to the floor.

The blonde vamp moved to do the same to her. Greylyn's hand shot out and punched her so hard that the vampire's body flew back and crashed into the bathroom stall door. Despite the noise, she knew that no one outside the bathroom would hear anything, as the walls pulsed with the volume of the music on the other side of the door.

The vampire women paused momentarily, as they considered her with more wary eyes. The blonde scrambled up from the broken stall; her eyes changing to slits of red and her smile revealing sharp, elongated canine teeth. Her red-haired companion unsheathed a long switchblade from the front pocket of her black jeans.

Two can play that game.

Greylyn withdrew her own special dagger from the holster sewn into the back of her bra. Her club clothes had not been conducive to her usual hiding spot at the small of her back, so she had made a few alterations. Even in the harsh light, its blade glistened with a cold blue energy. Power surged up from the hilt into her palm and up her arm.

Waving the knife in front of her face menacingly, Greylyn quipped, "Yeah, I got one, too. You wanna play?"

Snarling, they both rushed at her. The bathroom was tiny, making maneuvering difficult, but no more so than when she had taken down a ring of Leyak inside a coconut nursery on the outskirts of Bali.

But these were not primal Leyak demons – a type of werewolf that can shapeshift from human form into a hideous flying monkey. These were vampires; quick, intelligent, and cunning. Greylyn struck the first blow with a slash to the blonde's chest. It did not even slow her down. The vampire tackled her and threw her back against the pedestal sink, smashing it to pieces. Water spurted from the wall making the floor slippery. Greylyn lost her footing as she pushed her opponent backward. Both fell to the hard, tiled floor.

The knife in her hand poised above the blonde's neck, she used all her strength to push downward, but was yanked back. A kick from the redhead's heeled boot to her hand sent Greylyn's dagger flying across the room. Without her weapon, she would have to play dirty.

Her legs swiped at her assailant's feet before kicking the vampire full in the stomach. As the vampire doubled over, Greylyn launched herself off the floor to land on both feet. She struck out with her fists, smashing the redhead's nose. The crunching sound and spurt of blood sent a wave of satisfaction through her.

A slender hand grabbed her ankles and yanked hard. Instantly, she crashed back to the floor. Pain ricocheted through her head, blinding her momentarily; just enough time to give the vampires the advantage. The weight of one of the vamps pressed down full on her chest, as her arms were held down by someone's bony knees. Desperate, she rocked violently back and forth in an attempt to throw off the vampire, failing miserably as a soggy, pungent-smelling cloth clamped down over her nostrils and mouth.

Kael's blood boiled with a mixture of fury and impatience. Burly bouncers decked out in all black ushered drunken revelers out into the humid, nearly starless night. He had stayed hidden from Jasper after Greylyn had dashed off to the ladies' room. No need to incite the male guardian's anger or curiosity. Still...Kael longed to punch his lights out and peel his skin from his bones. Every day since he had seen him with Greylyn in the alleyway behind the London pub centuries ago, his fingers twitched and ached to pummel the smirk from the bastard's face.

Now, watching the front entrance from behind a bus stop enclosure across the street from the club, a sense of unease crept through the fury.

Where the Hell was she?

KC FREEMAN

DEFYING HEAVEN AND HELL,
A GUARDIAN ANGEL REKINDLES
A DEADLY PROPHECY.

Rekindled
prophecy

GREYLYN THE GUARDIAN ANGEL SERIES (BOOK 1)

Reader's
Guide

1. Guardian angels, of course, work for Heaven to protect and save humans from their own inner demons (addictions, depression, anger, lower vibration energies, and emotions, etc.) and the more nefarious real demons. What purpose do dark guardians serve? Did you ever suspect these supernatural beings existed, and why is more not written about them?

2. Why do you believe Greylyn insists on maintaining a "just friends" relationship with Jasper? Do you believe he wants more? If she allowed herself, would she want more?

3. In Greylyn's first encounter with Kael, he saves her from the demonic goons but then attacks her before suddenly stopping and trying to apologize. What causes the extremes in his behavior?

4. The innkeeper, Maureen, is a hopeless romantic who sees the chemistry between Greylyn and Kael immediately. Despite Greylyn's attempts to dissuade her of the romantic notion and her pleas to stop matchmaking, why does Maureen persist? What does she see between them that Greylyn cannot?

5. If you were Greylyn and found the folder of photographs Kael had in his possession, what would you have done when Kael came back to his suite?

6. It is widely agreed upon that the smell of Sulphur signals demonic presence. If Kael is a dark guardian, why does he instead smell of citrus and sandalwood?

7. Over 450 years of being a guardian angel, and Greylyn still has not learned how to swim. Why do you think she hasn't done this? Is she being truthful with herself about her reasons?

8. Jasper and Kael have a deep-set hatred of each other. Aside from Greylyn and just being universal archenemies because Jasper works for Heaven and Kael works for Hell, what do you believe is the unsaid reason for their animosity? Is there an underlying reason they have not killed each other yet? If so, what is it?

9. Greylyn encounters Kael many times over the centuries. They have fought each other, but neither has ever gone for the death blow. Despite all the chaos and destruction he has wrought, what prevents

Greylyn from killing him?

10. Do you believe the woman, Isabel, intentionally performed an incomplete protection incantation for Kelly, or was she merely careless or incompetent? Should Greylyn have questioned her more before allowing her to leave the psychic's apartment? What would you have asked Isabel?

11. Despite Kael's existence as a dark guardian, he does a number of things that do not go along with his bad boy demeanor. He rescues Greylyn from the shadow creature. He tends to her injuries after the battle in Washington, DC. He charms the innkeeper and cooks a fantastic traditional Irish meal. He saves the small child in the wedding party from falling into the koi pond. Is his kindness an illusion to lull Greylyn into trusting him, or is it genuine? What is the basis of your opinion, either way?

12. If you were Greylyn, how would you handle Jasper's sudden appearance at the wedding?

13. Although Lucifer does not make an appearance in this particular book, he is mentioned a few times. If the prophecy is so destructive, why would he not want it fulfilled?

14. The prophecy was thought to be dead when Greylyn died (as a human). Why did her human death not negate the prophecy? Do you believe her death and rebirth as a guardian was a part of the prophecy? Or was her rebirth as a guardian angel destiny's way of keeping the prophecy alive?

15. What kind of things do you imagine a guardian angel does? What would you like to do if you were a guardian angel? Or would you be a dark guardian?

Author Biography

KC Freeman

After leaving the corporate world to raise her five rambunctious children with her husband in North Carolina, KC Freeman eventually found her way back to her lifelong desire to write paranormal fiction.

KC writes mostly fantasy and paranormal romance novels. She is particularly fond of writing about angels. She also spends a lot of time editing other authors' manuscripts.

When she is not writing, KC is running her children to practices, football games, swim meets, wrestling tournaments, and generally all over town. In her spare time ... who are we kidding? She does not have any of that.